Our Savage

OUR SAVAGE

A Novel

Matt Pavelich

SHOEMAKER & HOARD
WASHINGTON D.C.

Library of Congress Cataloging-in-Publication Data

Pavelich, Matt.
  Our savage : a novel / Matt Pavelich
  p. cm.
  ISBN 1-59376-023-X
  1. Alientaion (Social psychology) — Fiction. 2. Tall people — Fiction. 3. Immigrants — Fiction. 4. Pioneers — Fiction. 5. Outlaws — Fiction. 6. Wyoming — Fiction. I. Title
PS3566.A878)94 2004
813'.6—dc22

                                                 2004025865

FIRST PRINTING

Text design by Gopa & Ted2, Inc.
Printed in the United States of America

Shoemaker & Hoard
A Division of Avalon Publishing Group Inc.
Distributed by Publishers Group West

10 9 8 7 6 5 4 3 2 1

～ Contents ～

Then he harrowed hell,
Healed the abyss
Of torpid instinct and trifling flux,
Laundered it, lighted it, made it lovable with
Cathedrals and theories; thanks to him
Brisker smells abet us,
Cleaner clouds accost our vision
And honest sounds our ears.
For he ignored the Nightmares and annexed their ranges,
Put the clawing Chimaeras in cold storage,
Berated the Riddle till it roared and fled,
Won the Battle of the Whispers,
Stopped the Stupids, stormed into
The Fumblers' Forts, confined the Sulky
To their drab ditches and drove the Crashing
Bores to their bogs,
Their beastly moor.

From *Age of Anxiety,* W. H. Auden

⤚ Vuk Hajduk ⤚

1865

➤ TOO LARGE A BABY to pass through anyone's hips, he was cut out of his mother with a midwife's septic knife. His mother, in the week that was left to her after the birth, never gained the strength to nurse him, and she feared this beginning was predictive of all his days, that he was meant for hunger and hardship. "Marko," she told her husband, "you will be the one to feed him. It falls to you, so promise me he will eat." Marko Lazich gave his weepy promise, but he had as yet no way to keep it, no milk for the child, and so his Angelene died to their son's dogged, hungry howling.

Desolate, Lazich went about and found three wet nurses and the means to pay them. They lived scattered at great distances, and for more than a year his days were consumed with the task of carrying the baby from one to the other. His grief eroded, and as he needed less distraction from it, Lazich, never by nature a very conscientious man, came to believe he would be the next victim of his son's demands. The boy was a writhing sack of rabbits to carry, livelier and a little heavier each day. Every obligation has its natural span. When the boy learned to walk he was expected to walk everywhere; when he produced teeth he was expected to chew with them. None of it made his company less burdensome. Lazich's son no longer needed to be carried, but the child's lunacy had always to be heard, more intricate all the time. The boy grew and grew, and talked and talked, and he was only ever lucid when penetrating his father's lies. The child, the creature, would not permit him any lies at all. For the sake of his dearly remembered wife, Lazich stood it as long as he could, but finally he told his son he must "stop it. Stop telling me what to do. You should speak when spoken to, but no, that courtesy is beyond you. And these pots, you think they fill themselves? I come home wanting a slice of the sausage only to find you have eaten it, all of it. What I bring into this house—no matter how much I bring into this house—you eat. I listen for quiet and it never comes. Now you are wearing a knife you've won wrestling with men, and what does that mean? Think of all of these things together. You behave as if you are such a shining intelligence, so tell me what all these things must mean. Come home as often as you like, but not to eat, I am done with feeding you."

August 22, 1873

Danilo Lazich, who'd been expecting his independence, had already noted places of shelter in the hills. He went around to a few of them to make himself confident, but it was summer and shelter was not his pressing need. He made a fire and left it smoldering. Already he had come to feel as his father had, that the duty of tending his appetite was too much. But for the boy there was anticipation and pleasure in it too, and for all his uncertainty he was content to leave his father's sphere of perpetual complaint. He decided to beg and descended to the road across Krbasko Polje where he expected to find an ancient lance or the skull of a cavalryman. It would be twice as efficient, he thought, to post himself in one place and let travelers come to him from each direction. Those he met on the road were as poor as he, had nothing to give, nothing even to sell. But they did have advice. "Go north," said a crone from under her load of twigs. "Go north until someone stops you. The Schwabes will take you in, and the officers will let you bring them their tea." "To the sea," a flockless shepherd told him, "go down to the sea and they'll make a fisherman of you." Lame Oresković came along, slowly. "You are waiting, Danilo?"

"For something to eat."

"I have nothing to eat."

"Tell me where to go."

"Why go anywhere?" said Oresković "It's all the same."

The boy waited by the side of the road. Travelers were rare and mostly afoot. He could not disguise his disappointment in them as they passed. He did not trouble speaking to them as there was nothing to discuss with the underfed. He walked in the night, but only to keep warm and preoccupied, and when he came to a village he either walked around it or turned and went back the way he'd come. There were any number of reasons he might go into the settlements, but he wanted charity and knew that in the villages any charity must necessarily be ugly. At sunup he found a paling fallen from a wagon, and he stopped to rest and to carve it into a weapon. Balancing the thing and making it sharp were as much comfort to him as any game he might take with it. He made a fire with the shavings, and when the fire was coals he hardened the tip of his spear in it. He sat by the side of the road with the finished instrument, flinging it occasionally into the embankment across from him.

At mid-morning a man came up the road leading an ass and a pony cart. In the cart were his wife and infant child. The cart seemed unequal even to its little cargo. The man had fixed a shade over it to keep his family out of the sun. Just behind them rode a large hamper so full that its lid would not completely close. They passed him without a word, and only after they passed him did the boy see the hamper. He followed along behind. He heard the woman speak to her husband, pose a question of some kind. The cart stopped and the man and his wife looked back at him. The woman asked, "Are you hunting this morning? Hunting with that?" Clear blue sky reflected on her eyes.

"It would be good if I could kill something. I am hungry."

The woman seemed sorry to hear it. "We have . . ."

"We are having a picnic," said her husband. He wore an ineffectual moustache and was stooped and thin and unlike a young man.

"A picnic," said the boy, "I've heard of that. It is a thing Englishmen do. The only intelligent way to carry food from one place to the next is in your belly."

"English?" said the young father suspiciously. He jerked his ass back into motion and started off.

The boy followed. Mother would tire soon, and then they would stop. The boy wished to be with them when that happened. The young father often turned to watch him, to smile, to frown. No emotion could gain much purchase in him, every thirty or forty steps he changed. The boy walked behind, curious, then bored. He smelled salami distinctly and could see the neck of a wine bottle. Why did they want to freight this around when they might be eating it? He followed, thinking he could not be turned away because he was only eight years old, thinking that they would tire and stop, and that they would have to offer him a little something if he was near. The boy was all but drooling when at last the young father turned his cart round in the road.

"We are going back to Bunić," he said. He was short of breath. "I have decided against our picnic, so we are going back to our village now. My wife's father, you may like to know, is a magistrate there. We are going back to Bunić at once. Good day and good luck. I must ask you to leave us alone." The man's wife and child were asleep behind him. He continued then toward his village and the boy continued to follow. The man glanced back at him constantly. His wife wakened again and began to hum dully over their baby. At some point the young father's legs began to tremble even as he walked, and shortly after that they'd become unsteady. His wife began to ask him, "Darling? Darling? Have you . . . darling?" The boy caught up with them and put it to the young father more directly, "Are you sick?"

"Take the basket," said the man.

"Should I make a place for you to lie down?"

"Take the hamper. Our hearts go out to you."

"Our picnic?" asked the wife. "All of it?"

"I don't want the basket," said the boy. "But I will take the food and drink. And a spoon if you've brought one."

"Please," said the young father, "just take it. Quickly as you can, please. And why would I want the basket now, to remind me of my cowardice?"

"Are you a coward?"

"He is not," said the wife. "He is a good man. But it seems he is afraid of you. Can you blame him?"

"Take the hamper now," said the slight young father. "Just take it now, if there's any decency in you."

The boy freed the basket from its bindings. The woman told him to use it well, to eat slowly the things he'd gotten. She said that her husband was the best of men, so generous. And her husband said, "We go, we go, we go now."

June 1880

In Agram, Father Bersa had been given a chestnut mare, an animal that provided more companionship than carrying capacity. Bersa prized its docile ways even above obedience, and the beast's weakness imposed a welcome, slow pace on them. The priest was not anxious to reach home. Just that morning he'd been on a lush Croatian plain, thrilling to a hundred shades of wild and cultivated green, but a half day's walk had brought him into this karst, a highland barrens strung inland of the Adriatic like so much corded hemp. Climbing into it, Bersa felt Europe as he understood it slipping behind. He was coming into the Lika, furthest frontier of successive empires, a district now populated by the descendants of stragglers and deserters and Hapsburg hirelings. Several cultures, forgotten elsewhere, remained like scarring in this appalling place, unresponsive to time. The district was a repository for old falsehoods, the land itself an eternal source of pessimism.

Somewhere on a promenade at the outskirts of Agram, Bersa had lost a heel from one of his new shoes. Four days ago. Limping pitifully, he wondered if he might not be owed some measure of enlightenment for his suffering. He walked slowly and with a certain, constant caution, still he gained on his destination. Rounding a face of Debela Brda, he came to a length of path littered with gravel, a schist scattered from the summit down and particularly cruel to walk upon. It slid underfoot as they crossed it. The mare had a moment of confusion here and pulled Bersa downhill with her lead rope. He wrapped the rope round his backside and planted his heels. The animal stopped and Bersa settled farther back until he was sitting on the ground, the rope caught under him, the naughty mare's head bent back and to the side. He looked into the animal's eyes and saw he was accomplishing nothing with his small rebuke, so he slacked the line. Having fasted the past few days, purely out of neglect, Bersa had made himself light-headed. He sat in the glinting dust raised by his exertions with the pony and which seemed to superheat and to thicken the mountain air so that he was unable to draw enough of it into his lungs. This, for all he knew, was dying, and he paid close attention to himself. When the crisis passed, as it did before very much drama could be had from it, Bersa surrendered to despair. It had been building in him for a long time, perhaps his entire life to this point.

When Bersa had first come to the Lika he'd had no animal and he'd carried on his back a crate of catechisms, a labor that cost him a year of unremitting pain. The twinging of his sacrum was benign, though, as compared with the ache in his soul that came of being anywhere in or seeing anything of his sterile parish. Immersing himself in duty, he had rebuilt the bell tower over the shell of a church in Gospić, caused a bell of French origin to be hung in it. He administered the sacraments, endlessly heard the confession of all those sins that had accumulated since his parishioners last had access to a priest. He'd heard also of the many recent sins they seemed almost conscientiously to commit. Bersa hauled grain in a sling, helped with the milking and castration of goats. In time vertical creases had appeared on his cheeks and he was widely mistaken for a mystic. After five years of it, he'd returned unbidden to Agram for an audience with Archbishop Strossmayer. Bersa believed he'd reached the end of his endurance. "It is," he told the prelate, "like living on the face of a butcher's block. Remember, Eminence, I was trained as a botanist."

They were in the prelate's study, a room cluttered by the man's enthusiasms. Everywhere were parchments rolled and tied with ribbon. A creel stood open on a desk, and within that Bersa saw a row of hooks mounted on yellow satin. The great man had allowed for an hour's interview. His Grace, some red leather text in hand, sat on a chaise lounge under the only lighted lamp in the room. Bersa could not afford to be overawed. "Reptiles, Eminence, lower-order reptiles, and perhaps a few small, hooved animals. That is what my district is fit to sustain. Not men. Those who live in the Lika are, in every way imaginable, lost."

"*Maté*," said the Archbishop softly, "we must have someone there. Their faith is their only comfort. You must admit that in some ways your work is easy. You have less competition from the world than any priest I know."

"No, Eminence. They take no comfort at all in the thought of God. God for them is an excuse for strife. If you could see them kneeling before me, their tongues extended for the host . . . their bovine regard for me. I struggle daily with the sin of Pride, and every day it defeats me. The poverty terrifies me. And, do you know, they consider each of the sacraments a specific for casting out one of their demons?"

"*Corpus Cristi*," said the archbishop. "Can you tell me, honestly, that anyone's beliefs are odder than our insistence on the resurrection of our Savior?"

"It is not the posting for a man of my limitations. I spend what moral energy I possess in self-pity. I am not the man, not the Christian to succeed there."

"You are tired. You are something of a sybarite."

"I am, more than ever, out of my depth. My vocation has been uncertain in much better circumstances, Eminence."

"You will do very little for that parish, *Maté*. It is an impossibility, I
know. But it is your impossibility. You may find in time that it has made
your spirit quiet. In any event, you are the Church in the Lika." The
archbishop went to the glass cabinet that contained a collection of chal-
ices and crucifixes. They were, he explained, like Bersa himself, of Slavic
origin. He opened the case and removed from it the largest of the
crosses, with its chain. "This was found in your parish. The best esti-
mates place its date of manufacture in the tenth century. Hammered
gold worked into a species of hardwood that has become, I believe, extinct." He hung the thing from Bersa's neck. "Wear it every day. Let
them see it."

"It is quite heavy."

"Yes," said the archbishop fondly.

And, so burdened, Bersa was returning, the crucifix tapping his chest
at each step as if he had acquired a second, cold heart. He looked down
from Debela Brda, across the wrinkled foothills. Below, living invisibly
in the torturous seams of this country, were his Catholics, the Hrvati, and
the Serbs who were Orthodox, and a scattering of Muslims. Lićani, collectively. An absurd, resilient people. Peasants on untenable land, each
spring they would carry dirt in wooden buckets up to their plots on the
terraced hillsides, earth that washed away with the first rain, or in
drought might yield runt cabbages. In the Lika, no one was weak; the
weak did not survive infancy. It was a region fertile only with suspicion,
and its people had all their stimulation and much of their sustenance
from brandishing their respective faiths at each other. They could not
skirt each other in the narrow valleys and so, for a Lićani, travel anywhere meant a fight. Barley gruel and figs. The severity of their lives
condemned many to early death and the rest to longevity. His own life,
what was left of it, would be spent among them. It was like thinking of
the distances to the stars. Bersa took a cheese from one of his panniers.

As he ate of it he grew thirsty. His canteens were empty; the mare had needed to water often and she drank wastefully from his cap.

A figure Bersa took to be a goatherd climbed toward him, not running but advancing as quickly as a runner directly up the face of the mountain. There were no goats about. Bersa called down. "Hallo." The climber gained definition and Bersa could see more clearly his manner of moving, that he was not climbing so much as trampling the mountain into submission. Bersa called again, "Hallo, there." He had the impression that the climber was approaching from out of some antiquity when men consorted with their gods. The fellow wore a jerkin cinched at the waist and his boots were of rough hides wrapped round his feet, not the habit of the Lika, or of any region Bersa knew. Bersa understood at last that it was not a man coming, but a boy, the predatory boy who was called *Vuk Hajduk*—the wolf, the highwayman. Said to be one of the better reasons never to travel these lonely roads alone, the lad loomed up. Bersa raised his hand in a greeting that was not returned. The boy came to within arm's length and looked down at him with the neutral curiosity he might have given a wounded bug. A tassel of down grew along his jaw. A current of fear shot up through Bersa's legs and settled heavily in his bowels. "I know who you are," he told the boy with some effort. "I have heard of you." The crimes attributed to Vuk Hajduk were of an especially curious variety. He looked to be capable of them. The highwayman breathed slowly and heavily. His breath was scalding. Bersa, unable to return his gaze without feeling nakedly foolish, confronted instead the boy's monstrous chest, sheaves of muscle only partly covered by the jerkin. Bersa recalled from childhood the sheer subjugation of being very small, and he suddenly longed to be forgiven. No specific transgression came to mind.

The boy took up the mare's halter. He lifted her head and inserted his thumb at the back of her mouth, which promptly opened. Her crusted teeth were revealed. The young giant was not pleased.

"I have only just been given this animal." Bersa didn't know what moved him to apology, but he could not refrain from it. "She is in a pitiful state, and it is a shame. But I will see that she has better care from now on." It was said that Vuk Hajduk could crush a man's skull between his hands, and Bersa saw that the child despised him, by instinct. "I will build her a corral. Would you like to come to the rectory with me? To help with the building? I would see that you got some decent clothing from it. Whether you know it or not, your reputation needs much repair. You should be seen doing honest work." The boy smiled. Possibly an idiot's smile. He looked into each of the panniers but found nothing worth taking in them. There was an unpleasant efficiency about his eyes. "At least," said Bersa, "you might lead me to potable water, if you know of any nearby."

The boy caught up the lead rope and walked off down the path with the mare. Bersa followed. Wherever he was going, he was going much faster than was his custom. The skirts of his soutane restricted his stride and forced upon him an awkward, skipping progress. He began to fancy his predicament, whatever it might be. Bersa thought he might even be slaughtered now, but he didn't very much mind or resent it, and he'd found a mood more serviceable than his faith had ever been. He sang a secular hymn, a single line of it, over and over again. "Here I sit, drinking and smoking, bothering no one." His voice carried and echoed. It occurred to him that he might have made a wonderful wastrel.

The boy, the giant, stopped in front of him on the path and turned back. "You learned that at the inns?"

"I have an occasional cognac." Another apology. "For my circulation. Even the clergy are allowed their small diversions. Where are you taking me? Where are we going?"

"You've heard the song the young men sing? When the inns are closing, they sing, 'Lamps out, knives out.' "

"There is no tune to that. Young men assume that everyone is so captivated by their capacity for violence. But for me it is only tiresome. For me there is no poetry in violence."

"No poetry in the violence done to Christ?" This and a look of evil complicity and the boy was on his way again, a child of unimaginable corruption. Bersa felt a fresh issue of sweat on his forehead, new seepage from the blisters on his heels. "Do you really think I fear you?" It appeared that the boy was no longer thinking of him at all. Bersa hurried after him, his impulse to sing spent, his buttocks knotting with effort. He jealously noted how well the mare moved along with the boy leading her. A child with absolute authority. The highwayman walked at a terrific pace and soon left the main path to follow a snaking series of fainter trails. Bersa meant to close the gap between them, but he could not. He meant to take the boy to task for his impertinence, though impertinence was the least of the damage he might inflict. Rage was in him, and he was enjoying it though it contributed to the searing of his throat. This could be martyrdom coming; his life would amount to a small loss. Was this courage? *Maté* is there nothing you cannot complicate? Would even death relieve you of uncertainty? "Young man, that horse is neither yours nor mine. She belongs to the diocese. You must tell me what you have in mind." He struggled into a dogtrot to keep up.

They came to a stream and a collection of huts that had been, apparently, their destination. It was an Orthodox settlement, icons lodged in pathetic shrines, Byzantine grave markers. No wonder, then, that in coming here Bersa had lost his bearings. He would not have visited this place before. He joined the boy just upstream of the first hut and they knelt together to drink. The water tasted somehow of tin and was tepid. Bersa in his greed and thirst sucked it into his windpipe and it came bursting out his nose. The mare also snorted wetly. Bersa lowered his head into the water to rest his cheek on the streambed. He resurfaced only when points of green light began to swirl on his eyelids. The boy sat across from him, his arms wrapped around his knees. In this compressed posture he was still immense. "Are you hungry, priest? This is my father's village. I can have him feed you."

"I have heard of you," Bersa announced again.

"I have heard of you. And I've seen you out on the trails before."

"Before? When?"

"I don't keep a calendar. Before."

"Who are you?"

"You said you knew."

Bersa brought another handful of water up to his face, to wet it again, to soothe himself. "I said that I'd heard of someone called Vuk Hajduk. But I had never heard that he talked like a Jesuit . . . 'the violence done to Christ.' I've been thinking about that."

"Think of this, Bersa: you will never do as much in service to God or man as the mercenaries who marched Christ up Calvary."

"Don't be vulgar. What are you? It isn't necessary. Can't we talk?" Bersa could not recover from the shock of hearing his name in this highwayman's mouth. "Is this where you're from, then?"

"We came from a place like this. He lives here now."

"There are no places like this," said the priest. "This is the worst I've seen." He knelt to drink again and managed to scoop a beetle in as well as water. It lodged beneath his tongue, and his fingers, like a clumsy dentist's, pursued it. He was to have no dignity here. "I had hoped to reach the rectory tonight. Would you take me? I may need your help to find the road again."

"You'd find it," said the boy, "but then you'd lose your way in the dark. It will be dark with no moon before you could reach Gospić."

"But with your help . . ."

"Am I your acolyte now? We've abused your horse just getting you here. She'll quit you if she isn't given some rest."

"We can't stay here."

"You can," said the boy. "You'll have to now."

Molting chickens paraded in front of them, the mare followed like a dog, and only when they were well into the settlement did Bersa realize that neither women nor children were anywhere to be seen. Outside the doorways of several huts men sat or squatted, smoking long-stemmed clay pipes. *Here I sit, drinking and smoking, bothering no one.* Smoke of differing densities issued from everywhere and clung stubbornly to the ground. There were low huts of dry-laid stone roofed with shallow thatching, some with no windows at all. The village looked to be in possession of all the refuse it had ever produced. One of the pipe smokers called out as they passed him, "If you eat the priest's heart, Vuk, be sure to boil it. Scrape the black off and boil it or it will make you sick."

Bersa's giddy moment was gone. Capable of terror again, he privately canonized Cyril and Methodius. Room in his theology, as ever, for whatever might be useful there. But these Orthodox would cherish their hatred for him no matter what he did or thought. He had only to wear the Roman collar to endanger himself. He was unable even to spit on the ground as he intended. "I am not welcome here," he said.

"I am welcome nowhere," said the boy. "I can smell the stench in their guts, just as I've smelled it in yours."

"Only see me out of this. I would give you anything."

"You have nothing I want."

"Not here, but in Gospić there are—"

"You have nothing I want. Nothing will happen to you, Bersa."

"Father Bersa. Or—whatever you like. Can it matter so much?"

The water in the stream became more silty as it passed down among the huts, and where it reached the settlement's downstream edge it smelled of animal waste. The boy stopped at the last of the huts. A pony nearly as wretched as Bersa's animal was tethered to a post. A small wagon stood by the open doorway, one of its wheels propped against its sagging box. The boy lifted the wagon and slid the wheel onto its axle, he drove shims into it with the heel of his hand. He looked in under the lintel and called, "Marko Lazich, wake up." Distractedly, as if it were a toy, he rolled the wagon back and forth to check his repair. Bersa peered around the boy and inside the hut. A small man sat prostrated at a table built of sticks and twine. "Wake up," said the boy impatiently. The man lifted his face away from the table, considered his company, and stood. He came to the door and cast his ruined eyes up at them. It seemed he'd been weeping. "The Terror of the Velebits. Have you brought me anything this time other than shame and trouble?"

"The priest from Gospić, I'll pay you to feed him."

Bersa now recognized the hut's resident as the itinerant cobbler he'd often seen, adrift in his black clothes and invariably cursing. He was not a third the size of his son, bore him no resemblance at all. "We are Serbs here," he said. "How do you think it would be for me if I took you under my roof? Even for an hour? Because of this hajduk my neighbors think little enough of me. Now I'm to entertain Catholic priests?"

"I said I would pay you, Marko."

"In any event," said Bersa, "I'm not hungry."

"He says he's not hungry," said the householder.

"And I say you are to feed him and feed him well." The boy removed a canvas pouch from his belt and emptied it into his father's hands.

"Twenty dinar? I hear of one robbery after another, you are hunted through the mountains, and then, when you come to my house, you come with twenty dinar? How is it possible to fail as a petty bandit?"

The boy tied Bersa's horse to the post where his father's pony was tethered. "Feed these something as well. With what I've given you, you can buy some feed for these horses. See to it, or you'll wish you had." Danilo Lazich turned and walked away in that abruptness of his that left Bersa feeling erased, and Bersa watched him almost out of sight before he remembered his host, still standing there beside him. "As I said before, I'm not hungry."

"You mean that a Serb's table is not good enough for you."

"I mean," said Bersa, "that I am not hungry."

"Danilo has said that you will eat. He has paid for it. If you leave now, maybe he will run you down and drag you back by the scruff of the neck. He told me to feed you and I will feed you."

"I don't believe he would pursue me."

"No," said Lazich, "he's gone. He won't come inside my house. It is so poorly built, he says, as to offend him. That is the opinion of a thing who sleeps in the snow."

"I'll tell you, if you don't know, that he is not safe and won't be until he is taken in somewhere. You should be ashamed of yourself. Your son is likely to come to harm with all this nonsense. It's bad enough that the boy trades on his reputation, but you with your talk of bandits—that talk is believed, and improved upon. You can't begin to know the stories that are told. This is just the kind of foolishness that can have mortal consequences, you see. Because he lives apart as he does, people are free to imagine him as they like, and they have imagined the worst."

"The worst?" said the householder archly.

"I had heard, for example, that he is a capricious killer."

"And you think that would be the worst he might do?" said Lazich. "Come in. Come in at least so the neighbors won't see us talking."

Stone, the hut was cool inside. Bersa reluctantly settled on the fragile chair that was offered him, and when it didn't splinter with his weight, he settled back. He'd been too tired to go on. The boy had saved him from his own stupidity. He watched Lazich lay a fire in his hearth.

"And what was your opinion of my boy? What was it, again?"

"He is very casually blasphemous. That should be cured."

"Would you see to his piety? Take him in, instruct him? Do you know how fortunate you were? You must know something of original sin. He has never been an innocent."

"You have confused me," Bersa confessed.

"I hold to no understanding." Lazich threw his thin right hand before him like a length of rag. "I profess no creed at all. The Turks chased my grandfather across the Sava, so I call myself a Serb, but I am not Orthodox. I cannot express myself because I am nothing but unconvinced, the perfectly unconvinced man."

"That is very likely the reason we've met," said Bersa.

"We met because Vuk Hajduk found you in the mountains. You must have made a good impression. He went well out of his way for you."

Lazich took a shank of lamb out of a boarded cavity in his dirt floor. He spitted it and set the spit over the fire. The meat began almost at once to drip fat, and a thicker, harsher smoke rolled off the hearth. The chimney barely drew. Bersa excused himself and went out into a night that was, just as the boy had predicted, almost absolutely dark. Lazich followed with a candle. He set it on his wagon seat and drew the tarp off its box. In addition to his cobbler's lasts and hammers and leather, there were hundreds of dirty, shoddily bound books in the wagon. "Select anything," he told Bersa, "and name your price. That is all you'll pay."

"I have no money," said Bersa.

"I will happily extend you credit. As much as you want."

"I will never have money," said Bersa.

"What is your opinion of them?"

"Opinion? Of your books? I am not literary, sir."

"Let me donate something to your library." Lazich blew the dust from the spines of *Caesar's Account of the Gallic Campaigns* and *The Sorrows of Young Werther* and put them on the wagon seat. He added *Problems in Arithmetic,* and *Isaveta's Fondest Memory,* and *The Poets of Illyricum.* "I have so much," he said. "So many."

"Yes. Latin, German, I wouldn't have thought . . ."

"Part of a man's estate. They were given to me. My only windfall, ever. You say they aren't good books, then? Is that the problem?"

"I believe some of the soldiers at the garrison should read the German. Have you tried there?"

"Many times," said Lazich grimly. "I've humiliated myself in Gospić and Ubdina and everywhere, trying to sell them. I think I am going to give it up. It has been ten years. Pure profit, I thought, but only if I sell them, and that has been impossible."

"That little pony of yours," said Bersa, "will be so relieved at your decision. It is sad, isn't it, that you'll never find these books their readers? They might be useful as fuel."

"Danilo read them. My son, the reader of books. What he cannot take into his mouth, he devours with his eyes."

"You were able to teach him? Then your library has served a purpose. You should be proud for having given him that. It's an education wasted, though, and I begin to understand your frustration with him. Still, he is your son."

"I taught him nothing," said Lazich. "He taught himself. He read the books. There was nothing else to do, going with me from place to place, so he read the books. The idea of teaching him something—no one has ever taught him anything. It's just that he doesn't forget. He remembers everything, so he learns whatever he wants."

"Never to forget," said Bersa, "how . . ."

"How vile. He claims to remember events from when he was in his mother's womb."

The men returned to the hut to eat. The meal was the shank, basted in olive oil and rosemary, with a single cup of wine, and was as perfect as any Bersa could remember. He had grown hungry again, standing out in the cold. There were no utensils, so he tore at the meat with his teeth, leaning well forward so that the grease dripped from his chin to the table and not onto his soutane. So much chewing used the last of his strength. He finished, rocked forward, rested his head on his arms, and slept without dreaming. He woke alone in the hut and went outside. Only just dawn. Lazich had already driven his wagon away. Bersa freed his own horse and set off, purely grateful for the cool morning, the sweetening air as he left the village behind. The priest's pleasure in himself so absorbed him that he'd walked half an hour before he noticed that the old crucifix no longer hung from his neck.

July 1880

When the Streifkorps moved, it jangled. From time to time, the barracks in Gospić released a column of the Empire's soldiers to sweep the district for brigands. Each of the soldiers so assigned was required by regulation and the petty diligence of sergeants to carry half again his weight in gear and arms; the chain of command raced constantly, shouted orders traveling from the front of the file back, and with it all rattling in the brutal limestone of the Lika, the noise of their coming preceded them by hours. No one believed that any but the dead would ever be apprehended by these expeditions. "Route step. Eyes up and moving. Keep a sharp lookout." They marched out for weeks at a time and made a great show of examining the milky rock.

Sergeant Reuben Munch was brought in one particularly fruitless summer to reinforce the command with his mountain howitzer. Munch, dispatched from near the Tyrolian frontier, came alone, his gun strapped to a caisson that was so warped his horse had to drag as much as draw it. A day after reaching Gospić, he was sent with a patrol back into the roadless, punishing countryside. They advanced through it for the prescribed ten hours a day, and each night a camp was pitched in conformance to manual 85-s, complete with a low breastworks. And each night, at a certain point, the patrol's fine discipline broke down. Munch was troubled at learning that no night watch was ever set, that the entire troop was allowed, was expected, to sleep from dusk to dawn. The captain in command explained it to him, peremptorily, the first night they were in the field. "We are alone in this waste, Sergeant. Against what do I set my watch? Who would come into this without being ordered to it? We are alone. And if I set a watch, then there must be sentries and a Corporal of the Guard, and a Sergeant of the Guard, and an Officer of the Day, and when would any of us sleep for all this watching you would have us do?"

Munch's gun, again by regulation, was to be placed a hundred full paces outside the camp's perimeter. He could only believe that the howitzer, left unattended all night, would be vulnerable to theft or sabotage, so Munch assigned himself to sleep with it, and still he dreamed of courts martial, saw himself in the dock, accused of losing the Emperor's artillery, facing years at hard labor. He remained awake most of most nights, and alone; and as the patrol went on he began to look forward to the exhaustion, the aimless reverie that filled his nocturnal watches. For company he liked to talk into the night, which was entirely patient with him, and he'd listen to the drone of himself and be pleased by it. The problem was in thinking of things to say. Munch found that there was really very little on his mind and that tricks would be necessary to extract even that. To that end he challenged himself one night to remember and describe the best hour of his life. "Grandmother's girl," he recalled, "brought the lacquer tray into the conservatory. She was flirting with me, that girl, like I was her last hope of happiness. A room without shadows at that hour. A room filled with light. A black lacquer tray with roses. Cakes, compote, cream. Eat as much as I wanted. I was her special one, it was all for me. 'Eat it all,' that's what she said. Grandmother smelled of violets. There were silver napkin rings . . ."

"Very pretty."

The voice was close behind, strange to him. Munch yelped in alarm, but he did not turn to it, and an impulse caused him to bring his carbine to port arms. That was as far as instinct moved him. With the first thought that entered his head, he froze.

"Quiet. Stand as you are and stay quiet."

Munch thought of the three operations necessary to fire the carbine. It might take as much as a second to perform them. He was not infantry, not very deft. The voice was so close. Behind and, strangely, above him. A voice pitched and accented like nothing he'd ever heard. His heart felt like a rock set rolling down a rough hill. "What do you want?" he whispered.

"I haven't decided."

"I think I am supposed to shoot you. You failed to identify yourself."

"Don't turn around," said the voice.

"I have my duty. To raise the alarm or . . . Identify yourself." Munch's eyes shot to the compound of tiny tents, a crushingly futile sight.

"They don't like you, Sergeant. Your field piece adds to the misery of their marching. If you call them down on me they'll never come in time to help you. They may not come at all."

"You address me by my rank. I am not wearing my rank." Munch was on guard, but informally, in just his breeches.

"I know you to be Austrian." The voice seemed to enter Munch not through his ears but at a more sensitive point on the back of his neck. "A sergeant from Austria."

"How would . . . who are you? Are you alone?"

"Who is not?"

"I think I must call out."

"No. If I have to quiet you, we'd both be sorry for it. I hear them address you, and so I know your rank. I hear you talk at night, so I know you are from Salzburg."

The voice knew more of Munch, had taken a greater interest in him, than any of his current comrades. Munch, in turn, knew nothing of the voice except that it was coming from that odd, elevated location just behind him, and that it had gotten its German from some very queer source.

"Salzburg. They must play very much Mozart there?"

"Yes," said Munch. "Especially in spring and summer, Mozart everywhere. To me he is like chain being dragged on cobblestones. Deedly, deedly, you know. Give me the music they play at the masquer's theater. That's more to my taste."

"In the Lika," said the voice, "there is seldom the luxury of preferring one thing over another. I have no tastes."

"I regret that. Very sorry to hear it. As for me, I was a printer before, only a printer. It's still printing I know best."

"A press is an interesting machine. But soldiering, I have never heard a soldier say a worthy thing."

"My father played the concertina," said Munch, desperately. "You've heard me talk at night? How long have you . . . I've seen no one. The outriders have seen no one. You've been following us?"

"I have never heard a piano," said the voice. "A clarinet once, but at too great a distance."

"Everything I have," said Munch, "is issued to me. It would be very serious if I couldn't account for it, if you took anything from me."

"I know the waste of soldiers. Why do you think I follow the column? A traveler can feed and outfit himself just by following these Schwab troops around. Don't tell me these things are dear to you, not when I live off your leavings."

"And you are to be commended," said Munch. "Fine. Take something, if that's what you do."

"Put your carbine on the ground."

"That you may not have. I'd be shot for letting you have my weapon."

"Why would I want it? It's done you very little good."

Munch bent to lay the carbine down. It seemed his brain was sloshing in his skull. "You've given me a killing headache, isn't that enough?"

"Before you were in the army, Sergeant, you lived among women?"

"Yes," said Munch. "But, if you're accusing me of—"

"How was it? How were they?"

"Women?"

"You lived among them."

"One is an angel, another a shrew. I don't know anything that is true of them all."

"You lay with them?"

"I thought you meant to rob me," said Munch.

"What do you have worth taking?"

"Nothing."

"Nothing? So—we are both disappointed."

"I thought," said Munch, "that you were asking for lewd tales. I'm sorry if I was mistaken. But go away now, can't you? If you go away now, you won't be a thief. By morning, I won't be sure you exist. There would be no need of a report."

His carbine on the ground, his back to a voice in the night, Munch waited. This was not what he'd expected of himself as a soldier, not what he'd wanted. When at last he turned, there was no one.

September 1880

The offices of the prefecture were several blocks from Ubdina's central market, still one could smell vegetables deteriorating at this distance. Bersa stood in the civic building's courtyard, the flagstone cool beneath his feet though the day was well advanced. Some part of this structure was an infamous jail, and all of its windows were battened and shuttered. Solemnly he mounted the stairs to a mezzanine where offices were tucked behind unmarked doors. He stopped in at several of these before a clerk told him that he had found the offices of Prosecutor Ritz. "Do you have an appointment to see His Honor?"

"No," said Bersa, "but I had received word that he wished to speak to me."

"No appointment?"

"No," said Bersa. "But I will await his convenience, if he is in."

The clerk shrugged and one side of his collar became detached from his shirt. He did not bother to reattach the collar, though he had to know of its condition. A soft, round, sleepy man, he sat at his desk carefully making diagonal marks across the top of a sheet of foolscap. In time Bersa decided that these marks were completely without significance and that the clerk was a simpleton. "Would you be good enough to announce me? I am Father Bersa."

"You have no appointment."

"No, but I received word that I was to come to him. No time was specified. And so I would like to speak with him if I may."

"If His Honor does not expect you . . ."

"If he does not expect me," said Bersa, "you must tell him I am here. Then he will see me, or make an appointment to see me later, or send me away altogether. But unless he knows I am here, none of these things can happen, can they?"

The clerk pursed his lips, placed a finger lightly upon them, and seemed to think Bersa's point well made. Still, he did nothing.

"So, would you be good enough to announce me to the prosecutor?"

"Of course," said the clerk, officious now, "for that is my duty, is it not?" He stood, gaining little height by it, went down a short hallway hidden from Bersa's view, and knocked at what resounded like a very heavy door. Perhaps a minute later Bersa heard a brief exchange, inaudible as to its substance but clearly unpleasant for the clerk. The heavy door was closed. The clerk returned to his desk where he at once resumed his methodical marking of the foolscap.

"Is it the prosecutor's intention to speak with me?"

"Yes," said the clerk.

"When?"

"When he has finished."

There was on the east wall a portrait of the Ban of Croatia, Count Khuen-Héderváry, as a young cavalry officer, born, no doubt, riding crop in hand. Otherwise there were only the clerk's empty desk, two empty chairs, and a bookcase containing many of the manuals the Austrians so loved to publish and distribute. The room suggested to Bersa an utterly indifferent universe. He gave some thought to passing the time in prayer, then thought better of it. He and the clerk entertained each other with an exchange of furtive glances. At last there were voices again in the hidden hallway, one of them high and feminine and coquettish, "What if Milutin knew? If Milutin should find out what you've done . . ." A girl emerged from the hallway, and as she came into the outer office she was stuffing something into her bodice. A pretty girl who caused Bersa to think, "someone's daughter," she wore the Lika cap, a fashionable dress, and no shoes, and when she saw Bersa she raised her left shoulder to her left ear, grimaced, and burst into tears. She ran out of the office and her feet sounded lightly on the tile outside. Borne on a cloud of rosewater, the prosecutor appeared. "The people, Father. Always the sad lives of the people, which we are expected to remedy." Ritz raised his eyes and a squared goatee thirty degrees toward heaven; they were comrades, after all, in a lost cause and could therefore become immediate confidantes. "We are expected to save them from themselves when that is impossible." A decoration depended from the prosecutor's lapel, a construction of ribbon and enamel and gold leaf, but beyond that there was nothing of the Empire's glory about the man—a morning coat hanging dejectedly upon the body of a lifelong bureaucrat. "Slomski," he said. "Would it have been too much to bring the father a cup of tea while he waited?"

The clerk looked up at him equably. "Tea?"

The prosecutor pressed his fingertips to his eyes. "No," he said. "Anisette, I think. Join me please, Father."

Bersa followed him into an office recently painted in two horizontal shades of brown. The prosecutor's desk, not half so large as his clerk's, was piled with writs and pleadings. A severe wooden chair stood behind it. In the sunny corner of the room were a love seat and a low mahogany table. Preparing their drinks, Ritz behaved as if he had been the party kept waiting, painfully deprived of their special friendship. He joined Bersa on the love seat, comfortable with their proximity and the way they had to twist to face each other. "What was your crime, Father?"

"My . . . crime?" The first words Bersa had spoken to the man.

"Surely the Church sent you here on the heels of some scandal."

"If I am being punished, I don't know why. I am only here."

"I, at least, have warm memories of the improprieties that got me here. Embezzlement, you know. It was prison or an assignment to this prefect. I've been told I might redeem myself if I am very conscientious, but even with that I wonder if I've made the right choice."

"Do you wish me to hear your confession?"

"My confession? I'm leaving that kind of thing to the other fellow from now on." Ritz opened a humidor and withdrew two dreadnaught cigars cured black in brandy. He circumcised them with a small, silver-plated knife, and with some ceremony lit them. He smoked and let the silence build, and finally said, "I must know that I can rely on you."

"In any way that I might be of service. Of course."

"Where do your sympathies lie, Father?"

His sympathies were entirely for Bersa, but that was an admission he made rarely and only to himself. "I don't know that I understand what you are asking me."

"Do you support the administration here?"

"I am indifferent," said Bersa.

"To the things of this world?"

"Yes."

"But you live in this world, more particularly in this hideous prefecture. Can you tell me that you have no interest in seeing order maintained here? No interest in your safety and the safety of other innocents? Why did you make no report?" The prosecutor had summoned a functional anger.

In Bersa's mouth there was a sweet new residue of smoke and liqueur. "Report?"

"You were apprehended in the mountains by one of our most notorious hajduks, and yet you made no report, Father. Don't you see how irresponsible you've been? It is so rare that an articulate, a credible source of information becomes available in these cases. Your silence is wrong."

Bersa had spoken of the incident with the hajduk only to the woman who cleaned the rectory. He now realized that everything he'd ever said in her presence had been ill advised. Talking to Jella, he'd imagined, had been like talking to the walls. What else might the authorities know about him? "I didn't think that anything worthy of official attention had happened." Bersa, within the ambit of the prosecutor's personality, felt strangely virtuous, but nervous.

"In the two months I've been here, Father, not a week has gone by when I haven't had some news of this Vuk Hajduk. He is a giant, he is a child. He is a prodigy, a heretic who may at times go on all fours."

"Yes?"

"This is a criminal with no confederates, no ties to anyone. Because he is so variously described, for me he has no real identity at all, no identity I'm willing to credit. So, Father, you can see the value of your account."

"May I have another anisette?"

The prosecutor poured generously into Bersa's glass. He did not cut the liqueur with water as he had before and it was nicely astringent on the priest's tongue, in his throat. "We met on Debela Brda," Bersa said. "As far as I know, he did nothing worse than guide me and provide me with food and drink." Bersa did not entirely trust his current recollection of that day; it had been in his thoughts so much that he now remembered more than had actually occurred.

"You've left something out."

"I hadn't finished telling it."

"He stole something from you, Father. That is a crime. Shielding the criminal is another."

"I don't know that to be true—that he stole from me."

"He intimidated you?"

"Yes," Bersa allowed. "At first."

"And then you established friendly relations with him?"

"No. Not friendly. He took me to a village of Serbs, an unusually degraded one. I am quite content if they are merely unfriendly to me in such places."

"You went into the village with a crucifix, and when you left it was no longer in your possession?"

"I may have lost it. I didn't trouble to go back and look for it. It was very old, and crucifixes are widely available here."

"Father"—the prosecutor's tone was fraternal again—"forgiveness is an element of your profession. It has no place in mine. He stole from you. He must be taken in hand."

"In hand?"

"Hanged, probably."

"And the law condones this, the hanging of children?"

"The codes are curiously silent on children who also happen to be criminals, though criminals, the worst of them, will be criminals from the cradle. So you confirm to me that he is a child?"

"An adolescent, yes."

"What else?"

Bersa remembered that he had been afraid on the mountain, afraid in Marko Lazich's village. He was afraid now and growing very tired of it. The aroma of a recent copulation rose from the love seats. He'd been true at least to his vow of celibacy and wondered how it was that he knew this essence with so much certainty.

"His appearance?" Ritz prompted.

"He is," Bersa said, "as you've heard, a giant."

"How do you mean that?"

"The person you want is the largest human being I have ever seen. He should be preserved on that account alone. For study. I doubt that anyone has exaggerated his size. But his career, his exploits, I think most of that is unlikely. The things you've heard."

"If it's the noose that bothers you, that's a barbarity we can often dispense with. The people here make unruly suspects and frequently don't survive their arrests. But if they do, there's a surprisingly gifted judiciary. We'll have a nice trial for him, though he won't begin to understand or appreciate the great pains we've taken for him, to preserve his endless legal rights, you know."

Bersa, to that point merely warmed by the spirits he'd taken, was suddenly drunk and aware of some anger of his own. "He would understand them, I assure you. If anything, he understands more than is good for him. It is on that account that I feel sorry for him. A little."

"Well," said the prosecutor, "it can be a grim business, but we are not inhumane. He'd be permitted to choose the manner of his execution. I can think of no compelling reason to allow this Vuk to reach his majority. I will find him."

"You seem quite set on it. Oh, have I been . . . rambling? I don't ordinarily take this much to drink." Bersa was only a little ashamed of himself as he spoke. "I can show you, I think, just where his father lives; the man's name is Marko Lazich, the father."

"Lazich," said the prosecutor, mildly surprised at his good luck. "The Empire registers all births, takes its census. Nothing could be more useful to me than this, a registered name. So, you see, you knew something essential. You'll have to let me decide what is useful and not useful to know."

"He stained my soul." Bersa's thoughts had begun to reveal themselves to him only as they left his mouth, and he did not feel very responsible for anything he might say. He held, he now saw, an insoluble grudge toward the child . . . *the opinion of a thing who sleeps in the snow.* "Vuk's given name is Danilo," the priest volunteered, "and I would assert that he is in some sense a thief, some species of thief."

"Let's take lunch," said the prosecutor happily. "The woman always prepares more than I can possibly eat."

Sardines had been frying in a nearby room, more acrid and more tempting as they burned.

～ Therefore Viennese ～

1880

～ IT WAS MIDNIGHT and he was numbed and enervated by the cold when he reached the blazed spruce notifying alpine travelers they'd crossed into Austria. Having escaped the Slavic-speaking corner of the Empire and perhaps his local fame, he held a moment's ceremony there to rename himself Daniel Savage and then by moonlight followed a vague old track down the north slope of a Carnic Alp. Morning brought him to Öuloo, a village where there happened to be a tailor skilled enough to make him, without benefit of patterns, a workman's pants and jacket. At nightfall he put on these clothes and slid his feet for the first time into the hard-soled shoes he'd had his father make him. He hadn't been long on the road before he decided that he might, wearing his conventional new clothes, travel by daylight if he wanted. His few meetings with Austrians had been that cordial. He made the entire trip to Vienna in this remarkable way, never once in hiding, never having to hear or issue a threat.

Savage found work within an hour of his arrival in the city, carrying hod to a pair of masons who thought him their animal, their machinery. Ruined for any obedience during the prodigious loneliness of his youth, he was strained to the utmost even to cooperate, and he quickly discovered how much he hated doing any one thing all of every day. He became bored, then mortally bored, and then to endure it he took an interest in the technical elements of the work. Soon he was telling his employers that they mixed their mortar too thin, that they were laying it in an improper rhythm with ill-formed trowels. One of them, a stout man accustomed to having his way among the laboring classes, took such strenuous exception to these criticisms that he attacked Savage one morning with a rake, and had his arm broken for his trouble, and there ended Savage's association with the masons. A pattern was established, the boundaries for all his years in Vienna set, and narrowly. In the city, to subsist, craftsmen and criminals and performers of every kind fell into webs of alliance that Savage, by his annealed nature, could not join. Not guild, not gang, he found his living on a scarcely habitable fringe of the capital's economy. As a purveyor of odd goods and very odd services he earned his way into, then out of, the tenements. In time he secured subscriptions to lending libraries, season tickets for the Mingusian symphony. A strong constitution sustained him through almost constant dalliance with women; he expanded very much on the mystery of them. He rode a bicycle, built a cello, painted and was painted, and with it all he was never to find anything half so satisfying in Vienna as the high esteem and good air he'd enjoyed as a boy, as an empty-headed highwayman.

October 28, 1896

There is a bend in the Danube where the river in a time of flooding will wash the silt off the bank, leaving a long strand of clean pea gravel, a great trove of pretty little missiles. Curs and urchins could be companion to his business, so Savage, when he happened to be in this district at an opportune time, would make a riparian stop to rearm. He kept a vest pocket filled with stone rounds, and they rode, pleasantly clacking, waiting to span the distance some careless tormentor might think safe. To launch this sparkling message was one of the bare pleasures to be had from his career. Savage drew a cart through the streets, and if the cart was often piled with the fruits of his genius, still he pulled a cart through the streets, common as a ragpicker or even his father. There were small combats. Today he'd come to the Eggenspburgh, an unusually peaceful neighborhood of artists and artisans and linden-lined streets where he'd once thought he might like to live, but as he turned onto the Mosser-gasse and was again assaulted by the smell of boiled braunbraten, he was reminded that it was all of a part, a single greasy profusion. One never achieved a vista in the city or escaped its cloying smell.

Savage came to 940 Jillenstrasse where Kirt Krueller kept his suite of rooms and a staff of servants who labored somewhat vainly to humor him. Krueller himself answered the door. "At last," said the councilman. Still in his dressing gown and slippers, his hair standing uproariously on his head, Krueller stepped at once into the street to examine what Savage had brought him, a pair of disconsolate birds perched in a cage large enough to have housed twenty of their kind. One faced east, the other west. "Is this their color, man?" Even in his delight it was impossible for Krueller to quit maneuvering. Everything must be contested. "I can show you *Fleury's Field Guide*—these are not true Bohemian thrushes."

"I'll set them loose," Savage offered. "If they're not perfectly to your liking, I'll set them loose."

"No. Would you have them try and make their way among the city's pigeons? No. I'll take them, but you can see that I won't be able to pay you as if they were of the species I'd wanted?"

"I will set them free," said Savage again. "I don't know that they're Bohemian, but I did ride with them by livery carriage all the way from Klatovy, and I doubt the slackjaw I bought them from would have gone very far afield to capture them. I don't know even that they are thrushes, I am no ornithologist. But they are nice, stoic little birds, and you will pay me the price we agreed upon, or I will set them free. They will be safer with anything they find in the trees than they would be with you. You are a stupid man, and we both know how misguided your affections can be." Savage fingered the latch of the cage door.

"I am a councilman of the City of Vienna, Third Order of the Interior."

"That hadn't escaped me, Krueller, you mention it each time we meet. But, more to the point, have you nineteen silver gulden?"

"You offend me. You offend my office."

"Why don't you pay me now? I've grown fond of these birds, Councilman. You'd better not neglect them because you suspect their pedigree. I'd rather see them circling the chimney pots."

Krueller's eyes seemed to follow his birds through the possibility of their freedom, scanning the sky unhappily. "Come inside," he said. "Bring them inside. That cage was never mentioned. I owe you nothing for the cage."

Liveried members of the household gathered near them as they came in, pretending fascination in the birds. Krueller sent them to fetch a bowl of distilled water, a bank draft, a pen. "You must not be insolent in front of the servants," he told Savage when they'd gone. "You'll grant me that at least. I am paying full price even though I shouldn't, so you needn't be insolent. I don't call you stupid, do I? I don't call anyone stupid, or at least no one who is my superior."

Savage opened the cage door, and Krueller tapped at it until the thrushes reluctantly quit their perches and hopped out into the larger confinement of the man's house, which was also an aviary. The councilman's initial enthusiasm had been for large tropical birds, and in his home the shrill report of cockatoos was constant, never less startling for being so. A kestrel hunted mice off the carpets, and a murder of crows had been let inside. All the birds made a braking sound with their wings whenever they took flight. When flying inside it was necessary for them almost always to backpedal. In every room buckets of water and rags stood at the ready, and these the servants brought to bear all of every day, bombarded by an inexhaustible rain of white droppings, or Krueller's just deserts. The household could not have been more dominated had it been filled with apes or tigers.

The councilman watched the new arrivals come to terms with their situation, their heads swiveling with the witless dignity of their kind. "They seem lethargic. "

"The air, Krueller. You've got to screen a few of these windows so you can open them. I'll put in a system of louvers for you. Upland species cannot survive this heat. I'm surprised that you do."

"The lovebirds do very well here."

"They come from a stifling climate. Let me ventilate these rooms or they'll be lethal. It wouldn't cost so much. The lovebirds, if necessary, can keep each other warm. It will give them something to do."

"You can never leave well enough alone, Savage. You are relentless."

"Well—enough? I've never seen it. Let in some air, let in some light. You and the whole menage will thank me when I've . . ."

"Ah, money."

"Or . . ."

"No," said the councilman. "I've told you before, I can have no part of a passport for you, even a visa is out of the question."

"What would you say to a falcon? I will acquire and train it for you, train it to land on your wrist. I could make you a dashing leather cuff. These others are only so much poultry as compared to the bird I could bring you."

"How am I to pay for it?"

"With your signature."

"No," said Krueller. "No, to all of it. If the empress were content to have you leave the Empire, she would see to it herself. Wouldn't she? You are the empress's man, and far be it from me to send you away on papers bearing my signature."

"Have one of your subordinates do it, Krueller. Surely you know how to deflect responsibility."

"For very little trouble you have a home and the freedom to pursue your—pursuits. An income, all the benefits that come of being near Her

Highness. Do you think that you'll blunder into something better somewhere else?"

"I think I'd better," said Savage.

June 31, 1896

They had insisted she must have more than milk and oranges; she must
succumb at times to sleep. Fretting physicians. Science annoyed her, as
did those who clung to it, unable to accept the grinding truth, that
one's fate waited, and if that fate was essentially tragic, no adjustment
of habit, medication, or diet was going to substantially vary it. Elisabeth
had just now done the best she could for herself, and her best was an
admirable, nearly odorless coil looped in her chamber pot. Who among
her advisors could honestly claim to defecate this well? Ever. And they
with all their gorging. She palpated the hollows at her hips where skin
and muscle were still smooth. Even in the Hofburg, with a thousand
minions interfering, she had her covert pleasures. Such perfection as remained to her was hidden, and was hers alone.

Elisabeth went to her escritoire to attend to correspondence. She
flexed her pen's steel nib and thought to write a poem instead. Verse had
long lain dormant in her, but this morning, cleansed, she was alive to
the howling of her muses:

Sister Persephone
We are wed to rimed realms
And we are ever cold
In every season duty whelms
Our misery to enfold.

You in clinging vines do lie
Your heart in thrall to hell

I alone need not ask why
You fell, my dear, just fell.

They want our radiance every year
Upon their clotted earth
Want grass and grain and cheer
So much beyond our worth.

We arrive with a sigh, leave with another
Always good-bye and good-bye and goodbye.

Of all her delicately balanced family, though several had been sui-
cides, no Wittlesbach had suffered melancholy to equal her own. Elisabeth, too, saw extinction as a possible approach to happiness, but she
was keenly indisposed to mortal sin and so had restricted herself to poetry and flirting with destruction.

She pulled twice, then twice again at the bell pull, and Frau Freifalik came with her rattling cart. The little woman, all in white, went
round to her back and worked her hands through the storied fall of her
mistress's hair to her neck; she kneaded its flesh upward. The women
believed that fresh blood could by this technique be forced to the empress's brain, which needed refreshment. Frau Freifalik was filled with
the importance of her work, sure and practiced in doing it, but she
could not be other than tender with the empress's person and therefore
made a bad masseuse.

"Thoroughly, please. Deeply. I like to feel your thumbs on my verte-
brae. No, harder." Elisabeth had always attracted servants who, desperate to please, brought her tea too strong and stockings too long, and
their many misfortunes. As empress, it would never do to do for herself,
and she had been their hostage, having always to ask for what she
wanted and never quite receiving it. "Harder," she said, but Frau Freifalik would not be driven to effectiveness. "Oh, stop. We will shampoo."

Frau Freifalik broke a half dozen eggs, separated their yolks, and floated them on a quantity of Armagnac in an earthen bowl. She included drops of humectant and an Egyptian henna. Elisabeth lay out upon the divan provided for the washing because her hair, when saturated with the mix, overburdened her slender neck. Reverently, Frau Freifalik made a great wet rope of it, formed it into a knot, and wrapped it in toweling. She crushed strawberries to paste in honey and spread it on the empress's face.

Elisabeth closed her eyes so the mix could be applied also to her eyelids. "Frau, bring me the countess. Make further inquiries about my giant. I feel they wish to deprive me of my Savage. Let everyone you speak with know that I will not accept excuses or lies. He cannot be so difficult to find as they are telling me."

There was the frau's murmured assent, and the empress sensed she was alone again—preciously.

She was in the forty-second year of her marriage. At sixteen she had married to the throne of an empire still reeling from the wounds of '48, and the young Elisabeth, the empathetic Elisabeth, had almost accidentally wooed Hungary so that the Dual Monarchy could be engineered. A temporary stay of the inevitable. In this generation, or in the next, the atrophied carcass of the Holy Roman Empire would be shred and fed to a nest of ravening nations. Their domain. The children were gone now, married off to their own dutiful alliances, the Prince perished by his own hand. Shopkeepers were rising up in every province, wanting to create jejune little parliaments where they might argue small, shrill arguments in their native tongues. This was a class that wanted an evenhanded world and would be dangerously disappointed when they found they couldn't make one. Grand things were passing away, institutions well endowed with love or tradition constantly slipping under. The institution of the Imperial Marriage, however, persisted. Elisabeth was awed, if not much pleased, at her life's accomplishment. Her mere survival entitled her to more, she thought, than this being wheeled out for display like an old canon. Recumbent, Elisabeth felt the weight of her loyalty to her husband pressing down along her whole length.

The Countess Irma Sztáray came into the room with an aromatic broth. "Oh, oh, oh," said the empress, as unhappily as she could, "take that away at once. My handkerchief, please."

When the countess returned, she was full of gossip intended for the empress's ears. They had been long away from the capital, and during their absence everyone at court had fallen into a liaison with the perfectly wrong person. It had become this season's fashion. Irma was aglow at the prospect of the evening just before them. The countess, had she not been Elisabeth's companion, would most probably be glittering in this firmament. She loved pomp and the company of the *haute monde*, loved them above all, save the empress. To remain at the empress's side it had been necessary for her to abandon all else in which she might have had a part. Irma's great sacrifice. Thinking about it often made Elisabeth sharp with her. "Irma, do you see how you have thickened over the years? Every part of you."

"My ankles," said the countess, "like the trunks of small trees."

"Have they found my giant, Irma?"

"Captain Jolewicz has been dispatched, Majesty. They say he always succeeds."

"A woman," Elisabeth said, "knows just two stages of life. She is transcendent, then ugly. There are no gradations, nothing intermediate. You and I, my dear, are ugly, and have been for some time."

"Majesty, many wonderful desserts are made with overripe fruit."

"All of them requiring that the fruit first be pulped."

Frau Freifalik wiped the empress's face so that she might lay slices of cucumber over her eyes. The light that came through them was a simple explanation of repose and quiet. Oh, the longing. "Irma, is she lovely, the tsaritsa? Does she inspire confidence?"

"Not so lovely as the tsar. Even at the Russian court she is considered gauche. But Nicholas is remarkably . . . pretty. Reminds one, almost, of our emperor in his younger years. There is something so definite, so identifiable in an imperial lineage. The habit of long sovereignty."

"Yes. I've reconsidered the advantages of breeding as we have always understood them. Mr. Darwin would tell us that the great houses have bred themselves into a very tight spot. Soon we'll make children who bark like dogs."

"Majesty."

"At intervals we should have permitted an infusion of good, turgid peasant blood. There are certain sensibilities too fine for this world."

Irma smiled kindly. Her mistress was a woman of many interests, many opinions, and might be expected to wander into sacrilege. "The seamstress tells me, Majesty, that she must request a final fitting. Your gown drapes listlessly yet. She's sewing a taffeta underlayment that should lift it quite impressively. A simple thing."

"I have decided to wear the blue gown, the Jurgen."

"That was given to a charity. Several years ago, when it was fashionable."

"At my request? I don't remember it, Irma."

"It should have been. Majesty, you have worn that gown at least twice previously to affairs of state, and I believe that protocol demands—"

"The blue gown," said the empress, "fits me. And it suits me. The Jurgen, then, and the Pianini jewels."

"Yes, Majesty. May we take it in at the waist?"

"If you like."

"May we add—"

"Leave it alone, Irma. It will certainly do."

Like her empress, the countess had been a horsewoman. Unlike the empress, the strength in her hands was apparent. Hands like cudgels. She was wringing them. "Yes," she said. "You are zestful this morning, Majesty."

"I am resigned. But not so resigned that I will be seen at this event without my giant."

"Majesty, won't you give yourself over to this? The city is alive. Ribbons are being displayed in the windows of even the meanest shops. Bakeries have prepared cakes in your likeness."

"They ask themselves in my absence, 'What is left?' "

"You are adored."

"But tediously so. I nod and approve everything I'm told, hardly understanding a word of it. That is what I do in Vienna."

"The prime minister has asked if he might meet with you sometime this afternoon. The Balkans, he says. He'd like to speak with you about Serbia."

"Badeni? There'll be no time for him. I'm visiting the stables today."

"Of course, Majesty, only you hadn't mentioned it before, had you?"

The Countess Sztáray shifted from foot to foot, having taken up a fan she did not think to use. Elisabeth had begun to take a slight chill beneath her beauty preparations. "Rinse me, dear," she told Frau Freifalik. To Irma she said, "I shall do nothing while my hair dries. And if you won't collect yourself a bit, calm yourself, I wish you would go off somewhere."

"But I've brought a surprise."

"More food?"

"Friends."

"Can we not?"

The countess put her fingers to her lips, minced ridiculously to the door, and opened it. The empress feared her heart would fail—there stood Lorelei and Heidi upon their two useful and proportionate legs, women now. How tall and brave they had become. When had this occurred? Why hadn't she been notified? Lorelei's mature head, depending as it did from the less erect of their necks, burdened them terribly. Elisabeth was saddened to see that no surgeon had been found to remove their forelegs. She remembered them as fawn's legs, and voluminous skirts engulfed them now, but they remained apparent enough, thrusting from the girls' single, wide pelvis. The empress found it difficult to imagine how she had ever become interested in this horror. These horrors.

"They have been asking, Majesty, for a number of years, to be allowed an opportunity to in some way show their gratitude."

"Gratitude? To whom? For what?"

"Their wonderful lives. They have been trained to play the pianoforte."

Heidi, except for her deformity, was the blushing alpinist. Lorelei was equally hale and pretty, but, because of her head's problematic relationship to their body, seemed abject.

"You are so very sweet," Elisabeth told them. "And I am so pleased to see you again. But you're lovely, aren't you? Stature, that's the thing. So important. They are so lovely, aren't they, countess. Country girls."

Heidi and Lorelei curtsied, a complex act for them. Elisabeth had grown tired already of reproaching herself about them. "Are you capable of conjugal relations?"

"No, Majesty," said Heidi. "We cannot and have no wish to."

"We are with child, your Highness," said Lorelei. "Our lives are full in every way."

"Girls." The countess clapped; reflexively the twins curtsied again, nearly failing this time to recover from it. "Think," said Irma, "of the lives they might have led."

"I cannot prevent myself from it," said the empress. "They live here?"

"They have everything in the Hofburg, their own chapel."

"Do I understand you to say, Countess, that they never leave the palace?"

"Majesty," said Lorelei, "we lack for nothing."

Elisabeth felt as if the floor were opening beneath her. "There should be some useful thing I could tell you. You were only girls . . . We'll visit these rooms of yours before we leave. Do you like flowers? Irma, see that those are delivered, and the hyacinths. Have they had a sitting?"

"They have declined a portrait, Majesty."

"Quite their prerogative," said Elisabeth pointedly. "Yes, very good. I am so happy to have seen you again." She stroked her throat by way of signaling the countess that the audience was ended. The girls were taken away.

As bad as all the rest, she had been mad for oddities. Elisabeth had collected lives to no better purpose than to consign them to various of her closets and forget them there, all with the best of intentions. As the victim of similar intentions, she thought, she should have known better.

The countess returned to her, well satisfied. "Friends, Majesty. You see, you have them everywhere, from every station and in every condition."

"Do you remember the little black fellow, Irma? That boy we had to purchase from the Ottoman? Is he . . . still about? Unhealthy, wasn't he?"

"He lives at Ischl. There is a crofter's cottage there."

"He must be grown by now."

"He did not grow so much, Majesty, as further contort. Like a vine twining round himself. But, do you know, he still calls himself by the name you gave him. His most prized possession is a rotogravure of the Silver Wedding Anniversary. He raises chickens."

"Dear God. Contentedly, Irma?"

"I cannot say, Majesty."

"Where are the seeds of contentment ever sown?"

"In service," said the countess with conviction.

"I am never allowed to forget the extreme privilege of service, am I?"

Irma sat without permission. Her underlip crept forward, her chin down, and she looked up through a well of abuse at her mistress.

"They have not found my giant, Irma."

"No, Majesty."

"I will not relent in this. I am available precisely to the extent my giant is available, and I must have him in time to see him properly groomed. That excess of his last May, the thing with the orange feathers—the emperor wanted him on bread and water after that."

"There are armies that would conquer Africa at a word from you,

Majesty, and yet you . . . your Savage, Majesty, never knowing what he may say or do. Why not a squadron of the Hungarian Guard? They could be assembled at a half hour's notice."

"Savage," said Elisabeth. "Our Savage and no other. We will have such fun as we can."

⟶ ⟶

The back wall of the Café Unklug was all mirror, and in that mirror Captain Jolewicz tracked his shako as it split the crowd. He emerged from the crush of patrons and was reflected in full above the counter. He wore his beribboned regimentals as well as any man and was, particularly by contrast to the louts lounging at the tables behind him, fabulous. Theorists they were. Cripples, irreligious Jews, and artists with their talk, talk, talking and their deplorable hygiene. How did they, how could they presume to such arrogance? These were not men of action. Some thought themselves dangerous, but none were more than unhappy. Kropotkinites, Bakuninists. There was among them a prevalent and maddening conversational tic: they presented their hands to each other like upturned bowls. Each of them seemed to think his every utterance sacred.

Now that Jolewicz had been generally noted, a dumb show was in progress. The café's clientele hid their mouths behind their hands and remarked upon his presence. He knew the laughter—abrupt, muffled, at his expense. Few ever imagined they might hurt Jolewicz, and yet nearly everyone did. He desired the day when citizens like these attempted more than incivility, more than talk. He'd order them against a wall. A cigarette and a blindfold, and then let them espouse, briefly, anything they liked. They affected here, almost universally, to smoke workman's black tobacco. Many of them could afford better. It was as if an artillery duel had been fought in the room. Worse, really. It wasn't honest smoke.

Jolewicz lowered his gaze to the marble countertop and considered the calming, swirling mosaic in the polished rock. He ordered a glass of water. The little waiter trundled by several times like a cask on wheels, smoothing a gray apron over his belly, serving others. Where a younger Jolewicz might have drawn his revolver, the captain only repeated his request. "Water," he said. Having regained the waiter's attention, he looked into his upturned nostrils and knew instantly that here was a man who would be tempted to rash expressions of stupidity. The man held a water pitcher to the light from the only window. Sand and vegetable matter swirled in it. He placed a glass on the counter, carefully filled it to overflowing, then moved toward cleaning the mess with his rag. Then, conspicuously, he decided against it and stood there with his woman's fists planted on the shelves of his womanly hips, as if to snatch up the glass the moment the captain had finished drinking. Jolewicz could not be turned away from the Unklug, but he wasn't welcome here; idiotically, predictably, he was stung.

The Café Unklug was, in its way, the most exclusive of Vienna's coffee-houses. In a city filled with malcontents, few were sufficiently weighted to sink to this depth. It was a society that disdained the idea of society and to which, therefore, no one could truly belong. Who would wish to? Nihilist pap, and what could come of it? An emptiness in the heart, the head, the belly. Jolewicz ached, however, to be taken in, even here where no one was taken in. Admitted everywhere but nowhere accepted, the captain was by his own estimate the most alienated of men.

"I am looking for the giant," he told the waiter.

"You must have very few informants in the quarter these days, my Captain, if you cannot find Savage. No man is more visible." The waiter did something with his mouth that gave rise in Jolewicz a desire to grasp the corners of his moustaches and stretch his fat cheeks into a grinning semblance of humility.

"I know that he is your patron, your regular patron. And you should know that I am the empress's envoy this morning."

"Jolewicz. I know your work. We know your agents when they are here."

"Agents? Well—you are obviously the author of penny operas. Agents, phht. Of what would they inform me? What of any possible interest to anyone occurs in this quarter?" Jolewicz, in violation of standing orders, often lost track of the district's more significant characters. He did not enjoy being reminded of it. And this business of having personally to consort with the motley each time Savage was wanted— that the continued success of his career should hinge on such an assignment, such a soldier. The empress's ongoing whim was as odd and urgent as a nightmare. "I see half a dozen persons here whom I should probably arrest on suspicion of seditious acts. I see gazettes displayed without the censor's stamp."

The waiter stroked his torso to wipe away the sediment of his profession, then to soothe himself. A further impertinence came to his lips before he abandoned it. "If you wait," he said, "the man will surely be here. He sells things. There are those who come here only to let Savage berate them, they enjoy it. How could he stay away? But while you wait, my Captain, you will have coffee, and pay for it, and you must offer your cigarettes around. That is a custom we follow here."

"Your custom? I must? Do you know, good fellow, that I once had command of the muddiest outpost in Galicia? I kept a man very like you in my employ, and he spent his days scraping the mud from my uniforms, assisting my laundress. I arranged to have him indentured to me. Surprising how easily that can be done. In time this Galician fellow came to think of me almost as his father, but that was after I'd been forced to give him quite a hiding. We were on maneuvers, you see, and he was found eating grubs. At any rate, the customs I most enjoy originate with me."

"Shall I stand tall at attention, my Captain?"

"Vienna," Jolewicz despaired.

"We live here," said the waiter, "therefore we are Viennese."

As a boy, Jolewicz had marched in his mind many times toward the Prussians' needle guns, marched in the company of innocents. Gloriously dismembered, they marched on until the day was won, the field of honor secured. Had he ever imagined his talents and duties would wend this way, he'd have become a milliner. He ordered *schnecken*, a *café nature*. He let his eyes wander the room and was gratified at the effect they had on those they fell upon. He was the wind from the north, Jolewicz. He had a finding instinct that told him to remain where he was.

At just past noon the giant entered Café Unklug. There was a sense of constriction upon his coming into the room. He'd let his hair grow since Jolewicz had last seen him, and he looked the brutish musician. He saw Jolewicz immediately and came to him, as if during their absence from each other they had become the closest of friends. He carried an open crate containing kidney-shaped metal objects. "Zoltan," he said, "you have become bloated. I know an herbalist who could help you with this. An emetic is needed."

"The proper form of address, Corporal."

"That again? Captain Jolewicz of the Emperor's Secret Police, Brigadier Colonel of the Hungarian Royal Guard, Master at Arms? You'd have me spend half my day speaking your name."

"You know why I am here," said Jolewicz. "As usual, there has been scant notice, and there is very little time. We will now have to waste an hour of it at the barber's. Your . . . compact, I believe the empress calls it, prohibits you from letting yourself go as you have. You are to remain presentable at all times. Now, what are those in the crate? Do we have here the evidence by which you will finally be exposed? Are you making bombs for this crowd of fiends?" Jolewicz took up one of Savage's canisters. A weight shifted within it and it threw itself out of his hand. He leapt back as it struck the floor. More laughter.

"Bombs," said Savage, "anyone can make. Bombs are not an enterprise of the analytical." He set his crate on the counter and retrieved the thing the captain had dropped and showed him how its fatter end contained a panel that could be opened and that, inside, there was a steel ball with a coarse surface, free to roll about. "Mortar *and* pestle, I have integrated them. One lets the weight of the ball do the milling. One no longer leans and grinds so laboriously. I will be regarded by history as a fine and useful development, don't you think, Zoltan? You can tell your grandchildren—you have grandchildren?—that you knew me."

Grandchildren? Possibly. Scattered bastards. "The empress requires your services again tonight. Why have I been unable to find you, Savage? Where have you been?"

They went out of the café together and down the Enderplatz. Three-story tenements rose out of each side of the street, new buildings draped with cast grapes and cherubs and already dark with the city's historic dust. From many doorways persons emerged carrying slops. From a thousand windows a rattling, collective exhalation could be heard. Vendors stood in kiosks, making no attempt to hawk their wares. "You are to remain a pace behind me and to my right," Jolewicz said, "and stay in step. In my company you will behave as a soldier, a soldier of inferior rank."

"If I were to stay in step with you, I'd have to take my strides from the knee down, like a mechanical doll, and wouldn't that be ludicrous? Regulations are your comfort, Zoltan, they have nothing to do with me."

"I have always wondered," said Jolewicz dreamily, "how many lashes would be necessary to make you lose consciousness. Someday I will put a team to work on that back of yours, have them work in shifts until there is nothing left of it."

Savage smiled at him.

"Enjoy yourself," said Jolewicz. "You may as well for as long as you still can. But remember, my term of service will outlast the empress, be sure of it, and the moment you no longer enjoy her protection I will be coming for you with the hounds of hell. You'll stand before a select military tribunal, charged with a thousand instances of insubordination. And then—locked away. I'll have you locked away, I think, rather than shot."

"Get your passports in order then, you and your hounds, because you'll be looking for me under a cloudless sky where the desert has been made to bloom. Look in some harmonious place far outside your authority, Zoltan, and if you come without friendship in that potmetal heart of yours, then hell will consist of finding me."

They passed leering prostitutes. Children. Jolewicz wished that he had brought his horse or ordered a carriage. His boots were badly scuffed. Gradually the city opened and sunlight seemed to gust down on them. They came to scattershot neighborhoods, through different formulations of misery. The city should never have exceeded its ancient center, should never have permitted itself to be surrounded by these adhesive layers of squalor. He heard fragments of many conversations and arguments, none of them in German. Finally, they came to the cottage where Savage was supposed to be readily found; the corporal posted at its gate saluted Jolewicz happily. They passed through the neighborhood's only garden, where there were rows of string beans that had reached an obscene maturity, strung along a system of stakes. The cottage was painted blue, all out of keeping with the drab or entirely unpainted huts surrounding it. Dark blue the shutters, a grid of stone walkways. Savage reached up into the door to manipulate a hidden lock that needed no key.

It was a single large room inside, the coolest place Jolewicz had been in a month. Cool, well lit, and pungent. A young woman reclined, the odalisque, on an elevated pallet in one corner. She wore an aquamarine silk robe. Jet black hair, also silken, fell across her shoulders. Her bangs were cut short and severe. Just as they came in, she'd put a match to the bowl of a pipe. Opium, then, was the sweet component of what Jolewicz was smelling. Chilies and large cloves of garlic hung in bunches over one counter, and along the opposite wall another counter was outfitted with shears and punches and hammers of differing weights. There were springs and screws in jars, virgin sheet metal, metal in stages of being shaped. A hammered steel wren hung from a string, approximating flight in the draft from the open door.

"Isolde," Savage told the woman, "this is Captain Zoltan Jolewicz, another exalted lackey. We are off to the Hofburg. I should not be very late. The empress never stays long at the ball."

Isolde unfolded from the pallet and removed from the closet a uniform jacket so heavy and large she might have lived in it like a tent from the Arabian Nights. She held it before her. "So I'll finally see you in this. It will be like finding myself on stage at the opera." She took up the cape and pressed her flush cheek to the ermine trimming. "And they say that artists are the voluptuaries. Soldiers, given the slightest opportunity, are the most flagrant sensualists. Wouldn't you agree, Captain Jurtek?"

"That is Captain Jolewicz."

"Captain Jolewicz," she repeated sternly. "Believe me, we are all toy soldiers here, addicted to the bright paint they daub on us. Files on parade, don't you think? And don't be so angry, little fellow, it is wearing when you are so angry." Again the tart pressed the venerable uniform of the Guard to her cheek. She pursed her lips. Her eyes were as bright as a bird's. It was not necessary to disguise that he was watching her, she did not mind his stare. She thought herself so clever, merely for having seen in him the obvious. If the girl were really astute, if she had even the slightest appreciation of his depth of feeling, she would be running now, running into the street, her eyes big as saucers, her heart full in her mouth, strangling a prayer for mercy.

～

They wore every sash and decoration to which they were entitled and every bauble they could afford. Nobles, notables, and ministers of state were milling in an anteroom of the *Grand Saal*, awaiting the sluggish formalities and the ball. Franz Joseph stood apart of course, alone in the rigorous misery of his most formal uniform. He perspired and regarded his subjects with the usual disappointment. The emperor, trained from infancy to close observation, saw that his wife would be difficult tonight. Elisabeth sat glazed and somnolent in the room's most cluttered corner, the nucleus of a swarm of fairylike attendants. Mountebanks posed nearby, watchful. The empress would neither wear nor allow anyone in her service to wear perfume and so the scent of opportunity was pure and strong around them. Just behind her, her bodyguard was propped with his back to the wall. His arms were folded, his leg cocked, a foot also bracing him on the wall. The plume of his busby bobbed atop his slowly descending head. Franz Joseph caught at an adjutant's sleeve. "Hinterlander. Remind that man where he is."

The adjutant pulled at the skirts of his tunic, maneuvered through the crowd to the giant, and spoke up toward his ear. The giant opened an eye but could not, in his boredom, sustain the effort. Hinterlander backed a step away and made a slight adjustment of his belt. He glanced toward the emperor. Franz Joseph nodded. Hinterlander pulled at the man's elbow. The bodyguard shrugged, then as an afterthought, he lifted his great arm and brushed the adjutant away, into the ambassador to Sofia, who could not decide if he was outraged. Hinterlander apologized to the diplomat and collected himself. Once again he glanced toward the emperor. Franz Joseph lifted his palm to the adjutant to signal retreat. The giant, in the emperor's experience of him, had never failed to promote chaos; he must not be given the slightest opportunity.

Franz Joseph was an actress's sometime beau; he was husband to his wife and to his wife's enduring hysteria. Whose energies would not be devastated by such women? Like any man he lacked the power even to alter very much those things, those people, he could actually touch, but in an emperor this seemed a shameful limitation. He hated having it particularly drawn to his attention. He was at times, usually ceremonial moments, struck by vast ambitions—form a commission, join a cabal, build a rail line to Romania. He'd be happier, he thought, if he found more to do. But his days were short and filled with irritations, and he typically reached the end of them having accomplished nothing. Franz

Joseph was just at the point of resigning himself to it once again, and assembling the proper mood to enter the ball, when Prime Minister Badeni trickled before him and presented himself. An example of this new nobility, a progressive, the prime minister made a quick mechanical bow and went straight to his preoccupations.

"Your Majesty. What a splendid meeting that was. Your time with the emperor was more successful than anyone had hoped it could be. Even your admirers underestimate you."

"Only God knows me perfectly."

"There was . . . sympathy. It was productive, Majesty, your conversation." Rich as Croesus, Badeni came out season after season in the same frayed frock coat.

"Productive of dyspepsia." Franz Joseph hoped to discourage Badeni before he thought to brief him on sanitation in the provinces or the price of bread. The prime minister was a chronic bore.

"To see titans making history, Your Majesty, few men are privileged to witness such exchanges as I saw today."

"There was history? I thought it was tea and toast. And that flask of his."

Incredibly, Badeni leaned in, his breath redolent of onion. "I'm certain I saw some deep feeling shared. There are treaties—and there are understandings. Which is the more secure arrangement?"

"A treaty is the more secure arrangement," the emperor explained. "With Russians, one wants something in writing. It means very little, Count Badeni, when some Romanov or other drinks your health. We're thrown together, and so we get on. Nicholas is a great improvement over his father that way, one can get on with him, but it would be a breach of duty to trust the fellow." Lacking a fundamental skepticism, Badeni would never grasp statecraft. Unseat the prime minister, another project Franz Joseph had left undone.

The emperor crossed the room to his wife and the crowd melted before him. Sleep was become a rarity for her, but Elisabeth could still manage it when it was especially inconvenient. Too frail now to walk as much as she liked, and long denied the pleasure of riding with any frequency, she was no longer sun- and windburned as she'd been when she'd lived her life out of doors. But the crepe, crosshatched flesh, that stunned countenance—irreversible now. He stood before her and made hushed expressions of love until her eyes opened; they were without luster, not rested, not wakeful.

"Darling, it's your little Franz." They never spoke but in a whisper. It had been decades since they'd been alone together. He gave her his hand. She gripped it between her chin and collarbone.

"No more," she said. "As I am, I contribute nothing. You must put me out to pasture, as they say."

The emperor touched his wife at the part in her hair and on the bridge of her nose. Like a cat she rose to his touch. Her endless wanderings, her swift attachment to arcane enthusiasms—cloud climbing he had called it. It was reported that various of his subjects described her habits less charitably. Elisabeth was expensive. Always reluctant to do her part, she'd been half her life in one conveyance or another, between destinations. Even her arrivals had a quality of departure. But while she was away he could at least imagine that he missed her. "You have been," he told her, "a riddle to me. But at last I know."

"Do you, Franz?"

"You're home at last, and I've wanted to tell you how I've unraveled the great enigma. It is only that you are shy."

"Yes."

"So very shy."

"Well . . . yes. Hadn't I told you?" Elisabeth sat suddenly forward as if to receive the rest of some very bad news. "I must have told you, or it must have been so . . ."

"That charwoman in the Ringstrasse, for instance."

"Franz?"

"Our little stroll yesterday. We passed a charwoman, and of course you wouldn't remember it. But the obverse is my point exactly. She remembers. Charwoman, someone like that, sees the emperor, the empress, remembers every detail of it—the empress was so fine-boned, so tired, so unearthly—that woman and millions more of her kind, they wait to pass some piece of you on to their children. The mere sight of you is an heirloom. All the details. Forever. Tiring to be seen in that light. Remember our courtship, dear? Didn't we surprise them?"

"I remember when the balls were only for dancing. But if I remember carefully, I know that was never the case."

"Given you an awful life."

"Yes," she said. "They kept taking my babies from me. Training them."

No one ever sat a hunter like his wife. Franz Joseph had seen her just twice at the hunt. Busy otherwise. Every detail. She rode, at least, like she meant it. Mother of his children. He wished she were away again. She could be a brave, pleasant creature while she was away. They heard a Slavic fanfare out in the *Grand Saal*, the tsar and tsaritsa were making their entrance. "You and I," he said. "Let this be your last ball, and we'll be together through the evening, just you and I. In my eyes you remain the most beautiful consort alive."

"I am alive," she agreed.

"Just you and I. Dismiss your . . . Dismiss that man tonight, won't you, dear? And we'll face them as we once did. The two of us against all comers. Remember?"

"Franz, you make such a point of allowing everyone in the building to touch you. No, I'll need Savage."

"I don't like him. This isn't the first time I've let that be known."

"No one likes him. If anyone liked him, he'd be of no use to me."

"The man is in constant dereliction. Not remotely a soldier, and yet, there he is, elevated to a lieutenancy, dishonoring the uniform of the Guard. The uniform I wear. He has no place here."

"Nor have I," said Elisabeth. "And yet, here we are."

"Empress of Austria, Queen of Hungary, the, you know . . . You are . . . and he is inconsistent. With our mission."

Elisabeth said nothing.

"Not necessary, he is not necessary. Every man of the Empire is your sworn protector, so the addition of this—person—is not necessary. You there, Lieutenant."

The man tilted negligently away from the wall. "We're going out?" A great deal of milk white virgin wool had been wasted in the construction of his uniform.

"You see? An imbecile. Lieutenant, recite your Twelve Basic Orders."

"I don't know them," said the giant. "Would the Ten Commandments do?"

"We needed him," said Elisabeth, "in officers' whites tonight. I hope you don't object. For our palate. Enlisted blue was so wrong for tonight, we just had to promote him."

"He will honor us and he will honor what we are about." But the emperor heard no authority in his voice. His was the voice of an old man who needed to urinate frequently and who had always, in the end, permitted his wife all her eccentricities. "You are not to speak again," he told the bodyguard. "Not a word from this moment on."

"Not ever, Franz? How can you . . ."

"No. While he is in attendance, he may not speak. No speaking, is that clear enough for you? You will follow an order as simple as that."

"But that," cautioned the giant, "would mean the end of our conversation."

"No. Conversation? No. I am the emperor. We do not have conversations. I am the emperor. I talk, you listen. Not a word from your mouth until . . . I'll make it very simple, not a word until midnight. You see, dear, how everything must be described to him in such infinite detail, or he is incapable of . . . the human, the . . . incapable."

Franz Joseph knew the latter half of the giant's life through a dossier compiled by his intelligence services. Nothing could be discovered of his youth. Savage himself had told them that he'd been born and raised in the city, which would mean that he'd somehow grown nearly to adulthood without coming to civic attention. His birth was not recorded in Austria. The parents he'd named for himself were vanished from the face of the earth. Franz Joseph knew to a certainty that the man was not Viennese, was not Austrian, and that he was an inferior specimen even of the pond where he'd hatched, somewhere in his realm, probably, one of those provinces his imagination had never quite encompassed. Slovenes, Slovaks. His was an empire, frankly, with an abundance of backwaters.

The giant, suddenly, independently, took an interest in his duty and came round and offered his hand to the empress. She took it and he brought her very easily to her feet. Franz Joseph did not know what to make of them. His marriage had been a saga in sum largely chaste, and it remained even now unsatisfying in that old, taunting way. He took Elisabeth's free arm, and together he and his wife and the giant formed the last rank of the queue behind the doors to the ballroom. The emperor admired the women's shoulders. He sometimes wished that his own costume could in some way be abbreviated, made lighter. What might it be like to join them? He loved the women's chirping. But Franz Joseph was losing sympathy for his wife's histrionics. She kneaded his fingers painfully. "The tsar," he told her, "has asked for a short processional. We won't be waiting long."

Elisabeth smiled that thin, tiresome smile she wore when anything was asked of her.

Hinterlander came down the file, dressing the ranks, looking for details of uniform and possible indelicacies. He came to the bodyguard and said, "You are to lead Their Majesties in. You must enter before them, not at Her Majesty's side." As before, he took the giant's arm. As before, Savage repelled him. The adjutant lost his footing and went down. Admiral Schoenbrun and several other gentlemen broke ranks to help Hinterlander to his feet. At that moment the doors to the *Gand Saal* swung outward onto the ball.

"Look at this," said Franz Joseph. "Look at this, dear."

His wife traveled the world over, insisting always that there be nothing more than the Countess Sztáray between her person and bedlam. But in the Hofburg she wanted personal protection, and necessarily that protection must have its carnival aspect. Franz Joseph went out to the Romanovs like a shepherd behind a scattered band of sheep. All went forward as best they could. Elisabeth had not released the giant's hand, so he remained at their side, where he was, if symbolically, their equal. Franz Joseph's heart pounded at his tunic's collar. But it was his fanfare being played, his personal anthem. He adjusted his chin. Applause accompanied them in; applause followed them past the Romanovs and the length of the *Grand Saal*. Plaster nymphs chased themselves across the vaulted heights. Everywhere gilt, gilt to burnish the light. With every measured tread, the emperor felt all his batteries fire at once beneath his feet. He was rather made for this. The emperor and the empress and her hulking attendant reached the end of the room, turned, and acknowledged the assembly. Franz Joseph was so very excited that he thought he must use the occasion to issue some proclamation, declare a small war. But the bodyguard was misbehaving. "Get behind us, man. Elisabeth, let him go there, would you?"

The Romanovs advanced to be received, the dapper little tsar and his wife. They smiled gamely.

"I said," the emperor hissed, "*behind us.* Get those hands clasped neatly in the small of your back, Lieutenant."

The Romanovs and their retinue came on, and so splendidly; for Franz Joseph a comforting revue of things-as-they-will-always-be. Their peers from Russia. The emperors clasped each other, hand and wrist. The empresses touched gloved fingertips. The orchestra had at some point fallen silent, and there was a hush over the assembly.

"The pipe," Tsar Nicholas whispered, "that pipe your valet supplied me, where would I find more of those?"

The royals released each other and turned to the room. Cheers were begun, ragged at first, but swelling, rising soon enough from every throat until a hopeful roar was achieved. Franz Joseph, buoyantly imperial.

Also, for as long as the general euphoria should last, he would not have to trouble with making conversation. The emperor noted the moment well, hoping to recall it during more tedious work. This was one of his many duties, to absorb the bottomless affections of his people. They were cheering him, the dear things, and he felt large inside. He raised his arm, as did his wife, as did the Romanovs, and their hands floated like maple leaves on a June breeze.

An odor came to Franz Joseph's attention. It lingered, accumulated, became more detailed and powerful and alarming. Scraps from the charnel house, scattered over the sulphurous floor of hell. He saw the tsaritsa discretely retch. Nicholas's eyes grew large. Elisabeth took obvious pains to breathe only through her mouth. The smell would not go away or even much abate. Franz Joseph's stomach roiled urgently. The cheering and the stench continued to wash over them. Swallow after swallow slid down Franz Joseph's throat. What had happened? What was to be done? He turned to see if his alarm was communicated to the bodyguard, to see if the giant seemed alert.

But not at all. Savage was, if anything, serene.

February 1899

Madame Fuhr had commissioned Havazelet to make her a bronze peafowl. The thing should be a hen by day, but she required him to duct it so that a mist could be pumped through its tail and broadcast over clever lighting, making at night a peacock in full display. Havazelet had a thousand gulden at the onset of work, would have five thousand more at its completion. Completion to Madame Fuhr's satisfaction. It was intended to be the centerpiece of her formal gardens; "scale it," she had said, "grandly, as if it were Field Marshall Radetsky." Havazelet saw no way in which to execute the Fuhr woman's wish without crushing his reputation, but, as he had sold nothing else in months, he took the commission. He sought Daniel Savage to plumb the bird. The man would do anything for money. It was over money and art that they had their little squabble.

"Hammered sheets," said Savage, "and the plumbing can serve also for a frame, a skeleton if you like. That would be the right apparatus. Carve a model in wood, hammer the sheets over it to shape them, rivet, braze, and polish the joints. It shouldn't weigh more than a large horse, and think how easily transported."

"I am sure," said Havazelet, "that she intended it to be cast."

"Did she say that? Cast it? Does she know what she intends?"

"It wouldn't have occurred to me to ask her. She'll want it solid. I somehow think that's the whole point of it for her."

"You are making it improperly."

"How does one make a flightless bird properly? It cannot be done." Havazelet referred to the poor piece of taxidermy serving as his model. "It is a feathered rodent, it represents a small, sad profit."

But, before he was done, there was not to be even profit in it for the sculptor. The work went on too long, even more pointlessly than he had expected. Castings rolled out of his molds, vaguely animal shapes. There were problems of anatomy. With its great melon of a body thrust so far over its twiggy toes, the bird was tremendously nose heavy, and each model he made of it wanted only to dive forward. Havazelet thought to stabilize the thing by making it even larger. He set out a hillock of wax and built scaffolding. He went around and around it, carving, fusing wax to wax, carving again; the piece would not yield the first pleasing line or shadow. In the early stages of the work Savage had been in to design the plumbing for the bird. He came after that only to see, as he said, the abomination born. He came and spoke of America, where, Havazelet was given to understand, large animals stood in desolate places. Savage spoke of making a silken wing and plying three dimensional space with it. The sky would be his. The wing, he said, would likely keep even an ample man like himself aloft for hours at a time. He predicted that the earth would not miss his absences.

Havazelet required only art for his days and something nice to eat and drink at the end of them. The thought of his possible ascent was too remote even to frighten him. But hearing the giant's imagination reel out relentlessly as the coin driven cinema had been welcome distraction while he worked on the pea thing, and it was shortly after Savage quit coming around that he decided he was finished. The sculptor needed very much to visit his dentist, and this was as good an end point to the piece as any, so he ordered a ton of coal and told his assistants to be an hour early to work the next morning, to have a fire banked in the furnace and be ready to cast upon his arrival.

On his arrival, however, the studio was cold.

A small soldier had backed Gruber and the others against the work table along the south wall, near the vises and tube benders. The soldier was alone, but details of his uniform suggested he could summon others if he wanted. He behaved as if those others were already there. He introduced himself to Havazelet as "Captain Jolewicz, in His Majesty's service." The little soldier went on to say that he knew only too well that he'd interrupted an important work in progress. His deepest apologies. But the emperor had become curious.

"About . . . ? Surely, I know nothing. I have my work and nothing else. I am entombed here in this studio. The same is true of these other fellows, Captain. We are not well-informed people."

The soldier revealed two perfect ranks of teeth; there was a milky film over his left eye which he seemed to see through well enough. "This concerns your friend, colleague, whatever he is to you. Savage."

"Oh. Savage? What of him?"

Jolewicz dismissed the sculptor's assistants; when they failed to disperse at once, he told them, "You fellows, no more idling. Do you think Herr Havazelet is paying you to malinger? Do something useful."

When they'd busied themselves to his satisfaction, Jolewicz asked the sculptor, "Aren't you ashamed of yourself?"

"Frequently. But, could you be more specific? Ashamed of what?"

"I know what you have here."

"It's something I have? If there's something I shouldn't have, please, take it away. Who did you say you were?"

The soldier turned on his heel and marched directly to an old *Winged Victory* that stood on a lonely crate. "This breaks my heart, Herr Havazelet."

"Well, yes. My first work in hard stone, actually, I . . . sentimental thing. I look at this and I can see that I've made some progress. A little progress, at least."

The captain blew on it, produced a kerchief and lovingly wiped at the little statue. "This has integrity," he said. "There is nothing delicate about it, is there?"

"No. No delicacy at all."

"I am a student of contemporary sculpture," said Jolewicz. "You wouldn't have thought that of me, but I am. I am quite fond of your work. At least the earlier things. Like everyone else, I prefer your vigorous period." He lifted the stone harpy by her sturdy wings. "To actually touch it in this way. I am so excited by this. Pleasure of this sort, I can tell you, is the great exception for men in my line. I prefer yours to the bare-breasted ones."

"My *Victory*," said Havazelet, "was modest. Would you like it, Captain?"

"You are speaking with a soldier now, whose existence is financed entirely by a soldier's pay."

"Yours for the taking."

"Why?"

"It makes you happy. I would never ask more of my work than that. It's intended to please, you know. I think it is yours by right, as you like it so well."

"Well, then, good. I will take her, but only because you'd neglected her so. We can't consider this any kind of gratuity, can we? You expect nothing in return. What were you thinking, sir, to make such a wonder and then neglect her in filth? My little barracks room cannot do her

justice, but I will keep her and cherish her there. She'll be kept immaculate. I know that I am only holding her in trust. For posterity."

"Not posterity," pleaded the sculptor. He had taken up a square of
paraffin to warm in his hands and was working its edges down. "About
Savage, Captain? He was discharged from the military, wasn't he? He
said he'd been."

"Lucheni," said Jolewicz. "Do you know the name?"

"How could I not? The man who stabbed the empress?"

"You read the newspapers?" the Captain asked.

"Yes."

"Like everyone, you've developed a theory?"

"Yes, but . . ."

"Did you ever hear Savage speak of the man? Lucheni?"

"No one spoke of him at all. Until the assassination. No one knew
of him. He was Italian."

"These revolutionaries often think of themselves as internationalists,"
said the captain. "What did Savage have to say of Lucheni?"

"Nothing—to me. I do not speak of murderers with anyone. But,
Lucheni, he was Italian."

"Savage?"

"No—Lucheni. Italian. Wasn't he?" Havazelet hardly knew how to be
careful in this, the captain was so thoroughly and dangerously stupid.

"Yes," said the captain. "And what do you think that means? That the
assassin himself appears to be Italian? Was Savage Italian?"

"I don't know."

"Where was he from?"

"He would never say. The man was a legend of capability in our little set, but he would work only where no one would demand papers of
him. He did what there was to do."

"We know at least," said Jolewicz, "that he has been in Vienna a number of years. But you, Herr Havazelet, have known him, we believe,
longer than anyone else."

"Years? How many years did you say it has been?"

"Your earliest contact with the giant? You've been doing very well so far."

"He started as a life model, came and offered his services. That was when the empress was filling her Achilleon. We needed heroic bodies. Zeus, Apollo. And Herr Savage, in my opinion, was made to be made over in rock. I'd be carving him still if he'd let me, but he posed for just the two pieces before he said that it was unendurable work for a man of his energy and that he disliked wearing the beard I provided him. Later, he worked for me in other ways."

"But he was not Italian?"

"No," said Havazelet. "Or—perhaps he was. I never thought to ask after his nationality, it was of no interest to me."

"So," said Jolewicz, "you too are an internationalist."

"These are not the sort of things I think about."

"God bless you, sir," said the captain.

"Much of what I do is heavy, much of what I make. Even many of my tools are heavy. With Savage on hand I needed less hoisting equipment. He loathed lifting, thought it beneath him, but he could lift anything. My *Deer Park*, solid bronze, he took it off the floor and placed it where you see it now. Cursed me all the while."

"He worked as your laborer."

"And then as an assistant. In fact, he behaved from the beginning as if he were somehow my mentor. That was his manner with everyone, including the empress." Savage, comfortably naked in a room of clothed strangers. Condescending to them. "He was imaginative," said Havazelet, "and useful. And irritating. Should I have reported him to someone? Is that it? That I failed to report him?"

"Not at all," said the captain. "How could you have known? Lucheni, as you say, was an unknown quantity."

"But, Lucheni—Savage? They have something in common?"

"Yes," said Jolewicz. "I've made a clearheaded survey of facts, many

known only to myself, that can lead to no other conclusion. No one be-
lieves Lucheni acted alone. A raving lunatic. Surely someone else sharp-
ened the file he plunged into the empress's heart."

"Savage?"

"No one else is so clearly linked to the conspiracy. He must be found.
And now that the gravity of all this is before you, I must ask you again,
where was he from?"

Fear kept Havazelet patient. "I don't know anything of his origins. I
don't know. I don't know. I asked, he rebuffed the question. Long ago.
I suppose I lost interest then. He was just Viennese, like the rest of us.
Did it matter? And wasn't it just the empress's companion who was
there when she was killed?" The sculptor had been as cooperative as
possible, craven in his cooperation, now he wished to be left alone.

"But you did not know that he was not an Italian?" Jolewicz asked.

"I did not . . . Or . . . what? What is it you are asking me?"

"He was uncommonly strong, Savage."

"Yes. It made him useful. The man would do anything for money."

"Extortion?"

"Not that."

"You said he would do anything."

"But, I meant . . . not that. He wouldn't do that."

"There is an unsettling fact in your file, Herr Havazelet. You cannot
know how anxious I am to have your explanation. A man of your eminence—suspicion should adhere to you for the briefest possible time."

"Suspicion? Of what? I am suspected?"

"You are only a piece of a very large investigation. One of very many
pieces. Almost insignificant."

"And you are investigating . . . the empress's death?"

"Among other things," said Jolewicz. "But, as to that fact, that unsettling fact—it was you who introduced Savage to the empress."

"Of course I did. She asked to meet him. By letter. I have the letter.

She was present every day of his second posing. They got on famously, made me feel drab in my own studio."

"Could you see at that time the traits of a murderer?"

"In whom? Would I have recognized them?"

"Where is he now?" Jolewicz asked.

"He wanted to emigrate, to become Swiss," said Havazelet. Switzerland was one of very few places the giant had not expounded on or desired. Egypt, the Antilles, yes—Switzerland, no. The sculptor savored his tiny deception.

"He has crossed no frontier," said Jolewicz. "I am certain. He can't cross any border unrecognized, he can go nowhere unnoticed."

"I should think not."

"You can see that I must, at the very least, talk to him? He was close to the empress, but no one was ever certain of how close they'd become. Except you."

"But, I wouldn't think . . . I do not think . . . there was no opportunity. They were here when he posed, that is all I know. And she was . . . the empress. Rather old, wasn't she, for that sort of . . . ?"

"And they got on well?"

"Yes. She never tired of him. She stood him better, really, than anyone else. They talked of everything, or he did."

"Of love?"

"Everything except love. He would have considered that a digression. The empress, perhaps. She sometimes mentioned it, she spoke of it. Love for her was like a bad day at the races."

"She talked of love? Did they make love?"

"No," said Havazelet, gratefully. "Not in my presence."

"But, outside your presence? You're a sensitive man. A man of intuition. Don't confine yourself to telling me of things you've actually seen. There were hints, I know. They spoke volumes."

"It is not entirely true," said Havazelet, "that I am confined to this studio. I have a circle of acquaintances, I am conversant with the city. Savage was a useful acquaintance and that is all I know of him. An acquaintance."

"Of several years' standing," said Jolewicz.

"If you insist. I find even that much hard to credit. Years?"

"Years," said Jolewicz. "The empress's Achilleon is built, furnished, sold, and abandoned. Years. You knew them both. You are unique in that respect, Herr Havazelet. And, yes, since I'm sure you've already guessed it, I can now tell you plainly, you are the keystone of my investigation. I don't take you for a halfhearted fellow. This studio—your studio—do you know that you live in a wonderland? You are the father of uncomplaining children, free to discard the ones you dislike. The artist is a god. I ask your permission to visit here often. Only let me watch you work."

"Watch me work? That . . . if you watch me, you see, I will not be able to work. Not at all. No one watches me."

Absently, Jolewitz fondled the butt of his sidearm. "Your career has declined, Herr Havazelet, as you've moved away from the vigor of your early . . . how can I say it? Vigor. Your *Seven Hills of Rome,* that was the kind of work we all loved. Why aren't you working in that manner anymore? With the immense . . . the bold . . . everyone laments the passing of that period."

"It's not as though I'd become a watercolorist, Captain. I'm only trying to work smaller now. It's the cost of materials. Adequate marble is outrageous, good marble is not to be had at any price."

"You knew them," said Jolewicz. "Both of them."

"I was often in their presence. But it would be well beyond my poor powers to know either of them. Apart from what I saw of them in this room, I do not know what they may have done, or not done, together or apart."

"Tell me," sighed Jolewicz.

"What? What, Captain?"

"Anything."

"He may be anywhere. I wish I could tell you more." The paraffin was now oblate and pliant. Havazelet pressed it with the heels of his hands and the balls of his thumbs and quickly formed a cloaked figure onto which he pinched a tiny nose. He elongated and spread the bottom of the cloak to form a base upon which the figure might stand.

"Captain," said the sculptor, "shall I cast this for you?"

"Yes. But I can't offer the slightest favor in return."

"Well," said Havazelet, "I am an artist, and long accustomed to pauper's pay."

His Own
⌐ and Some Other's Blood ⌐

February 18, 1899

⌐ HE MADE AND SOLD a slivovitz at his inn that often brought men to grief. Ordinarily, such foolishness as Branko Prpa needed could be had with the aid of milder intoxicants. There were times, though, when he wanted to feel the particular heat, to know the particular consolation that was the foundation of his small wealth. Prpa stood at the door of his establishment, glass in hand, regarding the empty street. The morning's silence, there was the world's response to a man's ambitions. Soon, however, there would be a thunderclap in Belgrade that would be heard around the world, a bang authored in small but essential part by Branko Prpa. He had longed only for God to find him some difficult task. No one knew, and how could they, what it cost him to be merely an innkeeper, an unrelievedly hospitable man. He had longed for a situation where his lion's heart might be of some earthly use. Prpa was subject to episodes when for days and even months at a time all that came to his attention reminded him of his obscurity, and he ached with it. Revolution, it was the very thing.

A man wearing a black beret and a black cape appeared at the end of the street and walked toward him, picking his way with some agility through the rubble of cobblestones that had not yet been carried away by ignorant villagers. The nearer he came, the more astonishing were his dimensions. Over his shoulder he carried a large canvas sack. He looked backward often, and when he came to Prpa, he nodded to him quickly and stepped inside the door of the inn. Prpa, mildly offended, did not follow him. The man hadn't even inquired if the inn was open, if Prpa was of a mood to serve him. Two Streifkorps rounded a corner and strolled toward him now, coming from the same direction as had the traveler, one of them wearing a poorly belted sword that ticked the ground as he walked. Garrison soldiers, they were sharing a joke. The Empire's sweepings were posted to the Lika, but once here they behaved as if the uniform made them superior to all, and they wandered the district aware of no duty beyond that of mitigating their boredom. Branko Prpa was as worthy of their notice as the tilting lampposts. He backed inside the door and brought the wooden plank down to secure it. The traveler was at a window, pinching the oilcloth just enough to see the street without being seen from it. He was, after all, no stranger.

"I didn't know you," Prpa told him.

"Didn't?" the giant said quietly, suspiciously.

"Not at first." Prpa was deliberate even to the way he moved his lips, he meant to convey a cool reliability. "You were a boy when you were here. But I should have recognized you. Who else could it have been?" He watched the traveler's eyes and knew that the soldiers had passed by the inn.

"Who else?" said the giant. "I ask that of myself, but not too often, Branko Prpa."

"In the Lika," said Prpa, "most men's wealth can be measured in the length of their bones. We have many big men. But none to equal Vuk Hajduk. That was true even when you were a boy. Welcome home, Vuk. You are more unexpected than ever."

The hajduk straddled a bench and leaned back against his great canvas sack. There was still something of the child about him, and Prpa guessed that, should he sleep, his slumber would be as deep and debilitating as a child's. "The Schwabes," said the innkeeper, "they come, they go. There are none here now who would remember you."

"And, surely, no Lićan would recall for them my history. Not my loyal countrymen."

"There was a reward," Prpa conceded. "But that was withdrawn years ago. You are safe here now. The Schwabes are concerned with new outlaws. But the people thought you had died, so you've been made a hero. What do you think of that? You have survived yourself and are the subject of guslars' ballads."

"Guslars? I am sorry if anything I've done encouraged them. It is impossible to exceed mediocrity on an instrument of one string. Let me have something to drink, not that slivovitz."

"Why not my slivovitz?"

"To burn holes in the lining of my stomach? A milder brandy, if you have it. Or wine, or water. Anything wet and reasonably clean will do."

The order wounded Prpa with precision. He'd seen this one when he was nothing more than a feral goat, and now the bastard had returned with worldly airs. Prpa customarily served those who liked a bit of pulp in their wine or did without. Here, any use of water not involving crops or animals was considered vain. Prpa gave him a brandy he kept in reserve. The giant held his nose to it, grimaced, drank, and paid.

"If you're looking for your father," said Prpa abruptly, "he's gone. All who lived at Magia Selo are gone."

"I've been there."

"Their spring vanished one day, swallowed by the rock. Some of them came here and, though they were Prećani Serbi like ourselves, we could not have them. They were too wild. The loss of their spring—we knew that to be a judgment on them. Except for you and your father, I could not have given name to a single man of that village. They made themselves a people apart. That was their mistake. They were ghosts." No man, thought Prpa, can discover without regret that he has been orphaned or abandoned. The giant's only remaining connection to the world was his own two feet. Bearing the news had not given the innkeeper the satisfaction he'd wanted. He only felt petty.

The hajduk looked solemnly upward. "You must know," he said, "that your rafter beams will give way very soon. They are buckling. The purlin is unsound."

The building was roofed in fired earthen tiles. Its collapse might prove fatal to all within. Prpa noticed the decay of his inn from time to time. As it had never been of any consequence to his custom, he was himself very little concerned by it. Dust, flaking daub, splintering tables, to fuss with such things was beneath him, intruded on his inward habit of mind. But it was true that the ceiling sagged, that it was dangerous. The timbers his father had hewn and placed were failing. An outrageous truth. "We have carpenters here," he said, "who are also sots. This is a problem easily fixed."

"The improper fix is easy," said the giant. "They would fill your inn with support posts. Or they would take the roof away altogether and rebuild it. Either solution would cause you to lose business. I can shore it up without all that trouble. I can build in knee braces. What would that be worth to you?"

"Vuk Hajduk would lend himself to my most trifling task? You are the little craftsman now?"

"What would it be worth to you?"

"What would you ask? What is it you need?"

"I don't haggle," said the hajduk.

"Why have you come here?"

"It doesn't matter, I am only passing through. But the fact that I have is your good fortune. If not for me, you might have been buried in your own neglect."

"Passing through?" said the innkeeper. "The Lika is not along the route to or from anywhere. There is no destination that can't be reached more easily by avoiding these hills. One comes here to come here. And if you had it in mind that there was danger—suppose there was some danger for you here . . . Vuk had reason enough to stay away, but not to return. To see his father? Marko Lazich? Marko Lazich has never been reason enough to undertake any kind of journey. I came to know your father well."

"Citizen, you seem to have mistaken me for someone I myself have never met, someone unsavory. You should give less thought to my itinerary and let me concern myself with that."

"No," said Prpa. "The fact that you are alive tells me you are not careless. Something has drawn you here. Let me know about it, I can help. I have influence. I have influence well beyond this district. You would be surprised to learn who I know. This," Prpa spread his hands and held them with perfect contempt toward the several beaten corners of his inn, "this is the least of my endeavors."

"You have more to offer than I could ever use."

"You are," said Prpa, "harried by someone, by something." As this was true of all men, it was an observation he often made. All seemed ready to believe he would make their troubles his own, just by hearing them. As an innkeeper he had at least learned the uses of a sympathy.

"The snow falls when I travel," said the hajduk. "If I ever fall sick, I am sure the sun will shine on my sickbed. Of course I am harried. But in all that I see no reason why I shouldn't be away from this district as fast as I comfortably can. It would make perfect sense to me if the whole population of the Lika were to vanish. There's a mystery no one would trouble to investigate."

"It is not such a good place to be," Prpa conceded, "but there was a time when Vuk took a good harvest from the Lika. Times are better now. For those who know themselves to deserve it, there is a little something for the taking almost anywhere. Even here. I'll show you what is to be done."

The hajduk was slack on the bench he'd chosen, beginning to recline against his sack. It appeared a weight hung elastically from his chin. A spasm bolted through him; startled, he sat upright and the bench squealed with it. He looked around and remembered where he was and yawned.

"What would you say to a featherbed?" Prpa asked him. "A cloud of goose down. My bed. The finest room in my house."

"Too generous."

"You know better. But we will do well by each other. Rest, then listen to what I will have to tell you."

"The bed, how long is it?"

"We can put chairs at the end of it. For your feet."

"Why not a room at the back of your inn?"

"I have only a few poor benches in those rooms, some flimsy cots. And the Schwabes are in and out; they come often. They do what they think is singing when they drink. I'd rather you were well rested when we talk, you will be more open to my ideas that way."

The hajduk fingered the sole of his boot where it was disengaged. "Would I dream of the Streifkorps, Prpa? Do you see me peaceful in my sleep, waiting for them even as you await some reward?"

"I told you, the reward is long since withdrawn. You may not be worth all you think you are. And, as for Schwabes coming to my home—I am a man of importance. Even the Ban of Croatia would not come to my home. Except by invitation."

"Don't invite him then. You see that I have more than enough society already?"

"Yes," said Prpa.

"You know that I will be gone as soon as it is convenient for me to leave? If you had some work for me . . . But, no, I'll be going."

"The Schwabes do nothing in my behalf, I do nothing for them. You and I, Vuk, we may have dealings. Only give me a little time to think of them. You have troubles, that I can plainly see. Let us say that Vuk Hajduk is dead. Something, someone still troubles the man who sits here before me, whoever he has become. I know we could be of use to each other. But, go if you like. Drag yourself to the road and down it. I would not prevent that even if I could."

The hajduk stood, oppressed by his own bulk and the weight of his baggage. "Look into the street," he said. "If it's empty, we go."

Prpa went to the door and lifted the bar away. It was possible, he thought, even at this early juncture, that they were under observation. By someone. Carefully he lay the plank on the floor. He cracked the door and looked out. During the night a thin blanket of snow had fallen over Ilmograd, three hours' traffic was recorded in it. Prpa raised to significance every footprint, every track. The street gleamed with low sun. He had never seen it just so before, in this very special light. He swung his chin forward. Prpa had always expected that one day he would be called on to command men in desperate circumstances, he had practiced the essential gestures. They went out.

He chose a route to his home that would keep them well away from the village's common wells. He also avoided the tobacconist's—the Sephardi lived in his shop. They reached the edge of the village, unobserved as far as he could tell, and slowed near a drayman's barn, which, though partly collapsed, was still sometimes in use. Tracks led away from it. Between those tracks, not far along, lay a steaming pile of dung. Prpa grabbed at the hajduk's sleeve and attempted to pull him back around the corner of the building. "We are only minutes behind that cart," he whispered.

The hajduk plucked a brass button from Prpa's jacket front and idly bent it into a pair of hard lips. "I am pleased, old man, that you are so well amused with our morning walk; but I have only to concern myself with soldiers and gendarmes, and I am not even sure of that. But if you continue to entertain yourself by behaving like a footpad, we will soon be noted by everyone, suspected of everything. I am not built for lurking. Get me to this bed of yours."

There were four paths leading up the long hill to Prpa's house, none of them situated to permit stealth. And the house itself was a dwelling made by his father for the sake of display and maintained by his wife for whom their prominence must be quite literal or it was worth nothing to her—four great rooms on each of its floors, its exterior whitewashed bright as the new snow. Prpa approached his home as if he were coming to it soaked in his own and some other's blood, as if there were a stag on his shoulder. He'd made an infamous friend. Now the women of his house might see at last how frivolous were their concerns compared to his.

Prpa's daughter, Stoja, sat on an upturned hogshead under the eave just outside the kitchen door, tatting, ignorant of the chill and of its effect on her flesh. She shivered without knowing it. But her ears were keen enough. She did not for their sake improve her crabbed posture or look up from her work, though she clearly heard them coming. Lace spooled in tiny, steady increments from her fingers.

"Daughter," Prpa said. "A guest. If you want to be uncomfortable and cold, that is your affair. If you want to be immodest, then that is my affair. No matter how old you have become. Go inside and put on a shawl. And then you will stay inside with us out of respect for our guest." The woman gathered her piecework and went into the house. She drew the door to behind her. Prpa stood looking at it for an absurd length of time. "She was young when you left the Lika, but I think she knew you. If only by reputation."

"This reputation of mine, am I tragic in it? Is it for love or noble ideals that I suffered?"

They went in. The Prpas had a maid two days of the week, but Augustina, Prpa's wife, dressed herself as if she were always exempt from the work of the household. A bright orange stain on her lovely dress. Such observations sometimes overwhelmed Prpa with tenderness for her. "Augustina," he said, "a guest."

"Stoja has told me. She says he is an outlaw. An outlaw, Branko, we send on his way with our best wishes. Sir, I am sorry that you are an outlaw. I dislike shooting very much. Let us make up a package for the poor man and—"

"He eats here," said Prpa. "Eats here, sleeps here, does whatever he likes here; he is my guest."

"If you wish," said Augustina.

She was the sparrow deviling the hawk, Augustina. She had better, he thought, offer them a drink.

"The inn?" she said. "Did you ever think of that, Branko, that these Austrian demons, the Magyars, they will use any small deviation to steal the inn from us?"

"They will take nothing from me," said Prpa. "There are too many consequences to those who take things from me." His daughter had kept away thus far from the kitchen. "Stoja," he called. "Present yourself." She came to them wearing a shawl, and she had put her hair up. Prpa appraised her for the hajduk. "You can see that her tastes are simple, she costs little to maintain."

"Why," his daughter asked, "when you know the things he has done, why do you bring him here? We are taxed so that the authorities can imprison men like your guest and keep us safe from them."

"Permit me a brief moment of sanity," said Prpa, "and I will explain to you how you are to think of this. First, if I recall, Vuk Hajduk was never apprehended, never stood charges. Do you suppose that, even if he enjoyed just a tenth part of the successes of which he was accused, if he was such a glorious villain, that they'd let him slip off with his spoils? They are administrators, the Schwabes, and they don't coddle criminals. It is only too obvious, if you think of it properly; this man is as much entitled to his freedom as you or I. If you think of it properly you will see that mistakes were made. A young man made his mistakes; the police in their hysteria made their usual errors in judgment. Mistakes, that was all, and those long ago."

"I think of him properly," Stoja said. "I think of him as do the dead. They know."

"The dead?" said the hajduk. "They must be consoled by your esteem for them."

"He behaves," Stoja told her father, "as if I am the one to be mocked, as if I am the senseless one. And in my own home, in front of my own father."

Prpa strode to his daughter and fixed her with a stern look she returned in kind. Prpa slapped her.

When the hajduk was settled in his bed, Prpa left the women a warning. "Do nothing to disturb his sleep. Move about on little mouse feet. If he should be wakened now, who knows how he might take it? He might break you like the dry sticks you are, and I wouldn't hold it against him. The man needs his rest. No one is to learn of his presence here. No one. Today you will forfeit your trip to the market, and there'll be no gossip with Lydia and the others. Keep to yourselves today. Tonight I will come back from the inn and take my supper at home. I expect we will have something at least as good, Augustina, as you would feed your mewling relatives. Tonight, I will make everything known to you. You will know my purposes."

Prpa, having briefly imposed order on his house, returned to the inn and went about the remainder of his morning's work, charmed and warmed by his possession of the giant. The inn's earliest arrivals that morning, the village's most devout drunkards, found plaited mats set out on the tables for them, a refinement usually evident only much later in the day. A good assortment of gamblers arrived, no one of them much blessed with skill or luck, so that all of them were announcing winning hands at regular intervals, "thirty-one." They made a separate competition of buying each other food and drink. Radić the waiter came in, and when he saw how hard the inn would use him this day he exaggerated the limp he claimed to have got soldiering. Old Marie came with a basket of the bread and pickled meats she prepared in her filthy way and brought daily for sale at the inn; Prpa advised her to bring another large basket that night. Profit, profit. Today would pay for a month's inventory, and from there on—sheer profit. Success of this sort made Prpa claustrophobic. As was his habit, he retired alone to a back room. He congratulated himself. The people of his village entirely lacked imagination: once out of their presence, one ceased to exist for them. In Prpa's village a man could have all the privacy he wanted, and if he wished to entertain furtive persons out of sight, this too went unremarked.

Prpa awaited the arrival of an operative known to him as Archangel.

They had grown so daring, he and Archangel, that they now adhered to a schedule that brought the agent to Prpa's inn at three-thirty many Tuesday afternoons. Today the young man came unusually careworn, his face folded and pallid as the base of a melted candle. He had a rabbit's active, red-rimmed eyes. Prpa's morale soared every time he met with him. Archangel was a sufficiently serious man. Together, Prpa thought, he and Archangel and the others must act remorselessly. "I have everything ready," said the innkeeper under his breath. "Tickets for America, connections in Butte, Montana. They will be as safe as if we'd sent them to Atlantis."

"No," said the agent. "It's all off. Gabriel and several of the others have been found out. And why don't you quit whispering? Is someone hidden in the wall?"

"Found out?"

"Betrayed, of course. Gabriel was apprehended last Saturday. They drove rusty spikes into his heels. You see now why we wouldn't let him know your identity until after he had acted. When a man is spiked, he will divulge anything, give up anyone, if only they will grant him a bullet to the brain."

Prpa's stomach rumbled. "Others? You say others were apprehended?"

"I am the only one," said Archangel, "the only one of us who knows of your existence."

This might well be true. Prpa had never been given a code name. "What of the man's wife? What will happen to her?"

"She knew nothing, not even that Gabriel would be taking her away. She has now disappeared, and we feel that it would be dangerous to find her. She is on her own, God grant her safe passage. And for you, brother, this business is finished. We won't be striking the King, only Milan. Gabriel and one of the others who was taken, they were the ones who'd been assigned to kill the king."

"Why do an incomplete job of it?" Rather than falling out of the conspiracy, Prpa thought he might now inject himself further into it. Perhaps to the extent that the organization would give him a name. "Joshua," he thought. "I have an agent," he said, "who would be ideal for our purposes. Let us use my man if we truly want the house of Obrenović to fall. Clean the whole nest of them out. This fellow is deadly and experienced, and I believe his talents can be cheaply purchased. Let me arrange an introduction."

The agent suffered to hear him out, but said, "It is not so simple to kill a king. Or rather, it is all too simple. We may not create a vacuum without having someone, something in place immediately to fill it. We are a shadow government, or we were. Alexander and his whore are safe until we have rebuilt it. For now, we are content to keep him frightened. But we are certain the army will rise and applaud as one man when we kill Milan. The Serbian army has had more than enough of Milan Obrenović."

"Branko Prpa remains available for any service. I will be with you until a Karadjejović is once again on the Serbian throne, and then you may rely upon me to live out the rest of my days humbly, grateful to have been of service."

"There is nothing left for you to do."

Prpa had never been privileged to know the name of the organization. If it had one. If it actually existed. For all he knew, it was nothing more than the Archangel's invention. A foam collected at the corners of the agent's mouth whenever he spoke at any length. Perhaps he was mad. "What about you?" Prpa asked him. "What becomes of you now? Can you be safe?"

"I am consumptive, my brother. My safety is a small concern. Have you any of the money left?"

"Money?"

"We gave you a great deal of it."

"Oh, that. All spent."

"Five weeks before we were to go forward?"

"As I told you," said Prpa. "Tickets are bought, arrangements made. I spent all of the money you gave me and that much more of my own just to see that things were done well and secretively." In fact, it was not so costly to get a man and his wife to America, even to spirit them there. Europe was leaking like a sieve. "But see my waiter," he told the agent. "Radić is instructed to give you anything you require." The Archangel, on leaving, kissed him reluctantly but three times, in the manner of the true believer. The Archangel, should he be apprehended, should he be interrogated, could give Branko Prpa no more than five minutes of his loyalty, whether he'd had his money back or not. Should the police offer to feed him his own eyes, the Archangel would provide them the name of Branko Prpa quick enough.

Prpa remained alone, brooding in his back room. Serbs across the river. He was the child of an expatriate nation, citizen of a kingdom where neither he nor his father had ever set foot. Serbia. Prečani Serbi. How long could a people, a family, nourish themselves on the paradox of their existence?

Prpa thought to see if Archangel had left the inn. He had not. "Have they given you such a little bundle? I mean to see you off comfortably." The anxious agent's hamper was supplemented by a bottle and a loaf, and then Prpa directed him subtly but unmistakably to the door. "I have already forgotten that I knew you," he said. "You are vanished from my mind, friend." Again they exchanged kisses, and the Archangel was off. Old before his time, in his own mind epic. Archangel—may boils blossom on his ass. Prpa thought that he must try to find a better class of conspirators next time.

He walked up to his house on the hill. Disappointment and indignity, the theme of all his days. Every window in his house was ablaze, as if lamp oil cost no more than water. Why couldn't Augustina embrace even the simplest precepts of economy? The woman managed somehow to keep them always just at the head of a pack of creditors, and without ever enriching their lives with her profligacy. Prpa wished to take something from someone, anyone. He wished to harm some deserving person, and if none could be found, then he was afraid he'd have to hurt an innocent. At the end of a day such as this, a man did not want a gaudy house to come home to.

The giant had awakened and was sitting on the floor of Prpa's kitchen, surrounded by plates. Augustina explained that she'd chopped everything edible into finger foods for him. He ate with one hand, and with the other he grasped his naked foot, and, with the off leg curled behind him, he stretched himself. "The pliant hamstring," he said with authority, "is the nearest thing there is to a panacea." Stoja was just finished washing pots. This was only the latest of several meals the man had taken. Augustina hovered over him, offering everything that was theirs to offer. She informed her husband importantly that she must have a feathered hat. In Vienna all the ladies were wearing them. The hajduk had said as much, and the hajduk knew.

"Even the shop girls," the giant said. "A month's wages sitting on their empty heads."

To hear such prattle in his grief—the real Serbia might never more be, and Prpa found them talking of hats. Within the half hour, he suspected, one of them would accuse him of being impatient. They lacked understanding, gravity. He was very near tears, could feel them welling. "I see crumbs on the table. What has happened to the supper I asked for?"

Stoja brought out a loaf of black bread and a knife. She took a cheese from the pantry, carved off a patina of mold, and set it before him. On an exhausted sediment of Turkish coffee, she boiled water. His daughter traveled in arcs around the giant as wide as the kitchen would permit. The giant stretched his other leg. Rested now, he was talkative. "The buttock," he said, "the buttock and the hamstring, that's where the largest residue of static energy gathers in the body. I release it regularly in this way. It is an electric poison. You should try this, citizen. Anyone can see you're not at home in your skin."

"This," wondered Prpa, "this is all he's left me to eat?"

"Whose fault is that?" his daughter asked. Stoja's ear, as ever, was cocked for insult. "The larder is empty because you told us to stay away from the market, and because we have fed this apostate, just as you told us. You must be happy with whatever is left. We have nothing more to give you, and we're glad of it."

His first child, Stoja had been for a time a rare proof that God might have some existence beyond the words. When Prpa's Stoja seized some toy, there was divinity; the girl might have become any kind of woman. As she was becoming a woman, though, just when her breasts started to jut, an itinerant monk came to Ilmograd at the height of a summer when the hills were being beaten with lightning. The man, when asked his name, would only say that he did not deserve one. He owned but one habit, and it was heavy, and while he was among them he was constantly aglow in fresh sweat. Rumor soon had it that the monk, beneath his shirt, had banded himself with wet leather thongs, that he was killing himself as slowly and painfully as possible. His skin was as colorful as oil on water. The nameless one, however, never managed to much diminish himself through his sufferings. The people of Ilmograd began to speculate as to how he fed himself, the most popular theory being that he was a thief. Stoja, who was prone to fascination just then, fell under the ascetic's corrupting influence. Even after the monk was driven from Ilmograd, she continued with a set of proscriptions and hardships of her own contrivance. She slept and ate little and grew into a long, coarse, and altogether ridiculous woman. Prpa had never been able to assemble a dowry sufficient to rid himself of her. The first of his children to be born, she would be the last to leave his house, if, and here Prpa always offered a sentence of prayer, she should ever leave. Stoja prowled his home like a ferret. The bread she had given him had sponged all the moisture from his mouth and he could hardly risk swallowing it.

The hajduk took the chair across from his, made himself erect as a grenadier, and, with numb pleasure let his head droop sideways to his shoulders, right, then left. Augustina watched him for a bit. Prompted by another sad enthusiasm, she took a chair for her own and copied him. The giant, lips slack, eyes rolled back, rotated his head through his neck's full range of motion. Augustina added her own touch to the ceremony, a soggy little moan.

"False," said Stoja. "Unclean. Mother, he may have you worshiping his idols. He may be placing you in a trance. Stop."

"I feel quite well," said Augustina. "Pliant."

"Muscle," the hajduk said, "is a peculiar engine. The clock, the generator, they wear away. The animal engine swells with use, swells and strengthens. It contracts, however, with disuse."

"I am beginning to think," said Branko Prpa, "that you are not the man I thought you were."

"I have so little for which to be grateful," said the giant. "But at least I am not the man you thought."

"I had several plans in mind," Prpa told him. "But all of them require some daring; we thought you had daring. When I was younger . . ."

"When you were younger, Branko," Augustina said, "you kept your business in good order. When you were younger, you did the proper thing. You will always do the proper thing because that is the kind of man you are. Proper and devoted."

A man's wife, thought Prpa, comes to know him not at all. "During this respectable life of mine, I have come by information. I have been, you know, twice the mayor of Ilmograd. There is a small defile a little south of here on the road to Zadar. Do you know it? I could tell you, to the hour, when the tax collector will pass through it, heavy with coin and scrip. If you had ambition . . ."

"The tax collector, he goes about with his bit of the emperor's treasury and no escort, no one to protect him from the enterprising?"

"Certainly, an escort."

"How many, then?"

"Four Streifkorps," Prpa allowed. "Five at most."

"Armed?"

"Obviously."

"Mounted?"

"A gig and . . . horsemen. Yes. You wouldn't expect them to walk.'

"You are right then," said the giant. "By your standard, I lack ambition."

"Where are you going?" Prpa asked him. "What are your intentions?"

"You assume I know. I'd never expected to find myself here again, but . . . I will go where I go."

"It seems you have come to us through Vienna. If you were returning there, I think I could arrange to have you deliver a package."

"Not Vienna. I have exhausted Vienna."

"Greece?"

"No."

"Macedonia?"

"No. Macedonia?"

"Where?"

"The Seychelles, I thought. Trinidad. Iceland. I may ply the Yangtze. Somewhere else, citizen."

"What of America? You may be suited to it."

"America," Stoja shouted. "They paint their faces and worship the moon. They keep Moors as slaves and shoot each other for pleasure."

"No," said Prpa. "That is no longer true."

"Where everything is for sale," said his daughter.

"Ignorance is her treasure," Prpa said. "But she is not so bad when you learn not to listen to her."

"We went to Rijeka once," said Augustina of the Prpas' travels. "We stayed at a fine hotel there, ate fish that had not been dried or pickled. Fresh fish, right out of the sea. Branko drank sherry like a gentleman. The men wore such beautiful coats. Graceful coats, immaculate."

"Remember, little mother," said Stoja, "that they sneered at us in Rijeka. Italians. Fine coats. I spit on Italians and their coats and their opinion of me. People must live where they are born, as they are born, knowing that they are good enough."

Stoja was not the monk but the monk's leather bands. Prpa's daughter—a woman so mean she found blasphemy in the meager pleasure to be had from a handsome jacket—his daughter was slowly crushing him. "Vuk," said Prpa. "Vuk Hajduk, to call a thing by its right name. He wants only to be away from here."

"When I wish to see the Lika," said the giant, "which is not often, I have only to close my eyes. Away, yes. I'll like leaving here."

Branko Prpa drank the silt from the bottom of his cup. "I thought I felt some fate at work from the moment I saw you this morning. America. I could see you there, I could arrange it. If you'd be willing to call yourself Mr. and Mrs. Regocidivić for a time, I could arrange passage for both of you."

February 27, 1899

Her mother had bought her a hand mirror in which to prepare for her wedding, and for several days, at every private moment, she had been absorbed in the thing, in the face of a woman who should not be trusted with even the mildest temptation. The little mirror, Stoja thought, in anyone else's hands, would be nothing more than a convenience. She'd courted herself, enjoyed the aquiline nose, the gray eyes behind which so much could safely and even attractively be hidden. By simply causing her lips to repose together she could invoke the benediction that God had settled on her, her beauty. But He had also made cinders of her teeth, and there was another, more complex pleasure to be had in smiling into the mirror. To smile or even to speak caused this other face to present itself to the world. She was Prećani Serbi, bred for contention, and her mouth was seldom closed.

With a forked twig Stoja secured her hair in a loose knot at the nape of her neck. There were creamy crescents of newly revealed fabric at her shoulders where her dress had been let out. Her mother and each of her sisters had married in this dress. As the family's oldest daughter, Stoja was entitled to take it with her to America. She could not imagine herself so unlucky as to bear a girl child, and she had heard that in America many women never married at all. But Stoja herself would take her turn in the durable garment, the white dress, though she knew that there were those who would say that on a woman of her age it was either a lie or an obscene boast; they would say that her maidenhead, if she had one, must by now be like bull hide. During her engagement Stoja was told very often that in the giant she had found a perfect mate. Her life was become the substance of a common joke.

Augustina came to her with the ring she was to give to the priest, who would give it to the *kúm*, who would give it to the hajduk. "You see what this is, Stoja? It is a circle. And that means?"

"Eternity."

Augustina gave her a sheaf of pressed, dried irises. "These are what you carry," she said, "when you marry in winter."

"I don't need flowers."

"You do," said her mother. "We must add any color to this that we can."

On short notice the women had assembled the rudiments of a wedding, all but for a satisfactory white carpet on which the wedding party should stand. Stoja had met this shortfall by insisting that the portable altar be taken outside, that she be married on the snow. She reasoned that, if she as a woman was not allowed in the church sanctuary, then the hajduk should not be allowed in any portion of the building. If the snow melted in time, she had thought, then she would quit this plan at once, she would not marry. But the snow did not melt; it had only become dirty by the day of her wedding.

Stoja considered her veil, set it aside. Her mother had raised none of her daughters to languish in virginal disuse, but neither were they made to be taken off to America. Her mother's anguish—she would survive it. Augustina had told her that when she left with the hajduk she would be gone from them with all the finality of death, that surely the hajduk would never return here again. Augustina had reminded her that she would remain her own woman until the moment the words were spoken, that Stoja had made no commitment, only her father. "You don't have to go off with him," she said. "My prayers are with you, whatever you decide."

Stoja, when she first understood what her father intended for her, had kicked her own dog so viciously as to cripple it. The next day she poisoned her little Lilja and buried her in the hills. She came home and broke every piece of crockery in her mother's kitchen, stuck her father's best knife deep in the wall by her bedpost. During these several days she had told all who would listen, and all who would not, that no decent man would give a virtuous daughter to a heathen, to a heathen country. What was to prevent her from going into the mountains and teaching herself to hunt? Why not cut her hair and join the army as a man? Why not simply die? She had been handed a fate, if not a man, that she might have chosen. But she hadn't chosen any of it, not marriage, not Savage, not another protracted contest of wills. She was simply obedient to the several patriarchs, even to the least of them, her father. For purpose, on those mornings when she lacked it, she had only to revisit her many resentments.

Stoja collected herself, her flowers, her shawl, and went out and stood beneath an arch of hand-squared stone that was the principal entry and exit of her father's house. She stood there for a long moment as if shy or ceremonial but really to enjoy the shuddering wedding party. A little boy, the nephew whose name she could never remember, tore himself away from his mother and ran down toward the village. When he'd gotten a little distance from the others he began to skip. Stoja marched out. Let them all shiver, she was not cold. This was the greatest and cruelest mystery of which she would ever partake.

Danilo Lazich still wore the silly cape he'd worn when he first came to Ilmograd, and someone had provided him a tie, its tails reached just to the second button of his shirt. He was smirking, she thought. He liked to think that he was so hard to understand, but Stoja understood him well enough. He would find this not so funny. She would educate him as to the meaning of this, and then he would think back on this day with hard reverence. Her candles, symbolic of sacrifice, guttered in the wind.

Branko Prpa wept openly, repeating in a pitiable voice not his own, "My little one." Since the marriage had been negotiated he had been drinking steadily. The smell of him was strong, distinctly evil, and Stoja wished him dead. What kind of man was it who, when the Antichrist came to his door, said, "Come in, eat, drink, take my daughter to wife"? To be governed by the wishes of such a great and undeniable ass—he had on his lapel the decoration he had won as a gymnast.

Her mother drew abreast of her, wearing a dress completely out of keeping with the season. Chiffon. She had nothing else for such an occasion, no protection from the cold. "Keep your eyes to the sky," she whispered, "where your heart truly lies."

The Reverend Laza Šantić opened the Holy Scripture. The book would bear witness to pledges signed. Stoja made her mark beneath a promise she could not read, a promise recorded nonetheless until Judgment Day and which she must keep in all its particulars. She would not be found wanting.

From Father Šantić's roseate lips, from deep within his matted beard, came sweetly a song of the marriage ceremony. She saw that the hajduk's ring was of sufficient diameter to make a baby's bracelet. Branko Prpa had chafed at its cost, arguing long into the previous night with a Syrian goldsmith who had made it to order and whose argument had been, "Find another like it before tomorrow." An hour before the cock crowed, Branko Prpa finally paid his price. "Two rings," he said, as if he'd swindled the jeweler. "And I will be *kúm* into the bargain. Let nothing interfere with my daughter's happiness."

Stoja gave her father the hajduk's ring. Prpa fumbled it, and it rolled off the pillow. Women's cries went up. The giant leaned down, picked it up, and put it on. Stoja took her own ring from Branko Prpa. She pushed it onto her finger, and it rode snugly there. Father Šantić told them, making a song of this, too, "Jesus went down to a marriage in Cana, followed by the curious, and when they asked for wine they were told there was none. So it was at a marriage that Jesus performed his first miracle, turned water into wine and the curious into disciples. In that moment the Church was born. Danilo Lazich, drink from the common cup." The giant drank.

"Stoja Prpa, drink from the common cup." Stoja drained the chalice and became Stoja Lazich.

"You have a wife," said the priest to the giant. "You are the savior of her body, just as Christ is the savior of our souls."

Stoja could detect no change in herself. She set the empty chalice down on the ground, profaning it for all she knew. Father Šantić led them in the dance of Isaiah the Prophet, three times round the altar. For the sake of joy.

As a wife now, she attended the men's table. Together with her sister, Stana, she moved among them, leaving no plate long empty, no glass long unfilled. They served their men so well it became brutal. With just a little assistance, any man would harm himself for pleasure. The sisters abused the principle, feeding them, bringing brandy and wine until the company was nearly subdued. Only then did Stoja let her sister lead her away from the table. Stana had been waiting all night to tell her something privately, and the moment they were a little apart from the party she became grave. Very slowly, as if it were something to be memorized, she said, "To have that man's child would turn you inside out like a cloth purse. No matter what you must do to avoid it, never let him touch you. They can't expect you to be a wife to that."

Just then their father, summoning the last reserves of his strength rose to make another toast. "To love, gentlemen. For what else is there? Without love, we are only carrion." He swayed left, caught himself. "Torn carrion beside life's road, our eyes pecked out by life's constant vexations. If not for love, we would be even more awfully scarred than we are now." He would, Stoja knew, soon begin to vomit. She awaited that blessing.

She had watched her husband watching her. When the eating was finished, the drinking and singing continued. Two of her nephews came to the giant with an iron rod, and he bent it round his knee for them. As this cost him little effort, the boys went off to find something more durable he might destroy for their pleasure. Her husband. His calm on their wedding night. Nothing was right. Within half an hour after Branko Prpa finally choked the flowing spirits, the last of the guests were gone and the householders were gone up to bed, and only the bride and groom were left at the party. "We'll have no rest," Stoja told him, "until we go to bed." She went into her room and began to undress. Her husband followed and also made himself naked. They sat, back to back, on her bed.

"We are nothing to each other," he said, "but a way out. Once we're shut of this, you can quit me at any time, sister."

"I am not your sister," Stoja informed him.

March and April 1899

There was something unobtainable in the woman but it was no part of her body. They submitted to each other in Ilmograd, Trieste, Marseilles, and even more gruesomely at sea. She bruised him with her enthusiasm for it. Grimly she rode, hands on his chest, muscle gathering and twisting at the small of her back and along her haunches to drive her down onto him. Savage supposed that he would take as much of this as she might care to offer; she was made for it. Still, there were places in her out of reach and chafed beyond his soothing. Never, before Stoja, had he heard a human being snarl with pleasure. She seemed to want to extinguish him, and after their every uncoupling he would lie there feeling that she had partly succeeded, and that it was, whether intentional or not, a gift.

They were twenty-three days aboard *La Tintina Nova*, a freighter of Italian provenance and British registry that was widely mistrusted in the merchant marine and therefore lightly laden, thinly crewed. She wallowed in any sea not entirely becalmed. Mercifully, the Mediterranean was placid for them. One evening as they were making way toward Gibraltar on a coastal shipping lane, Savage took a turn on deck to escape the conjugal reek of the cabin. Across the water he saw Spanish lights, smelled Spanish lemons. Twelve hours later *La Tintina Nova* was well into the Atlantic and a hard, gray crossing. Savage went topside no more.

Branko Prpa had secured them a berth in the ship's deepest, aftmost hold, a cabin just an arm's reach wide. Savage and his wife lay long and long on their bunks, seasick, then seasick and dehydrated. The propellor shaft turned in bad bearings not far beneath their heads, rivets working incessantly in steel plate. The bulk of Savage's attention was owed to keeping a little of the ship's fetid water in his stomach. He did not like to suffer, much less to suffer in company. During the course of their voyage he came as close as he would ever come to prayer, wishing her absence. Let the bulkheads buckle then, and the sea pour in, it could not be more stifling than his wife, the gelid silence between them.

As Savage could not see himself slinking away from her, or killing her, she was his, and now, too late, he was properly impressed by the enormity of marriage. He was embarrassed at having stumbled into so dull and common a catastrophe. Closing at last on the new shore, where he imagined all things to be negotiable, Savage resolved to make of himself a sharper trader. A man could afford very few bargains in his life as expensive as the deal that had got him America, and, should he ever succeed in ridding himself of this woman, the cost of that would be even more extravagant. Stoja was as honest as the waves pounding the hull. Honest and faithful and somehow inevitable.

⟶ If It Is So Far ⟶

April 1899

⟶ SHE FOUND NOTHING to like in New Orleans. Stoja followed the hajduk off *La Tintina Nova's* brow and through a file of black stevedores ferrying hawser line on their backs and singing, some of them, as if their own and all the world's troubles were only a mistake. Their singing caused her to quiver. "The ground here quakes," she observed. "Where have you landed us? Is this Butte, Montana?" The hajduk told her that there were fluids still coursing through her inner ears and that it was muscle memory that caused her feet to clutch at solid ground. It was, he said, a rare sensation, and she should enjoy it. Butte, he said, lay far inland and to the north. Because she had not seen him acquire this information, she doubted it. "I am not mistaken," she said. "I am sick at my stomach."

Her husband conferred with official-looking men in a tremendous room where the machinery for lathing ships' masts was still in place. They were made to dump their tote sacks, her trousseau, into red bins that their few possessions did not begin to fill. "We have nothing to declare," the hajduk told her. Whatever this meant, it was mixed news. A little fellow in a well-made uniform smiled at them as they restored their goods to their luggage. They passed on to another room where a number of papers were pressed on the hajduk for his signature. Savage read aloud from them in such a way that the customs agents laughed with him. He translated a single passage to his wife: "Do you intend to overthrow the government of the United States of America?" When

Stoja gasped at this, the customs agents permitted themselves a little more friendly laughter and handed them the documents that made them the country's guests. Now she was deeply suspicious, a very small sea change for Stoja.

While Stoja had been sick at sea, God had taken advantage of her special attentiveness to tell her that He had stoked her fierce, that she was a thorn of His perfect rose bed, and that she must always be angry. He told her that He would forgive her almost anything so long as she was never angry with Him. There was license in this arrangement, but she hated it. What was His forgiveness to her when she herself lacked the capacity to forgive? She was unable to overlook anything in anyone, including the smallest of her own multitude of faults. For her prayers and penances she had been granted a life as a dark disturbance. She too had bargained for a departure, which she had received, and for a fresh start, which she had not. Her anger, it seemed, traveled well and would find its fuel in any company.

To be helpless in the hands of the hajduk—only he could read the road signs, and only he could offer her any direction through the thronging, sweltering streets. In the first mile of their overland passage he stopped three times to eat, once at a saloon to buy two small glasses of an amber liquor that appeared expensive to her. The man would empty their pockets. Already she had told him that they could afford to travel only by foot. At nightfall, filled with crab meat, shrimp, and bread, he set out on a pike road at a constant six miles an hour over the long alluvial flat of Louisiana. Stoja ran along behind, shifting the burden of her tote sack so often on her shoulders that she raised welts on each of them. He mounted a levee that ran through a marsh. They went on. A glutinous membrane formed in her throat and pulsed with her every breath. She recalled the distances that Vuk Hajduk was said to have covered as pursuer and pursued; perhaps he meant to run her to death. In the heart of the night, the hajduk pulled up suddenly in front of her. Stoja drew abreast of him and also stopped short at seeing a creature athwart the levee. "Now dragons," she said. "You have taken me where the night air never cools and there are dragons."

"It is an alligator. The tail, I understand, is edible."

Stoja found a knobbed stick and ran with it at the animal. It pivoted away from her on its blunt little legs, then stopped to make sure of her sincerity. Stoja had not slowed, she had commenced swinging. The alligator slid down the levee wall and into the marsh. Stoja let the thrill of this engagement carry her an hour or two. They passed through a cypress grove, its roots and mosses agrope in the moonlight, then descended again to the pike road where, despite the hour, a fabulous traffic was abroad. In this nation, she saw, movement was the fetish; even the ragged rode by well mounted. A light and some attendant noise labored toward them, a carriage like those she had seen in Genoa and Marseilles, drawn along by nothing but its own racket. The driver, for all his piddling progress, hunched over the wheel of the machine as if to urge it forward and smiled optimistically beneath the great, silly sweep of his moustache. Stoja ran on, past trusting even her own senses. Lights of no detectable origin appeared before her. Eventually the night produced a final specter—a morning sun that was cruel from its first appearance in the east.

From a roadside shanty, from its sagging porch, a fat man spoke musically. His chin had become enfolded in flesh, so he defined the lower edge of his face with a strip of beard. Stoja assumed he must be ill, dripping as he was. At the edge of the porch was built a system of andirons, a cauldron hung from its apex. The fat man stirred at the cauldron with a long spoon. It looked to be silage, but its vapors were stronger. "He wants to feed us," said the hajduk. Stoja heard children singing inside, saw them gathered at a window, skittish. The sick man called inside, and a ragged girl with skin and hair of the same beige coloring ran out into the yard. She shooed hens off the crates where they were roosting in the yard and returned to the porch with a handful of brown eggs. She sweetly intoned a few words to the fat man. In his own honeyed way, the fat man spoke to the girl, then to Stoja. "Spring water, ma'am." He nodded toward a pipe standing in his yard and discharging clear water into a brackish ditch. "That's pure spring water."

Stoja understood it as invitation and knelt to the pipe to let it spill into her hands. She drank, and the water was very cold, it savored of the bright beard of algae depending from the pipe's lip. She sat cross-legged on the ground and drank until the weight of the water in her stomach hurt her. She wanted nothing else.

The hajduk let the fat man fry him two of the eggs and serve them to him floating on the green sauce from the cauldron. Her husband winced at the first bite, but went on happily, whistling inward to cool his lips. The fat man was seized with laughter. They hadn't yet made a human contact in this oven of a country that did not result in laughter. Stoja had come with her husband into the land of the Lotus Eaters, a place for which he was well suited.

When the hajduk finished his breakfast, the fat man gave him a gazette to read. Her husband sat near her on the ground and remarked, all morning it seemed, on its contents. "Several different models of internal combustion engine are offered for sale here. Here, you see, engines compete for supremacy. That is all to the good."

Trailed by the household's children, they set out north again. The children's games were also song, song apparently all they had. The hajduk joined their singing, seemed to know or divine their melodies. They came to a stretch of road paved in crushed shells, and the children turned back. The shells were too sharp even for their tough little feet. The hajduk went on, whistling. At last he let her catch him, and he asked, "Bruckner? Do you like Bruckner? Dvórak?"

"If you must squeal," she said, "squeal. Just don't ask my permission to do it."

The hajduk slowed after that so that she might walk beside him. But they had nothing to say to each other. She let herself fall behind. Her husband forgot her and strode out again. Stoja jogged along briskly and at this pace could not smell herself so much. The front of her dress was white with her body's many salts. She understood herself to be a creature approximately in God's image, secreting foulness. At shorter and shorter intervals new roads met the road they traveled. As pedestrians they were forced to the shoulder by a thickening stream of traffic. Not all the sun and the noise and confusion, not even the pitying regard of mere teamsters, not all of it together was as hard for Stoja as this running in soft dirt. She called to the hajduk's back, "Don't think I don't know that we're lost. We would surely have been there by now if you hadn't lost us."

At last they came to a small rise. They topped it and the hajduk brought her attention to a horizon where the red brick of several prominent buildings was just beginning to emerge. "Baton Rouge," he said.

"Speak to me in our language."

As they neared the city, the pike road began to run parallel with and generally in sight of a wide river, a river she would have called a sea except that she could see it flowing. The hajduk turned down to a boat landing where a scow was onloading cattle. He talked with a herdsman on the dock, and they were permitted to board the thing. They went forward to the bow and a deck somewhat elevated above the one where the cattle were penned. The cattle bawled, gulls dipped at the water, the scow swung out to make its slow passage into the current. Stoja lay down and dreamed of things familiar and things faint and far away until the engine she had slept over shut down, and the hajduk was at her again. Again he was saying, "Baton Rouge." They had come to another waterfront. When she stood, when she weighted her right foot, she understood at once that she had somehow broken it during the course of their walk. It had swollen inside her shoe, and she found that she could not prevent herself from limping. But she wouldn't allow the hajduk to carry her or to hire them some conveyance. Let no one deprive her of her pain, as that was all, it seemed, she could expect to have for her own.

The hajduk led her to a train depot, a busy little building of naked brick. She lay down on one of the long benches inside, squarely in a draft from an open door. Again she slept. She walked Ilmograd's few little avenues and saw again the walls of her village, the long, soft slopes in them at their foundations, where they met the earth. And she was gentle too in this dream. Gentle and fortunate. She discovered a Roman coin, had it between her teeth, and was just about to test its quality when she next woke. For a moment she could not quit her curiosity regarding the coin, but then she was completely among the wakeful. The bench had hurt her. The hajduk was across from her, eating crumbs from a crumpled paper. It was night and their fellow travelers, reduced in number, were draped all around the depot in abject ways. Merciless night, with gaslights and electric lamps. From time to time a man in a blue fez mounted a platform and called like a muezzin through a long cone, at which the depot would stir, and some left and some arrived.

Stoja was not happy, but the effort of moving anywhere else, she knew, would make her less so. "Where are we?"

The hajduk stood with such emphasis that she thought at first he meant to leave her there. But he did not leave. He lifted her foot from the bench and showed her how it had ripened—how useless and vulnerable she had made herself. She felt herself drawn a little closer to her man. She saw it in him. No matter who Danilo Lazich thought he was, or what he thought he might make of himself, he was Prećani Serbi, her countryman, and there was that hatred in him like burning dirt. At least they would always understand each other perfectly. She let him slip his arms under hers, allowed him to lead, then carry her to the far end of the depot. He placed her on the floor there, just before a wall on which was painted a vast tan map with hatched lines, blue and red and black. There was a good deal of infidel lettering. "The routes of the Southern Pacific Railroad," he said. At the bottom of the map, near the floor, a frayed peninsula spilled out into a field of blue, the Bay of Mexico. He pointed to a dot there. "New Orleans, where we made landfall." His finger slid up a bit to a second dot. "Baton Rouge. We are here, just here, having walked much of two days and a full night." He drew himself up to his full height and placed the flat of his hand well up on the wall, as high as he could reach, on a cold gray expanse into which no line or color of the map had ventured. "Butte would lie here. Or perhaps even farther north. And we would be forever getting there, walking."

"If it is so far for you," she said, "then we will ride."

"You've crippled yourself," he said.

"I can make my way. Always."

"And where is your way? Have you the slightest idea?"

"The worst that can happen to me," she said, "has already happened."

He addressed her where she lay on the floor. "I do not admire the uses of cruelty, but with you, woman, to do a kind thing is almost impossible. You said 'walk,' and we have walked, so now you see that your ignorance must not be our guiding principle. Never presume to tell me where I am going, or why, or by what means. Avoid that, and we may stay on friendly terms."

"Buy the tickets," she said.

April–May 1899

Stoja expected to find countrymen. Many of the ambitious Lićani of her generation had sent money home from Butte, Montana. They sent descriptions of their progress and invitations to those they'd left behind. No such invitation had, of course, been offered her, not that she'd wanted one. She was going anyway. For a woman with a pile driver for a husband, the mines seemed a sensible destination. She settled her swollen foot on the seat across from hers and held both seats for her own against all comers, including the hajduk, whose comings and goings were her most constant irritation. But even Stoja could be lulled by a long train ride.

Savage's mission to the city was more ornate. Gold, silver, copper, and zinc. An immensity of copper in Butte to tax his mind, marketed to a world intent on wrapping itself in copper wire and propelling itself with copper windings. That year the United States of America and all her territories and holdings had produced seven hundred and fifty million dollars' worth of ores, and a full tenth of that had come from the richest hill on earth. Butte sat up in a remote country Savage had craved since he had encountered it in Professor Ornbaun's thirty-volume treatise on the Americas.

The Silver Bow, Ornbaun had written, *is the uppermost and easternmost of all those drainages that feed the Clark's Fork and Columbia rivers, and ultimately, the waters of the Pacific. By virtue of its altitude, its stony soils, and the terrible toils and contamination man has brought to it, the city of Butte is a blasted setting quite in contrast to the lush upland valleys that surround it for hundreds of miles in all directions, and here wilderness presses close upon an already fabled destination where even the patterns of corruption remain youthful and vital. Wilderness or city, the Montana highlands may yet yield to the stout hearted a fortune* non pariel, *and will surely continue to crush the faint and the merely desperate arrivals to its precincts.*

There are in Butte, to be certain, cultural elements as glorious as anything known to her older sister cities of the West. The ballet that is danced in San Francisco makes its way soon thereafter to Butte. Denver proudly boasts of playing host to three vaudeville circuits; Butte entertains four. The city is the greatest concentration of sporting events on earth, the earth's latest excrescence of new wealth, and always in such circumstances and to such places is a certain breed attracted. It is a place of industry; it is a place of meritless gain. Granite and brick, also abundant near about, are the basis of all its civic architecture. If the city is new, it is not insubstantial. Butte's social structure is one of egalitarian brutality. The have-nots of many lands have assembled here and come into their own. Outcasts gravitate. Ulstermen play fan-tan with Chinese; Finns enjoy the services of Hasidic tailors.

Winters in the region are typically difficult. However, one descends from any snowbound pass leading into Butte to find a mile-high plain and a hillside ablaze with light that is profuse, profligate, and in no mean heedful of the trackless reaches of darkness in which it rests. Narrowly cosmopolitan, Butte offers every pleasure and every privation yet devised by man. The industry that creates so much possibility here also casts over its environs a pall through which the sun only rarely penetrates. It is a dangerous child of a city, destined to perish of its own exuberance or to someday rule the earth. Neither outcome would be, perhaps, entirely regrettable.

Savage had seen in Ornbaun's passage the face of the twentieth century and wished to see it again, close to hand.

But it was difficult to wait for it, hard to stay on the train. From Fort Worth, he sat behind Mr. Harriman's paired locomotives, and minutes and degrees of latitude fell behind, and marshlands and woodlands and farmlands and prairie fell behind them, and the boundaries of the various states were of absolutely no consequence. Forty miles on this train every hour; never an hour passed when he did not see from his window, or from the top of the mail car, curiosities he should have stopped to examine. Texas, New Mexico. His fellow voyagers, fellow Americans, sought him in the club cars, some with promotions in mind, productions to turn a buck.

"You could wrestle rubes at the carnivals and have a nice living from it." This was McNeil of Iowa's notion. "Or even just by putting yourself on display." Of late, McNeil had been on the road with perfumes, a perilous gift. " 'Rub the Gentle Giant for Luck,' " he said. " 'Man or Beast? Guess Correctly and Win a Cupie Doll.' Mister, you could be part of many an easy presentation. Remove your shirt." Fired by the thought, he made as if to remove his own; ". . . there, you'd have done a night's work."

In Colorado, Savage was offered the chance to sell crop and life insurance. Where the mountains rose up, he began to meet men who wanted him to go lumbering with them, partner on a crosscut, blow log jams. Enterprise was all in the nation. America, precious federation. He would be welcome here. He could have gotten off the train at any point and been home, at all points he was tempted. America. Savage was very sorry now to have been given just the one life; he'd never see any creditable part of all that needed seeing.

Skirting the eastern front of the Rockies, the train slowed. From Denver, passengers of their class became part of a mixed freight and were at all hours shunted onto spurs where they waited for their always lengthening train to take on more tonnage. They made connections in Cheyenne with the Western Flyer to wester with efficiency and élan through another several ranks of mountains and on into Pocatello. Then, running brightly behind the engine Pandora, they went beside and, sometimes with goatlike patience, upon the mountains' western slopes. Savage was never completely within the train, not during the whole trip through Idaho's fat toe and into the Bitterroots and Montana. He rode on top now, or on the shimmying platforms over the coupling knuckles, and he smoked prodigiously. He thought he was approaching a perfection.

⸺ ⸺

Savage went down in the shafts just the one day, to see the rock and to powder monkey. He was sponsored there by a cousin-in-law, Dragan Prpa, a Serb lumpen in make and outlook whose approach to the mines was military: Prpa saw himself the proud corporal in a civil army at war with the very earth. "We will see what you are made of," he told Savage, "when you are six hundred feet down the *Rarus*." It was important to Prpa that Savage understand every misery the industry might inflict on a man, and it was important that he appreciate the continuing largesse of the Prpa family. Savage should keep foremost in mind that he had his position here through Dragan, who, as a gesture to family, had made it possible to share his hole. They descended in a squealing man-lift, the cousin-in-law lopping cheese, close work in the cage, and manfully chewing black bread. When they reached the stope they were to mine that day, Dragan had already left himself with just a half canteen of water to sustain him through the next ten hours. Two stopes below, at the mine's deepest level, the thrum of a Worthington pump and the monstrous engine pushing it.

Afoot, they followed a horizontal shaft, Savage bringing up the rear carrying lengths of narrow-gauge track they would set and spike at the end of the tunnel where the crew had blasted and mucked the day before. They went about it in an efficient stupor, thinking their own thoughts, which would make for, in Savage's estimation, very poor refuge. Finished with the track, they fitted and set shoring timbers, brute work, performed almost prayerfully. Savage was assigned to heft the timbers. The day's engineering done, the foreman called lunch. Some of the crew slept. Savage ate, an overturned ore car his stool. Dragan Prpa settled in beside him. "Give me one of those boiled eggs, cousin." He stroked his nose thoughtfully, then again, more dramatically. "Every day we go farther," he said. "Do you know what we have directly over our heads, Lazich? We believe we are now under the Savoy Hotel. Give me one of your eggs."

"Why?"

"Because this is the direction of the seam. We follow the seam. It has taken us under the Savoy, if you can imagine that."

"Why should I give you an egg?"

After lunch they attacked the face of the shaft. Happy about it, Prpa rode a pneumatic drill, with godlike effect into the rock. "I make my holes. Sweet, neat little holes. And then the powder goes in. Fuse it, pack it, and then—boom, boom, boom—set them all off. That's what I like. Every day it's boom, boom, boom, and we have gone a little farther."

Down in concussive rock. Savage had not been an hour in Butte before learning a useful dread of silicosis. One breathed very little ore dust, it seemed, before the miner's pallor was on him and the scarring in his lungs. And it was well for Dragan and these others to think of themselves as afflicted but necessary, to have whatever satisfaction they could find in lives spent below ground. But Savage, as a miner, would address the work crouched, or kneeling. No. Not at all. There was never a moment when he thought he might be one of them.

He spent the following week at the end of a calcine oven, another noxious spot, and then took flight from the industrial arm of the labor force. One evening in the New Star he hired out to collect a delinquent gambling debt. Such metal as came his way thereafter was mined, smelted, and minted.

As his first step toward real participation in the fruitful land, Savage got himself ready cash and its emblements, all the personal finery he could think of. From the haberdashers at Henneseys he ordered a gray homburg, size eight and a half, and a pearled device, a coursing hawk, to pin to its crown. He bought twelve pairs of suspenders, as many starched collars. He went among the city's debtors, sleek as well as large, and at his first quiet request for it, even the most recalcitrant of them assembled some means to pay. Many seemed gratified by the experience, this chance to make good. "Never again," they would tell him. "From now on, I pay as I go, huh?" It was during the first few months of his life as a dun that he began to style himself Danny, a name that particularly struck his ear.

Savage and his wife had settled first in the Cabbage Patch, a neighborhood built on Butte's most weather-beaten hillside, but when he had the means to do better he rented a suite at the Arlen. Stoja would not accompany him uptown. He resided there without her interference, living at the charming velocity of easy affluence. And he prospered. Out on the town, bets were made as to the volume of food he might consume at a meal. In Butte, a man's hunger was respected; the ravenous were celebrated. Considered a jack of all the violent trades, he was finally fully fed, and everything was expected of him. He was asked if he would like to conduct bear-baitings, dog fights. His opinions were sought and attended to. In all his haunts women of varying age and persuasion found ways to pass slowly and closely by him. Curious, prettily scented, close. Such a shame, the hours wasted in sleep and waking with just two hands.

To supplement himself, Savage took thugs into his employ. First, despite the rumors, he hired Karl Ullmer. Ullmer effortlessly implied the Teutonic doggedness and did exactly as he was told. Savage took on a man whose *nom de guerre* was at that time Zed Strizich, and who looked the thug but did not sound it. Strizich was garrulous and enjoyed very much the confusion he caused with his Etonian drawl. A remittance man with a tiny Devonshire estate of his own, he owed much of his character to formative years at St. Bosco's, a school whose pedagogical premise was that no well-born boy is ineducable or incorrigible. St. Bosco's approaches to Strizich had fouled completely when it was found that Jeremy—he'd been Jeremy then—rather coveted the good caning to be had for bad behavior.

Savage, his thick-browed staff assembled and loyal, had become a small but persuasive agency. In the twenty square blocks where his group held sway, the deadbeat, that usually ineradicable weed, was all but extinct. Savage and company expanded their range of services, proving themselves indispensable to the resolution of any truly intractable negotiation. They became officers of a court that, while not official, had its jurisdiction wherever he and his cohorts happened to be. His circles of acquaintance arced higher and higher through the several arteries of the city's population. In Butte, in those places where its capital accumulated, most men thought themselves unique, and Savage was very little alienated among them. He was, most importantly, a fellow who got the right result, and made a fine associate on the sticky fringes of any business. So Butte curried his favor, and he was content with her though she was ugly. Danny Savage.

Domestically, he was less successful here.

April 26, 1904

On the feast day of St. Cyril, he rode the trolley in brisk weather over Park Street. The morning cloud cover was unimaginably high, torn to wraiths by winds aloft. "I will meet any man," he heard a child whisper to a pal smeared with axle grease and plum jelly, "on any terms." The boast had been in town several weeks now, wrongly attributed to Savage. He was often misquoted. These boys, he thought, were hoping he would kill one of them and thinking it would be delicious if he did. He was the source of a thousand specious thrills, infamous to all but the city's law. It was for Savage oysters on the half shell, and champagne and soda crackers, and whatever else he might like, and the only blot on it was his continuing entanglement with his wife. She had sent word that he must squander an otherwise promising afternoon.

For the benefit of his admirers, he made a handsome, sweeping dismount of the trolley at the corner of Idaho and Gold. He stopped to assess the progress made by the Orthodox in mending the onion dome above their church. Their first and irretrievable mistake had been to build it of plaster and lath. He went deeper into the Cabbage Patch, toward the place Stoja and he had once called theirs, though he was paying for it and now only she lived there. Of late, he had been an infrequent guest. Ohio Street, not a daub of paint in sight, and all along it lay the shadow of what by now should be his long forgotten home. Savage smelled Lika here, heard it, heard what had been the litany of his nursery, the only story Marko Lazich ever told him.

On the evening before the battle of Kosovo Polje, Danilo, a Serbian hireling crept into Sultan Murad's tent and skewered him in his sleep. Heaven was incensed, and a rude angel was sent to Prince Lazar to tell him that, because he had commissioned so foul an act, he had just one of two fates from which to choose, and he must choose immediately. The angel showed him Serbia as she might be on the morrow, his army's pikes heavy with Ottoman gore, and in the midst of that triumphant army Lazar saw himself standing bloody—victorious, but cloaked in the shadow of damnation. The angel showed him the same day again, but another battle, and here the Serb's regent is fallen, his army vanquished. Lazar saw himself, fallen in that latter dream, but also rising straight toward a seat at Jesus' feet. Our Prince was no coward, but he chose the serene eternity. That was five hundred years ago, and to this very moment Turks infest every fertile valley of the Old Kingdom. That, Danilo, was our people's first great betrayal. But only the first of many. Do you think Lazar aches in heaven at seeing still-loyal Serbs riding out from their black forests, century after century? The Serb rides out, never more than a clan at a time, always undermanned, always insufficiently armed. Year after year he rides out, wild-eyed and happy to present his bull neck to the Pasha's Guard, the Janissaries. It was the Serb who dulled the Ottoman scimitar so that Northern Europe might have her Reformation, her Renaissance, her Industrial Revolution, while in the Balkans a bet- ter people advanced not at all. Where is our reward? Ask yourself, Danilo.

Savage stood on a roadbed frozen hard as macadam. Of course they would live here, find this contemptible place to squat and nurse their grievances. *So for the Serb, Danilo, it comes to this: like Our Cherished Savior you will instruct the world by your suffering; if you are Serb, you are, like Our Christ, available for the killing but very hard to kill.*

Savage had married one of his own kind, of the kind he would not be, and he was determined that his further difficulties should not include anything so complex and wearing as this marriage. All along Ohio Street, dirt the brightest thing in sight. Not for the Serb any investment in temporal grace, and not for his neighbor. The Serb would live just here, oppressed by someone. And his Stoja would live here.

She had bought two new washing machines. There were now seven treadle-drive Sturgis and Philpot agitators fitted into the room. She sat among them in a red mackinaw and a pair of brogans—got, no doubt, through close trading—waiting for him in shoes that may or may not fit her. Each week Stoja built a thirty-quart cake of lye soap in this room and shaved it into flakes. She sank tons of blackened denim, bachelor's clothes, in scalding water and her acidic soap. She had made the room antiseptic. Wringers stood in a row, awaiting her labor. She was an industry, his wife, successfully in competition with the local Chinese.

Potent, incurious, awful. The awful woman, his. "My bed," Savage said. "My lamp and stool. My periodicals, my anesthetic. What have you done with them, Stoja?"

"That corner is not for your use anymore."

"I would tell you to go to hell, but that would be an improvement over what you've done here. You will go after my things and return them to the place and condition in which I left them."

"Why? Why would I do that?"

"What sort of party is it that you'd go to, dressed as you are? What sort of celebration? We must stop somewhere along the way now, somewhere downtown, and equip you like a woman. You've given me little enough to work with."

"I am wearing a four-dollar dress, hajduk. More than good enough to be seen with you. Save your money for the harlots."

"The bed. My bed, I'll have it back, or one of these moonlit nights you will find me in yours. Your little bed, the two of us. What would come of that? Show me another washerwoman who has kippered herring as often as she likes. These biscuits you like so well, these tinned goods, they come from me. I'll have something for them, won't I? In exchange for the small luxuries. Bring my bed back. I am paying for a residence and I will have a residence, whether I choose to live in it or not."

"The man begrudges his wife her little scraps of fish? The idler. What a wonder you are."

"Wonder of wonders," said Savage, "to be sure. Yours is the quotidian, I am not charged with that."

"To speak so on a holy day."

Savage drew two crumpled bills from his trouser pocket. "Again I tell you, come out of this. Move down the hill with me, Stoja, nearer the conveniences. Why do you work like an animal when I can provide for your comfort?"

"I choose to live among my people, where the old ways are understood. So should you. But you are ashamed of who you are."

"The old ways? I see. Then, by all means let's find a cave where we can crouch among the dogs and piss on our feet. The old ways. Come out of this, Stoja. It unsettles me. Come up to the Arlen and have room service, why don't you?"

"I will outlive you. What is mine is mine. I make an honest business. No one will shoot me for what I do. But you . . . when you are gone, then what becomes of me? I will see to my own needs, in my own way, among my own people. You don't have a thing to say about it."

When she wished to reach him, just three occasions in the two years they'd lived apart, she caused one of her customers to call the switchboard at his hotel. Each of the messages had arrived fantastic. *Wife says bring five big buckets and goose today.* And, *Wife says boobonik flag in Butte. Wife says stay away.* The latest: *Wife says St. Cereal day Saturday. Pick her up at ten.* Which meant, he knew, that Stoja wanted him for her seemly escort at the holy feast of St. Cyril. In truth, even his wife's interest in the mysteries and observances of the Faith had grown wispy here. It was for the sake of form, for business, that they should attend the feast as man and wife. To Savage's thinking, not reason enough to mingle with kith and kin. Yet here he was. "Well," he said, "come."

She would not ride the trolley because she believed it brought her near contagions. At the edge of town she prevented Savage from renting them English ponies to ride out on. Horses were afraid of her and behaved badly when she was near. They walked two miles before Savage tired of it and hailed a buckboard. "Climb on," he told her. Then again, adamant, "Climb on." The old sorrel at the head of the rig turned skittish, just as she'd warned he would, the moment Stoja pulled herself up onto the wagon box. They went on to Columbia Gardens, the animal straining constantly to see the new thing behind it. An abrasive wind pushed them across the flat and toward the pleasure grounds. They rounded a thumb of the gulch that sheltered the pavilion and the winter remnants of gardens limned in gray and white. There were hothouses here where international banks of flowers were in bloom even now. At the lane's turning a field of playground equipment danced empty in the weather.

Most of Butte's several hundred Serbs had come, and they stood in their clusters on the pavilion's long veranda. Savage and his wife were driven up to, then beyond the crowd, their driver cursing, reining back with little effect. He began to shout at them, "Get off. Get off." They alit at a stiff run, slowed, and turned to walk back to the party on the veranda. As they gained the summit of its sweeping central stair, Stoja identified for him the various factions where they stood. At the end of history every Serb would have his own flag and be patron saint of his own orthodoxy; until that final, perfect fracturing, they were settled into their fraternities. "Those wearing the wide red-and-white ribbons," Stoja said. "All from Belgrade, all no good. And the ones in the soldiers' jackets call themselves the 10th Serbian Fusiliers. They play like children at soldiers, but I wash for them, wash those uniforms after every wearing. It is necessary. They let Bosnians join them, Muslims. Filthy." Stoja and her husband belonged, in his case by default, to the Prećani Serbi. Their little group did nothing to distinguish itself except to stand apart from the others.

Serbs across the river, Danilo. Prećani Serbi. The good families massed in 1804, the best families rode into Belgrade and made it their own, as it had been anyway. At their head, the noble Karadjorj, the pig-broker risen through the ranks despite his belief that he was too angry a man even for military purposes. But he led us into Belgrade and into a golden era of eight years' duration. Then, by a treaty to which Serbia was not signatory, she was ceded back to the Turk. The Ottomans returned to Belgrade with their gifted executioners. They impaled us on their stakes, Danilo. Along every street patriots stood impaled, stakes driven rectum to clavicle, but ingeniously so that the lungs and hearts were spared and each death was a long, instructive drama.

So we wait. But for what? Serbia? We'd be strangers there, just as we're strangers here. We wait, but we wait for nothing we could name or put our crooked fingers to. Prećani Serbi. What shit.

Dragan Prpa came to them and gave them papers to pin to themselves, St. Cyril's stark, cruciate crest. The cousin had established himself as liaison between the Prečani and the other groups at the party. Shamefaced, he reported that no one had a key to get inside. No one was completely sure who should have the key. Of all the food and drink that had been ordered, only the milk had been delivered. Savage saw himself in a window and was pleased at how obviously he did not belong to the assembly—but their language was the language he understood most perfectly, the first he'd learned, and they talked of how hard they worked, as if more explanation was necessary than the sight of their best jackets hanging from their muscled backs. Muscled backs and hollow chests—no tailor would ever make a suit to hang handsomely on a miner's body. Serbs. In their leisure they talked of the atrocities committed by Hrvati who lived, in many cases, just across the street from them. The old hatreds, they had found, were true and necessary, and old enemies had relocated each other here, become neighbors to make a distillate of the Balkan idiocy. Their talk was very familiar to him.

Stoja stood near the veranda's railing as if she were in a sentry box, staring off at the upsweep of the Continental Divide or, probably, at nothing. Savage shuddered. There were times when she appeared wistful, fragile as a hatchling chick. Complaint was general around him, tending now toward menace. Standing out in this wind it was impossible even to roll a proper cigarette, and where was Obilovich? Hadn't Obilovich rented the hall? What of the box lunches, the beer? What had become of the orchestra? They had been wanting a fine day of eating and drinking above ground but were instead huddled in the blistering wind.

Having guessed he might become captive to just such muddling, Savage had bought an *Evening News* upon departing his downtown rooms that morning. He retired to an isolated section of the veranda, pulled the *News* from his belt, and refolded it into a quarter sheet to make it rigid against the wind. He put his back to the wall and slid to the floor. The lead story had to do with *News's* discovery of what it was calling the bohunk problem. *There are 3,000 bohunk miners in Butte today. Of these*

*2,175 are working, and the balance are being supported by their brothers and are
ready to slip into every job where a white man is laid off.* Whole areas of the
city were infested by *these black men from across the water,* and yet the *News*
seemed to feel it should be specially commended for having located
them and for having the courage to beard the disaster they represented.
The paper's house artist had illustrated in pen and ink the interior of a
shanty occupied by crop-headed, hollow-cheeked Africans in long un-
derwear, but the story was more accurate in many particulars. Savage had
come with a sorry lot to Butte. Many recent arrivals were living eight
to a cabin, sleeping in shifts on their cots or on dirt floors, and paying,
each of them, full rental as if they had the place to themselves. There
was a class of landlord, men who were also mine foremen and who, in
exchange for the larcenous rentals they charged, would guarantee each
of his tenants a job. *The bohunk miner,* the *News* reported, *never adapts
himself to the American way of life any more than does a Chinaman. Gambling,
white slavery, prizefighting, licensed prostitution, horse racing, and every ill, al-
leged or otherwise, that one can conjure up, palls into insignificance before this
black peril which has Butte by the throat and is dragging it down to the level of
a grading camp.* An accompanying editorial said that even a city as gre-
garious as Butte must have some standards, that it was time for decent
men to rise up and speak, to encourage these dark people to move on
and look for a place more amenable to their brutish ways.

"Alone again. Off laughing again." Stoja stood above him. "You sit on
the floor like a poorly behaved child? How am I to hold my head up
when you behave as you do?"

"Let's be off now."

"We have only just got here."

"See how unhappy they are? What do you suppose they will be like
in an hour when they are still waiting to be let in, still hungry? No one
will come to let them in. No one will bring food, and there will be no
orchestra."

"Stand up," she said. "When things aren't as you want them, you cannot wait. No, but always, let's be off. As if all things must be arranged for your convenience. You brought me to this, you must stay."

He joined her to stand again among the Prećani Serbi. Nearest them was a group he had seen before, a little cell of Bolsheviks that had been standing just outside the door of a church and cursing as loudly as they could, and smoking, while inside, also loudly, a priest read a sermon over one of their order who had died. Today, it seemed, some doctrinal problem had arisen among them, and they were about to splinter at least in half. Division and division and division, the endless, sexless genesis of political man. Savage was moved to analysis. "Serbs across the river," he told his group. No flattery was in his tone, but they listened because this was, at least, more interesting than the other had been, the waiting. "Did anyone bring a *gusla*? Isn't it time for sad songs? Isn't it time for *Ladé Capitané*? Sing, why don't you, but never anything to cause dancing, no, keep to your gray little airs, and sing them, and bicker with a neighbor who resembles you, and that is what you'll have in this country, the same you had in the country you left, because that is who you are. While you have been at each other's throats, the world has come to despise you collectively, you and the Hrvat, and even Czechs and Magyars—bohunks here, all of you. A united slavdom at last, united in condemnation. Now you may sing the old dirges because, once again, no other music is coming. Why should the good music of the world be wasted on your ears?"

The Bolsheviks murmured at this.

"How little you know," said his wife. "No music for us? No food? Well, who is that coming now, coming fast because they have made us wait?"

Three open automobiles approached down the lane toward the pavilion. Two of them bore the markings of the Silver Bow County Sheriff.

"Stop that, hajduk. Laugh and laugh when there is nothing to laugh at? Stop it. Do you laugh at me, you mud? You have a sickness."

"Watch now," he told his wife. "We'll have a comedy so broad that even you will be entertained."

He raised his voice again, this time so as to be heard by all on the veranda. "Is there even one here who is descended from those heroes who died at Kosovo Polje? Is there one such among this crowd?"

Up came the chin of every man and the several women and children in attendance.

"Then you are Serbs? You did not look like Serbs to me. On St Cyril's day, Serbs—men—know how to celebrate." Savage leaned out from the veranda and discharged his pistol three times into the endless sky. Similarly armed celebrants, their majority, also fired, dutifully, three times apiece, affirming the trinity. Damage was done to the veranda's roof. The oncoming cars accelerated. The third and most powerful of these wore no official markings and was full of riflemen in mufti. The cars came to within fifty yards of the porch and were drawn up in a sort of barricade; the passengers discharged and hid behind them. With his countrymen momentarily fallen silent, Savage could hear the newcomers just distinctly enough to know that they too had taken up some disagreement among themselves. Their shouting reached a crescendo, stopped, and a moment later a single, unarmed man walked out from the rampart of automobiles. The sheriff.

He came to the foot of the grand stair and looked up mournfully. "My name is John D. Boyle, and I am the law. I mean to collect every shiv and sap and pistol and knuckle duster on that porch. If you people think you can go around heeled like an American, then you are wrong . . . Oh, hell, is there anybody up there speaks a white man's lingo? Yeah, you, Savage, you tell them what I'm saying."

"This is an Irishman," Savage explained. "Who says he wants every weapon in your possession. As soon as he has them, you can well expect to be tithing to his pope. He has come to interfere with your celebration and your manhood."

"Keep it simple," said the sheriff. "I didn't have that much to say."

A captain of the fusiliers stepped to Savage's side. "No. No," he told the sheriff, the only words he had that might convey his desire for peace. To Savage he said, in their common tongue, "Tell him we want no trouble. We'll do anything he likes."

"He says," Savage told the sheriff, "that they have nothing they wish to give you."

The sheriff came up the stairs and walked directly to Savage, rattling as if poorly assembled of the wrong parts. Tired and vicious, he walked like a lawman. Stoja pulled at the tail of her husband's jacket. "I can see what you are doing. You are making a fight. Just for your fun, a fight. I will not mend you if you are beaten, I will not mourn if you are killed."

The sheriff was before them, his badge a tiny nickel star. He decided to take up with Stoja now. "Ma'am, I'll start with you. You can give me that baby pig sticker."

She had made herself a heavy necklace and hung from it a small sheath knife and a small, unreliable compass. These things belonged together.

"He wants your knife, little wife. Says you are to give him your knife."

"Quit laughing, hajduk." She fingered her necklace, the sum of her vanity.

"In just about three seconds," said John D. Boyle, "I am going to disarm one of these others and pistol whip you, Savage. You can't behave any better than this, I will just have to lay you out."

Stoja touched the knife's handle, slipping it just half out of its sheath. Then, slowly, she exposed for the sheriff her black smile.

"What you want," Savage told Boyle, "you will have to take. And isn't that always the way, Sheriff? Nothing given?"

"I know the nature of your business, Savage. I know who you know. You've gone ahead and made me mad, so who you know doesn't mean a thing anymore. Not to me. But I am everyone's sweetheart, and I don't care to see innocent blood shed. Not in Silver Bow County. This bunch down here, they think this is a shooting party. Wouldn't take much confusion before that's what we'd have. Gunfire, probably a lot of it. Not one of these men with me is interested in the formalities, Savage. So I will have to wait on you. Otherwise, I'd haul you back to town right now, down to the basement of the courthouse. You can shriek down there like you was Nellie Melba, not a peep of it reaches the street. The next time me or any one of my deputies see you—or her—we'll have a warrant in hand. We'd see you the next time you set foot in town. Now, if you are truly curious, big man, about how tough you are, you just let that happen. Let me find you."

April and May 1904

Late that afternoon, Savage and his wife, collectively thirty-five dollars richer than when they had come to Butte, left from a cindery switching yard on a southbound freight. They climbed into a boxcar filled with loosely bound, scraped cowhides. For warmth they burrowed in the hides, and there, during several days of otherwise negligible travel, their union returned to its old, lusty footing. Between them, he and his wife had not a single reliable instinct as to the rest of humanity, but they could be certain enough of each other. Lying in the hides with her, there were moments when Savage felt as if he'd never previously been warm, and their enchantment was in high relief as they came south. Their train, beset by a run of mechanical problems, took thirty hours just to crest Pipestone Pass, and days passed on the halting, jerking boxcar with nothing to eat or otherwise do. Bound for what? A man might escape much, but never himself. Savage was growing tired of that, of his person. He saw mountain meadows through the slatted walls of the boxcar, snowfields that under any little sun or moonlight glowed like sterile heaven. A limitless nation; he willed himself to believe it.

The hides, and therefore the Savages, were destined for Idaho Falls. Their car was switched onto a siding at the edge of town. They slipped off and made their way to a bank of the Snake River to make what camp they could in a backwater where a bit of privacy could be had among cattail reeds and Russian olive. They bathed in icy water, Stoja lengthily. She was afraid they might never again smell like human beings. "Tonight we sleep on the ground. We smell like butcher's scraps." When darkness fell, they huddled near a driftwood fire and each other. "Tomorrow," she said, "we will find work. You will pretend to be an honest man, pretend it from now on. Have we been anywhere where there are more farms? Where there are farms, there is work."

"Where there are farms," he said, "there is monotony. I do not see myself husbanding animals, splashed with their feces. It always comes to that. Farmers. Do you know the uses they would have for me?"

"Work, I said." Stoja drew apart from him. "That for you would be even worse than this? You will not dirty your hands?"

"With the soils of my choosing. To my own ends."

Of cold necessity, she placed herself against him again. In this way they slept, warm only where they touched. The first daylight saw Savage headed into town proper, Stoja calling at his back, "If I don't see you in five hours, I'm off. I don't wait here forever." Because he couldn't tell her exactly what he intended for the day, she would not follow him. Would not follow, would not wait.

At seven in the morning the streets of Idaho Falls were as busy as they would be at noon. Freckled Mormon farmers plodded out of the recent dawn, striving already. Savage went first to the railroad depot and was told that passenger trains ran only north or south from there, and expensively. He decided that he would go east, and he went around to cartage companies and freight depots where he learned that Idaho Falls made no welcome for gentiles, but offered no way for them to conveniently get out. Ferguson, of Fuhr and Ferguson, Haulers, told him that he should ride shank's mares, the farther and sooner the better, to any place where he, Ferguson, was not. Savage bruised the man a little for the sake of better decorum. Wanting a diminished presence then, an hour of warm contemplation, he set out to find the town library.

Even such as these, he thought, must have attempted a library.

Somewhat sore of heart, he was making his way down the boardwalk when he came upon a wagon sunk to its rear hubs in Garnet Street. A four-horse team stood wearily before it, still in harness. A muddy man lay face down on a lead horse's back. At Savage's approach the man sat up and said that he was Baxter Ness. He asked for a name in return. When he had it he said, "Savage? Bet you made that up, didn't you?"

"Yes. Do you like it?"

"I can say it anyway." Ness's jaw was crooked, and along one side of it ran an old gray slash of scarring. A toothpick pistoned in and out of his lips, accelerating with the onset of any new thought. "You're a big one, aren't you? They used enough material on you, mister, to make two or three regular people. Never saw anything like it."

"Where are you going?"

"Looks like nowhere. Not any time soon. This mud's got me beat. Me and my girls, we're wore to a nub." Of middling age but ill-used, Ness dismounted carefully. "Bought this load last October, thought I'd get it into Wyoming for spring roundup. All them horses over the mountains, right around roundup time there's a big demand for horseshoes. And a short supply. I would've done fine. Would have is one thing, though, and done is another. Guess I discourage easy."

"Two of those animals have hurt themselves, citizen. But, through the mountains? I'm going that way myself. My wife and I. Will you take us?"

"I'd drive the circus out of town if I could. Sure. But, mister, you're right about Honey and Sis. I done em so bad, wouldn't ask em to pull over the flat now."

"Fresh horses, then. It is not so much. You'll have three . . . five dollars from me toward their purchase."

"Not so much, you say? Now I have got to unload this wagon entirely and lay my wares in the gumbo. I must've had me one hell of a plan when I come to this. Right now, I'd just as soon see the whole deal sink out of sight. Then the other thing, we got a late spring. Get out of this, there's still snow up in them Tetons, just mile after mile of it yet, and knee-deep in the passes. Might get there in good fettle if you could fly, elsewise, it's a damn rough old ride. And I don't guess I calculated too good how much this iron weighs. Load I got here, on this side of the mountains, I might could sell it for a nickel more'n what I paid for it."

"We are going the same way. We should collaborate."

"The hell you say? With your wife? You'd take a woman up there? It can be birds singing one minute, and a minute later your nose is froze black on your face. That's how it is even if you got some good way to go and a light load. It ain't worked out for me, let er go at that. Believe I'll just sit on this until summer's come, more or less, and try and make what I can of it then. Won't be much, but I like that better than getting stuck and froze. Four hundred pair of shoes. You want em?"

"We'll make clamps to bind these wheels. How would that be? Make skids of them. Snow is a fine medium of travel. One of the best."

"Skids? You put this proposition to me when I'm stone cold sober? They'd be . . . skids? And over we go, huh? "

"With two fresh horses. Stallions, if possible, to be harnessed one in front of the other. That combination will draw weight, I assure you. A small increase in elevation? Think how pure the air would be. It is always invigorating to climb."

"You must be wild to reach Rainey," said Ness.

"I don't know it, but if that is what you have in mind, then I will go there."

"Lot of them boys like you over there—can't even say 'howdy' to you, most of em. Eat that lamb like there was no tomorrow."

"I don't know the place," said Savage. "I do intend to go over the mountains, but I could not accurately say why. With or without you, I will be going."

Ness unhitched his compromised pair and led them off, cooing to comfort and be comforted. Out of harness the horses were much diminished, and even on dry ground their gait suggested the suck of mud.

Off slow, sad and slow, to the stock pens. Savage unhitched the other pair and rubbed them down with sack cloth. He grained them and led them in circles. Matched Belgian bays, bred to work and keep working, these were far from done. He led them out into a lot dressed in the year's first sprout of grass, and they cropped it, and with two hours of grazing they'd reclaimed their strength.

Ness returned, a hackamore grimly in either hand, walking between two very large and stupid colts. "They ain't been broke to harness, so that could make it kind of hellish. But they're good and strong." He had their heads, but that was all he had of them. They cantered out sideways from his grip, and they were extremely but uselessly alert, and nothing impressed them nearly as much as their own vitality.

Savage held them while Ness harnessed the Belgians into the left half of the hitch. To harness the colts they eventually hit on the strategy of hobbling them, front and back, and having Savage drag them sideways into the tree. Ness buckled and cursed. The animals were deeply confused. These colts would live and die confused; Savage had lost all confidence in them. Ness stepped away from them. Savage let slack a lead line. The young stud at the rear of the rigging dove for the rump of the young stud just before him, and he nipped it, and as he dove to do it again the whole team, startled, drove as one into their collars, and the wagon lurched and rattled symphonically, horseshoes chiming on their racks, and the team surged forward again, and they were out of the mud and running, running on, terrified of the clamor they kept raising just behind them.

"Well," said Ness, "I guess we're in business."

—✦—

They heard in Jackson Hole that they were in the best of Wyoming already, that the passes they'd traversed thus far were nothing to Togwotee, which might yield to mountaineers on snowshoes but would certainly swallow greenhorns and an overburdened team. A dry goods man suggested they rent a room or pitch a tent. Everyone told them to wait, everyone. Savage wouldn't hear of it. "We are going east at once." Unable to account for his urgency, he was pleased by it, and he drove his party up into the Tetons as if the vast blue indifference of the mountains was itself a prize.

The weather turned warm. They reached snow line, and the snow was heavy and wet. They jammed the wagon's brakes and locked its front wheels with Savage's simple clamps, and they made it a sledge. It tended to sink, to push slush up in front of it, and even after Savage had built a prow for it out of short logs, the going was very hard. Three full days the men had walked beside and in front of it, shoving, shoveling, stripped to the waist like a threshing crew. Driving, Stoja became snow-blind, but not before she had brought the team to an understanding. One night, having reached that altitude where dusk brings on cold like a knife blade, they sat huddled under Ness's buffalo robe, listening to the horses breathe off in the trees.

"You don't want to think of it, but you do," said Ness. "Bears. They ain't too long outta them caves; and don't you think they'd say whoop-de-doo and make a meal of us if they found one of us dead out by the wayside? You seen them winterkill carcasses, they're picked clean. Between the birds and the bears and whatnot, picked pretty damn clean."

Neither Ness nor Stoja had asked to turn back or even broached the possibility, still they seemed to think that Savage should hear hourly of their every discomfort and alarm. He'd spent half his remaining wealth on wool undergarments for the party, but Stoja wouldn't wear hers, preferring the cold to the hives they gave her. Ness was drawn everywhere close to the bone, without much heat in him to contain. Because they were miserable, Savage had been patient, but maybe too long. Their morbidity would never do. "Is that all that troubles you, Ness, the fate of your corpse? Only give me the details, and I'll dispose of you any way you like. Unfortunately, you are in glorious health, so there is the risk that your funeral will come to nothing."

"I'd like about ten hours of sleep, layin'-down-in-a-bed sleep. That's all."

"Moonlight," said Savage, significantly.

"Yeah, woods are lit up like the Grange hall on Christmas eve, what of it, though? I am tired. Them animals are tired, and your woman here can't see a lick. It is nighttime, Savage, and awful goddamn cold out there."

"In an hour or two there will be a deep crust on this snow. Ice. Over the ice, don't you think?"

"When do we schedule a little sleep, I'd like to know? You want to take out in the middle of the night? That what she wants?"

"We can reach the summit in five hours on the crust. The same climb could take all of tomorrow if we let ourselves be caught in soft snow again. On the ice we can fairly fly. The remainder will seem effortless. The summit, and then the rest is descent. So you see how it is."

"Oh my," said Ness, "then I better brew up a pot of coffee. First things first. And, from here on in, I'll walk them downhill stretches. This wagon gets away from us just one time and we'll fly indeed. No, I'll just walk along behind, thanks all the same. Oh, but it's cold. Get out from under this robe and it'll be just terrible cold."

Stoja could see to drive again in moonlight, and at her direction even the colts seemed to have a sense of mission. The party, traveling in the efficiency of a strange, crisp dream, mounted the final easy pitches of the pass; fifteen miles brought them to dawn at the top of the world. They hadn't come to a stopping place. An unremarkable day saw them out of the snow, out of the pines, and into Dubois, where they stopped at last. But they'd driven themselves restless. Spread like a catch of fish under the wagon, they napped. They woke, took on water, and headed out into richly mineralized foothills where escarpments reared randomly near the road, appearing to ooze blood. They descended to high prairie, ground, Ness told them, that had been contested by Indian tribes just a generation or two ago. Chief Washakee, dancing with a Crow's heart on his lance—Crow Heart Butte. "They died for this? Why, it hardly makes for good antelope range. Be just like an Indian, though, go and die for something like this."

The country became more barren as they went on. At a great distance the Wind River Mountains broke the horizon a little, but only a little. High, dry land, this was home to the pitiless light Savage remembered from the Lika. And this, somehow, would be home to him. He bowed to terrible instinct and felt himself swell to fill an emptiness.

— The Soils of His Choosing —

— UNDER MUCH OF WYOMING there is a memory of lusher ages, a succession of jungles that lived, lay down, and eventually compressed themselves into life's carbonate essence, coal. In 1903 a factor for the Chicago Railway Company located such a deposit very near the surface of Fremont County, under ground that was otherwise worth nothing. Mr. Bell reported an extensive shelf of a bituminous suitable for firing the Chicago Line's latest steam locomotives and that it was to be had, essentially, for the taking. Mineral rights were bought, a lease obtained. A spur line was built to the site, and a subsidiary firm was formed to lay waste to ground the company did not own and would never wish to own in fee simple.

Then it was only workers that were wanting. The country had been much traveled through but only lately and lightly settled. Its value had previously been only that by climbing any little prominence one gained clear view of the miles and miles of wasteland lying in all directions. There was a certain safety in so open a landscape, no surprises but the petulant weather. The tribes had used it for a gambling grounds. Trappers rendezvoused in the area, making loud encampments in the looping bends of a river they called Little Popo Agie. Then, when the world was finished with long hunters and the various Indians were being run to ground, settlers came, but very few to stay. Most had only detoured from the Oregon Trail to a spot known anciently as Stinking Springs, where grease to lubricate their huge wooden hubs oozed from the ground. The cow towns of Riverton and Lander were feebly established, and midway between them the outpost of Rainey came into being as a stage stop. It was near Rainey that the Little Popo Agie Coal Company began its existence, its first order of business being to explain to Chicago investors a locality where there was, simply, no labor force. Among the region's cowboys and Arapaho and Shoshone, not a local soul of them was interested in mining coal.

This was the void that Savage and his wife and other unsuccessful immigrants of that time came to settle. They built a coal camp, and they could not make it anything but wretched. But they made it theirs.

September 7, 1914

Though she was a vaporish soul whose purpose in life was to disappear, for her first day in the fourth grade Angelene Savage was dressed in patent leather pumps, an organdy dress, and a lace pinafore that her mother cinched to her knotting belly with a big pink bow. Satin, the thing would whisper repulsively whenever she moved. Strands of Angelene's hair lay coiled at either side of her face. Stoja gave her a pasteboard box loaded with her lunch and several Mason jars, remedies for ailments the girl did not have. "Drink the green tea at ten. That is for the kidneys and the eyes, it's what makes the hair so shiny. Ten, I said, and if I find out how that Mrs. Clark made you wait until the lunch hour again, I will go down there and choke the life from her neck. I am supposed to think she knows something? Schoolteacher. Does that make her somebody? And I better not hear that she made you go out in the sun to those machines of theirs. Teeter-totter? Merry-go-round? Who ever thought of such wicked things for children?"

In ringlets Angelene was even more acutely the outcast; when the mousy flourishes swayed at the edge of her vision she held herself so still and erect that she looked for all the world like a girl putting on insufferable airs. She stood her mother's inspection uneasily.

"Get rid of that look on your face." Stoja's thumbs lifted her cheeks, rolling her lip up into a ludicrous sneer. "You be proud, you hear me?"

"I am, Mama. Kind of."

"Never let them see you looking like that. You got no reason to be the gloomy one, and I won't have it. Here's a kiss . . . now go. When he brings you home, you can have your cookie, and we make some of that bean soup you like for supper. I got two nice ham bones."

Her parents were only ever in agreement regarding certain details of her misery. Her mother could see no reason for her to walk and arrive at the schoolhouse like a tinker's daughter, run down at the heels. Her father had said that he would not be deprived of the daily pleasure of her company. He was waiting for her now, his truck quivering in anticipation. Most mornings Angelene was given to ride while the other children of the mine had the better fortune to walk, to joke and bully each other, to muddy their shoes and be children.

Angelene went out to him. Danny Savage took her lunch box from her and gave her the pair of motorist's goggles he'd modified to fit her head. Last year the smoked lenses had got her nicknamed "bug" at school. When she came home this afternoon her parents might argue again about what a mess the apparatus made of her hair. Angelene slipped the goggles on. It was not in her to argue with anyone. Her father gave her a package done up in foil paper, a brick of a package. "Oh, you didn't have to, Daddy. How nice." Carefully she worked the wrappings off, they slipped out of her hands, out of the truck, and fell behind. Very nice. A dictionary with scallops cut into its thousand pages. To help her find her way.

"Darling, that belongs to you and to you alone, so you must keep it at your desk. Then, if they should bore you, you can page through it and profitably amuse yourself."

"Daddy, this is such a . . . oh, a . . . thanks a lot."

Midway to school, they came upon two camp boys who had just chased something under the rocks by the side of the road. The boys were worrying the creature with sticks. Her father slowed a little and offered to let them ride on the flatbed behind them. The boys shook their heads 'no.' Johnny Product and Tristan Jones. Lolligagging as they were, and still so far from town, they'd be very late for first bell. They might be truant altogether. Patched, truant, thick as thieves. As the truck passed them their eyes bulged and they cacked like magpies.

Men never laughed at Angelene's father. Grown men were careful even of laughing with him, scared of giving the least offense. But Danny Savage, when he was with his daughter, was sometimes mocked by children. She was so ridiculous. Angelene had hoped that as she grew older her mother would cease to dress her as a doll, or that she would develop some identity for her own, independent of the flounces and ribbon, or that the other children would grow accustomed to the absurdity of her. But now she was entering the fourth grade, a plateau at the end of childhood where all that had been bad before would be very much worse. There she'd be, the enormous dictionary at her elbow, silly and prim as Violet Crimmons. Like a banker's little girl, or worse. Now she must live in fear of everything again, chalk, ink, dirty children. What a festival of loathing.

They reached the schoolyard. "This year, my dear, without fail, you must master the multiplication tables. It may be the blandest information the mind can possess, but it is useful in everything."

Angelene lifted the goggles away from her face and collected tears slid all at once down her cheeks. Her nose ran copiously. She had no handkerchief and could not think how she would explain to her mother that her good cotton gloves had got crusted with snot. Jenny and Jessica were in that corner of the schoolyard they thought of as their own, already calling to her, "What's wrong, Anga—*leeeen?*" Jenny. Jessica. Homespun girls, waving and calling, frantic to have her with them.

"I can't, Daddy."

"You cannot . . . what?"

"I can't get off here."

"Too much bacon? I thought she was giving you too much bacon. I will take you home then, and your mother can—"

"No, not home. I'd have to drink something. Real bad. Or she'd make me sweat, or she'd bring the *Tuźba* over. Please. It's not I'm sick. It's just I don't belong. Here."

"Tell me what I am to do, Angelene."

"Everyone's looking at you—not you, me . . . oh, maybe you . . . But I can't stand it. Not right now."

"Who tells you this? That you don't belong? Don't belong to what?"

"They don't even have to. That's the thing. I know." Her father's eyes fell on the schoolhouse. She saw its roof sag. At a word from her, he would level it. Daddy, hip deep in the wreckage, wreathed in the dust of sudden justice. "It's just me," she said. "It's just me. Sometimes I don't fit in too good."

"What shall we do with you? "

"Just for today, that's all. Then tomorrow I'll go back and go like always. To school."

"You'll go about with your father then. I have sometimes thought of taking your instruction in hand myself. It disturbs me to see you so far forward in your education and still without a word of Latin. Here, give me those, I have a place for them where they won't be dirtied. Your mother celebrates you as best she can, poor woman. But as to those homely children, those schoolmates, tell them . . . Only try and remember that your mother is, even with the gloves and all of that, she is so much more than fond of you."

Angelene was not going to think of her mother just now. She believed she knew her mother well enough. Her father was another matter.

She had been, more than anywhere else in her life, at her mother's table, and at her mother's table she'd heard Stoja and Stoja's boarders speak of Danny Savage in one way when he took his meals with them, and in another, careless way when he was absent. Angelene knew what her father was not. A man who had much to do with the mine, he was not a miner. He was her mother's husband, but not in the manner of other mothers' husbands. He was often away, often unaccounted for, and he'd come home from his travels talking of torque and warranty deeds and Glen Livet. At her mother's table he would talk, and the others could listen or leave. Their eyes would wander while worlds they would never visit bubbled out of him, Belgium, magnetic flux, the Furies. He did not especially intend even to be understood.

With all their coming and going to school together, and with all those times she'd crawled into her father's lap and made a gymnasium of him, still they were strangers. She wished to know him. He was quite as odd as she, but she saw that he liked and cultivated his life apart, and Angelene thought that if she could know him he might teach her how to live happily within herself, happily alone.

"Eight times eight?"

"Daddy. Most kids my age don't know hardly any times tables yet. Not even their ones and twos."

"Three times eight?"

"Three times eight is . . . twenty-four?"

"Yes. Good. We are not interested, darling, in the attainments of other children. That is no standard."

They drove and drove through the brush and a silicate dust. To find water, he told her. It did not seem to her that they would ever come to it, traveling in this direction, over this ground. Her father asked if she knew the origins and the tenets of the United States Constitution, and when she admitted that she hadn't heard of it, he told her of men called Magna Charta and Tom Paine, and how farmers met one summer in Philadelphia and decided to have a nation where every Negro was just three-fifths a man. Angelene was not good with fractions. She'd heard of Philadelphia and knew that it was far from them. They were far from everything this morning. For most of an hour they approached a windmill—slowly she understood it as a windmill—and when they reached it at last, a freshet was thrumming in its vanes and the mill rod was spinning hard. The pump pumped dryly, squealing.

"Quite as noble as a horse, Angelene. It would work itself to death."

Her father disconnected the pump and the prairie was quieter for it, but the wind engine above them whirred on, eerily. At the base of the tower, cows stood near a dry stock tank. They had come to drink. The animals seemed so stupid and obstinate that Angelene was afraid they'd die here, waiting. "Shoo. Shoo, cow." They looked at her and looked away and waited.

Among her father's tools was a long branch of cured alder, forked at one end. He said they were going to do some witching with it, that it was as sensitive as hickory, better than hickory for readings at the higher altitudes.

"It's a wand?"

"A divining rod," he said.

"But . . . magic?"

"If you like."

They walked an expanding circle round the windmill, her father holding the point of his rod just off the blistered clay, quiet with concentration. She felt free to follow, but not to interrupt. Rapt, then dubious, then bored, she walked along with him. There was nothing to say, nothing to see. Her father could be as adult and tedious as anyone. Five miles later and they were still within a half mile of the windmill. She worried that his face had been so immobile for so long; she fretted her cruel shoes. Finally he whispered, "We have it." The stick strained down from his hands, wanting to replant itself.

"Daddy?"

"The aquifer is fifty feet beneath us where we stand. We'll be paid in beef for finding it. I think we will build a drill someday. Soon. Rivers of the sweetest water run beneath our feet, darling, what do you think of that? A fortune worthy of the Americas—flowing quite close at hand."

To mark the spot he drove a yellow stake. They walked back to the truck and rode away as if there had been no miracle there. Her father began to plague her with questions again. Was she acquainted at all with the periodic table of elements? No. He told her of the heaviest and the lightest elements and of atoms and their importance. The entire universe, he said, was replicated infinitely in the palm of her hand. The universe. She had not begun to comprehend the house where she lived. Rivers under ground.

Though it seemed to her that they had already finished a full day, he took her to a machinist's shop in Lander where he bought a spool of cable for some purpose at the mine. They went to the cellar of the courthouse, to the plat room. Under pale and purely electric light he examined books as big as furniture. Penmanship flowed over their pages like row crops. Here was the only legal proof, he told her, that the earth was owned. He said that he searched from time to time for properties that were about to be auctioned for taxes due. Invariably worthless plots, they could often be had for a fifty-cent filing fee. "My scattered estate," he said. "Gravel and bog. But who knows where the road may be built or the transmission line raised? One day, Angelene, we'll be selling rights-of-way all over this county." Her father was constantly hectored by possibility, by what might yet happen or be done or be gotten. Though he'd been speaking to her, she thought she should remind him that she was there. "My legs hurt, Daddy. I think they're too tired." She sneezed and sneezed again. The plat room smelled of fungus and dust.

He took her to a restaurant where the tables wore checked tablecloths, and they were shown to one where a sweating pitcher of ice water awaited them. Angelene felt at once that she too was become cool and ornamental. Her father introduced her to their waiter and to diners smiling on from nearby tables. How pretty she is, Mr. Savage. Bright as a new penny. They made no mention of the grease that striped her dress, shoulder to knee, her black souvenir of the machinist's shop. They kept their eyes on her face, though that was dirty too. What a little orchid, Mr. Savage. They glanced at his hands, hard and horned and spread over so much of the table, and they said she was pretty. She didn't care why it was said, she didn't care if they were wrong, she liked hearing it. Chops were placed before her, steaming, oozing fat. In ten minutes Angelene had reduced them to bone.

"Samuels, bring my girl an ice cream sundae, will you? Tell them to be lavish with the nuts and the cherries."

"Daddy, I'm so full. I'd like to try it, but I am awful full right now."

"Let's be profligate, darling. You're not at the mine camp now, you are with your father, and you must have a spoonful of sweets, at least, if only to aid the digestion. "

The man in the apron returned with a gleaming confection. The marshmallow syrup and cashew nuts were new to her, and there was chocolate of course, dark and light syrups, banana, cherries, applesauce. She took it bite by bite, and only when the very last of it had traveled the length of her tongue would she admit that she did not feel well. Her father dabbed at her with a wet napkin. It was not effective against the caramel; she was beyond cleaning now. They went out and stood on the boardwalk as if they'd accomplished some singular labor. Angelene maneuvered upwind of her father's cigar. The street was alive for them.

A man in a yellow vest and strange, tight breeches approached them and asked Angelene if she'd ever met an actor before. No. He gave her several tickets for a most edifying and heartfelt diversion, a limited engagement. He asked her father if he hadn't toured with the Kirov circus at one time. No. Never tried show business? No. The actor walked on, his boot heels somehow soundless on the boardwalk. Not the mine camp now, not the school yard, this was afternoon in downtown Lander. There was a cowboy, drunk, his arms bowed up in plaster casts, his big horse throwing its head. A sun-red automobile rolled by, filled with women in bonnets. "That is Mrs. King and her daughters. Mrs. King, as you see, is a very able woman at the wheel."

Men of some blunt order turned off Second Street and came marching in a group under and around a yellow banner with a slogan Angelene couldn't read. Even the lettering was strange to her. Someone across the way set up a camera. One of the marchers labored a tuba, another an accordion. All were intent on coming in good order. Though it was her first parade, it was clear to Angelene that this one was entirely flawed. She resented the musicians' mounting failures. The marchers made her sad.

Her father stepped down from the boardwalk. "Kraft, what good do you think you will do the Fatherland, five thousand miles from the war? You must go and offer yourself to the guns. You must die if you wish to advance the cause. To the trenches with you, all of you."

The marchers would not look to him but only steadily ahead to the exalted thing awaiting them at the end of the street, which was, she saw, nothing. "In Berlin," her father told them, "frauleins wait impatiently to receive the French army." The instruments stopped, and now the marchers' feet, a slightly lesser confusion, could be heard. The men straggled on, none looking back, but her father raised his hand above the rail of a hitching post and brought it down, and the rail snapped, and finally the marchers spun to him, their lips twisted. A banner bearer forgot himself and his half of the sash folded and fell.

"Germany is Bismarck," her father said, "and Bismark is dead."

Two of the demonstrators, one red of face, the other pale, separated from the group and came back toward them. Heat and light and bile passed through Angelene as they came.

"Kraft, you are calling yourselves the German-American Bund? Whose idea was that?"

The red one answered. Kraft. "You think we are the only chapter, Savage? What do you think is happening in St. Louis and Seattle and all over Texas? This is a very big movement. You are not for Germany, is that what you want to say? Not for the Germans? That would be stupid of you."

"There is nothing in nature quite so stupid as a patriot. Your father let you drink beer from his stein and fed you bratwurst, so now you think you are the Kaiser's man. Go home. Do something useful."

"You should mind what you say." Kraft was a little larger than before and shading darker all the time. "You Slavs, you start the wars, but we'll see who finishes them."

Her father breathed them in. "Patriots, Angelene, can be found in the street. They will walk abreast and make as much noise as they can, and they won't be satisfied until every last one has stepped in his share of horse shit."

"Did anyone ask your opinion, Savage? Has anyone ever asked your opinion?"

"If the war is your business, then go off and fight it. But I am an American, a neutral, and I am not at war, and I don't like to be bothered with it. Unless you must absolutely become a hero today, Kraft."

⚊ ⚊

Going home, Angelene rode under his arm. It was stifling there, but by keeping very close, she hoped to keep her father quiet. He knew everything, and it was no great gift, and she was so tired. With nothing else to offer, and no other defense, she rode under his arm.

November 6, 1919

Neither man was gifted at repair, so neither thought of making any. They wore sportsmen's shoes but not of the sort for sport outdoors, so they waited in the car, hunched and breathing visibly. Their noses and hands and especially their feet soon felt crystalline.

Juro Capich had not come to America to be a sideman in anyone's business, but prospects had been so bad of late that he'd fallen in with this Miroslav Mlinar, a bohunk who spoke his English like a *chuvar* because he was in fact Cleveland-born, and things broke the man's way just because he believed they would. Capich envied him more than he liked. It was demeaning. In the months since the temperance people had bullied their foolishness into law, bottled-in-bond had been exhausted in

Rainey and was running low in every town, and it was just too obvious that a man like Mlinar, who could make whiskey from any grain or fruit, such a man would soon be printing his own money. He'd smell of juniper and money. The success Capich foresaw for Mlinar was too rigorous and too repetitive to be anything he truly wanted for himself. Still he envied him his luck, and when the man's Model T shuddered and stopped on the prairie, just inside the reservation and nine miles short of Ethete, and would not consent to start again, Capich had taken it as something of a good thing.

"It was supposed to get better," he said. "After the war. Remember what was said? Better. That was wrong. This is the worst year since I been over. Then I let you talk me into wearing this duster, which I knew it was ugly, but also it don't keep you warm. Poor excuse for a coat, Miro."

"You keep gasoline and oil in these things," said Mlinar, "and they are supposed to just run and run. That is the whole deal with a Ford, supposed to be reliable. Gasoline and oil, and keep the tires patched, and off you roll, but my outfit, no. The one I happen to buy, there's a Ford that dies as much as Mary Pickford." The whole object of Mlinar's trade on the reservation was the purchase of a better car He would need one.

"I went from Denver to Vancouver and back," said Capich, "and what did I hear? No matter where I been, it's, 'Old So-and-so's dead. Oh, what a terrible shame, he was in his prime.' Gambler knows he don't stand a chance with this influenza, and he's afraid he will get it from the cards, so he stays away from the better tables, and a man can't get a game. What is it? What did it come to? The war, the influenza; what next? If the times don't get better soon, I think they will bore me to death. Let's hike. This car of yours is nothing but an icebox now."

Ten cases of poteen strapped to the roof and every fender, the thought of them gave Mlinar pause. "We leave this liquor, and it's gone the minute we're out of sight. I'll be lucky if Terrence Badeaux and that crowd don't come out here and take everything down to the buttons off my upholstery. They'll take anything they happen to find, unless it was you and me. You and me they might leave stranded."

"What do you want with this automobile, Miro? You say yourself that it is your enemy. You like to be out here when night comes, is that a good idea to you? What you should have did with this coupe, did while we was still in town, was bet it on a bad hand. I'm making for Rainey, and you can stick with the liquor if you want."

"Let's take what we can carry."

"That would be a bottle each, if it was worth drinking. We are a long way to the first warm place, and I am going as light as I can."

Mlinar rubbed with his sleeve at the frosted windshield, made a transparent smudge, and in it, as if he'd known just where to look, they saw help coming. An angular, yellow thing, bumping in and out of the coulees, coming at cross purposes to the road. Capich thought that if he'd been alone in this fix there'd have been walking to do and plenty of it. But Mlinar, as he was used to his luck, did not find their rescue surprising, not even their rescuer. "That's the one and only Savage."

The man approached upon a small, open-air truck that he rode as if it were a child's pedal toy. The vehicle ground patiently on beneath him. "In the Lika," said Mlinar, "there can't be more than four or five Ličani left, if there's any, but on this side we got about a hundred and thirty-five million of you. If it's a real hardhead, I always ask, 'Lika?' And if it's a *real* hardhead, that's always where he's from. You people are like dandelions, once you got over here. You're everywhere."

"I know who that guy is," said Capich. "What did you call him? Savage?"

"You hear stories, how he used to be this that and the other thing. But he's been Danny Savage for some years. Best leave it at that."

"We had a giant. In my father's time there was a giant in the hills. They said, 'Vuk Hajduk—and he is still out there. He don't let himself be seen anymore, but still we see his work. He is out there, more terrible than ever. He is out there, and he is out there, and he is out there.'

Vuk Hajduk. I never believed them. But now I see. If this one is from the Lika, that's who he must be. As big as they said, but not so ugly. They used to talk about him when they wanted to scare the children."

Mlinar and Capich got out of the Ford as the giant drove up. He switched his engine off, which seemed unwise to Capich. The cooling motor ticked while he looked them over. "Once again," he pronounced, "all is vanity. What has happened with your machine?"

"Do we look like we know? Just skip the foofaraw would you, Savage, and give us a ride into Rainey."

"I may. If it seems necessary."

"If? Don't be a ass. This is Juro Capich, maybe you knew his people in the Lika. Me and him need a ride. I need this stuff hauled out of here, too. What'll you want to do that for me? Want a case of this? I got it all cased up, bottled up, and I wouldn't recommend you drink it, but the stuff's negotiable."

"I would not drink it. I would not sell it. Unless you're taking more pride in your work than I remember. You showed no early promise in this line, Miroslav."

"Find a need and fill it, that's me. I make good liquor," Mlinar said, "and I make bad liquor. This is some of the bad, but it's worth something. So what'll it be, Savage?"

They had amused him slightly. "What you are offering is worth nothing to me. You might appeal to my sense of decency, but you were on your way to sell this sickness to the aboriginals, weren't you?"

"They buy it from me, that means they like it. It's just a kind of whiskey."

A jay flew by, its wings audibly stirring the air. "Vuk," said Capich at last, as if it were the first thing said among them. "You are Vuk Hajduk."

Savage stepped off his truck, and it squeaked in relief. He came to Capich and Mlinar and stood before them and looked down.

"Was I supposed to still be afraid of you? What is Vuk now? Not much. They used to say you could fly if you wanted, but . . . no . . . I ain't scared of you."

The giant seemed almost sad. Capich had seen this look before on men about to do violence. But Savage only looked down at him, and then through him, and then moved past them to open the Ford and examine its engine. "You ran without sufficient oil pressure until it seized. You've completely seized it."

"And that's real bad?" Mlinar supposed.

"For the salvage of the wheels and running gear I will tow you. And your goods."

"Don't you think you better ask for my firstborn son, too? What? You mean to have my goddamn car just for giving us a ride?"

"As it is, it is a small consideration. But you can ride for nothing if you want. On the back of my truck. We will leave the rest where it is stalled."

"Vuk," said Capich.

"See what I mean?" said Mlinar. "You people are just everywhere."

Savage produced a chain from one of the boxes on the bed of his truck, and he fixed an end of it to a point under the flatbed. The other end he secured under Mlinar's coupe. Capich and Mlinar squeezed back inside. Scraping and scraping at the glass to see what little there was to see outside, they were drawn on at twelve miles an hour in a direction that looked no more promising to Capich than the unremarkable place they were leaving. The distances in this country had often conspired this way to make him feel the fool. He turned his collar up, tucked his chin into it, and slept for a time. Miserably. Miserably he woke.

"Savage turned off toward the mine a while back," Mlinar said. "Roundabout way to Rainey, but that's how we'll get there now, by way of the mine camp, or by way of Greenland, or wherever he takes it in his head to drag us through."

"The sonofabitch. Did we say that? Go up there? That wasn't on my way." Capich could find no point of reference in the countryside. He was lost, the hajduk's captive and, unaccountably, a little thrilled by it. "I been around Rainey three months, and I never have set a foot up in that camp yet. What do they do up there? Dig in ugliness all day. And for what? For their ungrateful women and their brats. I got to go see something like that?"

They came at the mine up a long slow rise so that they couldn't see it until they were immediately above the broad gully that contained it. Then it was inevitable. Company streets marched toward the mouth of the mine in several ranks of identical, square, shiplap shacks, echoed by ranks of identical, square, shiplap privies, all painted mustard yellow. The mine's tailings were everywhere, the mine's grit on everything. There was livestock, unfettered and underfed. Not an animal in this bottom, it seemed, had been successfully penned, and pigs, cats, dogs, chickens, sheep, and goats circulated warily among the houses and the husks of old hoists and trucks. Half finished skinning a goat, a hawk-nosed man looked up at them. Both creatures, the living and the dead, seemed embarrassed.

"Savage built this," Mlinar said. "He showed up, and they had a crew of our people and Calabrians and Cornishmen and what-have-you, and he was the one guy who could read a set of plans and talk to everybody. So he told em what to do, and they built this. These houses came in by train, in crates. It was just a mountain of crates when Savage showed up. He told em how to put it together. Since then everyone has had to put up with him because he knows how to keep it going. He knows how to keep the mineworks fixed, so he lives here pretty much on his own terms."

"He told them to do this?"

"It ain't that bad. It's how me and many another bohunk wound up here. You should see the old neighborhood. There's parts of Ohio, believe it or not, the parts they'd let us into, that make this look nice."

"Little Popo Agie Number One," said Capich. "They wasted a pretty name on it."

They were a spectacle now. Three boys had fallen in beside them, their faces slack with that peasant wonder Capich knew so well of old. "Christ, they're like maggots, these people. Why did I ever got to see this?"

"It ain't so bad," said Mlinar again, sounding less convinced of it.

Savage went all the way through the camp to stop in the shadow of the tipple and go into a large shop building. There were barrels filled with steel scraps, a fenced garden in fallow. The boys had nursed their fascination and followed this far, and, as if they'd snuck backstage at a geek show, they looked in on Capich and Mlinar where they waited shivering in the car.

"Get away," said Capich. "Get away you children, or would you like me to gut you? Come on, Miro, we got to go in after him. That hajduk, he forgot we are out here or something."

"Bring us here, and then just leave us sit like this? It's rude. Big bastard never had to learn any manners, did he?"

They went into the tremendous warmth of the shop, an interior favored by light from windows and skylights. Capich did not know the use of most of the tools he saw there, and many of them seemed malevolent to him, invitations to a maiming. A girl stood partly hidden behind the potbellied stove, the stovepipe. He saw her left eye, a doe's eye. Looking at him. A pleasing slope of shoulder, a length of hair, a length of thigh. A girl. Not for long. She'd soon be perfect, and from that she would deteriorate. A girl, perfectly unrealized.

Savage stood at a bench, twisting a yard of black tubing.

"What the hell?" Mlinar asked him.

Savage achieved a certain shape with the tubing and cocked his head thus and thus to see it from several angles. "Something has occurred to me."

"Take us on down to Rainey," said Mlinar. "We ain't got time to be fooling around."

"Why you brought us here?" Capich wondered. "You. Vuk. Nasty place you made here. Bad as home. You did this? You came here? You stayed here? Goddamn, and now you took me here, too."

"Angelene, this is a man from the Lika. A Capich. He would come from among those squatters at the northwest foot of Debela Brda, the mountain's dark side. Turnips, Capich? I believe that was your family's ambition. But now look at you, citizen, a hem in your trouser legs and all. And you smell just subtly as if you'd been to a Hindu's funeral."

"I am Juro, that is what you need to know. There are no more of me. Inside of my family or out of it. No more like me. And you can forget my family, too. I did. It was very fucking easy to forget them bastards."

"Keep a civil tongue in the presence of my daughter or I'll use you to lubricate something."

"Yeah, fuck you. I told you before, Vuk, I ain't scared of you."

"You made us wait," said Mlinar, "while you fiddled around in here. You run us way the hell out of our way, out here where we got no business, and then you just leave us sit in the car? Like I was telling Juro, that's rude. It was Rainey, remember? You said you was taking us in."

"I ask you again, old man, why you come to live here?" Capich stepped to the giant. "You couldn't do better? You were Vuk, for Christ's sake. Now you are this? I can't stand it. Why you didn't die before you let yourself come to something like this?"

The girl shifted behind the stove. She did not favor the giant in any way, still Capich would have known her for his daughter. Just a girl. But not.

Savage lifted a polished steel rod from a rubble of less likely parts. He held it in his left hand, the black tube in his right. He beheld these objects as a pair and took very much pleasure from the pairing. The pieces of a complicated machine were spread in some radiant coherence on the floor at his feet. "I now believe," he said, "that I can make the Merrick Compressor, for all its faults, run without pause for weeks on end. That would be very liberating."

"Rainey," pleaded Mlinar.

"And this?" Capich wondered. "For your girl, this? You were Vuk Hajduk, and now this is the best you could do for a child you got?"

January 17, 1930

Though it was nothing more than a gravel thread through the sage-brush, it had a name compounded of Serb and Spanish parts—Pút Puta, the whore's path. Savage climbed toward his holdings on the ridge overlooking the coal camp, a bat and board building backed by a permanent bivouac, tents pitched on platforms and bristling stovepipes. The tents had been Mrs. Delongchamps's embellishment. Frost glittered on their canvas roofs. In the bar, however, where Savage had installed a great stove from a failed foundry, potted rubber trees were thriving. Several early patrons were in their sodden shirtsleeves, and Mrs. Delongchamps was reduced to a threadbare dressing gown she'd cinched tight across her plunging paps. "Shit," she said as he entered.

"Remember the thermometer, Deloris. Have you seen? Eighty-eight degrees Fahrenheit."

"Think I gotta read that thing to know it's hot? That stove of yours runs outta control. Especially if Maggie gets at it in the morning. Stay out from behind my bar, Savage."

"That would be my bar, I believe, while you are in arrears."

"Yeah? Why don't you have some normal appetites, then? Every once in a while take something out in trade?"

"Your fallen farm girls with their barrel hips?"

"They're clean," the madame claimed. "But everybody's home with their mittens on these days, and I'm runnin in the red, so I can't pay you like it was good times."

"In good times they celebrate, in hardship they console themselves. It is all the same to you."

"Nah. They're drinking," and the madame could only acknowledge the three men at her bar, one of whom, Cecil Jones, had passed the night on her billiards table and risen early. At ten of a Tuesday morning he'd done twelve hours of drinking interrupted only by a three-hour nap. Still, whatever consolation he sought had plainly evaded him.

"But whoring's way off with these troubles, and that's where I make my nut. It's the girls." The madame's gray cheeks were stamped with rounds of rouge so that she looked like a corpse prepared by an apprentice mortician.

Beyond the tall bank of mullioned windows Savage had set in the south wall lay broken sandstone, a series of gulches stepping down to Lyons Creek. To no one in particular he mentioned the morning light. That same light had fallen inward, where it did no flattery.

"You know what some guy told me, some Fuller Brush man?" Madame Delongchamps removed a crumb of tobacco from her lipstick. "He said the whole world is owned by thirty Jewish bankers in New York. It's just on loan to the rest of us. And every now and then they take it back, repossess it, you see, just to show us they can. They're showin us who's in charge, that's what this crash is all about. That's why we're all in a hurt, too."

"Gentlemen," Savage offered, "your pleasure?"

"Step out of there, you big ass. I'll handle this. You can knock that off your damn rent, and I'm having a toddy myself, also on you."

There was agreement on one last thing: Finley's Grey Label. The madame set out five fresh glasses, and poured, and the stranger among them said something about the Lincoln Brigade, and they drank. Savage ordered up another round, which was taken less abruptly and with much less ceremony. The work of a real Canadian distillery, and expensive, Finley's was to be savored.

"Mabel sent me up here this morning with two bits in my pocket," said Michael Dušan, a miner with the poor luck to break his ankle just when the continued operation of the mine was in doubt. "She told me, 'See if you can mooch a drink, if you think you need one so bad.' So, here's to you, Danny, no matter what they say. When I'm at work again I'll do you right." His mouth closed like a trap, he'd reached the end of his imagination. For Savage, Dušan would always be that young man he'd glimpsed one night, just off shift and sitting in a galvanized tub in his parlor with his young wife pouring basins of water over him. A squat fellow who could be, and for most of his life had been, perfectly happy with a day's work, the shelter and food that came of it, and the small luxury of being occasionally idle. Savage had not intended to buy a taste of the man's fear. Dušan incessantly fingered the cheroot he kept in the pencil pocket of his bibs. "This'll work out," he said vaguely.

"Work out?" said the stranger, a born Westerner by the sound of him. "No, comrade. You got to *work* it out. You've got to take a hand in history."

"History?" Dušan was stricken. "Here? Friend, you're in Wyoming, don't you know?"

"Everywhere. You are part of the historical struggle, brother, whether you want to be or not. You, me, every working stiff alive, we're all part of it." The stranger was handsome despite a livid strand of scarring along the line of his jaw and an ear missing half its circumference.

"What is it you make?" Savage asked him.

"Make? What are you gettin at? Why don't you come right out with it?"

"To accurately call yourself a worker, shouldn't you make something, provide a service at least?"

"I'm *of* the working class, mister. *Of* it. And, never you mind, I'm with the right outfit. Or what about this—what if I tell you I'm makin a world where no man is a wage slave? That product enough for you?"

"That would be all right," said Dušan.

"Most ambitious," said Savage. "But your name?"

"My name is James Shipp, if you need to know it. I've got a serial number too, courtesy of the United States Army, and who I am, and what I've got to say, are all right out in the open. It'll only scare you if you're afraid of the truth."

"Yes. That much rectitude is always frightening."

"I want you all to get a good look at this," said Cecil Jones, and he thrust his right hand up for their inspection. Its thumb and forefinger were missing, the remaining three fingers twisted violently away from each other. Purple and glossy over much of its length, the hand might have been something from the vegetable kingdom.

"Put it away," suggested Dušan. "Why do we have to see that thing every time you're drunk, Cecil?"

"That mine got its piece of me when I was nine years old." There was something of the torchbearer, the old-time orator, in Cecil Jones's stance. "Just a breaker boy, nine years old, when I watched that conveyor carry my fingers off, and I said right then—hell—what did I say?"

"Do you know what your beloved company did with those fingers of yours? Ground em up, made sausage, sold it back to your mother at the company store." This Shipp was a man, Savage saw, so taken by his own metaphors that he would come to embrace them as facts.

"We never have had a company store," said Dušan. "Wish we did. Be nice not to go five miles every time you needed a pencil or a stick of gum."

Shipp, also in oratorical fashion, spoke almost entirely to himself, but loudly. "You ever hear of Ludlow? That's where I started my education. Saw em bring in the National Guard to shoot down miners for wantin a wage that might buy more than a little grub from one payday to the next. Shot em down, their women and children, too. So now I organize, damn straight I do."

"To what end?" Savage asked.

"I've told you, mister." Shipp wanted very much to find a fight in the name of justice. He had come to require the pain of his calling. "These men need to join with a larger brotherhood, get the weight and experience of the I.W.W. behind them, and strike."

"We got a union," said Jones. "I'm a steward in it."

"A union," Savage offered, "that sells citrus fruit and offers its members group rates on their burial insurance."

"You work clean, Cecil," said Michael Dušan. "That changes your outlook. You're a bookkeeper, and it's not the same."

"What do you mean, Michael? That I don't . . . ?" Jones, having drunk himself sober, was drinking himself drunk again, and his head was unbalanced on his neck. "All right. Then I'll put it to you like a book-keeper. In about two months' time we've lost half our markets. The ones still buying coal don't want it either, not unless they can get a 30 per-cent cut in their cost. Now where's that supposed to come from? Com-pany's took in its belt till there's just one notch left, and that's labor."

"Here's a union steward taking the company line," said Shipp. "You know that snake in the Garden of Eden? It crawled out of its tree and fucked a hyena, and the result was the whole race of capitalist stooges. The result was you."

"Ah," said Savage, "the diligent provocateur."

"Fucking Wobbly." Jones's own head wobbled as he spoke. "How bout that brother of yours over in Washington State? Castrated him, didn't they? There's some that think it's a fine job of work to make you boys sing a different tune. Bet I could find fifty guys at the American Legion that'd be happy to escort you to the state line."

"Your kind are good in the dark," said Shipp. "When there's a bunch of you."

From behind the bar Mrs. Delongchamps retrieved an oak stave half again thicker than her wrists and a yard long. She held it so that she might bring it quickly to bear and said, "If this gets started here, I'm giv-ing you a whack just for good measure, Danny."

"To the art of conversation," said Savage, "may it rest in peace."

Shipp and Jones were turned to each other, their cheeks twitching. Both men were breathing quite hard, face-to-face at a distance that might instantly be closed, their eyes bright but growing regretful.

The door flew in to bang on the wall, and there was a sharp draft and a woman came in bearing raw steaks on a platter balanced on her up-turned palm. The woman nodded to the madame; Mrs. Delongchamps nodded to her in turn. "Put em right there," she said. She placed her finger on the bar midway between Shipp and Jones. The woman came forward in a long, orchid-print skirt that parted finally at mid-calf and gave way to unlaced field boots. Her hair was black, and coarse, and long, and lustrous as the tail of a well-groomed horse. Her glance was dismissive. "I don't do this no more," she said. "Carry this meat. Cook it. Nothing like that."

"We all do our part here, honey."

"I know what is my part—honey. I work in my tent, that's all." The whore, the specialist, swept out of the room and back into the cold outside.

Cecil Jones returned to his drink, suddenly no one's enemy. "So that's the new girl, huh?"

"New to my house. Calls herself Annie Contreras, and she ain't gonna be one of the friendly ones, Cecil, but I'm gonna charge for her like she was nice as pie. Fact, I might charge more cause she's mean. You goddamned men, you like that."

~ ~

Annie Contreras held back the flap of her tent to let him inside. He entered and stood, deeply bent at the waist, and though she liked him bowed that way she offered him her chair. "You," she told the john, "you got to pay extra. For how big you are. You pay something extra to me. Like a tip. And we gotta do it on the floor. We break that cot, then the madame gonna make me pay for it, buy a new one like it was my fault she is too cheap to buy a real bed to put in here. She is a chiseler, that woman. I got to pay for this and that, and by the time I get done paying expenses there's nothing left. I pay and pay until I don't get paid."

"We won't need to recline," said the giant.

"Mister," she said, "I fuck, that's all. I don't do nothing funny." She did not know that he owned the tent and the ground beneath it and the platform where it was pitched. She did not know that he'd planed these very floorboards but never so smooth as to accommodate naked, striving flesh. None of that mattered to her anyway. She had never seen a man as large as the man who'd just come to her with the madame's chit in hand. That didn't matter either, except that she rarely liked the weight of even one man upon her, and now she would find herself under the weight of two. "Bad enough I have to fuck a *cavron* like you. I don't do nothing funny."

"I think," the giant said, "your integrity will be safe."

"I bet you one of them never goes to confession. You got no religion at all."

"You are very loud," he said. "Were you always so?"

"Something don't say nothing you can have for free. Rocks don't say nothing, they laying around all over the place. But a woman will talk. You can't pay enough to have it any other way."

"I take your point."

She'd made a nightstand of packing crates, and on it she'd set out her mobile shrine. There was a honeycomb candle and three ball bearings and a darkly painted Pieta. There was a silver frame containing the first photograph that had ever been taken of her. A girl staring at the first camera she'd ever seen. She saw the giant's eyes on the picture, felt them when they returned to her. "Third from the left in the front row," she said. "That was me." A girl in a Yaqui skirt, kneeling behind a Spanish Mauser. "The fat one just behind me, that was Villa. He called me *soldadera*. I didn't even bleed like a woman yet, I was so young when I went out with them." A girl in a huge sombrero, draped in bandilleras. "The general, he liked to have pictures. Once you in a picture with the general, you got to fight with him, cause once you in that picture, the Federales gonna shoot you anyway. Might as well fight. Villa's a pig like every general, but he was better than Huerta. That was good years, too, we had with him. The cadre took what it wanted and rode away." In the memory of that danger and abundance she fell backward through her life so far as to become shy. Her hand rose to the flat plane of her chest above her breasts. "All right. Enough. Take you clothes off."

"That won't be necessary."

"You don't, I don't, mister. That's a rule I got."

"Look at me," he said.

"I was in the Revolution," she said. "Know what I would like? Put a big Colt to your ear. That's how you find out what's what. Now, for true, what you want? Let's get it over with."

"Be quiet please."

"Or what? You hurt me?" She began to undo the buttons of her dress.

"Leave those alone."

"Maybe someday I will blow your brains out." She wanted very much to push on with the usual transaction now, to move to that point where their business would suddenly conclude. "You making me sick."

"Quiet."

Cured like an old skillet, she could endure being touched however rudely. Nothing stuck to her. But she had no crust against what the giant was doing. Looking at her. Seeing her. Whatever it was he wanted she did not want to give, but she was confused into silence, frozen by a tenderness in him. So she stood it. She was a professional and she stood it, and sold off yet another piece of herself, one she hadn't even known she'd owned.

January 18, 1930

It was shortly after Angelene left them that Stoja first discovered the stock market and began to visit Lander to trade her hoarded quarters with Lonny Bennet, a broker willing, at least in the beginning, to take jars of pickled produce and pots of soup for his fees. Her early gains were modest but constant. Bennet saw her as a blue-chip client, and he invested her entirely in companies with assets of fifty million or more. Adhering to what he called the gravitational law of finance—money makes money—he'd partnered her with Standard Oil and Bell Telephone and rolled her every dividend back to the great maternal warmth of these firms. Stoja bought nothing on margin, took no risks, and when

the market broke and ruined other speculators, the spasm only strength-
ened her portfolio. She'd become rich but could not imagine taking
any of her wealth out of play and so, except for a rattling new set of
teeth, she lived much as she always had. On very cold mornings like
this, when water froze in the cisterns as fast as it could be pumped from
the company trucks, she got up to chip ice in the dark. She'd go out into
a night twelve hours old, the hair freezing in her nostrils, and break ice
with a short-handled pick and carry it back to the steel bin in her
kitchen. Every fifty pounds yielded her five gallons of water.

"You deserve to prosper," her broker had told her many times. "And
you will prosper, see if it isn't so. Measured greed is a wonderfully re-
warding thing."

She breathed plumes loudly. Her tool rang. All the noise of her was
borne off at once into the immense quiet of the hour, and in such deep
privacy she could imagine herself another woman, a graceful creature
who did not quit the warmth of her bed at five, but at nine, and then
only to take delivery of coffee and pastries. Stoja saw a window overlooking a clean street in a clean city, a window seat, and curled into it
was a woman who could read like a bishop, a Bible in her lap. A gilt
Bible, a view of a park. Tap water would be available on demand to such
a woman, she'd run it into a porcelain sink. Sometimes for her lunch she
might bother about an apple, sometimes not. This would be a woman
who lived where her radio drew a clear signal, and she'd have the time
and temperament for long afternoons with all those sawing violins. At
night she would sleep contentedly alone.

Now that she had money Stoja went through the work of her days
knowing that none of it was strictly necessary. The water. The fire. There
were other places where she might have these things without having to
first manufacture them. Here in this home that was to her husband only
another place to stand out of the rain, everything was more trouble than
it was worth.

She made smaller chunks of ice to put into the coffee pot. To melt.

To make coffee. She made breakfast for her boarders, and while they were eating it she made their lunches, put them in linen sacks, and put the sacks in their buckets. She washed the breakfast dishes. She bought five chickens from Mabel Dušan, wrung their necks, scalded, plucked, and butchered them. At intervals she stoked the stove. The hajduk had been off somewhere since this time yesterday, and she was feeling his absence as if it were something new to her. Her husband had no sense of shame; her sacrifices made no impression on him. For twenty-five years, at every meal she'd made, she'd laid him a place at her table. A place at her table, a place in her bed, and he came to them only as often as it suited him. He owned her yet as if she were a brush or a scissors, and all because she needed at times to scrape and to nip at him.

Stoja had just ripped an unintended hole in the bottom of a flour sack when a meek knocking sounded at her door. "It is open," she called. She heard no one enter or call back to her. "It is open, goddamn you, come in." The knocking was repeated, no louder. No one, she thought, with any legitimate business here would think to interrupt her like this. It must be the *krinac,* a quaking little man who came occasionally to try to peddle thread and needles and notions that she never bought. He came to be turned away each time with an insult for his trouble. This time she would go so far as to put her hands on him, leave white hand-prints on his peddler's jacket.

She went out to the parlor and opened her door. It was her daughter. Angelene. She held a snot-nosed boy protectively in front of her. He would be, Stoja calculated, about ten, and was already as tall as his mother. Too tall to be held in such an embrace—decently. His eyes, if he could have forced them to it, would have turned all the way round to regard the back of his skull rather than look upon his grandmother. Thick-tongued, Stoja said, "I told you, come in. What, I am supposed to heat the whole world with my door standing open?" Angelene pushed at the boy, and they came in together and stood just beyond the threshold, still attached to each other. Angelene, only a lavish promise as a girl, was as a woman fulfilled, a beauty; life had defined her. Life was not finished. She still had the look about her of someone longing for a wreck.

"All this time I don't hear nothing, not 'Good-bye' not 'How are you?'—nothing, not even, 'Kiss my ass.' But now, now you come. Wanting what from me, I wonder?"

"Mama . . ."

"You leave when you want, come back when you want. The whole time, I'm just here. But don't think I was waiting. I wasn't waiting. I didn't wonder, too." Stoja was not aware of backing away from them until she had backed nearly out of the room. "What did you . . . ?" She was at the kitchen. Angelene followed.

"I'll help you get supper out, Mama."

"That why you came? To help me? You gonna help me?"

"I named him Radé. He's your grandson."

"Think I didn't see that? Big. Too big, like the hajduk. And the face on him, like that Hrvat gambler of yours. Where is now your Juro Capich?"

"Dead. He's been dead a while."

"Good. What do you want here?"

"Couldn't you go out and say . . . something? He's your grandson."

"To me? No. He was a tumor in your belly. Now he's pieces of all the worst bastards I ever knew. You stitch that shit together and bring it to me? How many years of nothing, then you bring me this?"

"That's my son, Mama. And I'm no little girl anymore, so you watch how you talk about him. Maybe you got a beef with me, but not with him. He never did nothing to you, or anybody. He's just a real nice little boy, so you come on out now and say something to him. I told him you're his grandma."

"What I'm gonna say? You got the words for me, Angelene? Why I'm gonna say something to him?"

"Why? You have to ask . . . I'd forgot, Mama. I guess I made myself forget. How you are."

The women were separated by a table. On the table was a mound of dough, waiting to be kneaded.

"All right, I tell him . . . I tell him, 'Hello you little sonofabitch, you got some of Danilo Lazich in you and some of Juro Capich, and I bet you got some new way to cause me grief. So welcome to my house, I'm so glad you came.' " A strange pressure had pooled in Stoja's fingertips. She was not well.

"He's a little boy. He doesn't look like it, exactly, but he's just a little boy. And a sweet one at that. I can't hear you say bad things about him."

"Then you shouldn't bring him here."

"Maybe I should have started by telling you I'm sorry. Because I am. I didn't think you'd want to hear from me."

"What you want?" Stoja asked again, but this time because she meant to provide it, whatever it was. Angelene had come to her knowing that her mother could deny her nothing. Nothing, at least, that was hers to give. The table stood between them. It was not so wide. Either woman might easily have reached across it to touch the other.

"Wanted to tell you I'm sorry, Mama. That's the first thing."

Her daughter was a woman, with a woman's mantle of regrets. They had now everything of consequence in common, and Stoja was just beginning to see how much peace might be had from saying so when she heard her husband come into the parlor. Now they'd never make sense of anything. Angelene cocked her head and smiled. There was a murmuring beyond the door.

"You women," the hajduk called in to them, "how can you leave this lad alone with nothing to eat and no one to praise him?" He came into the kitchen with the boy riding bewildered on the crook of his arm. The hajduk swept his daughter up as well and held them like a pair of babies. Angelene closed her eyes and kissed his cheek, and it was all very easy for them, as if she'd never gone away, as if they'd never made any pain for each other. Her husband could summon joy like this, but in all their years together he had never summoned it for Stoja.

"The fruit of us," he said. "It appears there was something to all that copulation and torment after all, Stoja." He jostled them. Angelene pressed her face to his neck and sighed copiously. The boy saw this and was gratified by it. The three of them were of a piece. The children were his. The hajduk had burst in, ever the thief, and made them his at once.

"You," she told them. "I don't got time for this. I got my bread to make and my supper to put out on the table. This day for me, it's like all the rest. I got bread to make and miners to feed and cleaning and all the rest of it. So get out of here. Get out of my way."

The hajduk had fixed a swinging door with tin kick plates for her kitchen. He passed back through it with his daughter and grandson still in his arms.

Stoja heard them through the door, the hajduk's japing, Angelene's lesser voice, and even the boy, almost inaudible but with warmth. She heard their pleasure in each other, the whole mute dialogue. And maybe she'd told them to leave, but how quick they'd been to do it. Never any argument from them about leaving her. Stoja scrubbed her hands at the sink, dried them, and powdered them with flour. She plunged her fists into the dough on the table, harder, then longer than necessary; it felt like flesh, and it changed shape entirely each time she hit it. This was a batch that would rise up light for her.

January 19, 1930

Savage applied blowtorch flame to the Republic's crankcase. "The lubricants in this engine have become gummy with the cold, and the crankshaft is somewhat mired. We warm it to its task." There were flares as oil and gasoline burned suddenly off the steel.

"Sorry." The boy stood back a bit, balletically, fascinated, poised to spring away.

"Steady, you don't imagine there's something unsafe in this, do you? A little faith, please, in my judgment."

"It's just when that fire shoots out of there . . . I . . . I don't know."

"You won't be burned. Now you."

"Me?"

"Take the torch," said Savage.

"Me? I better not."

"Then set the throttle, would you?"

"The throttle?"

Savage feared the boy might lack the proper spirit of inquiry, that he might be one of those children who waits to be told. "On the panel, just above and to the right of the steering column, a handle, a notched handle."

"Yeah."

"There's the choke just above it, pull it out. Set the throttle at full." Savage turned the crank, and the engine turned as well, then pinged, then raced. "Now that we have it running, it is running on oxygen-rich air. Cold air. Runs with a will, do you hear it? Back the choke off. Yes. Good. I think you may as well drive."

"I don't know how."

"It is not so much. If you are to be of any use to me, you must learn to drive."

"All right."

The boy was a reed bent on any little breeze, eager to please. Savage had never before undertaken anyone's reformation, but he'd decided to stiffen his grandson. The boy's breeding alone should have made him more resistant than he was.

"It's been a long time since we had a car," he said wistfully. "Since I was six, I think. Since we been in Chicago. I was pretty little then. Old Boolah, the guy who lived in the apartment above us, he had a car. A nice one. He was a Muslim, Mom said. He never drove it, though. I don't think he could. He just left it parked out on the street, and he'd take a stick to anybody who got around it."

Savage saw them but too clearly, his daughter, his grandson, living stacked with other refugees in a cubicle within a cubicle. A brick facade on a street of broken glass and gum wrappers and idle automobiles. "The life of a great city," he said. "Museums, libraries, and especially the symphonies—the wilderness has its deficiencies, I can tell you."

"We were always kind of broke, Grandpa."

"Money is no longer your problem." Savage and his wife had one good in common, they were competent, and it seemed to him that some of this ability should have passed down to their daughter, but in this as in all else Angelene had departed from them. She'd walked with the boy all the way from Lander this morning and never thought to protect their faces from the cold. His cheeks were still quite red from it. Such misadventures, Savage suspected, had been a constant in his daughter's life, and in his grandson's. "Wrap that muffler so that it covers your nose, Radé. Depress the clutch. That is your means of engaging and disengaging power to the drive train. Depress the clutch with your toes."

"I got it. It's depressed."

"Take the shifter. Move it to the left and up. Left, left."

"Left. Up."

"Now, slowly, but not too slowly, release the pedal."

They surged off.

"The clutch again. Pull the shifter straight down. Again, the slow release." As they moved on into the road gear, Savage mentioned pressure plates and their workings. The boy nodded, but not with comprehension. He simply would not risk giving offense, but he seemed to enjoy their increasing speed. He might do. He would have to do.

"Correct!" Savage caught the steering wheel and jerked it toward him. "It is a simple matter to avoid our destruction. Pay attention. Confine yourself to the road." The boy at once regained the wheel and resumed control. His muffler had slipped down and away from his mouth, and he was smiling, the happiest Savage had seen him. "That is quite enough of this 'grandpa.' I find it cloying. The linkage is loose, the steering linkage, so . . . no . . . you will have to drive with a bit of anticipation. We'll tighten it, but . . . pay attention, Radé."

He directed the boy to drive them down to Rainey, and through it, and to the one-room school at the edge of town, now the Union Hall. The union met but once a month, and its quarters, lacking much maintenance, was a blot on several adjacent lots. Banked tumbleweed had climbed well up the north side of the belfry, and in the belfry hung an idle rope. Meetings here, ordinarily, weren't much. But tonight the rank and file was to vote on the strike, and tonight the Miner's Improvement Committee was committed to distributing a shipment of grapefruit. Automobiles were scattered over half an acre of otherwise empty ground. A restive crowd stood outside and stared at the door, but did not move to it.

"I ordered mine in September," said Savage, "and now, in midwinter, they arrive, not a week off the tree. It is a promotion, you see. Fresh grapefruit."

"Don't let me drive into anybody, all right?"

"We stand on a plateau of history, Radé, where our commonplace was only recently the prerogative of kings. Fruit in midwinter. There are pink grapefruit now. Nothing is impossible."

Nolan Fergossi, a charter member of the International Fraternity and Brotherhood of Miners of the Little Popo Agie, stood with his back to the door of the hall, assigned to keep all but dues-paying members out. As Savage and the boy came up a broken sidewalk, Fergossi was again telling the assembly outside that "the Wobbly wanted in, wanted to speak. And we just couldn't see it, and we closed the meeting. Close it to one, got to close it to all. So here we are, neighbors, and I'm every bit as cold as you are, standing out here. Sorry. You can't come in."

The merchants of Rainey were there in force, convinced to a man that a strike vote meant the loss of the mine, and that in turn would cost them their businesses. "In all decency," said Burke the butcher, "let us in. We have a right to hear what they're saying."

"It's closed, Mr. Burke, that's all I can say. That's what they put me out here to say, and I'm getting pretty damn tired of it. They should've put one of the young pups at the door, but no, it was good old, reliable Fergossi."

Denied better access, the crowd strained to hear even the tenor of the meeting inside. They heard discordance. "None of the boys," said Fergossi, "had to play the firebrand, until that Shipp showed up. Now he gave em ideas, some of em. Goddamn agitator, he's who we got to thank for standing out here tonight. But it can't be much longer. There's only so much to be said, for or against it. We strike or we don't."

Savage stepped through the shopkeepers. "Are they ashamed of themselves, that we can't hear them, that we're not to be taken in on such a night? I've come for my grapefruit."

"Danny," said Fergossi in a swoon of self-pity. "Now you of all people? Why?"

"I've told you. To receive my merchandise. You liked me better when you were taking my money."

"Didn't we have trouble enough without you showing up? You'll just have to wait for it till they've got things sorted out in there."

"Give us," said Savage, "our grapefruit in good faith. And we'll be off for civilized company."

"But I've gotta stay outside," said Fergossi.

"I don't," said Savage.

"Just hold on, would you? Let these people hear what they can, they're trying to listen."

The crowd, as if upon instructions, grew even more quiet and intent. They heard themselves breathing, heard a new and especially aggrieved voice being raised inside the Union Hall, and when the brittle crack of a blast reached them from the mine, they flinched collectively. The shock of it rattled the windows, and they winced again. A huge explosion. Above ground. Three miles away, still echoing.

"I knew it," said Fergossi. "I told em, 'Let him talk. Talking's not the worst he could do.' Now look, he's gone and started a war or something." Behind him, the meeting was adjourning.

"I think you better drive going back," Radé Capich told his grandfather.

An unprecedented traffic streamed toward the mine. Savage fell in behind the sedan containing the sheriff of Fremont County and one of his deputies, and when the cruiser slid off the road in front of him he was obliged to stop and hammer its fender out so that it could go on. And so he arrived with the law to find women and children bringing wine into the company streets, and no one looked particularly cold, and torches traveled singly and in clusters through the dark. From his porch Michael Dušan told them, "We all thought it was that Shipp, we thought he'd done for us. The maniac. We should've run him off the minute he showed. Now we start over again, and we'll be talking about it like sensible men. Run that guy off and start over. Can I trouble one of you for a light?"

"That's what didn't happen," said Sheriff Selvey. "What did? Do you know?"

"One of Deloris's girls blew herself up."

"And she's . . .?"

"Finished. Well, you heard it."

Savage acquired a torch, and with it he and his grandson and the sheriff and the deputy walked up the hill to Mrs. Delongchamps's, then past it and downhill again toward Lyons Valley, toward a place in the brush where lights had collected like a jar of fireflies. They passed tourists leaving by the same route who reported there was nothing to see, a hole in the ground. A full moon over new snow, and Mrs. Delongchamps's voice carried clear for a hundred yards. She stood tented in blankets at the edge of a velvet black, shallow concavity. "Maynard, I want that ring. Get it off her."

There had been shreds of her dress and such an abundance of bloody hair that they had known at once it was Annie Contreras. They'd found her right hand, clutching sagebrush as if to arrest its flight. There was a gold band on its ring finger, supporting a yellow amethyst, a gaudy ornament that the madame, with her severe sense of personal style and economy, had never worn. But it was hers, that was the point, and it had been taken from her private quarters along with three hundred dollars in paper money that was only a dull confetti now, almost indistinguishable from the snow. "Right out of *my* bedroom," said Mrs. Delongchamps. "I want something done, Maynard. Get that ring off her."

"It's evidence," said the sheriff, "and you can't have it."

"Evidence? Who you going to arrest? Don't you have a pretty good idea who's guilty here? Now, get that ring off her. Why else do I pay taxes?"

Sheriff Maynard Selvey had soggy, narrow little buttocks and a melon for a stomach, and he'd worn his suspenders too long, but now that someone was violently dead he felt he'd come into his importance. "How'd she do this, Savage? This looks like some place you've been to."

"Dynamite sweats," Savage said. "If it isn't properly stored, it sweats. She must have found such a cache."

"Sweats?"

"Beads of nitroglycerine, Selvey. And then explosive that was benign becomes quite sensitive. She tripped, I think, and was no more. Sweated dynamite furnishes its own detonator."

"I wonder what she had in mind?"

"To take what she wanted," Savage said, "and ride away."

Mrs. Delongchamps pressed her palms to her ears, her blankets wrapped close around her. "I want something done, Maynard."

"You said it yourself, Deloris, there's not much that can be done. Wonder where she thought she was going, where she thought she could get to? "

"The ring, Maynard."

The sheriff approached the hand but he could only bring himself to look at it. A hand, a shattered remnant of wrist, then nothing. The concentrated mortality of it was too much for Selvey, and his recent supper

returned to his mouth, where he contained it until a second retch overwhelmed him. When he finished he said, "All right. That's about enough
of that. I've did as much as anybody could."

"Well, haul her off, anyway. Haul every last piece of her off. The
thieving bitch."

"You said," Savage reminded the madame, "that you couldn't pay
your rent. Do remember that?"

"I'm supposed to remember that now? Just how did we get back onto
that subject?"

"No cash, you said. Said you lacked the money to pay me," Savage
said. "Has it fallen to me now to keep you current with your various
lies?" He gathered up the mass of Annie Contreras's hair and used it like
excelsior to enfold the hand.

"The ring, Danny. Get it off her, or I will."

"That is hers. She died for it."

"Is that right? Well, then you just forgave this month's rent right
there, if that's how you mean to be about it."

━ ∼

There is no potter's field in Fremont County, no fund for the burial of
the indigent, so Savage decided that he would cement her into a me-
morial very like the sheepmen's cairns standing lonely watch all over
Wyoming. He set it near where her tent had been, the usual cumulation
of rocks, but taller of course and more complex, and a month after he'd
finished it the madame and her other girls were gone, and a month
after that he'd taken the hall down to get at the timbers in its foundation. So then her tower loomed alone on the hill over the camp, and in
death Annie Contreras was become a prominent citizen.

January 20, 1930

Her son would not or could not cry, but with her hands on each of his shoulders she could feel him tremble. Angelene would feel this forever. He hadn't said a word against her plan, but there was pleading in his eyes. "I'm not going to tell you to be a good boy," she said. "I know I don't have to." This was true. Much of what she was saying was not. "You'll do just fine here." But why would he? She herself had escaped this household at her very first opportunity. She gathered Radé once more in her arms. She told herself once more that he would never be hungry here. The boy's hunger, and his mother's hunger in its many variations, was all he had known, and he had never asked more of her. She didn't know how to explain to him that what he wanted was not enough, that what she could give him was so impossibly far from being enough. "Maybe next summer," she said. "I might be able to come back for you. At least for a little visit, huh?" She couldn't risk another word, and so she glanced up at Stoja, whose scorn would suffice to drive her out. Leaving was never easy for Angelene, but she'd made a life of leaving with no place to go.

"It better be today," she'd told them on the very day that snowdrifts and wind had made the roads impassable to all but travel by foot. Born to a job she lacked the stamina to perform, Angelene could be the light of anyone's world for only so long, and then she abruptly reached the end of her strength. No one questioned her reasons anymore, or even her timing. Her father had seen to it that she had trousers and boots for the walk into Lander, and as she began that walk he fell in beside her, upwind of her to shield her from the worst of the cold. He was to put her up in the Belknap Hotel, where she would stay until the next bus going anywhere could make its way out of town. Storms seemed to anticipate her movements; it was only fair. "You don't have to take baby steps, Daddy. I've been on my dogs a lot since I left home. I can keep up a good pace."

"You have done the proper thing," her father said, "by bringing the boy to me."

The snow was so dry their feet seemed to tear it. "I think he'll be all right here," she said.

"He will tolerate us, Angelene. We are who we were when you left, but the boy will tolerate it better, I think, than you did. He's keen that way, he seems prone to the necessary adjustment."

"You'll get to like him."

"It's not a matter of liking him. Though that would be pleasant."

His legs were so long. She'd been wrong about keeping up with him. It was still a struggle. But she'd do it, and she'd be heard, and she promised herself she wouldn't give up until she was sure her father understood her, even if only on this one point. "Just don't get too carried away. He's only a little boy."

"What do you mean?"

"You know what I mean. Things happen where you are. Take it easy. And don't try and train him or make him into an experiment."

"Oh, that. That has all been so exaggerated. I am all of a piece. Would that be the case if I were so hazardous? I have been in my own company forever and I am quite whole. Your imagination has made a painful little detour."

"Let's not be mad, all right? We got this walk together, and after that . . . We shouldn't be getting mad. I'm glad you came with me."

"I cannot be angry with you. That would be impossible, Angelene."

"I know, Daddy."

"I was there at your birth. I held your mother's hand as you were born, if you can imagine that. You remain perfect."

"Yeah. Great. You know, that's not even fair, to say that. Nobody's perfect, especially where I'm concerned."

In the flat beyond Lyons Valley there is a spring that sponsors a willow grove. The trees there were lashing themselves, clicking. It seemed to Angelene that they were a long time passing them.

"I'm as bad as ever," she said. "I'm that same box of rocks I was when I ran off with Juro. I haven't wised up one ounce since I was fifteen." Her face felt like she'd given it a scrubbing, but the good sting was mounting toward pain.

"What purpose is served by speaking that way of yourself? You must quit that, Angelene."

"Back when we were in Utah, Juro and me, we got in with another bootlegger. This guy was set up in the boondocks outside Orem. When they'd cook up a batch, they'd put Radé out in the car to be lookout. Little-bitty kid, up in the mountains, cold as hell and him out in that car, all night sometimes. By himself. Did I say no to that? I didn't. I let em stick him out there. 'The Fedth are coming,' poor little guy, that's one of the first things he ever learned to say in English."

"If he is intended to survive, he will survive, darling. Circumstances have vanishingly little to do with it. The boy has some cunning. We'll get on splendidly."

"But take it easy."

"I don't know what you meant by that."

"No? I guess not. But all I'm saying is, this boy has had it kind of rough. After Juro died I got us hooked up with a grifter, Tony Matolovich, who's pure shit. Used to hit Radé for no reason—all the time. That was another thing I never put a stop to. So one day two big Swedes came to the house, and they're saying Tony's knocked up their sister, which he no doubt had, and they wanted to know what he means to do about it, and pretty soon they've got their pieces out and they're saying he better take a walk with em. Tony didn't need that much persuading, he was only dangerous in his own little way. So he goes off with em, and I follow, wondering you know, and they've got him down in the lot where the big kids play ball, and they're talking about money, and I hear Tony say, "I'd be happy . . ." and that's all he ever got out. Went to his hip pocket for his wallet and one of them Swedes gut shot him. Thought he was pulling a gun, or maybe just got sick of him, and *boom*, Tony's gut shot. I never saw anybody hurt so much. Twelve hours it took him to die. We took him home and watched him die, and then we went to Chicago, which hasn't been a whole lot better."

"I heard your first cry," said Savage.

"Yeah, and it was just about then I got off on the wrong foot. Can you see what I'm saying, though? If you and Mama could take it a little bit easy? The little guy doesn't need a lot. Just kind of take it easy, would you? But who am I to say? You can't do worse by him than I did. So you see? Perfect? Think I'm perfect now?"

"Perfect enough," said her father.

⏤ Twilight Coming ⏤

March 27, 1937

⏤ At last there came a sustained chinook, and after a week of warmth blowing in from the west the Little Wind River was heartened and enlarged. The river shrugged and broke the ice that had been its back for many months, and great blocks of it surged down the channel. Savage stood on the bank considering the bridge he'd been hired to save. Its pilings were already listing away from the weight that had borne down on them, the broken ice. "No," he told his grandson. "No, you must . . . yes. Flip the wrist as I told you to do. There, it goes right in." He had designed a device like a fishing pole but with prima cord for line and bundles of DuPont Hi Velocity Gelatin and blasting caps for bait; each charge was tied to a piece of wood to make it float up to the underside of the floe. He'd instructed the young man to cast for the fissures. "Radé, with our fee we'll buy you a presentable pair of boots, me a bottle of Courvoisier." He relit his cigar and scanned the countryside off in the direction of the Gas Hills. "Snap, snap, that's . . . yes, snap, as I said. It is often the case, you know, that the flourish delivers. One wants that."

Savage had the use of an explosive that would detonate even when wet. Spring was greenly in his nose. Wet dirt and a reasonable cigar. He fretted a little that as an old man happiness came almost too easily to him, resided too much in whatever might be close to hand. He was pretty easily placated anymore. "Now, take in your line. Keep it taut." He directed his grandson through the placement of several charges and

spliced the resulting strands of prima cord together into a single circuit
that he grounded on the bumper of his Buick. He lifted a section of the
hood, hot line in hand, detonating cord. He took the cap off a spark
plug to which he wired his fuse. "Touch the starter, Radé. I'll show you
something beautiful."

There was the usual sound of a small motor chiding a larger one, then
the sound from the river, as if a weight had been dropped on an enormous drumhead. A cloud of powdered ice rose, a prism, a vapor. Danny
Savage turned to consider his grandson with a pleased and knowing
look, a bloody rose at his temple, blood dripping from his chin. He
smiled and pawed the air. He glimpsed an eternity no more profound
than the lobby of a fair hotel, a big, dull, comfortable place where he
would be underused. Savage pitched forward and lay there, listening at
some remove to the fresh whispering of the Little Wind River, free of
ice and flowing innocently now through the pilings under Clate Johnson's bridge.

⌐ ⌐

Radé Capich rolled him over and saw that he was still breathing, breathing easily. Near his shoulder lay a smooth stone with a shattered face.
But for the blood and the knot just above and forward of his ear, his
grandfather might have been napping. Capich pressed the heel of his
hand to the wound. When he felt the oozing quit he pushed at the old
man's cheeks to rouse him. The flesh was inelastic, as he had expected.
"Danny." His grandfather seemed like nothing so much as a piece of dis-
carded machinery. "Danny." Capich could think of nothing else. He
arranged several contradictory expressions on the old man's face. The
hajduk could be molded now, but not into that animate thing he'd been
a minute before. Capich waited as long as he thought he reasonably
could, then dragged him by the straps of his coveralls and wrestled the
liquid weight of him up and into the Buick. He lost control of the great

stone of his head and it bounced hard off the doorframe as he shoved him through it. New bleeding. The trouble with Danny Savage was, as ever, that there was too much of him.

Capich set out across the prairie. No speed was possible. The Buick's passing startled a small herd of antelope, a rabbit. Sage hens flew up. At every dip the old man's head lolled forward at the dashboard, wanting, it seemed, to hurt itself some more. Capich stopped to bind him to his seat with prima cord. This made of his grandfather a sight more desperate than he liked to see.

They followed a wagon track until it met with a good dirt road, and that they followed until it widened six miles later at Rainey. There Capich turned on to another, lesser road and mounted the shoulder of a rimrock. He drove along its face. The road and a railroad spur converged and followed the thread of a coulee and brought them shortly to Popo Agie Number One. At intervals the mute clatter of hoist machinery came up out of the earth. He went up B Street. Coal camp, in its perpetual self-made dusk. He came to his grandfather's house. His grandmother's house. The place where for much of his life he'd been allowed to eat and sleep. He let the engine idle. Stale and lazy, his soul was momentarily palpable within him. He'd done enough for one day. A sow passed in front of the truck, enjoying the fine weather. Capich had seen this decisive pig kill rattlesnakes and crush a litter of her own young.

He unbound his grandfather and slid him out of the car. The old man's weight was crushing. Capich lifted him from behind, arms round his chest, and dragged him so that his heels made two furrows in the dirt. He backed him in, eased him to the floor of the parlor, and was arching against the knot in his back when Stoja Lazich came out of her kitchen, a bowl on her hip. She looked down at her husband and was displeased. "What now?"

He'd heard that his grandmother, as a younger woman, had been a lyrical beauty. Capich did not believe it. She had the shoulders and the heavy brow of a prize fighter. She sweated easily and often. She was sweating now. "A rock came up out of the ice. Clocked him."

"Always with him it's exploding, or cutting, or drilling. The noise he makes. Pull those idiot shoes off and lay him out. Lay him out so he looks like something we don't have to be ashamed. Why you put him on the floor? He goes on his bed, don't he?"

"Yeah, but give me a minute, would you?"

"You put him on the floor?"

"He's heavy."

"You thought I didn't know that? Pick him up. I have other things to do this morning."

The hajduk's bed was a bed he'd built to fit him, oak strips he'd torn off the floor of the old telegraph office and steamed and bent into a spare, counterbalanced frame based on a Joseph Hoffman design he'd seen decades earlier in Vienna. Upon this elegance he'd put a ticking mattress. Upon that, Capich now lay Danny Savage, who was finally without an opinion on any subject whatsoever. Stoja came and washed his head. Capich arranged him in what looked like comfort and then sat there with him for the rest of the morning because he could think of nothing else to do. It surprised him to be able to sit in peace like this without his grandmother yelling in to require something of him. She remained apart, if not away from them.

Capich killed the light and sat in the dark for a time and then, just for variety, switched the naked bulb back on. The room, without his grandfather talking in it, was unfamiliar to him, and unpleasant. It had been wallpapered with pink front pages from *Daily Denver Post*s of April and May of 1926. The pink had warped a sore brown, and the headlines too had aged unpleasantly: COUNCIL SEEKS BELL, LAUGHS AT ACCUSERS; BIGAMIST FLEES NORTH; MR. PRESTON EMPLOYS THE BLIND. His grandfather's room, in fact this entire house, was as strange to Radé Capich as any place on earth. He sat in the sorry light and read the walls.

Dr. August McChesney lived in a handsome cabin down among the cottonwoods at the south edge of Rainey. There he enjoyed his improbable, abundant health. Each year at the first thaw he turned a strip of earth around his cabin, the beginning of a bed in which hundreds of marigolds would bloom all summer. This had been the work of his morning. Now, pleasantly fatigued, the doctor sat with his morris chair turned to the woodstove, drinking Oolong tea and eating shortbread, adrift with Odysseus on the wine-dark sea. There were three raps at the window above his sink, three more, more insistently. McChesney let his chin fall to his chest and closed his eyes. He felt rather than saw Radé Capich, grimly regarding him through the glass, blocking a slant column of sun intended for his kitchen floor. Making his reluctance as obvious as possible, he rose and opened his door to the boy who stood there like a suitor, a nosegay of small bills for his bouquet.

"Red. What is it?"

"We were blasting ice out at the Johnsons'. Rock blew out of it. A big one." The young man indicated his temporal bone. "Caught Danny right here."

"Kill him?"

"No. But he hasn't come to yet."

"Does he seem to be hurting?"

"I don't think he feels a thing. That's what makes you worry."

McChesney shifted slightly in the doorway and happened to catch a swatch of red reflected in his bifocals, the ghost of his own living nose. This common sighting startled him a little. "It's no emergency, then. You go on into Riverton and find Dr. Woodrell, or that new man. What do you expect me to do?"

They boy looked at the doctor, and then a little to the side of him. He was shy and unaccustomed to seeking favors. "It's been over four hours. Danny hasn't moved a muscle. Could you just come up and take a look at him?"

"Well, he's not going any place, is he? I can't see where I'm so desperately needed. Why is it you people won't recognize a man's retirement?" The boy's offer of cash was still there, his hand still extended. McChesney had from the beginning of his career seen the role of medicine to be negligible. Pain and death were part of a bargain struck long ago, a price everyone drawing breath would eventually pay, and so his little fund of sympathy was quickly exhausted and then, without it, he'd gone on to participate in decades of suffering and death very little mitigated by his occasional successes. So he'd quit the hell of doctoring as soon as he practically could and, having quit, McChesney could not see why on a lovely afternoon he must be the answer to anyone's bad luck. "I'll let you drive me up there. But, Red, I want you to know, if it wasn't Danny Savage, nothing could induce me to set foot outside this house. I guess a fellow retains his scientific curiosity."

The invention of the motorcar had in McChesney's opinion done much to rob the world of grace and leisure, and he'd never learned to drive, but he lived in a place that was distant from everything, and so he had often to trust himself to a machine he understood less than perfectly, to a driver whose skill he resented. In Savage's great, purring Buick he felt a child. He had a child's pleasure in rolling through an awakening countryside. But the point of it was to reach the mine camp, and Little Popo Agie Number One was for the doctor the seat of human futility. "These foreigners, I don't mind telling you, I've seen more foolishness up here than you can shake a stick at. You people have your potions, and compresses, and hoodoo, and god-knows-what-all, and none of it does the least bit of good. But you won't be convinced of it. I'm not speaking of you necessarily, Red, I don't know what theories you may subscribe to, but I do know that almost every time I've been called up here, it's been too late. I come up here to find some poor devil all but killed, and often as not it was somebody's idea of a cure that really turned the whole thing hopeless. See, I never have thought it was particularly my business to comfort the dying."

Lines bearing wet wash tied the houses of the camp together. Black tailings lapped everywhere as if the last of the miners here intended to stay on until they'd buried themselves in tailings. At the door of Savage's house a pair of scarved women watched the doctor coming in, a petty local deity who'd come to do them little good and then charge his fee. A mule deer's rack was mounted above Savage's door and to a tine of that was tied a barometer. They went in, passing through a ghastly parlor and into the sickroom, which lacked any ventilation or natural light, and there the patient had been stripped and was now being scrubbed pink as fish meat by his wife. McChesney had known Danny Savage since sometime before the war and remembered nothing of a wife. A wife, though, was the only thing this woman could be, angry and diligent as she was. These bohunk women stayed close to home, and in their homes they kept a terrible and terribly odd propriety; in their homes they were like badgers down a short hole. A man didn't go out of his way to meet them.

Capich spoke to the woman in a language that was to the doctor's ears all consonants and spittle. Their whispers contained force enough to propel screams. The old woman's nostrils worked like a bellows, her eyes like a drill. McChesney felt his sense of purpose calcify. "Well now," he said, "if I haven't fallen in with the goddamnest heathens. Be quiet, both of you, and let me attend to this man."

The old woman raised her hand to him and performed a small, vicious dance with it. It seemed she wished him to leave, and he'd have been happy to do so; the house smelled of boiled cabbage and old cigars and the caustic water in which she'd washed Danny Savage. The house smelled of death, probably.

"*Babina*," said the boy.

She hissed at them from her throat. A muscle at the hinge of her jaw flexed, and she left, and the room was instantly serene for her absence.

McChesney thumbed the patient's eyelid open. The pupil swam in its iris, the sclera was milk white. "Concussion, but I could have told you that much without leaving home. This hemorrhaging you see here, this big bruise—could be some of that on the inside, too. You can bruise the brain, too, just like anything else."

"So that's not too bad? If it's just a bruise it can't be . . . something he wouldn't get over?"

"I didn't say that," said McChesney. "It might be pretty damn bad. Or it might not. Depends on the amount of swelling."

"How do you know? One way or the other?"

"Wait and see. When what happens, happens, then you'll know."

"Is there anything you can do about it?"

"Pray if you pray. Otherwise, just hope for the best."

"Hope?" The boy was not keen on so pale a strategy.

"There's trepanning. You bore a hole in the skull, relieves the pressure if you drill the right spot. Did that a few times in my drinking days, successfully, wouldn't attempt it now. So it's just wait-and-see, Red. Best I can offer you."

"He will come around, though?"

"Oh, probably. Or maybe not. I don't know."

"What are his chances?"

"For the last time, I don't know. And that's about as good a medical opinion as you'd get on this thing. I can tell you he's not in as good a shape as he was before this happened to him. It was a good hard knock. You might think of it this way, he's already lived longer than he had any right to expect. Most men anywhere near this size don't see forty. " McChesney dressed the old man's wound. The damage to the flesh was incidental but all that was susceptible to his treatment. He wound gauze over hair that was at the crown of the head as fine as feathers and at the chin as coarse as the leavings of a file. "Must be pretty near seven feet of him, and stoutly made. About four hundred pounds of bone and muscle mass and brain, I'd say, and it takes quite the bonfire to keep that much machinery up and running. Gigantism, the pituitary gland goes kerblooey and you get . . . You know people your grandfather's size, even some of them no bigger than you, they're often clumsy and slow, and the journals aren't too optimistic on life span. Old boy's probably got a heart in him the size of a muskmelon, even so, the organism was never meant to achieve but so much. *Homo sapiens,* a limited beast if you ask me."

"He's never been too limited," said the boy of the patient. "That's never been his problem."

"The old scamp knew something about everything, frequently more than I, give him that. And he had that lovely trick of not giving a damn for anyone's opinion of him. Enviable life. Tears are in no event called for here."

"Now you're saying he's done for?"

"I'm saying we all are, it's just a question of when."

The boy drew his grandfather's bedclothes up to his chin. The doctor heard the long trestle table in the parlor being laid and boarders coming into the old woman's house to take their supper. These sounds and the warmth and odors accompanying them brought him comfortably home to the affairs of the healthy.

"You better stay and have some of her supper," said the boy. "She'll really raise a stink if you don't take a bite with us. No one's ever said she wasn't a good cook."

There was a protocol for leaving the mine camp: you broke bread first. Though McChesney had never been hungry here, he had never successfully refused the offer of a meal, and so, not one to bother with vain protest, he went out to the parlor with the lad and sat down to table. Steam floated on granite-ware pots filled with beans and sauerkraut. Sauerkraut, the miners' anti-scorbutic. From a blackened iron roasting pan they took thickly sliced beef. Stoja Lazich circled the table, continuously prompting, *Urdi. Urdi.* Eat. And, very efficiently, they ate their Saturday supper. The boarders were so recently finished with the week's final shift that their hair still glistened with the water they'd combed through it at the company wash house. They had nothing to say to each other or to him. McChesney knew them from that time, not so distant, before he'd given the world the slip.

Boarders. How it must be, never to eat at your own table. They'd seemed larger to him before, some of these men, when he'd known them in more public circumstances. The Welshman across from him was a tenor so pure that his voice had drawn McChesney one Sunday into a church where he had no other business. Eddie Rakestraw. Years had passed since he'd heard or even seen Rakestraw, but here he was and here he'd been all along, taking his thousands of meals in company with the Marković brothers who ate like slightly privileged animals. Nicola Marković had once come to McChesney with a foot pinched almost apart. The other Marković , the stranger of the pair, had shown up at his office one night with the underside of both his arms scored by a broken bottle. Connor Fariello, formerly a syndicalist and lady's man, worried soft bread in a toothless mouth. Since when? If Dr. August McChesney was not the McChesney of old, not the little brute who took his rye neat and could at three in the morning give you an hour of Robert Burns from memory, he was by no means so diminished as these men had become. He had known them, and they were not this before. The speakeasies and shacks and tents all smelled of liniment he had dispensed; he had known everyone then and specialized in treating the terrible wounds inflicted by large animals and heavy machinery, and that's how he'd been a man. It had seemed enough at the time.

At the head of the table, an empty chair.

The old woman went down to her root cellar and came out of it with a gallon of the zinfandel her husband had vinted that year. She uncorked the jug and set it heavily before them. "Sing," she demanded. This was the first the doctor had known she had some English, clear English if she felt like it. The men around her table were just then as likely to sing as draft animals. "Oh, are you thinking of that one? And that makes you so sad? You, doctor, you can tell them. He's dying, huh?"

Suddenly very weary and arthritic, McChesney drew himself up. "Maybe."

"Not maybe," said the old woman. "He will die now, I know. He has led an evil life, so he got a long time dying, but he is going to die. You think that is a bad thing? You don't know. You don't want to sing, you want to cry for him? Because you don't know. My tears will not be wasted."

McChesney touched the base of his wine glass. He'd been sober ten years. Tears? The woman's tears would turn all they touched to stone.

"Danny Savage," she said. "No. That is another lie out of him, because he was Danilo Lazich, and he was born a peasant or not even that. He was known to my village, and they said his mother slept with the unholy. They said this one, the hajduk, he was his mother's punishment. And sometimes at night he would come down to a well, and he'd laugh out there in the dark, for no reason. No one ever went out to draw water. 'See how white the teeth in him,' they said. They knew what he was. I was told what he was. I have been his wife. No one knows but me, and I say he has lived too much already. He will die now."

"*Night and day, you are the one,*" sang Red Capich with no accompaniment and no preamble.

"No," said the old woman, "no jazz."

"*Only you beneath the moon and under the sun.*"

"Shut up, you Capich, you Hrvat. How did any of my family's blood ever get into something like you? No more from you."

"*Whether near to me or far . . .*"

"Enough," the old woman shouted.

"*Darling, makes no difference where you are . . .*"

McChesney thought the young man's voice had an excessively reedy timbre, like a Negro's.

"Enough," said the old woman.

"*You're part of me, night and daaay . . .*"

"No," she said. "You do what I say now, because now I'm the one. The only one, and you gotta do what I say."

The young man stood, and the whole long table tilted away from the thrust of his rising thighs. Plates rattled dully. "Don't talk like somebody died. "

"This is my house," she said. "It has always been. But now I put up with enough. Long enough. So now you can take your *chuvar* doctor and get out. Get out of here. You're no good to me. You can take the car. I give it to you."

"It's not yours to give," said Capich.

"Yeah, and you can take that jazz, too, take it straight down into hell with you. Get out."

The doctor left without once meeting the old woman's eyes. She'd scrubbed her husband raw with that flour sack, and McChesney had reckoned on first meeting her that looking into her face was more work than he'd signed on to do. He left her house a little ashamed of himself on that account. The young man followed shortly with an apple crate full of magazines and a satchel.

"Don't believe she cared for me, your grandmother. She is your grandmother?"

"She is. You wanna go for a ride somewhere? I can take you wherever you want to go."

"Now, why do you suppose she thought she had to take that tone with me? What in the Sam Hill did I ever do to that woman?"

"You're an American, that's all."

"Wouldn't be otherwise," McChesney asserted. "What's wrong with that? What's she? What are you, for that matter? Hell, you were born here, weren't you, Red?"

"Yeah. But, you saw. She doesn't like me, either. And that's just one of the reasons."

"She's got a lot of grass, don't you think? If she doesn't like us, she could always leave, go back to wherever it was you folks came out of."

"Yeah, but I guess she didn't like them, either. Don't think you got picked on; if she did like you, then that would be something to worry about."

The doctor could think of nowhere to go but home, and he was returned there as the charm of the day was beginning to fail; hours before twilight, he could feel twilight coming. Sometimes in early spring he was subject to a nasty melancholy. McChesney was not prepared to be alone again. He invented a reason to prevent it for a while: when he reached his place he told young Capich, "I've got something you should see. It holds some sentimental value, and I believe you should see it." He led the young man out to his garden shed. A yardarm extended from its eastern gable and from that hung "an Aeolian harp. Your grandfather gave it to me, probably a little before you were born. Out of the blue he came to me with this item he calls an Aeolian harp. He said he thought I'd be amused. And I was. Have been."

"Oh. Is it art, or what?"

"It was just a paint can when it came into his hands. How did he know to do this? Cut these reeds into it—he knew they'd sing. Where does a man come by information like this? To do something like this? It's an Aeolian harp, something I'd never heard of."

"Pretty fancy."

"I took it out here and hung it as he told me to, and it turned to the first wind, and it's been singing fairly steady ever since, a little different tune depending on the pace and direction of the wind. So it's an instrument that way, a kind of weather gauge. It's pretty. You think by now I'd have tired of it, but not at all. A machine that runs without power or repair. Just runs. That old man required the gods to speak for him."

"They say anything interesting?"

"No, they sang. That's what I'm telling you. Or it does. This thing of his. This works better than anything else I own, and to better purpose."

"He should make more of these."

"The point is, he made one. Not many men are even as much as clever, Red."

—— ——

Miroslav Mlinar cleaned the bowl that had contained his oatmeal and returned it to its shelf. With the same methodical detachment, he pulled on a pale blue shirt and rolled its sleeves to a turn past his coolie's elbows, knotted a silk tie, and lined his lower lip with Sen-sen. He slid into his vest and suit coat and out of his bachelor's shack to walk to the club many hours before it was really necessary to be there. Turning down Main Street he passed the brick storefronts that had housed the Gilded Lily, Huson's Hotel, and Sanger's Fancy Bakery. Mlinar now owned the whole boarded row, had owned Rainey essentially, ever since diesel had come into favor and killed the market for soft coal. He wore Rainey like a hair shirt because he'd happened to build his club there; he owned Rainey and the club owned him. Mlinar's ice house in Lander sold ice by the ton and by the hundredweight, his powerhouse on the Big Wind sold direct current day and night, but the heart of his operation was the club. The club had been very good to him all through prohibition and the depression, crouched in her Moorish thickness of arterial red stucco, six thousand square feet of fine saloon. His moneymaker. To celebrate the repeal of the Eighteenth Amendment he'd torn out another block of Rainey's business district just to expand his parking lot, and a pair of neon palms were mounted on the roof, their fronds to waft nightly on a signmaker's zephyr. Mlinar's were the durable goods. He sold isolation here, repackaged as license. They came from all over because he sold the best steak in Wyoming and whatever else was necessary to a good time. Of course, no one came so faithfully as Mlinar himself.

He waited in an empty house, considering the emptiness and finding it once again intolerable. He watched morning make its way across the dance floor through the small windows set high in his walls. Waiting, as he arranged to do each day, made him anxious. He hated this daily wait for the help to come in because, left to his own devices, he got fidgety and bored. None of his better wits were available to him when he was alone.

At last Louise Kresovich came in through the back door to the kitchen. Mlinar heard the rattling of drawers and the soft pinging of pots and pans. He prevented himself from going straight to her because today she must have time to think of all the conversations there might be between them, and so he waited until he felt she'd had time to imagine the worst, and then went back to the kitchen to find Louise stirring a vat of tapioca, her stroke getting wild as he neared her. He watched her work, the pellets whirling wide of a wooden spoon. For sanitation's sake, and because her neck was still slender and pretty, she wore her hair in a heartbreaking wisp of topknot. There were holes in her stockings.

He watched her. Finally he said, "Where's your Eli? I told him to come in and see me this morning."

Louise, hedged by misery, thought of trying a smile. "He don't feel too good. Maybe he got this flu that's been going around."

"I saw him getting that flu. Got it off my back bar last night. Is he coming in later?"

"I . . . maybe," she said. "He'll try, I think."

"Try, my ass. Try don't do me no good. He's canned. You see him before I do, you tell him that." Mlinar took a twenty dollar bill from the fob pocket of his vest and gave it to her. "You can also tell him he's eighty-sixed. Gets a snootfull and then everybody in the place has gotta see how much hair he's got on his chest. Christ almighty. Enough of that Little Eli."

"He's a tough boy," she said.

"Didn't say he wasn't. Tough, and less than a dime a dozen. Big deal. I know you raised him the best you could, but he's no prize, Louise. You can make my coffee now."

"It's not perking yet," she said, "but I've got it on."

Louise Kresovich supported a husband whose legs had been crushed in the mine and two sons with no excuse for relying on her. The woman bought masses for everyone but herself and moved through her life like a pony at a pony ride. She belonged in a kitchen. Soon she would be pulling cabbage out of brine, and when she opened the crocks the smell of it would fill the place front and back. The smell would make Mlinar happy for a while.

Mlinar touched his coffee with brandy and returned to his booth, and with a red linen napkin he shaped a sand crane and a daffodil; this was a skill he did not remember acquiring. The paperboy came in with yesterday's *Post*. He read it front to back, society pages and all, and felt when he'd finished as if he'd eaten a tub of mashed potatoes. He fell into a reverie featuring scenes from a week at the height of his virility, the week with Brenda Lamouette. Her sofa, her bed, her kitchen counter, the gazebo in the park. Lawns and shade trees and a time before Rainey when he had been more flexible and susceptible to repeated satisfaction. Though he was not so very old, he could make himself feel that way by remembering the compensations there had been in being very young. Mlinar was relieved when Red Capich came out of the kitchen and made humbly for his booth. Anything to rid himself of his own company. "Throw your shoulders back and walk like Juro Capich, why don't you?"

"I don't recall his way of walking," said the boy.

"Head up, shoulders back, and I'm-God's-gift-to-the-world, that's how he walked. There was a swagger on him like you don't see anymore. Big as you are, you should be able to pull it off easy."

"It's not my talent."

"Yeah. But don't be moping like that. Pisses me off."

"All right."

"So, what do you want? You come in early for work, and hangdog like you are, I know you want something from me."

"I need a raise."

"Who's pregnant?"

"Nobody. Not by me, anyway. My grandmother kicked me out." The young man did not seem surprised or even disappointed.

"How'd you ever put up with her as long as you did, Red? I run into that woman exactly twice in twenty years, and I remember both times. What a nightmare she is."

"Danny got hurt. So she was mad, I guess."

"Bad? He doing all right now?"

"I don't know. He's alive. Was when I left."

"So why's she mad at you? You weren't the one who hurt him, were you?"

"No. We were blasting. She just gets mad. Makes it hard to stay out of her way, keep out of trouble with her. I'm not even sure what I'll need. More, though."

"I couldn't pay you a penny more than what I'm paying you now, not to wash dishes. A dishwasher's only worth so much, any dishwasher." Mlinar set his ankle on his knee. "Got an opening for a floor manager. Job's yours if you want it."

"What about Eli?"

"What about him? You want the job or don't you?"

"I want it," said Capich. "But I'd look like a fool out here, dressed like this. What I'm wearing, or stuff like it, is all I got."

"What size shoes you wear? Number thirteeens, fourteens? Must be something godawful."

"Biggest ones I can find."

"I'll get you a sharp pair of shoes, take you to my tailor. Kid, I hate to tell you, but you'll never buy a suit off the rack."

"What do I do till then? You want me out here looking like this?"

"Unless you'd rather wash dishes. Now look, I dropped around to the crummiest dive in Red Lodge, Montana, one morning with your old man, and he was wearing those kid gloves of his; I was sure he'd get us stomped in there. You know what those rummies did? Bought us a round. Point is, it's not what you wear, but how you wear it. You ain't out of place until you think you are. How old are you?"

"Seventeen."

"That's right. Seventeen years old, chest on you like a horse, nice head of hair, and you probably get a hard-on just walking into a warm room. And you're worried about how you look? Shit. Look at me. I'm ugly, that's all, and my threads don't do a damn thing about it."

"I guess not. But the other thing is, I'm kind of a poor scrapper."

"Did I say I wanted a bouncer? Said I wanted a floor manager. Fight's an expensive thing in a place like this. I got nice furnishings. The whole idea is to get these hooligans to bust up their own shanties if they just have to bust something up. They can save that shit for their own shacks. What I'd want out of you is a little finesse, little diplomacy. Got any?"

"Maybe. But one thing—I'm not my old man, if that's what you were thinking. From what I've heard, I'm not much like him."

"Well, I know that. Don't have to poor-mouth yourself about it. That guy was one of a kind. I wouldn't have trusted your old man to walk my dog, but I'd give my shriveled left nut to see him stroll in here tonight. Guy like Juro Capich don't work for you, he graces your business. You're a different story, Red. You'll have to earn your way. And that's all right. There's a place for that, too. You're a smart kid, maybe about half-assed honest. I can teach you a few things."

"I start tonight then?"

"You start as soon as you find somebody else to wash the dishes."

The young man turned and set off to do it. Mlinar expected to get good use out of Red Capich.

— ⁓

He wore for the first time the only shirt his wife had ever bought him. He knew he was wearing it and that it had been starched. She was speaking to him.

"Why do you open your eyes, hajduk?"

He saw her unclearly at the foot of his bed. Words formed in his mind, but he would not commit them to speech, afraid they'd somehow bind him back to that old, raw thing, his being. He was a swimmer through charged air, he was heat lightning; he liked what had happened to him very much.

"You got to be tired," she told him. "So much of everything all the time, you got to be tired. Why you always had to wear everything out? Everybody? Why you don't close those goddamn eyes of yours, hajduk?"

━ ━

Capich was about to knock at her door when Agnes Cirrio, as if she had been expecting him, opened it. Always she was like this, like a crow set to launch from barb wire. She stepped back to let him pass into the peculiar, heavy air inside. Her house was a mine shack moved down from the camp, the same cleverly partitioned square as his grandmother's house, with its parlor, two bedrooms, and the long kitchen at the back. But, for all that, Stoja had warned him many times of its dangers. "Stay away from them Cirrios," she had told him. "That Agnes, she likes you good enough now, but maybe someday she don't like you so much, and she don't say why, she just goes off in the corner, next thing you know, you're shitting snakes. And that boy of hers, he'd slit your throat for a quarter. Never mistake a gypsy for a friend." Stoja had educated her grandson with slanders against everyone they knew in common, convincing slanders, but he could not see how Agnes Cirrio, old and anxious and frail as she was, could be very hazardous to anyone. Agnes led Capich through the parlor and into the kitchen where her son, Julian Cirrio, sat at the sideboard sponging up a saucer of creamed coffee with bread. Breakfast fare, usually. Cirrio had acquired a jar of brilliantine and slicked his curls into a wave that crested an inch above and an inch forward of his forehead. Strange grooming and eagerness were his burden.

"Want to go to work, Julie?"

"When?"

"Tonight. Right now."

"Doing what?"

"What I've been doing, pearl diving. What I was doing."

"You quit?"

"Mlinar made me floor manager. Danny got hurt, blasting. Took a rock to the head and it cooled him. Then Stoja kicked me out. Then I got this floor manager job." Capich was and was not keen on himself as he recounted the day. "So, the thing is, I'm supposed to find a new dishwasher."

"He made you floor manager? Floor manager of the Alhambra? What is it about you? I just don't see it."

"Julie, it's a poor move, trying to do you a favor."

"What'd I say? Man, you're touchy. Don't worry, Danny Savage, he'll be all right. Danny? You gotta be kidding. How they gonna hurt that guy? And you can stay with us, too. We got room, don't we, Mama?" Julie's was, however, a recurring kind of envy, and he was never able to put it aside for long. "Floor manager. Red, you'll get your ass whipped in there, then what? Somebody's gonna cut you down like a tree, then what'll you do?" No progress was made by anyone that was not made somehow at Cirrio's expense. He never quite got his share—not for lack of trying.

"Look, Julie, I gave you first shot, but I've got to get back to the club now and I'll stop and ask a few other guys on the way. Don't say I didn't offer it to you first. But we need somebody right now."

"Slide around here and try and hire me? You? Hire me?"

"You coming?"

Cirrio sucked at his teeth. "I'd like to help you out, but they just appointed me secretary of state. Maybe, if you ask polite, my aide-de-camp'll wash your dishes for you." He rose from the sideboard to pump himself a glass of rusty water, graceful about it as a movie buccaneer. Handsome Julie. His mother sighed and said something corrective to him in Romansch. "Yeah," he told her, "I never said I wouldn't. Lay me out a change of clothes."

"It's kitchen work," said Capich. "You're fine the way you are."

"You think I'd go anywhere looking like you, Red? I'll wash dishes cause I got to. But I won't slop around looking like a dishwasher." He went into his room, let the curtain to behind him, and began to hum. Capich believed Julie intended this humming to make him seem carefree, but he worked hard at it.

Agnes Cirrio had come to Rainey at fifty, pregnant with her first and only child. She came with no man and no obvious means of sustenance. When she had the child they were a for a while a small mystery around town. As the boy got older, though, as athlete, scholar, and a pain in the ass, he gave them a more public presence. The Cirrio parlor was hung all around with ugly and unlike pencil drawings his mother had made of him at each stage of his life. There were two trophies on a stand, clippings from the Lander paper.

A quarter hour passed before Julie was ready to go. The Bay Rum was still wet on his cheeks as they left. They walked down the naked half-acre prominence from Cirrio's house and through the ruins of Bailey's Addition. Still evident on this block was the system of fire hydrants made to serve just four houses, houses surmounted by shingled turrets and girdled by porches decked in trim as intricate as lace; a hundred generations of bats had bred in them by now. This had been Rainey's best neighborhood, when there had been neighborhoods. Curtains moved in an upper window of the house that had belonged to Mayor Bailey himself, heavy old velveteen, sucking at the broken panes.

"So this is the schedule," Capich said. "You go in every night, four-thirty, five. You help Louise stuff her *sarma*. Then you check the tables. You know those lamps on the tables, bunch of little bulbs supposed to look like candles? Make sure none of those is out. Never skip checking the lamps. Makes Mlinar crazy if he sees a bulb out. Then you mop the dance floor, throw a little wax on it. Then, sometimes, you haul things around, stock the pantry. Big thing is the dishes, though. Believe me, they're a big thing."

"People are going to start seeing themselves in Mlinar's plates now."

"They don't want to see themselves in the plates, Julie. You gotta pace yourself. You'll be doing this six nights a week, swamping Sunday mornings."

"You do any cooking?"

"No, you're the dishwasher."

"Now, that's a trade," Julie said. "A cook can find work anywhere. I'll get Louise to show me a few things."

"She'll show you the door if you bother her too much."

"You bring me down here, start telling me what a crummy job this is."

"Well, it's fifteen bucks a week you didn't have before."

Capich took Cirrio in through the front door, the only entrance acceptable to him. The gypsy said hello to everyone in sight. He said hello to Mlinar, who tracked the boys' approach to his table with a tiny, ambiguous smile. "You joining my little family down here, Julie?"

"You'll be happy you hired me, Mr. Mlinar. I can go like a sonofagun."

"Yeah?"

"I never blew an opportunity yet."

"You never had one." Mlinar took a long pull of soda water. "Red, get him lined out, show him what to do."

They passed through swinging metal doors and into a well-lit affliction; the cook, her helper, and two waitresses traveled this kitchen like pushrods in an engine, and it was wilting hot. On any given night they might be called upon to make and serve fifty stupefying meals, four or five courses each. "Louise," Capich said, "Julian Cirrio is going to be back here with you now. Mr. Mlinar said to tell him what to do."

"You tell him," she said. Sad old Louise, corrosive thing. "Mlinar hires nothing but children anymore. Could you find no one else?"

"Mrs. Kresovich," said Julie piously, "I can do anything. I'll do the work of two guys back here."

"Could you find no one else?" Louise still wished to know.

"He'll be all right."

"While there are two of you," she said, "I want you to bring me a side of beef."

In the club's great cooler, halves of animals hung in a row, smelling metallic. Cirrio shivered. "Well fuck her," he said. "Children. She was talking about us. Me. She keeps talking that way, I'll flop old Henry out, then she'll see about this 'children' thing."

"Grab the hind end of this," Capich told him. "Matter of fact, take it yourself. You've got to learn to pack these things."

Cirrio bowed beneath the carcass, lifted it off its hook and shouldered it. "Man, that's a lot of iron, you get iron out of eating it. Beef, and pigs, and that's a lamb, isn't it? Think of it, lamb chops." Condensation billowed out of the cooler when Capich opened the door. Pumps switched on outside to restore the escaping chill. Cirrio staggered, all but hidden under meat. "We need to eat a lot of this."

"You will," Capich said. "It's the main benefit around here."

"We'll kill em next year."

"Who?"

"Thermopolis." The gypsy saw them glorious on the gridiron. "Greybull, Casper, all those pricks. We'll walk right over those guys, eating like this. Don't matter how bad everybody else on that team is, you and me, we'll be enough by ourself to wipe em all out."

"How you think we're gonna work here and play football too?"

Very slowly Cirrio tipped the carcass from his back and onto a long wooden counter. "This where you put it?"

"Ask Louise."

"Mrs. Kresovich?"

"That's too big for you," she said. "You're gonna drop it sometime. Hurt yourself."

"No, ma'am. I don't get hurt, do I, Red?"

The kitchen would hurt him soon enough. He'd put that rubber

apron on, it would hit him about mid-shin, and in five minutes the
whole front of him would be bathed in rancid sweat. The job was just
the thing for Cirrio. "Soap in one sink," Capich told him, "and clear
water in the other. Louise controls the hot water reservoir, doesn't give
you much of it. Lukewarm is no good. Lukewarm is what you'll have,
mostly. Glasses first, then plates and silver, then pots. Clean your sinks,
start again. The thing is, keep yourself elbow deep in bubbles. You can
use all the soap you want."

Cirrio's attention had wandered to a better place. "Remember that
Christmas party at May Percival's house? Cut the crust of their sandwiches and didn't even spike the punch. Was that nice?"

"Not that nice. That Sinclair guy ripped my shirt. Fred Sinclair, remember?"

"Yeah, but before that. It was pretty nice wasn't it? Remember those
little teeny bells they had in there? Those decorations? All the girls
with their hair so pretty?"

"It was all right."

"Now, why do you think we were there, Red?"

"They let anybody come."

"Not anybody. A lot stayed home. But you and me, we're right there.
Hell, I had a cup of tea."

"And we fit right in, didn't we, Julie?"

"No, but we were there, and that's the main thing. Right there in the
Percival home. And why? We were there because every time dear old
Lander High needed five, six yards, they sent me off right tackle and
they got it. That is the only reason we were at May Percival's party. Me,
I'm going again next year. I'll buy you a new pair of cleats. We'll be All
State. I'll marry May and you can marry her ugly sister. We'll live hap-
pily ever after, selling daddy's Chevrolets. Oh, we gotta play ball, Red."

"About fifteen minutes," Capich said, "and they'll be bringing dishes
in. If they stack up around the door, everybody starts yelling at you.

Especially Beverly. The others get cranky. Beverly's just mean. Keep the floor dry, whatever else you do."

"Do I look like an idiot to you? I gotta have an hour lecture on how to wash dishes?"

"You'll do it your own way, won't you?"

"That's right," said Cirrio. "Now what happens if you don't make it out there and Mlinar's gotta fire you? You think you're gonna come back here and take my job?"

"No. I washed enough dishes. Gets old after a while. You'll see. Wash dishes, mop the floor, scrub the toilets. It's just wading around in other people's shit."

"So when the position comes open, first one you think of is me?"

"You were the only one I thought of, Julie."

"Floor manager. Mr. floor manager." Cirrio bent at the waist and looked up at Capich through his lightly balled fists. His hands described small circles. His eyes were slitted.

"Julie, not back here."

"How many push-ups can you do? I can do two hundred." He weaved down into his crouch.

"I said, not here."

"You're big, but you got no style. Me, I got the Dempsey style. I come in low, let em hurt their hands on the top of my head." He weaved; an oily strand of his hair worked loose and twitched in counterpoint. "I got leverage. Hook with either hand. Bam, to the liver, and down he goes." Cirrio's right whipped around and stopped just short of Capich's ribs. "Joo-lee-an Cee-ree-ooh, the winnah and still champion."

"Save your energy, Julie. First night back here is tough. Floor's so hard, wears you out."

"Got energy to burn. Got conditioning. What you got, Red? Show me something."

"I need to get out there. Mlinar's waiting for me."

Cirrio threw his left, and Capich felt it push air past his face. He stepped back. Cirrio advanced again. Capich had retreated as far as he could, back against the wet rim of the sink.

"Julie."

"Let's see what you got."

Capich put a hand on Cirrio's shoulder and shoved him away. A lively thing, but small, Julie. He stood up, moving his chin back and forth repulsively. "You can't connect clean on me, see what I mean? I'm a mongoose. What are you? Just slow." Back into his crouch again, and forward. "You're slow, I think."

Capich rapped his knuckles on his friend's head.

"That don't hurt."

"I'll do it until it does. We got work to do, Julie, I can't be messing with you."

"Mess with me?" Cirrio moved as if blows were raining by on all sides; he shot a straight right past Capich's ear, shuffled back and to the side, bobbing, and in a sudden excess of evasiveness he slammed his face down into a work table. He remained crouched for a moment, cringing really, then stood, white and nearly tearful. He cupped a hand beneath his mouth and slowly unhooked his upper lip from the incisor it had snagged; the tooth came away in his fingers. He bled in earnest. Louise Kresovich came to him with a clean white towel. Cirrio, perplexed by her kindness, thanked her as best he could with his damaged mouth. Louise laughed, a sound sudden as breaking glass. It was just as well, Capich thought, that she was not much given to this.

"I can't believe they put that table there," Cirrio said.

"You okay, Julie?"

"I can't be hurt," he said again.

— ⁓

Capich went out to Mlinar where he sat behind the detritus of his supper. Mlinar pointed to the far side of the horseshoe booth, and Capich let the leather cushion receive him. Just to be allowed to sit here, this would be wage enough. A trumpet in the men's room spun out a series of arpeggios that spiraled into *Hail to the Chief.* Beverly and Nallie carried food and liquor and bussed tables and were constantly attentive and sweet-tempered to the custom. Capich saw them now as athletes; he could not imagine himself doing anything so well or so energetically as Mlinar's waitresses waited tables. They served families at this hour, sweetly formal families in their best bib and tucker, turned out for appetizers. Fresh radishes in April. Where else but the big floor of the Alhambra? Capich felt unequal to it. "What do you want me to do?"

"Get something under your belt first." Mlinar caught Beverly's eye and beckoned to her. She broke her rhythm to come to their table. Her mouth was made large and terrible with lipstick. "How long," he asked her, "am I supposed to sit in this mess?"

"I'll get it cleared." Her hair hung down her back, bunched in a net.

"First, you better take Red's dinner order. Tell her what you want."

"Fried chicken."

"Chicken? You got a dozen entrées to choose from, you ask for chicken? Let me tell you something about chicken. I won't charge people to serve it. I damn near give it away. A barnyard fowl, for Christ's sake."

"Okay," said Capich. "T-bone then. Could I get it rare, please?"

"And bring him a tall glass of milk. Kid's still growing, which is overdoing it, but there you go."

"Is that all?" Beverly's order book lay concave in her hand beneath her pencil. She hadn't the time for this.

"No," said Mlinar, "that ain't all. Clear my table."

She swept up the waste, and her hips worked angrily, carrying her off.

"Believe it or not, I was once shacked up with that woman. Couldn't begin to keep up with her, she wouldn't hardly let me get any sleep. Three, four months there, I looked like I had a couple figs under my eyes. Makes a fair waitress, though; lot of energy she's got. But remember, don't let her start thinking she's smart. She'll try and get cute if you let her. Don't let her."

In its signature arrangement the band's reeds rattled autumnally against the brass section; dinner music and nostalgia bore down on Capich while he waited for his meal and as he ate it. Too tired to be hungry, he ate because eating was all he'd been asked to do. Cut flowers were delivered to the tables. Relish plates, baskets of bread. Soup and salad and ravioli and *sarma*. And he, Red Capich, at the delivery end of the feast. Silver rang on bone china, good glassware chimed expensively. The dancing got under way, and shoe leather skated in rhythm on special-order sawdust. Mlinar's fake candles glowed in their thousands. Musicians and dancers—Capich, who had never danced a step in his life, measured himself against them. He was not much. "I don't want you to think I'm lazy, just sitting here. Could you tell me something to do?"

"What's wrong with doing nothing?"

"Makes me sleepy. We were up at five, Danny and me."

"Red, not everybody earns his keep digging coal or washing dishes. What I want from you is to keep your eyes open. What do you see out there?"

"Lot of smoke, for one thing. More than I thought there'd be."

"Smoke? That all . . . ?"

"Oh . . . excitement?"

"Is that good?"

"It should be," said Capich.

"You're not your father's son at all, are you?"

"No, I don't think so. Except, you know, in the technical way."

"That guy was the royal nonesuch."

"So they say."

"I saw him lose his shirt more than once, and the very next night he'd be back downtown with a fresh haircut and a new stake. He was an education, that Juro. Never careful, never really broke. See him walk into a joint like this and you'd hear em start, 'Say, Juro, have a drink,' and

'Juro, dance with me,' and 'Juro, take me home.' It was quite something to see."

"Then you're right," said Capich, "that's not me."

"Man was nothing but a knockabout, but he took his cigarettes out of a monogrammed case. Gold inlay. What a rounder. You had to love the way he carried himself. I was as good a friend as he had in this world, and he didn't give a shit for me. Kind of set him apart, made you hungry for him."

"He never did me any good."

"Never did anybody any good, never regretted it. Glorious sonofabitch. That's what I'm talking about, Red. Why you think you gotta live in service to somebody?"

"I don't think I said that."

"No, but you sit here wringing your hands, and you're asking me, 'What can I do? What can I do?' If I want you to do something, I'll tell you. Meanwhile, relax." Mlinar contemplated something magnificent and beyond him. "You know how your old man died?"

"He got sick. Died like anybody else. Got sick and died."

"We were in Telluride. It was . . ."

"February," said Capich. "February, nineteen twenty-five."

"This was back in the days before I bought out John Luck's half of the Alhambra, back when I was free to go off now and again, and so I was on a runner, and who do I happen to run into but your father. In Sacramento, of all places. Then we're here, there, and everywhere for a while, and somewhere we got hooked up with Abraham Roulier, and the three of us hit Telluride, and we hear about a card game way the hell-and-gone up the side of a mountain. There's a couple engineers sitting in, and some other yahoo thinks poker is a science—money to be made. But for me and Abraham, after we're there five, six hours, it's cold up there, and after a while we say the hell with it. Juro, though, he's up. Cleans out them engineers, and then when they leave, he starts in on a couple guys just hit it big with a placer operation. And he's getting sick. No food, no sleep, living on whiskey and cigarettes. It was cold in that tent—longer you sat, the colder you got. Little campfire at the flap, more smoke than heat. But Juro's sitting on about sixteen thousand dollars. So they keep coming in, and he keeps skinning em, two and three at a time. He's a bulldog. The man can't let go. Getting sicker all the time. Day by day, me and Abraham, we're in and out, and we're telling him, 'Juro, why don't you quit while you're ahead?' And he says, 'Quit? Then what'll I do, put my feet up and pet the cat?' When his time came he didn't so much as sigh, just put his head down on the table. He was holding jacks, king high."

Mlinar was not the first to recall to him so reverently the legend of his father's life and death, but it was another lesson lost on Capich. In Juro's courtship of the big beyond had he given any thought at all to his wife or his son? Did he imagine that his Angelene would know even worse marriages when he was gone, that she would see more and uglier death? Did Juro see that day when his heirs went to have a few of their teeth pulled and saved a quarter each by skipping the anesthetic? No. For Juro Capich, there had been just this moment, and this moment, and this moment, hardly even in sequence, and never another time waiting beyond, never anyone's need but his own. Juro was a man so unencumbered he was nearly capable of flight, and men of his time often spoke as if surviving him had been a mistake, as if they'd missed their chance to use themselves in that incandescent way and avoid old age. But for Radé Capich, Juro was only the man in the train station, the man standing on a polished marble floor. His bright black shoes. The net bag of oranges he'd handed down as a parting gift. Juro was the man on the platform, the man on the train, his yellow glove lifted in good-bye. Juro was the train huffing out of the station and passing very shortly round a bend.

"We took him down the mountain strapped to a toboggan; and we could have stood him up in front of the Catholic church and called him the Virgin, he looked that good. White as marble. You should've seen the wake they had for him."

Lifting Danny that morning, Capich had ripped a muscle at the back of his shoulder; for a long while that night the persistent ache of it under his right arm kept him awake. Mlinar had told him to keep his eye on the band. He watched them without knowing why. The sign at the door said they were Derry Heath and His Orchestra, on Very Special Tour with the Hot Thrush, the Lovely Miss Inez Perry. Miss Perry, when she wasn't singing, sat to the side of the bandstand, a cigarette caught rakehell in her lips, her head cocked to keep its smoke from her eyes. Flounces erupted from her bodice. Her right foot kept impeccable time, and when she was summoned to sing, even if it was a selection that caused her to roll her eyes, she sang with conviction enough to carry an otherwise modest band. She meant to be fascinating and was, but she was not particularly the girl in the picture that went round with her publicity, the picture of her on the placard outside.

"Something's a little off, right? You see it yet, Red?"

"No, I don't believe I do."

"You see anybody spending money?"

"It's late."

"I like it late," said Mlinar. "I like it after midnight, that's when they spend like they mean it. Liquor—first, last, and always, that's where the money's at. They should be three deep at the bar right now. You watch the bar and the cash register, that's what keeps the operation healthy."

"Okay. But I was watching the band like you said I should."

"Them too. You watch everything. So what are they doing, you see it? The musicians."

Stardust, the clarinet was taking its choruses. Six couples survived on the floor, clinging to each other and the sad, slow, durable tune. An up-tempo set had taken them out beyond fatigue, and they were returning ennobled, still red of face and breathing hugely. They seemed very fine to Capich.

"Goddamn dancing," said Mlinar. "They don't spend a dime when they're on their feet, and when they sit down all they want to drink is water."

"Then why the band?"

"Because it's a nightclub. They expect to have a big time. But these musicians—why these guys think they have to play all this goddamn boogie-woogie is beyond me."

Stardust was borne away on a soft chord. Inez Perry said something to the bandleader that caused him to turn away from her, then turn back with a craven little grin. Capich had watched her lacerating the bandleader and the men of the band all night, and he'd wondered what she said that was so punishing. The boys were afraid of her.

"Why don't you run everybody out of here, Red? Might as well make it closing time if we can't do any better than this."

They seemed a little relieved when Capich told them it was time to leave. Dancers, drunks. A man in a Tom Mix Stetson wheeled by, a high-ball in either hand and headed for the door, likely to a car crash. The band played on, sustained by its artistic differences, until Capich was specially instructed to, "Shut them guys up, would you, Red? And bring that Heath over here."

A bandsman himself, a clarinetist at Lander High, Capich heard frayed harmonies as he approached Heath and company; they'd played badly for over three hours. "Mister."

Heath turned to him, not very curious.

"The boss says wrap it up."

"Your boss, kid." His band had gone from bad to worse during the last half hour, but he addressed them again as if they might be more than the sum of their parts. He purposefully lifted his baton.

"Mister."

"What?"

"Mr. Mlinar wants to talk to you. Said you're supposed to go over and see him." Capich, in his small, unfamiliar authority.

"Now . . . ? What kind of . . . where'd they dredge a thing like you up, kid?"

"Come on," said Capich, and he walked back to Mlinar's table, followed by Heath. Some of the band played on behind them, a diminishing march. The others were already draining the spit from their instruments.

"Mr. Mlinar," said the bandleader, "we sure do enjoy the crowd you draw here. Just a real lively crowd."

"My crowd ain't the problem. You are, Heat."

"That's Heath. Heeeath." He held his baton at the oblique, his lips pursed with satisfaction. "A musician," he said, "does live for Saturday nights."

"Musician? That what you are?"

"Yeah . . . I . . . yeah." Heath had not been offered a seat in Mlinar's booth and he hadn't taken one. He stood now with his little feet close together. Surprisingly small feet for a man of his size.

"Pack these guys up and get em out of here."

"Oh, sure. But we like to leave the drum kit up overnight. It's kind of a chore carrying those drums on and off the bus."

"You don't need to worry about tomorrow night."

"Well . . . Ah, we weren't that bad, buddy. What's wrong?"

"What's wrong? You better not dummy up on me, you asshole."

On the bandstand there was discomfort. Their leader's posture was abject and they saw it, knew it boded poorly. Heath regarding his small shoes.

"Go get me that guy's coronet case, the guy on the end. Don't open it. Just bring it on over here."

"That's his property," said Heath. "If you want him to show it to you, I'm sure he'll—"

"Red," Mlinar suggested.

"No. That's fine. Don't get the kid involved. I'll do it."

As Derry Heath made for him, the coronetist's swollen lower lip trembled, and he stood with his arms tight round his chest, finding nothing comfortable to look at. Others of the brass section became brittle or elaborately indifferent. "Now what?" said Inez Perry, audible from across the room. Heath returned to Mlinar with the case and set it before him. Mlinar tripped the nickel latches. From a velveteen bed he took the coronet; from an inner compartment he took rags, valve oil, and a handful of glassine squares that he let slide from his hand. "Why would anybody want my whiskey when they could have this?"

"No," said Heath, mortified. "I don't tolerate that. Never have. If I . . . no."

"You didn't notice that guy going back to the can every fifteen minutes? You didn't notice my bartender standing around half the night with his thumb up his ass cause nobody's wanting anything to drink? They're all hopped up and busted from buying this shit. We had a sheriff's deputy in here tonight, too, having dinner with his wife. So ain't that wonderful? You idiots trying to put me out of business? I tell you something else, this is my club. I run all the concessions in this joint."

"He just joined us," said Heath. "I'll get rid of him, get rid of that stuff. I've said it time and again, not in my band."

"Before I hired you, Heat, I got your schedule for the year. Remember when you sent that to me? So now, all I have to do is make a few telephone calls and you boys might as well sign on with the Salvation Army for all the work you'll have."

Heath had now forgotten confidence. "Gee, that shouldn't be necessary."

"You didn't know he was selling dope?"

"No, sir."

"You think it don't piss me off when you lie to my face this way?"

"I suspected him," Heath admitted.

"You what?"

"I'll get rid of it," said Heath. "I'll get rid of Tim, too. Should have weeks ago."

"I paid your advance, didn't I?"

"Yes, sir."

"Think I should pay you any more than that?"

"Well we can't very well get down to Salt Lake without something."

Patiently, Mlinar said, "Do you think I ought to pay you anything more than that advance?"

"No," said Heath. "No. We'll pack up and . . ."

"You can stay, if you want."

"You want us to work the week without pay?"

"What am I supposed to do, bring in Ratko Dukich, have him play his accordion for me?" Mlinar bit open one of the packets and bent it further open and touched his tongue to the powder inside. "This is piss-poor. This is harsh. You bring something like this into my place?"

Derry Heath rejoined the band and explained its new situation. Defeated musicians began to leave, singly and in pairs. The band, reduced to its component parts, was almost nothing. Capich pitied them their need for each other; he pitied them generally.

"Your musician," Mlinar told him, "is a hophead or a drunk."

"I never saw a thing. I missed it all night. Will this be trouble?"

"With the law? That Ferd Wise has been a cop of one kind or another for thirty years, and he never saw a crime he couldn't ignore. Wouldn't know cocaine if he brushed his teeth with it. But, even if he's Johnny-on-the-spot, who's he gonna go to? The County Attorney. Which I own. No, we're fine. This was just a little opportunity to reduce my overhead. So, you getting the picture, Red?"

"I guess not. You mean about the . . . ?"

"The big picture. Management. What you're supposed to be doing."

March 28, 1937

He was not sure that he could move, or that he wanted to move if it was to be in the old, leaden way. Savage had always been a miraculous sleeper, and so he was not much accustomed to the press of the night, the dark stuffed with implication. He closed his eyes, opened them, closed them again. This would not do. Only a moment earlier he'd been a cloud, adrift over any landscape he could call to mind, and now he was a citizen of the depression he made in his mattress. And it would not do.

— —

They rode out along the road of shattered slate that followed the dry bed of Lyons Creek. Cirrio had bummed a Lucky at the club and was ritually smoking it, exhaling elaborately through his nose. Idling in compound, the Buick bore them just a little faster than they might have walked. "That singer," said Cirrio, "puts out." He thrust his head out the window and howled. Coyotes cocked their heads for miles around and remained silent.

"That what she told you, Julie?"

"She told me and anybody with eyes to see, Red. She puts out."

"Yeah? Well, you're not supposed to be seeing her. Dishwasher's not supposed to be lolligagging out on the floor."

"Why not?"

"You stink. Stinky people are bad for business."

"I'll sprinkle a little baking soda on myself."

"And there's that moustache of yours. That shouldn't be seen in public."

"On your whole body, Red, you might have a little dab of hair grow-ing out of your ass, and you're giving me a hard time about my mous-tache, which is an actual moustache? You think she puts out?"

"I think it doesn't matter. Not to us."

"You're not the one she craves."

"You?"

"Me. Exactly."

"Well sure, she'd have to go for a guy like you. Penniless gypsy dishwasher. A kid who don't know shit from Shinola, who she could get arrested for."

"It's an animal thing, which you don't understand. You got all the instincts of a bowl of milk."

"I better get you home, Julie."

"Let's stay out all night. I'll get my .22, we'll jacklight a deer. Let's go up on the reservation."

"For what? I feel like I've been awake forever already. No, the day's caught up with me now." Capich turned back for Rainey. He brought the country up before him, pale and sterile in the cone of his headlights. They raised Rainey and then the Cirrios' place, and there was another forlorn light, a gauzy one at the parlor window.

"I think I'll just drop you off. That's a little house. I'd be imposing."

"Where else you gonna go? Why are you being an asshole? She waited up for us."

"All right, just for tonight." Capich would not give offense, couldn't afford to.

The Cirrio parlor was cluttered with chairs, as if they liked to entertain there with their many guests knee to knee. Agnes Cirrio was asleep in one of them with a chocolate cake in her lap. She had changed into her better dress.

"Mama, we're home."

Forcing the slack from her face, Agnes Cirrio got up to offer the cake to her boy. She saw his mangled lip and put a question to him in some secretive tongue—Magyar? The woman was a league of nations, but Capich knew what she wondered, what she must be asking her son. She would want to know who had hurt him so.

⟩ A Thought to Caresses ⟨

March 28, 1937

⟩ DOVE JOHNSON smoothed the flannel sheets, and she smoothed the counterpane. There was something of her warmth left in them, otherwise the room was cold. She pulled on her cold, stiff jeans, a cotton jersey, a wool shirt, and wool socks, and then she stopped to sit in the dark for a moment. Her left hand nested in her right. She thought of the dream she'd just had, a dream no longer novel or dear to her, but still curious, of dragonflies teasing the surface of a pond still as gelatin. What on earth could it mean? Why insects? It was five-fifteen. On the other side of the wall her folks were straining to hear those small sounds she would make when she left the house, waiting for her to establish the rhythm of their day. Dove laced her boots up and tied them off.

Outside, the barnyard had frozen again into ruts, and her footing was a little uncertain. The moon had long set, and the stars were innumerable, cold, and dry. Habit guided her through a scrubbed darkness. A Johnson never needed to wait for sunrise to navigate the home place. During the eighties and nineties, Dove's grandfather had thrown up all the buildings here using the nearest available jack pine, logs hauled by wagon from the mountains and small enough that a single man could lift them and spike them into courses. The house and its addition were turned to meet first light, the barn and a half dozen outbuildings ranged along a perimeter so that there were very few steps from one job to another, and the corrals in the center of the circle were protected from weather coming off any point of the compass. The old man had died shortly after her birth, but Cyrus Johnson remained present in the logic of his place. His ranch, the ranch Dove was born to work, was as perfectly and expressively made as a spider's web.

Just outside the barn she came upon the disfigured car that had been driven by that huge old man who'd come around to talk with her father about blasting the ice out from under their bridge. Mr. Savage. Cautiously she neared the windshield. The lid of the car's trunk was removed, as was its rear seat, and the whole resulting space was taken up with equipment and books. This she could see in its gloom. But no driver. No one in or near it. She'd never been close enough to catch the specifics of the old man's negotiations with her father, but she'd heard his tone, inflections strange even for a foreigner, and he'd made her edgy, even at a distance. The long, indifferent line of his back. And now his empty car.

Dove whistled, and her whistle brought Tammy the milch cow in from pasture, her heavy udder swaying rhythmically under her, her face blank as a wall. Dove shot the bolt to the barn door, and, followed by Tammy, she went in. She took a kerosene lamp down from its hook, set the wick, and lit it. She lowered the lamp's chimney. Tammy, wildly impatient for a cow, nudged her from behind. Dove lifted the lamp to spread its glow. There was in the barn some other presence, not an animal's. "Hello," she said. "Hello?" She walked the length of the main bay, the sole source of light. Shadows fell away from her.

In the last horse stall, she came upon a man lying blanketed in straw and a loose pile of his clothing. The old blaster, Savage. But no, he was not quite so big as that. A stranger then. A thief? When lamplight fell across him, the man twisted away, wretched and cold as a titmouse. Dove had swollen for a fight, there was a sour paste on the back of her tongue, but she saw at once that the man was no threat and that there would be no fight. Now she felt she wanted one. "You'd better let me see you," she said. "Let me get a look at your face, see if I know you."

The man rolled back toward her, squinting. It was only Red Capich. Red Capich from school, the outsized underclassman, the one who had seemed so alone up there above the others in the hall between classes. She recalled that she had enjoyed feeling sorry for him. "You just about scared the life out of me."

Straw clung to his hair. He worked his eyelids extravagantly. "What time is it?"

"What are you doing here?"

"Came to get paid." He sat up and gently cleared his throat.

"At this hour of the morning?"

"It's morning? Could've fooled me."

"You scared me."

"Well, I can't help that now. You're not still scared, are you?"

"No . . . but the point is, you did. Scare me. I come in here, don't have the slightest idea who you are. You're a mean tramp for all I know. So I was scared. I don't get my surprises . . . many surprises out here."

"I'm about as scary," he said, "as a well-kicked dog. Or a throw rug. Have to trip over me to get hurt."

Dove's jaw slid to the right. "Did you do something to Sadie? I should have heard her barking when you came in."

"No. Like I said, I came to get paid. You knew we blew the ice out of the river for Clate? Me and my grandfather."

"We heard the boom. So he's your grandfather. But that's only obvious, now that I know."

"I just got cold in the truck. That's all it was. I sure didn't mean to scare anybody. And if your dog would've seen me, she'd have barked. They always do." Capich stood and shrugged into his jacket. His arms were too long for its sleeves. The size and prominence of his wrist bones nudged Dove's heart. He'd completely departed his boyhood. "If you could have your dad send me ten dollars at the Alhambra. I work there. Danny took a rock out there, so I guess I'm collecting."

"He's hurt?"

"Knocked him cold as a wedge." Capich stuffed a satchel with the clothes he'd used to blanket himself. "Tell your dad we didn't charge him for the explosives. That was courtesy of the Little Popo Agie Coal Company."

"You mean it was out here? Doing work for us?"

"Yeah, blasting that ice."

"I'm so sorry," she said in her mother's Methodist manner.

"Why?"

"What do you mean, 'Why'?"

"You don't even know the man."

"Do I have to know him to be sorry for him?" In truth, what little she knew of the giant she did not like. It was, however, a parallel truth that she felt sorry for him. A pale sympathy, though, and maybe not worth mention. "Daddy says . . . look, he'll be up and having his coffee in a few minutes. Long as you've come all the way out here, why don't you stay and talk to him yourself?" Her voice had flattened and she could find no other tone. "While you're waiting you could give me a hand with my chores. If you wanted something to do."

As best she could tell, he was offended. He went to the door and was stalled there by its homemade latch. Dove followed him, came up behind, and put her hand in the small of his back. With her free hand she jerked at the mechanism. "You grab this shackle. That's how you get out of here."

Then he was gone.

She led Tammy into the milking parlor, locked her in a stanchion, and fed her an armload of grass hay. The cow's tail began to switch happily. Dove hooked her snapbrim on a peg, and found fault in it, a faithful hat. Foolishness. She stood in the middle of the parlor's floor, her arms hanging limp in the sleeves of her great, ugly coat, and she listened for the car to start outside. When had she begun to reckon the passage of her life in months? A month since she'd worn her dress or Daddy had taken a good bath. Christmas since Mommy last went to church. Dove's head rolled back until all she could see was the planked ceiling, and she had almost surrendered to some richly unpleasant feeling when she heard

the barn door open again. Red Capich hadn't, as she'd thought, managed to leave without her hearing him.

   Busy now, very busily, Dove straddled the milk stool, brushed dirt
and dung from Tammy's teats, secured the pail between her knees, and
started to draw milk so that it ripped like the push and pull of a saw. A
layer of froth grew thick in the pail. Without a word he had come into
the parlor to stand behind her. She could think of nothing to say. He
offered no opening. Finally, when the silence between them had become
absurd, she asked him, "How've you been?"

   "Fine. You?"

   "Pretty good." She was unhappy about how she'd spoken to him earlier and feared that in her confusion she'd do even worse. Dove milked
on until the silence was intolerable again. She squirted a jet of milk
onto Red Capich's right foot, but he only stepped back, and she thought
that if he was going to be impossible this way, without a word to say
for himself, that maybe she didn't like him too well after all. She was
only trying to be nice. "Your grandfather," she said, "seemed very sturdy.
I'm sure he'll be fine."

   "You think?" He'd taken her too much to heart. As if she knew.

   Dove pressed her forehead deeper into Tammy's flank. The cow
spasmed enormously, lifted her tail, and sent a thick arch of manure out
behind her. Oh what a gifted pair, the milch maid and her Jersey brindle.

   Red Capich took a pitchfork down from where it hung by a nail on
the wall. He slipped the tines under the dirtied straw and flung it out
the window. He forked new straw down where he'd bared the floor.

   "You like fresh milk, Red?"

   "Don't like any kind of milk."

   "Me neither. But I do like cream on my preserves. Mommy's got some
peach preserves. You like peaches?"

   "Everybody likes peaches."

   Dove had the young man hold cheesecloth over the mouth of a crock
while she poured the morning's milk through it. He was big enough

that contact was inevitable when she was anywhere near him. She smelled straw dust on him, cigar and cigarette smoke, and a lighter, more fundamental scent. No one of her senses received him simply. "Could you set that crock up on the window ledge, Red? We'll leave it there to cool. And put that board over top, please. Keep the kitties out." This would need time. She turned Tammy out of the barn and rinsed her pail in the trough just outside the door. Dawn was under way, the horizon shading pale yellow to pale gray. Coyly, Sadie appeared at the far side of the barnyard, excited but not sated with the night she'd just passed. Dove spoke her name, and the dog threw its head in an aimless circle and came to them on a hard run, slowing at the very last to prance up and shove her nose into Red Capich's crotch.

"Down, girl. Down."

A porcupine quill was caught in Sadie's forepaw, and it flailed with her every step. Capich got pliers from his grandfather's car for Dove to pull it. Sadie, for all her yelping, enjoyed the young man's soothing attentions. "Hush now, hush," and she began to follow him.

They might have gone in for breakfast then; instead, Dove set about other chores, chores that would have waited until later in the day. Capich seemed willing to follow her, safe in being with her so long as she was working. A small parade, a girl and her duties, her dog, and a boy with nothing better to do. She fed the chickens, fed and watered the yearling bulls. They carried rolled oats in eighty-pound sacks up the barn stairs into the loft, Sadie ever underfoot. Dove had Capich hitch the hay-wagon behind the tractor, and they went out to the lower forty to feed cows that had recently calved there. Sadie darted among the calves, provoking their mothers to charge her. Capich forked hay off the wagon.

"Spread it out, Red. Spread it out more. Don't dump it such big piles, they'll just trample it that way. That's good alfalfa we're feeding." Spring again this morning. Dove was ready to believe the season was at last established. She thought of things left undone. When they came in from the field, she went to the toolshed and got the Johnsons' biggest claw hammer and had Capich carry out a cask of spikes. A week earlier her father and his two-year-old colt had burst through a section of pole corral. It fell to Dove, of course, to mend it. A stack of lodgepole lay on the ground near the breach. She lifted a pole to her shoulder and set it against a post. She placed a spike. "Drive it."

"What if I miss? I'd take your hand off with this thing."

"Don't miss," she told him.

When he'd seated the spike and she took her hand away, he swung big to impress her, and shortly he'd buried it. He stripped his jacket off. "It'll go faster if you just let me hold these up myself. That spooks me with your hand there."

"It's my job," she said, "the least I can do is help."

"You've got enough jobs, taking a break wouldn't kill you. Just stand off a ways, okay? The head of this hammer needs another wedge in it. See, it's loose."

He knew the use of tools, and it was nice, she thought, that he wanted to demonstrate it for her. In some things he didn't need much direction.

"If you scoop a hollow out of these poles with a draw knife, right where they meet the post, makes for a better seat. They'll fit together tighter. That's how Danny taught me to do it."

"What's a draw knife?"

His hands grasped invisible handles, and he moved them as if he were rowing a tiny boat. "A tool," he said, "for shaving wood."

She thought of thin chips curling away from a post, of the piney smell from long, bright wounds; his forearms would tense and tense, pulling the blade. "Sorry," she said. "Didn't mean to turn you into a hired hand."

Capich started another spike.

"You'll graduate next year," she said.

"Maybe."

"Grades?"

His hammer echoed violently. "No. I'm on the honor roll and all. Wouldn't be grades, but . . ."

"I didn't think so," she said. "You look smart enough to me. I liked school, myself."

"I don't mind it,"—he flailed at the nail head—"at all."

"I would've stayed in longer," she said, "if they'd let me. Not that I was the belle of the ball, but I liked the things they had you doing there. You could say I was the queen of geometry."

"Sure. You were valedictorian."

"You remember that?"

"I was in the band. We played *The Great Gate of Kiev.* You gave a speech."

"Boy," she recalled, "that was terrible. Felt like I was up there naked and not very pretty."

"Not a bad speech, though."

"'Now we go forward,'" Dove recited, "'into the greater world. Now our education truly begins.' Oh, that was a doozey. I've been to Cheyenne to sell our cows. That's about as far forward as I've made it. The greater world—man oh man."

"You weren't a bad basketball player, either."

"Not bad. What about you? I'd think they'd fall all over themselves to get a big galoot like you on the boys' team."

"I foul out."

"Oh? You don't look all that mean to me."

"Not mean—clumsy. So, where've you been? Since school? You keep pretty scarce."

"Here," she said. "Right here."

"You should get out more."

"For anybody looking, I wouldn't be all that hard to find."

As if she were timing him at it, Capich spiked another pole. He raised a constant clatter with his materials. Dove raised her voice to be heard over it. "Have you had any field trips, Red? That was my favorite. We went to Laramie once with Mr. Blackburn and saw the museum, saw the mummy they had there for a while. I still think about that quite a bit, kind of dote on it. You ever think about getting off somewhere differ-ent, somewhere where it's brand new to you?"

"You should try going to the pictures once in a while. You ever get to the show house?"

Funny he should ask. The Riverton Rialto. Her greasy fingers. The backs of heads in silhouette, leaning at each other; the whispering all around, none of it directed to Dove Johnson. "I used to," she said. "But I'm not so big on all these dancing pictures they do nowadays. I like a three-hanky romance."

When the corral was fixed, Dove felt that she could not in good con-science ask Red Capich to do anything more for her, especially as she was almost certain he would do whatever she asked. They returned the hammer and the cask to the tool room. There was in an adjacent shed a granary, and Dove led him into it, though she'd intended on taking him to the house to see her father. Sadie came in behind them. "Scat, girl. Scat."

Slabs of yellow light were let in through long gaps in the wall, light filled with yeasty, swirling dust. Dove sat in a bin of barley. She lay back in it. The grain made its own warmth. "My quiet place," she said. "You want to close that door?"

He looked around him as if to admire it all. Poor boy. What could he say?

"You have a quiet place, Red?"

"I guess, but I don't know where it would be."

"I come here to think," she said. "Sometimes I just . . . No. That's not really true. I don't go here or anywhere else to think. Maybe I should, though. See, I'm trying to make myself sound more interesting." Her eyes adjusted to the limited light. He had definition enough, one leg cocked, the other bearing his weight. She could see him well enough without windows.

"I remember you," he said. "You were somebody I'd remember."

"I was somebody? When was that?"

"You know what I mean. Kind of makes me blue, the way you talk. It's not that hard for a good-looking woman to go places, if that's what she wants."

"I'm not going anywhere, Red."

"I could see you on the streets of Paris."

"You had to think a long time to say something as nice as that."

"No, I just featured it. You, in a little different duds, strolling the boulevards."

"By myself?"

"If you're alone in Paris, it's only because you want to be."

"The way I see it," she said, "someone's waiting for me. I'm on my way to meet them."

"That's what it looks like to me. But you're in no hurry. In Paris, I think, you gotta stroll."

"I wouldn't be dawdling." She pushed up out of the barley bin and put her hand on his shoulder, not the top but the fleshy part, off to the side. A tiny shrillness had been inserted into her breathing, a little whistling in her throat.

— —

Once while serving a detention in the high school library, the most pleasant room he knew, Capich had spent the whole hour watching the student librarian. As a freshman he'd been invisible, a circumstance he could sometimes exploit. Dove Johnson was at the long desk at the front of the room, distracted and entirely available to his inspection, her chin at rest on her fist and her hair draped over her wrist, heavy and smooth as melting wax. Her eyes moved over the pages, and the progress of the book played on her face. A big, closely printed book, she brought to it an attention for which he was grateful, though it had nothing at all to do with him. There was a small piece of raw jade suspended in the cleft of her throat. The nap of her sweater caught and held light to her. She wore this same white sweater to school every day, the same pair of sensible shoes. She was fresh as recent rain. He'd wanted to touch her. In that moment, and every time after that when he happened to see or think about the Johnson girl, he'd wanted to touch her. Now she had touched him, and it had been a rout. All he could think to do was let her hand linger there, and it did, and it did, until there was that small, quick squeeze, her regrets.

She followed him out to the car, and he thanked her for the use of the barn. She thanked him for his work. After he'd driven away he realized he hadn't gotten paid, that he hadn't said good-bye or anything like it. He was a lad to whom even the tang of the morning air was on loan, and she'd taken him by surprise. A girl like Dove Johnson, he'd have thought, would set her sights a good deal higher than Red Capich.

Sunday morning. At Little Popo Agie Number One the hoist machinery was still, and the camp's several children had fled into the coulees to avoid their fathers' hangovers. From a long way off, Capich was able to clearly hear the *Tužba*, the woman ululating like a mountain Turk. She would be keening over his grandfather. The useful Mrs. Obradovich had once cased him in a wild mustard plaster to cure him of whooping cough. In some earlier spring she had shaved the hip bone of a lamb and read from the scraped surface the quality of his future, "Ah, Radé, you gonna get along in this world, but never too happy about it." Inevitable here, the *Tužba*. At every death she must have her black lace shawl, her silver dollar, and for this she would announce the family's bereavement. She must come and wail so that the dying one would know that the pain of death was not his alone to bear. She was the very face of that loud ignorance he'd intended to leave here. Capich went into his grandmother's house without knocking. The *Tužba* was rocking on her haunches just outside the door of Danny's room. Veins welled on a neck engorged with blood and air. Through her lamentations she offered him that same hopeful smile she wore as a midwife to live births. The house reeked of *litzky reba*. He went into the kitchen where his grandmother was boiling dried cod in olive oil and garlic. The broth smoked where it fell on her stovetop. "*Babina,*" he said to her back. She was butchering tomorrow's supper already, making cutlets with a cleaver. "Stoja," he said.

Her blade barked, parting meat and bone. An arm still like a piston. "You forget something?"

"You should get her out of here. Mrs. Obradovich, she's gotta go. Please."

"What?"

"The last thing he needs is that noise. He's not . . . is he?"

"Not yet." His grandmother had taken up a boning knife. "It only comes, and I wait."

"That's no way to be," said Capich.

"Who are you? Who are you to tell me how I got to be?"

"Do I have to take him with me?"

"Leave."

"I'm taking him with me if you don't do something about that. Send her home."

"Good. And who do you think will have him if it wasn't me? I tell you—nobody. Nobody."

"I could lay him out for the vultures, and he wouldn't be worse off than he is here. You know he wouldn't put up with that racket for a second if he was awake."

"Put up with, put up with . . . my house is such a bad place now? You stayed here a long time if you didn't like it that good. Take him if you want him. Save me a lot of trouble. You keep him clean. You move him around so he don't get the sores."

"Ah, now what would I do with him? I've got no place to keep him. Just get rid of her, would you?"

"No. You leave. Leave like I told you before. Two good-for-nothings.

Take him. That's the first smart idea you ever had. But when you get tired of him, don't try and bring him back. When he dies, you don't bring him back either, make a big fuss. Now he's all yours. Did I want you in the first place, any of you assholes?" Stoja's fists were tightly closed, she held them against her ribs. It was a woman's world, Capich thought, and he gave up on understanding it. Out in the parlor the *Tuźba* crawled up and down a minor scale over and over, her voice like salt in a cut.

Capich found his grandfather closely shaved and smelling of soap. Not a nick of the razor. Stoja was more careful of him than he'd ever been of himself, and yet Capich could see no choice but to deprive the old man of her excellent care. Gathering himself for another big lift, he thought of something less strenuous. "Danny. Danny? Hey."

The old man's eyes opened. Innocence had been restored to them, and if he saw his grandson's face there before him it was nothing he chose to bring into focus. "Hydrogen," he said.

"Hey," said Capich witlessly.

"Do you know what the Japanese will soon be doing with hydrogen?"

"No, I don't. You think you can walk? You want to get out of here?"

"Walk?" The old man swung his legs off the bed, pressed his feet firmly to the floor, and stood. He looked around him gravely. "Walk, waltz, whatever is necessary. As usual. Which is not to say I am satisfied." They went out into the parlor where the *Tuźba* stroked her bristled chin, contriving perhaps to take credit for the patient's rising. The loss of her voice was restful. Danny looked down at her. "That," he told her, "will be the fire brigade. Hoffman's underwriter is following close behind, and tonight they'll smother us in blintzes and knockwurst and beer. What good are your ethereal pastries now?" He turned on his heel and strode out to the Buick and was rummaging through the glove box when his senses failed him again. Capich came out to him just as he collapsed in the seat. He pushed him up so that he could slip in behind the wheel; the old man settled back onto his shoulder at once, pinning his arm and making it difficult to steer with any accuracy. But it was a fond and final farewell to Little Popo Agie Number One. Capich was never coming back. That, for now, was the full extent of his plan.

Capich returned to Dr. McChesney's door and announced himself and happened to see the man's shadow retreating through the house. Too humiliated to press the matter, he drove to the club and parked in front of it. Why? Julie would be there, swamping this morning, Mlinar doing the books, but they'd be of no use to him in this. He noticed a spool of cloth surveyor's tape in the back of the car and used it to re-bind his grandfather to sit more upright in his seat. "We can't keep on just driving around, Danny. What am I supposed to do with you? Wake up . . . snap to, okay?"

The old man's eyes opened a slit, reluctantly, and his head came by several small stages off of the seatback. While he was surprised to find himself bound there, surprise was not the first thing on his mind. "*Cujus et solum*," he droned.

"Aw, what is it now? What is it?"

"A formula from the common law: The American is the man who owns his little acre absolutely. Never doubt it, it is good to be here."

"So you're . . . ?"

The old man wobbled and fell back into a contentment Capich did not like. Danny Savage was, properly, a restlessness, and to see him otherwise was a sour thing, a glimpse of that gaping indifference also awaiting Red Capich. Until now, Capich had vaguely thought himself immortal.

In a gully near the Indian mines he had cached his savings, a finite pair of sawbucks faintly fluttering within the Prince Albert tin he retrieved from the scree. It was all Capich could bring to the party. The old man's assets had largely fallen victim to the depression and his withering indifference. He'd parceled off or spent his holdings until he owned just the contents of the Buick; Danny had claimed to prefer it, his latter poverty. So now, with Red's twenty, they were just well enough provi-

sioned to throw themselves on the mercy of strangers. Capich drove
them back through town and took the turning to the Johnsons'. He
went down a mile-long lane with its fence posts dressed occasionally in
boots worn heel-up. To struggle even a little successfully on such land
seemed to Capich a noble thing. Square miles of alkali and hardpan bore
their name; the Johnsons and their kind were the lairds of Wyoming.

Clate Johnson stood in his cuffed jeans in the middle of his barnyard,
devotedly smoking a hand-rolled cigarette. The arrival of the Buick
disturbed his pleasure very little. Capich pulled up to him and rolled his
window down. The man pushed up at the brim of his hat and bent to
look in. "He still laid up, is he?"

"Not as bad as it looks like."

"Dove told us he'd took a knock in the head."

"Yeah."

"He'll be all right."

"Yeah."

"Why you still haulin him around? Probly ain't the best thing you
could do for him."

"It's just worked out like this."

Dove and her mother stepped out of the house and came to them,
both women bent a little forward from the waist. Mrs. Johnson wore the
same chignon and ruffled apron as that doughty matron stamped on
sacks of Burnham's Best Flour. The two of them came and stood on either side of Clate and also bowed and looked in. A gallery now of those
pellucid eyes. A weathered family, looking in.

"Red?" Dove asked.

"How are you?"

"I'm fine. But . . ."

"I guess you were needing paid," said Clate.

"What are you doing with that poor man?" Mrs. Johnson wondered.

"You boys got to that bridge a little late," said Clate. "I went out and
had a look at it. Think I'll have to rebuild er anyway."

"We came when you told us. The ice was gone when we left. Most of it."

"Red?" Dove repeated.

"I never said I wouldn't pay you, son."

"I thought you might let us put up in your barn for a while. Instead of our pay."

"That might be all right." Clate Johnson held his cigarette cupped so that the cherry burned just a little off his palm and smoke welled out of his half closed fist.

"No," said Mrs. Johnson. She went around to the passenger's side of the car and opened the door and touched Danny's brow. Her daughter joined her, also reaching in, their fingers gently deployed on the birthplace of ten thousand offensive thoughts. Mute, the old man was unable to destroy their sympathy for him. "He needs a bed," said Mrs. Johnson, "maybe even the hospital."

"Yeah. I can see that. But you should hear him on the subject of hospitals sometime. If he woke up in a hospital, I don't even like to think how that might go. He's got quite a thing about bacteria."

"He looks like he's been well tended," said Mrs. Johnson. "Was that your doing?"

"No, not before. But it is now." This had been his only idea and it wasn't working. Capich steeled himself to slink off at the first request, waiting for any one of the Johnsons to come to their senses and send them away. An expression, possibly of gratitude, had claimed Danny's face. From his own family there had not been so much as a thought to caresses, and now the Johnson women, for all their country reserve, hovered as if they'd been awaiting such an arrival, such a need. "I can't," said Capich, "take him back. I think he'll come around soon, but in the meantime . . . I don't know what in the meantime. Gotta do something with him. Something kind of cheap."

Mrs. Johnson reached in to take up Danny Savage's right hand. She spread it and read it like a bill of fare.

"I think," said Clate, "you'd weather nicer in the pump house than the barn. We can let you use a couple of roundup cots and you'll be snug as ticks in a moustache."

Mrs. Johnson glanced sidelong at her husband.

"He seems to be coming around," Capich said. "He's been talking."

"Oh hell," said Clate. "Savage here, he's the biggest piece of gristle ever come down the pike. If he ain't up and at em in a day or two, I'll be just flabbergasted. I ever tell you, Mother, that story about me and Hoot Myers and old Savage. We was kids, Hoot and me, and we'd been at some foolishness that was boring us, Fourth of July picnic I think it was. Snuck off and wound up out by the railroad tracks. Hoot found a spike and set it up on the rail. The idea was the train outta Casper was gonna run over it and mash it or spit it out. But along comes Savage on this little handcar he's made himself. He's pumpin away and whizzin right along, and he hits that spike and just flies up off them rails. Him and that handcar both go sailin, lit in the rocks about thirty feet down the track. We seen that and hightailed it. Seen that, and I'll bet our eyes looked like baseballs. Hoot, you know, he's about half jackrabbit. Was in them days. Big deal. Savage run us both right down. Big as he was, he run us both right down. And we figure we're in for it. He's got us, one in either hand, and I'm about to piss down my leg, forgive my French. He's got me by the scruff of the neck, and my feet are plumb up off the ground, and that's when he starts in on velocity and, what was it? . . . inertia, and all that. I was never so happy to hear a lecture in my whole life. Nah, Danny, he's a rough old cob. If he ain't killed, he'll be up and chipper any time now. Shoulda seen him bounce up off that track and come runnin. That was a thrill."

Mrs. Johnson had taken her daughter's arm. "You know," she said, "I can see Dove getting hooked up in this; it's like her to try and help. And she has plenty to do already."

"I don't want to take advantage of anybody, ma'am," Capich avowed.

"Nobody," said Dove, "is trying to take advantage of anybody."

➤ Flesh Wounds ➤

March 29, 1937

➤ CAPICH COULDN'T SLEEP or find any reason to rise. Daylight leaked into the pump house and slowly revealed the old man across from him to be supine on his cot, less than conscious. In remembrance of some tool or agony his right hand clutched and released constantly at his side, all independent of the rest of him, which was still. To the gloom and their unmoored waiting he offered, ". . . to free *all* men from the bonds of earth . . . ," but no more. Capich lay numbly beside him, unable to detect in himself any grief or even very much sympathy for the man who had been so recently and for so long his principal benefactor, the overlord of his thoughts. What a dull watch it was, waiting, and Capich wanted any relief from it, but when at last Dove Johnson came and spoke his name at the door, he thought at first he would not answer her.

"Red?"

"Just a minute, I'll be right out." He did not want the girl to see, or smell, or guess at their situation in the pump house. It reflected so poorly on his good sense, on his luck.

"Red?"

"Just a second."

"Is he drinking? Are you getting any water in him?"

"I just about drowned him."

"Yeah, but . . . it's going okay in there?"

"Fine," said Capich.

"Are you decent? I'm coming in."

She appeared first in silhouette, framed in the door with the low sun at her back. The shape of her, all in proportion. She came in with a tin pitcher and some rags and sat with Capich on his cot. "You don't have the foggiest notion, do you?"

"Not as much as I'd like. You think he's going downhill, or what? I can't tell."

In movements slow and exaggerated she twisted the end of a rag and dipped it into the pitcher and held the wetted fabric to the old man's mouth and squeezed. "Do it like this. You know this is something you can't just make up as you go along, how to take care of him." Under the fabric tit Danny's lips worked in obscene appreciation.

"I thought he'd be all right by now."

"You've got to ask for help," she said, "if you need it. Which you do."

"Well, that's just the thing, I need it so much. Talk about a helpless mutt. I told your mother I wouldn't do this . . . have you do this. See that? His hand has been doing that, just steady squirming like that, I don't know what causes it."

"Me neither. But, how are you doing, Red? You all right in here?"

"Fine."

"Really? We better clean that window off a little so you can see what's what. It's not very warm, is it?"

"I was thinking I might build a little fire. Outside. To cook on. Think that'd be okay?"

"What were you going to cook?"

"No, I mean when I get something. When I got something, I'd cook it."

"When do you think that might be?"

"Today," he said. "We don't have much household stuff. But we got a frying pan, and I'll buy us a coffee pot. I draw my pay on Mondays, so that'll help."

"Is this all the blankets you've got? I thought Mommy was bringing you some more blankets."

"It wasn't too bad."

"Do you want to be miserable, Red, or what is it? I'm sure he doesn't. One blanket's not enough for guys like you. He's hanging out all over the place; that can't be too warm. A couple blankets is not much to ask."

"All right."

"And you don't need to worry."

"I don't?"

"You'd better figure on eating with us. I can just see you out here with a fire and a frying pan, I can just imagine the results you'd get from that."

"That's too much. Then you'd be taking care of us, and that's not what I had in mind."

"What did you have in mind?"

He said nothing.

"Listen, you'll be all right here."

⟶　⟵

From her room Inez Perry saw the tree, a cottonwood standing out in the featureless prairie between herself and the Arctic Circle. The desk clerk had told her to look for it. What was the story? A mail plane pilot, flying around in all that empty sky, sap ran into it and killed himself. Of course.

Inez was at the window to mend her stockings with M'Lady's Little Loom, a Bakelite gizmo for fixing rayon. The trick was to gather rips and runs, slip them in under the hot element, and clamp everything together while it was still aligned. The stocking fused and puckered, a caustic smoke gave off, and the repair was made. She often melted her material entirely. Inez had ruined more garments with this process than she'd ever saved. Rayon. Inez Perry—appearing nightly in rayon.

When she was on the road, especially when she was so very far on the road, a night off tended to make her heartsick. Inez had spent much of the previous day bathing, had bathed again this morning, and still she felt unclean. The hotel's fresh linens and towels were, apparently, for a better class of guests. She started a note about it to the management but decided instead to strip her bedding and throw it into the hall for the maid. Working around a smoking Old Gold, she brightened her lips. She smoothed on a little foundation, a little rouge, and went down to the lobby where the drummer known to her as Jackson was boring the desk clerk, his hands flailing over an imaginary trap set. The stickless percussionist. "Gee," she said, "you just lug bricks, don't you? Why can't you ever stay at one tempo for a measure or two? And quit that god-damned humming. If you can't do it right, just don't do it." Jackson stopped at once and found himself a newspaper.

"I saw your gruesome tree," Inez told the clerk. "What a landmark."

A deeply agreeable fellow, the clerk stood there almost invisibly.

"I believe," she said, "Mr. Heath has a phone in his room. Could you ring him for me?"

"He said no calls till ten."

"That's all right. Ring him up, would you?"

"Say it's you calling?"

"You're making this too complicated, buddy. Just hand me the receiver and plug me into his room."

"You've got some wires came in this morning," said the desk clerk.

"Just a second, I'll . . . . Derry? . . . Put your teeth in so I can understand you . . . I'm down in the lobby. No. You come down . . . we've got to get things a little better in hand . . . not just to complain, either, we're gonna do something. We've got to . . . Just throw a little polish on your shoes, and we'll . . . yeah. I'm right here at the desk, you can't miss me and you can't avoid me so you might as well just . . . yeah, come on down."

While she waited, Inez read her wires. The first of them was from her mother.

DADDY SICK AGAIN STOP THINK THIS IS IT.

What they wanted now, Daddy and Mommy, was money enough to

consult doctors until they found one who understood Daddy's latest peril, and then there'd be sugar pills, three dollars the bottle, or a water cure, or a prescription for codeine, and then the crisis would continue in some slightly new vein with or without Inez's contribution. Daddy had been sick since he'd quit the post office. He'd outlive the Rockies.

From the offices of Huarte and Nathan, talent agents, she learned,

NO IN NEW JERSEY STOP NO IN PA STOP CARNAHAN
SAYS NO STOP TRIED.

Inez scribbled replies on Western Telegraph forms. To her mother she wired,

PATIENCE.

Her message for Teddy Nathan was,

BAD BUS BAD BAND THREE HUNDRED MILES BETWEEN
GIGS STOP GET ME EAST COAST WEST COAST GULF
COAST ANYTHING POPULATED PLEASE.

She would have preferred to phone the agent and tell him in detail and volume how she was not the blossom for the great American desert, but she couldn't afford the long-distance charges. Out where the doggies, or whatever they called themselves, were howling. Inez preferred to be the only one doing any howling.

Heath came to her fresh from his Lutheran ablutions. He'd sunk his face in cold water to make it shine, and had a big red smile for her. The wholesome greasy, Heath.

"One thing I don't like, sport, is cooling my heels. We've got some things to get cleared up this morning. Business end."

"Every morning, Inez." Heath, from the set of his shoulders, thought he carried the burden heroically.

"Look, I sing for nothing, Derry, I sing for the pleasure of it, but when I haul my ass out to Bumfuck, Wyoming, for that I need to get paid a little something. This no-pay thing, I don't like it. Where does this guy get off?"

"He's got us over a barrel, honey. For now. Why don't I take you out to breakfast? You like some flapjacks, slab of ham?"

"Now, how do you go that, buy me breakfast? Where do you come by the scratch to do something like that when we're not even getting paid?"

"It's the Norwegian in me," said Heath. "Scandahoovian. I generally have a little something in reserve. Guess that's why I run the outfit."

"Sure. Look what you ran it into. You ran it into this phoney deal. Don't even try and think up some plan for this hunky, this Mlinar. Only thing we can do now is go back and tell him in no uncertain terms, 'no-goddamn-way.' If you don't tell him, I will. But if that's my job now, then I'm the bandleader, and you can sit down and play your little trombone. Third chair, Derry. If you aren't the boss, you're about third chair trombone."

With just the two of them on the bus it was capable of a reasonable speed. They made a steady sixty. Inez rode at the back of the coach on the resonant bench over the engine, and in the ten rutted miles from the hotel to the club they encountered no other traveler. She'd dine out on this story, tell it for laughs, how our plucky gal played a ghost town, and even there they'd tried to stiff her. For now, though, she was awfully serious, and had been ever since she'd been dropped into a country that looked to her like a desiccated crust of bread. There was something very serious about this place. Heath rolled up in front of the bohunk's club, a vast, liverish lump of a structure, and he killed the motor. They stepped off the bus. Mud, and dust, a little crabgrass, and an aggressive, smothering quiet. Not a bird to be heard, not the winding sigh of a distant motorist, nothing. Inez had never been more lost in her haphazard life.

The door of the club yielded to Heath's small tug at it, and they heard from within, "Heat, what brings you . . . ? Come to get some rehearsal?

Not a bad . . . what's it, just you two? Where's your jukes and your kallikaks? "

"Mr. Mlinar?" Derry Heath's voice rolled over like a dog presenting its belly. He'd be going nowhere with this.

"Hit that switch to your right," said Mlinar.

The houselights came up over a half acre of empty floor and vacant furniture and the bar and the bandstand. A dim, sepia light. Mlinar sat with his back to the bar, his elbows on its cushioned edge, and Inez saw as they crossed the floor to him that he found them cute, a minute's entertainment.

"We wanted," said Heath, "to come out and maybe clear up that conversation we were having last night. Beavers, that guy we were having the problem with, he's gone. We wanted to thank you for pointing that out to me, what he was doing."

"What was it you didn't understand?"

"You said something about . . . I think you wanted to adjust our pay . . . what were the details on that?"

"I said you'd have to settle for your advance. Your rooms are bought and paid for."

"But, that can't be right. We can't . . . we'd have to . . . that's wrong, Mr. Mlinar."

"I wouldn't think you'd like it," said Mlinar, "but that's what it is."

Inez had been grinding her teeth. She could taste them. "Not," she said, "by a long shot, mister." She'd have slapped a less forbidding man. "Whattaya think this is, a hobby with us? Sometimes you pay us, sometimes you don't, depending on how you feel about it at the moment? No, baby, you're gonna pay. We're gonna play, and you're gonna pay us. That was our arrangement, and it still goes."

"But what about the dope peddler you brought in my place? I'm stuck with this evidence; I'm a criminal now, just sitting on it."

"Oh no," said Inez. "No you don't. That was not us. That was one guy, and like Mr. Heath told you, he's gone. Small loss. He can pay for his mistakes, and I'll pay for mine. But so far I haven't made any, not where you're concerned."

"And the evidence? What did you want me to do about that?" The bohunk's small, bleak smile became almost genuine. "What's with the dungarees, honey? They have you greasing the bus this morning?"

"Evidence? Evidence? We don't care about that. You can do whatever you want with it. Wasn't my dope. Turn him in. Turn it in. You can be citizen of the month if you need to. Long as you remember, I work for pay."

"Inez, why don't we try and be a little more—"

"Shut up, Derry."

"But what if," said Mlinar, "what if I had to turn it in? Then they'd run down what's-his-name and arrest him, and an hour later they'd serve everybody in your outfit with a subpoena. What do you think you'd do then? The county don't put you up while you wait to testify, which could be a longish old time. All I'm trying to do is spare you some inconvenience. I'm taking care of the problem you brought me."

"Blackmail," said Inez.

"If you ever get sick of this crowd, honey, I'm sure I could always find something for you to do."

"Sure. If there's not a ditch to be dug somewhere. How do you live with yourself, sport?"

"Oh, pretty easy," he said. "Hungry? I think I could find us some cold cuts back there."

— —

When old Savage snorted and sat up like a sprung trap, Dove fumbled her embroidery. She thought at first that he was looking through her. But he was not. "You should be careful, Mr. Savage. You might be kind of woozy yet."

"Miss Johnson, isn't it?" The old man's long forearms lay across his knees, and his hands hung from them like birds of prey.

"Yes."

"And your father called you Dove."

"Yes."

"I see. Where are we?"

"This is our pump house. You were hurt. You got hurt up at the bridge."

"My grandson was with me. Do you know what became of him?"

"He's fine. He brought you here."

"And left me here it seems. I assume he's taken the Roadmaster."

"Your car? Yes. He had to go to work."

"He might have taken me home at least."

"He did. He took you there first, but there was some trouble."

"Trouble?"

"I think I should let Red explain about that. He's stayed right here and looked after you, but he had to go to work. It's Monday, Mr. Savage. Well into Monday. You've been out a long time."

"But Radé wasn't harmed. The trouble you mention, I suppose that had to do with my wife."

"He's all right. The rest of it, I don't understand too well. He's fine, but I think I'd better let Red tell you about all the . . . other. Does your head hurt?"

"My sinuses are engorged with phlegm."

"You were hit in the head," she said. "Are you hungry?"

"I will be soon enough."

"Red's been right here with you the whole time. Watching over you and . . . I talked the poor boy's ear off."

The old man lay back again. He smelled slightly of turpentine or pitch. "Has your father anything to drink, anything in the way of spirits?"

"He keeps a bottle in the toolshed. It has a name I forget. Hoge-booms?"

"Would you drink with me?"

"I'll sit with you," she said. "I was anyway."

Nick Brkvich could not tie a reasonable Windsor knot without the protracted use of a mirror, and so dressing for a night on the town was always a little cruel for him. At twenty-five he'd been half his life a coal miner and was the sum of the injury done to him in his work, a hammer of a man. His hair was as short and coarse as the fuzz on a knuckle, his arms bowed and powerful as an ape's. He'd scraped the grit from his hands with pumice and a jackknife, and he'd brought his Florsheims to a high gloss, but now there was the matter of this tie and the flat, crude face just above it, and with his tongue budding from between his lips he wondered why. Why bother?

Brkvich spritzed a cloud of mail-order cologne, stepped through it and out into the company street; two doors down he passed the empty shack where he'd lived as a boy, a duplicate of the one where he lived as a man. Brkvich had never really learned to read, he'd long since traded his radio for a rifle, and his world was only that small place he'd seen with his own hooded eyes; he'd seen it all so much that everything in it was as common to him as lint. He climbed up out of the coulee and passed the crowded plot where his mother and father and two infant brothers lay beneath a single wooden cross that he'd been intending these two years to whitewash. Since Mama died. She could wait. They could all wait. He passed his days, after all, in a grave deeper than theirs.

He went on as fast as he could, but the miner's great strength did not translate to speed. There was in his gait a torturous lifting and throwing of the torso at each step, and it cost Brkvich a difficult half hour to walk the two miles to the Alhambra. He went straight to the bar, unhappy. "Jimmy, what the hell are you people doing with this place? I saw one car in the parking lot that didn't belong to the help. That Mlinar, he's running everybody off with the way he acts, the shit he says to people."

Jimmy Svilar had served the sullen for thirty years. He had the face and patience of a cigar-store Indian. "Shot and a beer, Nick, or you want a water back?"

"Beer. Where is everybody?"

"I don't know. It's Monday. Mondays can be quiet."

The Alhambra was the miner's church and his far horizon, and he came to move gratefully at the edge of a crowd; faces-in-a-crowd, the only certain pleasure his meager soul could devise. Brkvich felt he was owed at least that much. "What's with Capich? That guy's an eyesore. Sits there at the owner's table in his tee shirt and nobody says a thing to him. Is that right?"

"Eli got his walking papers," Svilar said, "and Red's the bouncer now. So the poor guy gets his little raise but has to sit and listen to the world according to Mlinar, which does get old in a hurry."

"Ah, that's crazy. Put that kid in . . . see? See what I mean? That's how he screws it up. Drags a kid like that out here—big, ugly, mealymouthed kid. Capich? In his tee shirt and tennis shoes? Like he was going out to play baseball? Now that makes quite an attraction for the place, don't it? Ugly fucker."

"I wonder why they ever do come," said Svilar, "I wonder every night. Would you? Come way out here if you weren't already here in the first place?"

"I'm here tonight," said Brkvich, "and I feel like I'm the only boob with nothing better to do."

"But for you it's just the corner bar, and a man's corner bar should be quiet."

"Bullshit. What's the deal with that band? They ever play or is all they do is just sit there and squabble with each other? Hit me again, Jimmy. Long as I'm here, I'm gonna have a few."

Brkvich took his glass to a tiny circular table just at the foot of the bandstand, and there he drank. Though he was not very hungry he ordered a porterhouse. He was having porterhouse and he was drinking good rye and still that bandleader glanced down at him as if he were

something to be scraped from a shoe. The bandleader with his shitty little smile and his shitty little stick and his band that wouldn't do what
he said. At a table back by the bar there were some railroaders sitting
around in their silly hats. They wouldn't be dancing. They'd have nothing to say to him. His meal came, tasting course by course of feathers.
Brkvich received and ate his *sarma* and his ravioli without pleasure. He
had another highball. His steak came, overcooked he thought, and dry.
The ice cream was like dust. And in the band they were making jokes
he didn't understand. Joke and play and joke and play, and this was
their work, and they didn't begin to appreciate how good they had it,
to be so worldly and light and lucky, to play at something for a living.
He slid his chair to the edge of the bandstand where he could tug at the
cuff of the bandleader's trousers. "Hey. You guys know any of the good
old tunes? You know anything a white man could tap his foot to?"

"No," said the bandleader. "We only do jungle music. We don't even
have a banjo player."

"What? What was that?"

"Just kidding. What do you want to hear? We might know it."

"What do I wanna hear?"

"You got a song in mind?"

"A song? No, just . . . What'd I say? Something good. Something
good is what I meant."

"Okay, then. Just for you." The bandleader. Looking down. Down his
nose.

"It better be." Brkvich tried to think of something more to the point,
and then he tried to think of the point, and then he felt a hand on his
shoulder, heard his own name spoken as a threat—Nick—he stood and
turned to it. Red Capich. Also looking down at him. Brvkvich felt like
a piece of soiled carpet. "You touch me? You . . . touched me?"

"Take it easy," said Capich nervously.

"Shit. Take it easy. That's what they all said. Eli and a couple before
him. They said that. Now you? You?"

"Don't do this."

"What?"

"You know what. Act like this."

"Who are you?"

"Who am I?"

"You think you can tell me what to do, Red? You?"

"I . . . just take it easy, would you?"

"You better go back and sit down with Mlinar. Maybe he'll tell you who you are. Meantime, you better go back and sit down. And shut up—boy."

— —

The girl brought him her father's last ounce of whiskey. She brought Savage sandwiches and coffee, and when he mentioned in passing that he might like to read, she brought him a lamp and editions of *Timon of Athens* and *Riders of the Purple Sage* and a digest of veterinary medicine. He was, she said, no trouble. Savage saw to his regret that the girl was wary of him, thus the many reasons to leave and come back. He liked her very much and so, to put her at her ease, he seized on the most neutral observation he could make: "While I was indisposed, Miss Johnson, I dreamed of flight. Free flight. I was almost constantly aloft. What do you make of that?"

"I've done that, too. I'm a regular barnstormer in my dreams. But without the airplane."

"One drifts. It is delicious."

"Yes," she said. "I think so. Like the back of your britches were tied to a big balloon." Her coat collar cupped a long, weather-sweetened face. Her hands were chapped and expressive. "Of course, when I'm awake, and if I get up on the roof of the barn or something, then my knees just start right in banging away. They say the fear of falling, that's your deepest fear."

"'They,' as usual, are wrong."

"What is it, do you think? The deepest fear?"

"The old familiar, my dear. We are, and we fear to be, alone."

"You mean country people? Cause this out here, I have to say, this can be a lonely old deal."

"I believe you know what I mean."

"Yes, I guess I do," she said. "There's some that take great comfort in their Bible. And Daddy and me, we kind of like our critters, so . . . but . . . yes, I do. I take your point, Mr. Savage."

"Not completely," said Savage. "My grandson, Red, as you call him, don't you think he's a likely lad?"

— ～

Capich heard Mlinar out on the subjects of buck euchre and the fractious Cleveland of his youth and an old conquest named Flora. While Mlinar talked he kept an array of objects moving always through his hands, his cigarettes, napkins, a supply of paper clips to be bent into stars and letters and four-legged figurines. So little distracted by business, the boss talked until he'd bored himself, and then it was just his fiddling hands. A distant, disapproving look gave Capich to understand that he'd failed even as an audience. He'd meant to give good value for his wage, but now he'd been called upon to curb Nick Brkvich and he'd failed in that as well. Red Capich slid into Mlinar's booth expecting to hear shortly that he was not the man for his job, a fact that was in any case clear to him.

"That puke. What was he saying over there?"

"Told me to leave him alone."

"Then that's what you do. Until you have to do something else. You might end up earning your pay tonight, Red."

"I wouldn't mind." Capich considered the bony back of the Brkvich head and hated him. The sudden depth and darkness of the man's stupidity had frightened him at first, but he was over that now. To know

Nick Brkvich was to wish him harm. Persistent and durable in a fight, if only that, Brkvich had demanded several profound beatings during his career as a socialite, and he'd also been beaten occasionally at the mine. Capich noted a crate of Double Select, left for some reason on a bus tray midway between himself and the bandstand; he could feel the weight of the bottles in either hand, their cool bluntness. In all his life, all Red Capich wanted was the safety that he believed would come of being necessary to someone. Instead—this. He trembled, but not unpleasantly.

"Don't get your feathers ruffled, Red. That's the wrong approach. Smart, not mad."

Capich knew this to be good advice and that it had come too late. "I don't care for him, and he don't care for me. If I have to tell him to leave, if I have to tell him anything . . . the guy deserves everything that happens to him."

"What this town needs," said Mlinar, "is a dive, a hole in the wall where sonsabitches like Brkvich can go and run their mouths, and you could put your waddies and your half-breeds and them cheap hookers from Rawlins in there, too. Keep em outta here. Maybe you'd end up running it for me, Red. Call it the New Cleveland, call it the Stale Fart Saloon."

"Me?"

"It's slow," the owner despaired. "It's a pit. You might as well tell Beverly and Nallie and Louise to go on home, there's no point in them sticking around. We sold four dinners tonight, which didn't cover what it cost me to heat the building."

"What about Julie?"

"Tell him the grease traps need cleaning." Mlinar was cheered by the thought. "Don't you do it for him, either, showing him how."

"You want me to tell the band to take off?"

"No. That's what they wanna hear. I wouldn't give em the satisfaction. They come in here and piddle around and piddle around and piss me off, and that's what they want me to tell em—go home. No, the band can stay. If anything you can tell em to get busy and play something. The band and the bartender stay. When you get done sorting everybody out, Red, have Jimmy build me a martini. Have one yourself if you want it."

Inez had come only to avoid spending a night alone at the hotel; she was resolved not to sing another note in Rainey, Wyoming. But the small result of her small protest was that she felt especially irrelevant and bored, so she sat off to the side and smoked until she'd scorched her throat, and then she drank lime juice and seltzer to cool it. She eyed the old bohunk fiercely, to no effect. The old crook and his goon. Them, and some railroaders drinking, successfully, to forget, and that barking fool down front. Their audience. Not one of them seemed hurt by her absence from the bandstand.

A gal, she thought, who'd been born the least bit pretty, or ever learned to make herself that way, would not be playing the roadhouse circuits. If she'd been at all presentable she'd have missed the Alhambra entirely and also all those afternoons in the half light of her rooms, copying out arrangements at four bits a sheet. She was ruining her eyes, becoming more pinchfaced all the time; her fingers were permanently dappled with India ink, and she had the nails and cuticles of a field hand. She made do with what she had, and what she had, apart from the music, was increasingly pitiful. Inez still wore her hair like a flapper because she believed the lacquered bob, no matter how far out of fashion, made her head seem smaller and more nearly round. The head Benedetto had once admired as a freakishly resonant chamber. She had her art in spades, her discernment, her pipes, her power and range, but she'd have traded a little of each for a turned-up nose or a reasonably feminine skull.

With the boys finishing "Swanee" in their funereal way, she found she could no longer tolerate her own silence. Inez mounted the bandstand. The band had lost interest in Heath's direction, and the selection was falling to earth around them like a handful of flung gravel, a shopworn death for a shopworn tune. This sort of thing never put Heath much out of sorts. She'd seen him content to let them limp along like this for nights on end, uninterested and incoherent. From the beginning Inez had been unable to forgive them their sloppiness, could not like them, and so, of course, they didn't like her, and so it had been for the whole tour.

"Derry," she said, "let's do some of my things tonight."

"We've only read through those that one time, Inez." He wouldn't for the world disappoint her, but it couldn't be helped. "And that was quite a while ago."

"Right. When you hired me. And remember? Remember what was said then? I signed on cause you said we'd be doing some of my things, and now it's been months of nothing but the schlock from your book, and in the meantime these guys have played through my stuff exactly that one half-assed time. You know, lately every guy I meet is some kind of welcher. I'm getting sick of it."

"Well, sure, but . . . we'll need some more rehearsal on those."

"What do you think this is? Look around, Derry, you see any audience to speak of?" She drew very near to him, face-to-face. "This *is* a rehearsal, or might as well be. Hey, Purefoy, break out that portfolio of mine and pass that stuff around. We're gonna do a couple of my numbers."

"I don't know," said Heath, "I like to have things kind of worked up and polished before . . ."

"Her stuff," said the guy with the ham-hock face at the foot of the bandstand. He'd been heckling Heath for hours and had him a little rattled. "It couldn't be any worse than what you've been doing. Could it? Let's have some of hers." Her advocate's mouth, having said its piece, hung open and his tongue continued to work within it. Eyes like poached eggs and catsup.

Heath bore his sick grin to the microphone where he announced, as if the idea had been his own, as if they were before a large and eager crowd, "Something a little different tonight, ladies and gentlemen, for your listening pleasure." His pitchman's glad-handing baritone rolled through the empty room. "We're going to try some songs penned personally by the Hot Thrush as they used to call her in Kansas City, our own, well-traveled stylist, Inez Perry. So—shall we try that little blues, honey?" Inez told him its name, Heath named it for the band, and there was a rustling of sheet music, more pointless remarks, a moment of readiness; Heath raised his baton and let it fall. Having contributed that much, he slouched pouting to the back of the bandstand where he stood with his arms crossed, the patron saint of boredom, while Purefoy at the piano noodled a four bar introduction. Inez settled herself. Her lungs filled, her gut pushed in and up and:

> Did you ever hear of a garden
> Buried deep down in Underton Wood
> How the flowers there, they need no care
> And blossom just when you think that they should?

At her feet sat her awful fan, his chin in his hand, his mouth pursed and productive of foamed spittle.

> And how a rude boy went out to find it
> Traveling always by cover of night
> How he lost his way, forgot the day,
> But finally everything came out all right.

> Honey, I should sing you
> A song about seeing the light
> Why don't we try
> Something o-old?

The tune, she felt, was shapely and logical. The boys, despite themselves, had fallen right into it, and Inez was delighted to let Heath have
his snit. She directed while the sections took their verses. She'd make
men of this shambles, an instrument, an organization. She noted with
pleasure that Purefoy was taking none of his usual liberties with the
piano part. The last conscious railroader had found a second wind in the
music and sat studiously listening. The owner and the owner's goon
were listening, wearing that stricken look she liked to see, and at her feet,
especially rapt, was that rough specimen who had crawled out of some
unimaginable putrefaction to come in tonight and demand this song:

> In all your life there's only one thing
> Worth the trouble of being alive
> Now that garden's there, so soft and fair
> But it can't bloom until you've arrived.
>
> Honey, I should sing you
> A song about seeing the light
> Why don't we try
> Something o-old?

— —

"Man," said Capich.

"She'd eat you," said Mlinar. "Wouldn't she? Just eat you and spit out
the seeds."

"That raises the hair on the back of my neck when she . . . man."

"From the lowly seed," said the owner, "the tall oak grows."

Miss Perry said something stern to the band. As if to second her,
Nick Brkvich got to his feet. He rocked side to side. Now the singer's
remarks were caught by the microphone and carried to the room,

". . . put valves on those instruments just so you can find your way around a scale, and you still play out of tune. Listen to yourselves, will you? How about a little intonation? Okay, let's try going uptempo. Dig out the one that says 'Miss Simmering.'"

Nick Brkvich was before her, riven with abortive impulses. He sat, he stood, he sat. At odd moments his head careered back or to the side.

"Goddamn him," said Mlinar. "That's something you're probably gonna have to take care of, Red. And when you do, if you get the chance, just go ahead and kick his knees out from under him. "

Capich thought that he'd come to do a job and this was it. He liked the weight of his shoulders, he liked his considerable reach, but he was not quite so stupid and ready that, waiting for it, he didn't have a gurgling in his belly.

"Best thing you can do for a guy like Brkvich," said the boss, "is kill him and feed him to old Billy Peters' dogs."

Inez Perry looked out upon the audience that should have been and pumped her fist. Nothing happened. "Okay," she said. "Okay, you guys, get with me now. Ready, please. Ready? . . . and two, and three, and . . ."

Jackson, suddenly enraptured, leaned out over his tom-toms and pounded, already beyond himself, all for the cause, and caught on her whirling beat. The brasses joined. The reeds entered. Heath stood to the side, wretched and forgotten. The piano strode up through spacious chords and the horns began to call and answer.

"Christ," said Mlinar. "Imagine traveling with that woman. On a bus with her. It's no wonder they take drugs."

Capich felt the ghosts of dancers past brush past him to take the floor; his own feet pleaded with him to allow them to move in some pretty way. Miss Perry had her microphone by its throat and, with her free hand punching out the beat and the band pounding like an engine behind her, she dictated:

The only thing you have to fear is fear itself.

Brkvich stood and walked through his table to reach for her. Capich was up, moving.

So why don't you take yourself down off that shelf?

She swayed, and Brkvich, stiff little column of meat that he was, swayed also, almost elegantly, almost in time, still reaching. He caught the singer's ankle. Capich closed. Miss Perry kicked free.

Get up and dance, get up and try, if you really want to you can get up and fly.

Capich had the miner's sleeve, but not his attention. Brkvich lunged and caught the singer's ankle again, and this time when she kicked at him she didn't free herself but only fell back onto a music stand, which fell back onto the trumpeter just behind her, and a wave of silence moved through the band and stilled it. Capich turned him. The sleeve tore in his hand, but not before he'd turned the miner to him and away from Miss Perry. A handful of fabric, his whole authority. "Out, Nick. Now."

Brkvich looked at his sleeve.

"I said, get out."

"Oh. Wha'd I tell you, Red? Didn't I tell you . . . ? What?"

"Hey," said Miss Perry to no one in particular.

Brkvich let his head roll side to side on his neck. To ease some tension it seemed. His eyes closed.

"Nick."

"Hey," said the singer again, very sincerely.

"Look. Look what you did." Nick Brkvich had made the sleeve a badge of all the many injustices he could bring instantly to mind. He had been wronged again.

"Get out."

Very forlorn, Brkvich kneeled before him. Kneeled and went so far as to bow his head. Capich had a wild moment of hope.

Brkvich lifted the leg of his trouser. There was a razor in his sock, in the garter. A razor in his hand. Then he was up again, sober as a judge, and the razor was spread for business, the blade an extension of his forefinger. Brkvich on his feet, a single thought to animate him.

"Goddamnit, Nick."

"Hey," said the singer. "Now . . ."

Brkvich wore a dreamy smile. His chin had begun to slide side to side, his razor hand to weave.

"That's no good, Nick. We can't have that."

Brkvich, his teeth all revealed, seated in their dark and swollen gums.

Capich crouched to wait for him. The blade cut the air before him. Fluidly. "Put it away, Nick." Breath was coming dear to him, and he was wasting it.

"Put my baby away? You big sonofabitch, you'd like that, wouldn't you? Think I'm stupid?"

Stupid. Exalted. His movements were beautiful and ran ahead of his thoughts, and his first thrust at Capich drew blood. Capich thought at first he'd pissed himself. A spreading wetness. Blood.

"Stop. Stop." Even in this Miss Perry's voice was lush as the string section of the Rochester Radio Orchestra.

Capich bled. The warmth had reached his knee. The razor floated before him. He expected Brkvich would come in low again, slashing, as that had worked so well, and so he came, but this time Brkvich was repeating himself, and this time he winced to announce the move, and so Capich retreated that second, crucial step, and this time Capich caught the miner's arm before it could be withdrawn, and he caught it up and he brought it down to snap like dry kindling on his knee. The razor fell and Capich toed it away. Brkvich made a sound so frightening that Capich released him at once.

Brkvich sat on the floor, his legs splayed before him, his mouth a shocked portal. With infinite tenderness he cradled one arm in the other, an arm with a new angle in it midway between its wrist and elbow. Capich stepped back.

— —

Dove needed to believe that men and women came together by a process more complex and sweet than turning a bull into a pen with a

heifer in heat, but she knew that the wellspring of her sudden fascination for the Capich boy was mostly feral, estrous, and that it was obvious enough that old Savage had seen it in her. If she was embarrassed
she was no less curious for it. She did not trust herself at all.

She sat with the strange old man, the pair of them under blankets,
face-to-face at less than three feet, and the night wore on. He said he
couldn't imagine sleeping. He was very sad, he said, about the turn the
war in Spain was taking. "There is evil," he said, "never doubt it, and it
has its triumphs." He told her of the Inquisition, El Greco, and some
other things she couldn't follow at all, and then somehow he was off
on the unimaginable wealth to be had from the Amazon Basin, advis-
ing earnestly that she go there. Dove's usual bedtime came and went.
Nothing was sacred to the old man, nothing profane, his talk hammered into the quiet parts of her brain, and she knew she'd have long
since excused herself if not for the faint hope that Savage might return
to the subject of his grandson, information that might be useful. Then
at last, when she was very tired, she remembered that she was, after all,
a straightforward girl, and she simply asked him, "How was it that Red
came to live with you, Mr. Savage?"

"His father is dead and not lamented. We do not know what has become of his mother. She left him with me."

"And that's your daughter?"

"Angelene."

"That must be pretty hard on everybody. Not knowing where she is."

"Not so hard, perhaps, as knowing."

"But he knew her? Before she left?"

"He was her strength. He has never been so staunch in his own behalf."

"He is pretty shy."

"And you like that in him," Savage told her.

"I like him."

"So you see . . ."

"What?"

Old Savage waited her out.

"Yes," she said. "I guess I do. What do I do about it?"

"Wait for him," the old man said impatiently, "and when he comes, be plain spoken."

"You think it's up to me, huh? I'm not sure what you say."

"It won't matter," he said.

— ⁓ —

Capich fingered the soggy rent in his pants and looked through it as best he could. The cut transected his inner thigh, the softest flesh of his leg. Modesty moved his hand to it.

Mlinar had come with his .38, too late for the fight. The muzzle of the pistol traveled everywhere. He stood over Nick and told him, "Don't get up." Nick tried to answer, but could only gape and gasp. He wouldn't be getting up.

"Help em," said the singer.

"This is your fault," Mlinar told her. "Clear out."

"That guy on the floor is really hurt. What about you, kid?"

Capich was soaring, but on fragile wings. "I'm fine," he told her.

"You don't look it. For one thing, your lips are gray. See that, sport? See what's going on here? Why don't you put your thing away and help this poor kid out?"

"Why don't you shut your mouth? You know, this is the kind of thing that really upsets me. My luck, one dies of shock and the other bleeds to death. So I guess I don't need your advice, do I?" Mlinar raised the pistol and thoughtfully shot two holes in his own zinc ceiling. From within the smoke he said, "And didn't I tell you to go?"

"Pull yourself together," she said. "That's not doing any good."

One of the railroad men rose up from his table, up from a long nap on it. A red straw clung to his cheek. "Don't shoot," he said, "we were just leaving."

Julie ran out from the kitchen and was disappointed to find no one was shot, but there'd been a fight at least. A gray glob clung to his chin, hard upon a yellowing bruise there. Julie, too eager even to speak. Bruised Julie, bent Nick, even the singer had bloodied her lip. "Why don't you get em to the hospital," she said, "if you're through goofing around?"

"Yeah, and by the time I'm back from Riverton, you and that mess, you'll be gone, right? You, and everything you brought with you. And then I'm gonna fumigate the place."

"I don't have to go," said Capich. "I don't need to go anyplace."

"You sure? He didn't catch your sweets there, did he?"

"Oh, for crying out loud," said Miss Perry. "Let's just load em up and get em some attention."

"No," said Capich, "I'm all right."

To be certain of it, Mlinar told Julie to examine his wound. Julie bent before him, careful to touch nothing. "Quit shaking Red. Pull it back so I can . . . well, it's just . . . it's like a paper cut. You were just about nutted, but you're not even bleeding now, so quit trying to make such a big deal out of it. It's nothing, Mr. Mlinar, he's fine."

"I already told him that, Julie."

"Help me, Julie. Help me get this idiot off the floor." Mlinar and the gypsy tilted Brkvich to his feet. Brkvich wanted to scream, but there was a catch in his throat that would only let him grunt. By grunting he told them they were not to touch him anymore. They walked on either side of him, as tenders, and the group took a good while crossing the floor. Loudmouths all, they had fallen into a silence that made for a fascinating tension. At the door, Julie glanced back and twisted his chin in imitation of the way Brkvich had been writhing as he walked. He laughed gaily and followed the others out.

Bile rose in Capich's throat. He put his hands to his knees.

"Don't pass out," said the singer. "I don't see how we'd carry you anywhere."

Capich lowered himself to the floor and sat on it, much as Nick had,

his legs spread before him. From this stability he was able to appreciate the woman's gabardine trousers, her tailored shirt. She'd come to
work in trousers. Like a man. Not like a man. She knelt before him, curious. Her glasses were set in a slender gold frame, her temples lavender fields of old acne. She looked very much better at a distance. "I
suppose there's no first-aid stuff around, is there? A first-aid kit? Should
be a crime in a dump like this, not having any bandages around."

Julie came back in and told Capich to get off the floor, that he was
embarrassing himself. Capich waited out a wave of nausea. He got to his
feet and another spasm sucked his sternum inward, but he didn't vomit
and knew now that he wouldn't. The woman took a pack of cigarettes
from her purse, shook one out for each of them, and lit them all. It was
an odd routine for a woman.

"I'm Julian Cirrio," Julie told her.

"I'll just bet you are."

"Me and Red, we go way back." Two circles of smoke pulsed from
his mouth.

"Go and get me some clean bar towels. Your buddy's leaked quite a bit."

"And a beer," said Capich.

"No beer," she corrected. "Get him a glass of water."

"Well, how did I get to be step-and-fetch-it? Do this, do that? I
thought we were getting acquainted." Julie, still in his rubber apron and
gloves. And his ludicrous dignity.

"Chop-chop, will you, kid?"

"He's not even bleeding now."

Inez Perry pursed her lips.

"Okay, okay, jeez, you act like he's dying. You want a drink, lady?
Long as I'm at the bar?"

"Yeah, fine. Bourbon. But get it, would you?"

The singer took Capich by the arm and walked him back to Mlinar's
booth and sat him down. She slid in next to him. Her head turned to
him like an owl's. There was calculation in her regard, and she seemed

to think she could afford him. "What's it take to get rid of your buddy?"

"He's excited." Capich stubbed his cigarette cold. It had been horrible. "Which is not too good for a guy like Julie." The singer studied him. "Those were quite the songs you sang," he told her. Her accomplishments were old news to her. She studied him. Now there was nothing he could say that wouldn't sound utterly foolish, and Capich was relieved when the bandleader came to tell her that it was time to go. She told him that she would go when she was good and goddamn ready.

"You're a lot of trouble. You are a lot of trouble, Inez. We're not waiting around for that."

"I didn't ask you to."

"What that bohunk said, about how you caused all this, he wasn't far off, you know that? That was a nasty little turn, lady." The bandleader touched his blond pompadour without altering it in any way. "I think you'd better just get on the bus. We may not stay in Lander any longer than it takes to grab our suitcases. I feel like sleeping on the bus, on the road."

"All I did was come to work and do my job. I came to work and did my job. Just like anybody else, okay? So leave me alone."

"Inez, you're . . . how are you . . . ?"

"I'll manage," she said. "You know I will."

"No later than six. If you're not there by six sharp you might find yourself hitchhiking to Boise."

"Good night, Derry."

The bandleader left, trailing the others with his mackintosh over his shoulder, his horn case in one hand, and a highball in the other. He carried his shoulders in an exaggerated way like an actor afraid his meaning might not be taken. The door swung back at him at his approach and caught his highball hand and he cursed and was gone, the last of the band.

Julie came with the towels and three glasses and his cigarette still stuck in his mouth, a technique unfamiliar to him. He put the towels in the singer's hand. "What do we do now? Red, what do you want to do?"

"Not very much, Julie."

"What about you, lady? What's your name? Whatta you wanna do?"

"What's my name?"

"Yeah."

"Why don't you go somewhere, kid, and wipe that stuff off your face? You've got some goo on you, you really ought to clean yourself up."

Julie touched his chin. His mouth fell open a half inch and he left them.

"He's your friend?"

"Usually."

She slid to Capich's side and pressed one of the towels to his thigh. She pressed, and when he didn't jump, she pressed with more emphasis. "That hurt?"

"Not very much."

"I know something that can make it feel a lot better."

"Really, it doesn't hurt. Maybe later it will, but not yet."

She bent to whisper in his ear, "A lot better. You bring a car to work, jumbo?"

"Sure."

"Well?"

"Okay," he said. He checked the sentiment that would have offered her his hand. Capich got up and walked out, and she followed him into the parking lot, fell in beside him to cross to the far edge where the Buick was parked. "It's my grandfather's." Capich wished to disclaim all the torch work and clutter that had been inflicted on this recently beautiful automobile. The singer opened the passenger's side door and got in and patted the seat beside her. "Come on, Rod."

"It's Red."

"Okay, I guess you'd know. Get in."

"All right, but you know those . . . those things they use . . . I don't have any."

"Things? Oh. Relax, honey, I'm sterile as boiled water. Now, come on. Christ, what is that smell?"

"Solvent, I think. This is Danny Savage's car. He's got the better part of a machine shop in this thing, and quite the library. If you knew where to look you could find almost anything in this car."

"Except you, honey. Come on."

Capich leaned down to look in. She presented her face and he dutifully kissed it. Her mouth tasted of cigarettes, her tongue was rough as a cat's. The singer pulled him down and in and straddled his lap. He felt the cut begin to seep again. She held his face, her forefingers hooked back of the hinge of his jaw, and drew him to her again. She thought to take her glasses off and lay them beside her. Then she kissed him more athletically. "Ah, sweetie," she said. "You great big thing, you hero." Capich departed himself to hover above, to watch this, perhaps to remember. She pushed her face into the crook of his neck and sighed terribly. She pressed her crotch onto his swollen cock. Inez Perry held herself that way for a time and tears ran down his neck. "Come on," she said. "Let's skin these trousers off." They disentangled to do it. His legs, exposed, were unpleasantly cold. The woman mounted him again. She slid her hands up under his shirt and pinched his nipples.

"You don't have to do that," he told her.

"Wanna get right to it, don't you honey?"

"I guess. If . . . however you like to do is fine by me."

"I'll be damned. It's your first time, isn't it?"

"Oh no. No. Well, sort of."

"Do I feel good?"

Capich was unequal to the least conversation.

She reached down and put him in her and slid carefully down onto him. "How's that?"

"Fine." And it was, but far less than the spectacular promised by years of longing and ages of song. By some reckoning he must be a man. He wondered if he was expected to move now or if that was to be saved for later.

"And, honey, when I do this, do you . . . son of a *bitch* . . ." The singer twisted violently on him and Capich's cut ripped and he had the pain at last that he'd earned a half hour earlier. "Your little rat-face, dipped-in-shit friend was out there. Had his face pressed right up against the glass. What is wrong with that guy?"

"I don't know," said Capich.

"Now we practically have to start all over again."

"Well, I guess I'm game," he said, "if you are."

— ~

It was very late at night. Savage read an article treating on the removal of obstructions from large animals' bowels. *When the patient is well snubbed and tightly tethered in all four extremities* . . . Here was his intelligence again, revived to swoop like a pigeon, picking at almost anything . . . *will insert his bare, soaped arm as far as is practicable. If the blockage is still beyond reach, it may become necessary to fashion a makeshift probe* . . . These were the hours for doubt to crowd round, and Savage envied once more the gullible, the tractable, the fellow, his head stuffed with the cotton of acceptance, for whom the dark and silent prelude to dusk must be much less clamorous . . . *rare cases involving the prolapse of the rectal sphincter* . . . He was an old man, alone in an outbuilding . . . *resulting at times in an explosive release of impacted material.* He was an old man, and his limitations had been apparent to him for a very long time. Where was Radé? Savage stepped out into the night and heard a calf bawl in the middle distance, its confusion rattling up through a strictured throat. What if the constellations should remain constant? What good was that to him? This was the hour when he was so like to steal in and lie beside his wife and have her slap at him without quite waking. She was the altar of all the ritual he had ever permitted himself. In the night he would press her to him, not for that shocked release, that was more her requirement than his, but for her warmth, for the sense of being within something larger than himself, larger than the two of them collectively. Awake, she would not suffer this. He would not be suffered. But he had a woman who worked herself daily to exhaustion, to no better or other purpose, it had seemed to him, than to temporarily kill her resistance to it and prepare herself to be held. Sometimes her head would bang back against his chest. But lightly. And in the old tongue she'd talk to her sisters of matters entirely void of consequence. Close, parallel, warm. Warm. Her hard old back and soft old ass cupped in the length of him.

Savage heard the engine of his Buick, distinctive even at a mile. He stepped around the corner of the pump house to watch down the Johnsons' lane, and soon enough a light came on, swung into the Johnsons' barnyard, and fell upon him as he stood there, the unexpected specimen. The headlights switched off, the engine fell silent; Radé stepped out of the Buick.

"You are very late tonight. The girl tells me you have been promoted. Is it your new status that keeps you so late at the ball?"

"Danny," said the boy somewhat skeptically.

"She would not tell me, however, why it is that we are here. Just here, Radé."

"Stoja kicked us out. Me first. Then I got you kicked out, too. So I brought you here. It didn't work out too bad, though, did it? They're nice people. I guess you met Dove. She even plans on feeding us. You all right? Couple days there, I didn't know. But . . . you all right?"

"Kicked out? What did you do, tuck your tail between your legs and leave because Stoja told you to leave?"

"Let's go inside," the boy suggested. "It's chilly out here." They went in and the boy lit his father's gaudy lighter, which he carried with him always; and with that he lit the lantern.

"What has happened to you?"

"Nick Brkvich. He cut me. He's started carrying a razor."

"Where is he?"

"It's all right. I got him. He's in the hospital. But now I'm down to one pair of pants. For work and school and everything, I've got one pair of pants."

"Your wardrobe can be replenished. Why didn't you tell me?"

"Like I say, you've been out of it."

"About the pants, Radé. I would have bought you pants."

The boy removed the pair he'd been wearing, and got his other from his satchel.

"We'd better clean that wound. It will suppurate if you don't clean it."

"I need to use the car a little more tonight. I'll be back in the morning."

"You're in rut. The girl? Dove?"

"Dove? Oh, god no. Not . . . oh no."

"It should have been her, you idiot. What are you doing?"

"I think you'll be all right now." The boy raised his trousers. "Maybe I'll go for a drive. I need to do some thinking."

"You should have done that earlier."

"I'm gonna pass on school today. I did yesterday, too. But I can make it up."

"I see. And you are going out there somewhere to think? Will that be safe?"

"You're one to talk, Danny. I need to go for a drive."

"I'll go with you."

"I'm wound up," said the boy. "I need it to be just me. Can I have the car a while longer?"

"Of course. And then you will drive to that location, as yet unknown, where your thoughts will suddenly order themselves, and your testicles will resign as your chief advisor."

"I don't see why not," said Savage's grandson. He buckled his belt and went off again.

— Astraddle the Great Divide —

March 30, 1937

— MRS. JOHNSON brought him into her kitchen, insisted he call her Viola, and served Savage a long, complex breakfast. Her husband and daughter, she said, had gone into town earlier that morning. She seemed to miss them already and was almost foolishly happy for his company. He was given a pan of corn muffins, and to spread on them she gave him butter she'd churned, jams she'd canned. He drank her coffee with heavy cream and ate country sausage. Viola was unable to make herself even briefly still; she traveled the path worn in her pine floor between her icebox and her stove, her counter and sink, her bulging pantry. Savage had briefly known the first mistress of this household, a country-woman named Estelle, and he recalled some mention in her obituary of a joyous reward. A restless, endearing streak of kindness ran through this family's women; they hadn't notably profited by it. At the center of Viola Johnson's table were several knuckles of raw jade and a jam pot and salt and pepper shakers and a porcelain Dutch girl.

"They might have waited," she said, "to see if you wanted anything from the store. But it's the same every Tuesday, they like to be in and out of Lander before noon. They say it gets too busy after that. We're none of us very social."

"One ceases to be. My grandson and I are in your debt. What may we do for you?"

"Oh, don't be silly. We're just so tickled to have the chance to visit with somebody. We don't get off the place much, and there's not many come out this way, so we wind up hermits almost. And poor little Dove, I guess you know she can't be all that fascinated by now with Daddy's rheumatism and my lumbago. She's done more visiting in the last couple of days than—I-hate-to-think-how-long. That grandson of yours, he's a fine young man. And quite concerned for you, I might add."

"Yes. But he has my automobile. There must be something I can do for you while I await the return of the prodigal. Shall I tell you your fortune? Tune your guitar?"

"We don't have a guitar. Got a radio. You're only just now back on your feet, why don't you take it easy for a bit. And don't feel you have to hunker down in that pump house either. I keep that teakettle on all day long."

He saw the three of them round this table, Clate, Viola, and Dove, saw the Johnsons as they must sit together three or more times a day, almost every day of every year, unable with any decency to look away from each other; he was sorry for them, the girl most of all.

"I'll make you something," he told Viola. "Shall I make you a tool, something for your convenience?"

"Sure. If you want to."

That morning Savage had found a forge on the premises, and now he found a harrow gone to ruin out in the yard. Its teeth were spring steel. He unbolted one of these from the frame, the only one of thirty that wasn't welded with rust. He built a bed of coals in the forge, upon which he lay the tooth. He worked the bellows until his steel got bright, then brighter, and when it was an evil red he seized it with a pincers and lay it up on his anvil and began to work it with a smithing hammer. He intended a kitchen knife. He beat at his stock until it hardened, then thrust it into the coals to soften again, and by this process and by many hundred blows he shaped a shanked wedge, a blade. The ringing carried for miles.

Clate and Dove Johnson returned from town. The rancher let himself carefully out of the cab of their truck, threw a despairing wave toward Savage, and went straight for the house. The girl came to him, curious.

It was Savage's impression of both parties that they'd been arguing.

"My goodness," she said, "you bounce back fast. What's that you're doing?" She'd worn a dress into town and the front of it had gotten ripped.

"Tempering the metal." Savage dropped his piece into a tub of cold water and an oddly contained cloud of steam hissed up. "So it will hold an edge."

"You just hammered it out like that? Is that how it's done?"

"I have machines for grinding and polishing at the mine. With those machines one can make cutlery. What has happened to you?"

"Oh, this? It's nothing."

"That's blood at your waist."

"A couple drops. Cold water gets it out."

"All right then, what happened to you?"

"Well it was Daddy's hip, or not his hip exactly, but it went out, and then there was this spool of barbwire we had to get in the back of the truck, and . . . just the usual thing." Tears welled unfamiliarly in her eyes. She was herself again almost at once, circumspect, the restraint that defined her so would have crushed a lesser child.

"Why don't you take me home?" Savage said.

"You don't want to wait for Red?"

"Not here."

"Could I change first?"

"Whatever you prefer, do it."

"You're not leaving on my account? Because, really, I feel safer with you here, Mr. Savage. Oh, don't take that wrong. I just . . . you know. Somebody in the middle, kind of."

"Someone in the way."

"But home? Can you go back there? I thought . . . or . . . I guess you can if you want."

"There are difficulties from time to time with my wife. With Stoja there must be drama. But I would like to finish this knife for your

mother, and I'll need my equipment to do it." He'd become a burrow-
ing beast, and, worse, he'd become aware of it. "Home, you see, is the
place to which one returns, even when there is nothing whatever to
recommend it. Take me back, if you would. You have work to do."

"I guess so. If you put it that way, maybe that's how I should think
about it. All right then, if that's how it has to be, give me a minute to
get changed and . . ."

"Do you think you should? You must let him see you in that dress."

"That's what I had in mind, but not like this. Some kind of rough-
neck who can't keep herself nice for half an hour. I wouldn't want him
seeing me like this."

"Particularly like that. You are devastating that way."

"Mr. Savage. I'll be right back. In my overalls, thank-you-very-much."

‒ ‒

Capich followed the nurse down the corridor. She had called herself
DeSmette. Brittle, iron gray hair trailed from her fantastic cap. It was still
early in her shift and her skirts were taut with starch and made a great
rustling as she marched along, shoes squeaking on the waxed floor. She
did not like him at all. "This Brkvich is in a bad way. Don't you do
anything to upset him."

"No."

"We have no real surgery ward, so he's in here."

"They operated on him?"

"Yes. The bone splintered."

The ward was powerfully lit, rows of windows, rows of bulbs,
shadow largely banished; only two of its beds were occupied, one by
Brkvich and another by a lunger with his back propped against a half
dozen pillows.

"If he wakes up," said the nurse, "fine. But don't you wake him up,
you hear?"

"Yes, ma'am."

"And don't get Mr. Rossi fussing, either."

"All right." It was Candie Rossi. Or half of him. His cheeks leaned terribly inward and his gaze was steady and flat. When the nurse had turned on her heel and left, Rossi said, "You're Juro's kid, aren't you?" He was yellow, translucent. He'd been a lineman for the telephone company and was famous for falling from poles without being hurt. A smart guy. A tough guy.

"Yeah."

"You got any cigarettes?"

"I only use em once in a while. Don't carry any."

"What good are you?"

"You supposed to smoke in here?"

"I sneak em in the can," said Rossi. "And that's what I do for excitement. This your buddy they brought in?"

"No."

"Oh. Then you're the one that got him, huh? I hope he needed it, cause you did him up to a fair-thee-well; he is hurt. What if I gave you some money? I've got three dollars and thirty-five cents here, and you can have all of it if you'll get me a carton of tailor-mades."

"Now?"

"When you get around to it. I'll make it worth your while."

"Is that good for your condition?"

"What about it, kid?"

"I came in to see this guy."

"Why?" said the lunger.

"Like you said, I'm the one that hurt him."

"You won't be the one to fix him, kid. You know what that is they stuck in his good arm? That's morphine. He might not even know he's alive. They used to get me like that. When I first came in they'd give me all the dope I wanted, but I guess I asked for too much, and now they're sick of me, and it's, 'You'll just have to try and be a little stronger, Mr. Rossi.' Why? What have I got to prove? I was strong all my life and look where it's got me. I been strong and now I'm weak, and you want to know the only difference I can see? One takes more effort than the other. We like our shot in here. Should've seen this one about four-thirty this morning, had his back well up off that mattress, sweating like a pig. They missed his shot, see. What'd you do to him anyway?"

"Not that. Or, I didn't think . . . Boy. "

"You'd have plenty of time to run down to the commissary. He's not coming to anytime soon."

"Then what? Sit here while you smoke up the bathroom, act like I don't know what's going on? They'd run me outta here."

"If that's the worst thing that ever happened to you . . . shit. Do a guy a favor, would you?"

"Later. Before I leave. But I should stay long enough to . . . I thought there might be something I could do. I oughtta try to do something for him. I didn't know it was this bad."

"I think you did enough already."

"Oh, man," said Capich. "I don't like this."

"No," said the lunger, "but I bet you get over it sooner than he does." He hissed, once for effect and once in pain. Rossi was not quite so resigned to his fate that he didn't hate them, his fellow patient, the visitor, the nurse, or just anyone who'd be seeing the fireworks next Fourth of July. "If it was your old man, he'd have cigarettes, and no sneaking, either. What are they gonna do? Evict me? Fine me? Cut back on my stewed prunes? Bring me those packs of smokes, see if I do any more sneaking. I'm a grown man who should have his smoke if he wants it."

Capich thought of showing Rossi his father's lighter, for old time's sake. He thought better of it.

Brkvich lay with his arm suspended above his chest by an intricate rigging. His fingertips were lavender, and cotton batting poured from each end of the cast. He breathed in obedience to a distant command. Brkvich breathed, and Rossi breathed, and soon enough Capich noticed that he too was doing it, labored, conscious breathing.

Backing out of the room, he met nurse DeSmette coming in. "Not too chatty, was he?" There was a prominent mole on her chin, with hairs in it, and it conferred tremendous authority upon her. Behind DeSmette came a doctor on his rounds. The doctor came straight up to Capich, his pale, pleading eyes very much enlarged by his glasses, and he said, "What do you know about this, young fellow?"

"I know how it happened. I did it, I guess."

"You guess?"

"I didn't mean to. He had a razor."

"What was it," the doctor asked, "Monday night in Rainey, Wyoming? That the occasion? I don't imagine anyone has taken the trouble to investigate, have they?"

"They don't need to. I just told you what happened. But . . . his arm's broke. You can fix that pretty well, can't you?"

"You didn't just break it, son. You ground it into meal. He'll have debris in that arm as long as he lives."

"But that won't . . ."

"Oh, it's crippled," said the doctor. "He'll not have much use of it now. I hope you had good cause to hurt him so, because it looks like you've got completely away with it. But you've come to see him, have you? Well, that's fine. That's fine of you, I suppose. DeSmette, wake that man up. He's got a visitor. Visitor may do him more good than anything."

"Wake him up? Dr. Hewerly, shouldn't he be resting?"

"He'll be doing so much resting, it can't hurt to miss a little." The doctor was too mild a man to be indignant for very long, and now he only wanted to patch things up.

"Wake him up? That's what you want me to do?"

"Yes."

"Wake him up? Those are my instructions?" DeSmette was at the brink of mutiny.

"Yes," said the doctor placidly.

DeSmette knuckled Brkvich's sternum, her eyes never leaving the doctor's face. Brkvich resisted and resisted and then shot off his pillow, a dog snatching at flies with its yap. And he gasped.

"You've got a visitor," said the doctor on his way out. "Let's slow that drip, DeSmette. Traction settings the same. Broth only."

"Drip," she said to the empty door frame when he'd gone.

Brkvich drove his head steadily back into his pillow. His lips were compressed into a bloodless gash. DeSmette spoon-fed him crushed ice. Brkvich made constant, minute adjustments to try to come into some acceptable relationship to his arm. There was none.

"He could use a shot," Candie Rossi advised.

"Couldn't we all?" DeSmette took the miner's pulse. "Wake him up. For the love of Mike, what do they teach these guys? How a man can spend so many hours on the floor, see so many patients, and never learn a . . . Wake him up? You're up now, Mr. Brkvich? Comfortable?"

"Iiicce," said Brkvich. "Morrre iiicce."

DeSmette tipped the spoon at him again. To Capich she said, "You want to make yourself useful, then give him some of this ice. It doesn't take a nurse, and I haven't got all day to spend doing it."

Capich approached and took the spoon from her. DeSmette shot him a look that said she didn't think much of his contribution and she left the room, clipboard under her arm.

"She's not quite so nasty when she's on nights," said Rossi. "She hates that day shift."

Brkvich worked his lips like a fish and Capich slipped a bit more ice into the opening. Brkvich brought his tongue into play.

"How are you, Nick?"

"Oooh."

"I didn't mean to hurt you so bad."

"Fuck him," said Rossi. "A razor's no joke."

"Fugh you," said Brkvich. And to Capich he added, "Iiicce."

They listened to Brkvich slurp. Again like a dog, lapping.

"Redth?"

"Yeah?"

"Redth?"

"Spit it out, shithead," said Rossi.

"Ahhn youhh, shidhead. Ged you, too. Fuhgger."

"Where's your razor now, greasy?"

"Leave him alone," said Capich.

"Cominn. For youhh. Redth. Tomo'th pistoohl. Come. Youhh."

"What? Come and shoot me? Don't you think this has already got as far outta hand as it needs to get?"

At immense cost Brkvich sat up in his bed. The blankets fell from his shoulder, which was black to the neck. "Dollarday," he said. His face, so ill conceived for other uses, was perfect for this. There was a small trapeze for his healthy hand. He clung to it. "Me. Whagh ahm gonna do? Noh. Come. Godda gun, Redth. Wanna shood oud?"

"Why don't you just choke him right now?" said Rossi. "Why don't you just throttle him and be done with it?"

"I'd watch what I said. Gone as he is, he'll remember anything bad you say to him."

"I'll slap the shit out of him. And how's he gonna hurt me, huh? I'll slap you around you try anything with me."

"Why," Capich wondered, "does it always get back to this? Somebody slapping somebody around?"

"Dollarday,"said Brkvich.

"What?"

"He's saying dollar-a-day," said Rossi. "He's saying you made him a dollar-a-day man."

"Come 'n kiiilll. Youuh, Redth."

"He's sayin . . ."

"Yeah, I got him," said Capich. "I got that part."

~ ~

They traveled a road that passed within two miles of her doorstep, a road that, for all its proximity, she'd never traveled before. "I surveyed this," said Savage, "and it was graded with mule teams. An agony. We felt like the Pharaoh's gang. Now look, the alder is grown up on either side, and year by year the road itself threatens to disappear."

"It's a fine road," said Dove Johnson. She'd not been on it because she'd not been to the mine camp, and it occurred to her that she hadn't been very neighborly where the miners were concerned or gone even slightly out of her way to know them. "I envy your generation, Mr. Savage. You got here when there was still laying out to do, and building. You folks got to do so much more of that kind of thing. Every corner peg on our place has been set for thirty years, barns built and ditches dug and all that. I feel like now we're just keeping up what's already been done, we'll not have the chance to start new as you folks did."

"The world," Savage intoned, "and everything in it was very old when I came to it, and every last scrap of it was in someone else's possession. But, one tries to engage during his little instant, to be of some use. For me, it is metallurgy. That's my study now because one had better understand steel and aluminum if one wishes to accomplish very much." Like Jesus in the old tints at church, a hand and a face uplifted, he gestured to call her attention to three windmills that had reared as if by command on the rimrock just above them. "I had thought by now," said the old man, "that the Savage High Aspect Wind Turbine would be making heat and light for the multitudes. The warm, well-lit hovel, that was to be my doing, and I expected to become rich on the strength of it, and that would have been interesting, I think. Have you ever considered all the digging that is done for power? Digging, and drilling, and damming. A great deal of mess and trouble."

"I hadn't," she said. "Hadn't given it a thought to be honest with you."

"The wind blew," he said, "and blew uselessly by. One fears that will be one's epitaph. These machines grind through the best bearings I can make for them in under three months. The vanes are splendid, though, don't you think? I spent a week at the Carnegie Library in Pittsburgh, in the aerodynamics section, and came home with these in mind. See how long and thin, and with very little twist in them? I have added a kilogram of lead at each of the tips."

"They do fairly spin," she said. "Way faster than our old Delco did. Pretty, too. Like clipper ships."

"We live in the finest moment history has produced, don't you think, Miss Johnson?"

They descended into the coal camp proper, which was spangled with broken glass, and many doors flapped open to the weather, and a row of root cellars had been revealed where shacks had been razed or lifted away from their rock piers. It was the ugliest ten acres she'd ever seen.

"The one at the end," Savage told her. "With the maples. The saplings. They've been saplings now these three or four years. Just there, where the woman is hoeing. That is my Stoja."

The old man's wife saw them as they came but did not lift up from her work, not when they stopped in her yard, not as he called to her, "Come and meet the author of my restoration, Stoja. Let's have three glasses." And to Dove he explained, "I have a bottle of wine which was made from the first and the best crate of grapes I imported here. It was nineteen ten. It has occurred to me, however, that there is nothing to be gained by not drinking it." He stepped out of the truck. To Dove it seemed the well-bred thing to do to step out also, to shut her motor off, and step out and shake the woman's hand, and she attempted it; but the woman stood with her hoe at her shoulder, soldierlike, and looked down at Dove's proffered hand as a joint of spoiled meat and then into her face with absolute certainty and hatred. Nothing in Dove's life had prepared her for this moment. She was very grateful when the old man came nearer.

His wife asked him, "You think you could bring your chippies around to my house? Just because you are—"

"Stoja, may I introduce Miss Johnson. You are not to . . . Stoja?"

"Where do you work?" the old woman asked her. "Do you do something?"

"We have the ranch. The Johnson ranch?"

"So what? Did you know that one you're with is dead?"

"He's . . . how do you mean?"

"My spirit remains abroad, however," Savage said, "and it would like a glass of wine."

"Dead," the old woman declared. Her blood lay very near her surface; with that and working in the weather her cheeks were polished apple red. One corner of her mouth was ajar. Clear discharge slid from each nostril and out onto her curled lip. "So," she told her husband, "you come back, and you are talking your talk like always, and you think you can fool me, but I know because I saw. You are dead. Get away from me. And you, who did he say you are? You should save yourself if you still can, and don't give yourself to something like that. You are keeping company with a demon."

"Are you . . . ? Is she all right, Mr. Savage? She doesn't look too well."

"My name is Stoja." She seemed to be trying to hail them from across a field.

Dove backed away from the giant's wife.

"Stoja, why don't I take you into the house now? I think you are feverish and should lie down."

She thrust the hoe a half inch forward. Her knuckles stood bone white along the haft and the whites of her eyes were also too apparent. "I took the vow," she said. "For life. But that's all. You only got one life out of me, and when you die, that's it. I did what I had to do and I'm done. Don't come around no more."

The old man turned to Dove Johnson and absently asked, "May I prevail on your courtesy a while longer?" To his wife he said, "Until I return for my things you must try and remember to drink as much water as you can. Shall I bring you fresh water . . . ? Good-bye, then."

With that they got in the car and Dove drove them out of the coal camp. She drove for what seemed a very long time in silence. "You think it's all right to leave her alone?"

"She could buy your father and me and several more like us out of petty cash. She does very well by herself."

"Not really. Not if she's like this."

"No," said Savage. "Not really. How concise of you. But she will do what she will do. She has never brooked any interference from me."

"I never saw anything like that before. Did she mean that? She didn't?"

"She is never insincere," said the old man. "Always in error, but never insincere." He wore a haunted grin. "She has meant all of it, unfortunately, all of it."

— —

Capich pulled his blankets over his head to shut out the light and was only briefly aware of his stunning, captive rankness before he slid off into sleep. Irritants nibbled at the edges of a syrupy and undulant dreaming; at intervals he felt his shoulder shaken and was told to rise; something was said about cleaning his cut; he was called to supper; another voice spoke only his name, "Red? Red?" Capich was having none of it. He slept as long as he possibly could and when at last he woke again, it was dark. There was an unmistakable shape sprawled on the cot beside his. "Danny? You awake?"

"Well, then, everyone with his wits about him. What won't we accomplish now?"

"Do you know what time it is?"

"Late enough that you've missed another day of classes. You are also late for work at that defiled nightclub. Now I suppose you must scurry back to take up the cause of Miroslav Mlinar?"

"I guess I should. The man does pay. But I'm done there. He made me floor manager, and I was in over my head. I went and saw Nick this morning. He's crippled. That arm is. I was just too young for it."

"You are well out of that chaos. Mlinar cultivates it; he made you an entertainment."

Capich sat up and rubbed his face. "Nick says he's gonna borrow Tomo's pistol and come and shoot me."

"A *pistolero* now. A borrowed pistol in his off hand. The man is a lesion on humanity. He needs to be deprived of air and light until he disappears."

"You really are feeling your oats," said Capich. "I think if he comes, I'm gone. I'll say it again, enough is enough."

"That is more or less what your grandmother has said. To me. I am evicted, you know."

"You let her throw you out?"

"It was a kindness, Radé. She has exceeded herself. She is a bit more deranged now, and a great deal more generous than she has ever been before."

Red Capich contemplated the partnership his grandfather seemed to have in mind for them. He reached a conclusion. "There's a man in Riverton," he said, "who's a big fan of their football team. He's Bradstreet and he has that hotel. The Bradstreet. Says if I'll play for Riverton High School he'll put me up in a room, feed me. Says I could probably make some walking-around money, too."

"The game of football had been almost completely outlawed when I first came to this country. What a poor use of one's time."

"Yeah. But that's what I think I'll do. I think I better take him up on that."

"Why?"

"Well . . . can you think of anything better?"

"Yes."

"So you're all right now? You feel like you can do what you need to do now?"

"What do I need to do, Radé?"

"I thought you were going to tell me."

"Learn to operate the switchboard. If you're going to a hotel, learn something useful."

"All right," said Capich. "You staying here?"

"Going," said Savage.

"Where?"

"Majorca . . . The land of milk and honey . . . something pleasant, I should think."

— —

The girl came out to the pump house again and once more called his name through the door. She was beginning to resent always having to pry him out like this, or push her way in. The old man had told her to be plainspoken, but the young man hadn't yet given her the chance, and she was tired of waiting. "Red?" This was difficult. She knew herself as a patient, measured young woman. This was hard. Though it was late and their lamp wasn't lit, she had come out again to see if he might answer her call. She heard them talking inside, or the old one talking, ". . . no time now to wash . . . the least bit gracious, Radé . . ." Dove Johnson felt not so much bold as depraved. She did not feel very hopeful. "Red? Can I get you to help me with something?"

The lamp was lit, a slice of its light falling through the door, which opened and was filled at once with Red Capich, lantern in hand. There was so much of him. He seemed a very decent sort, but in fine what she wanted was the sheer mass of him. Against her. She hadn't made herself this pathetic on account of his possibly sterling character. It was not her usual way to embarrass herself quite so relentlessly. "Hold that lamp up a little higher," she said. "You look like Boris Karloff when you hold it down at your waist like that."

"What are you doing?"

"Doing?"

"You said you needed me."

"Oh, that. Well, I do. But just to . . . could we talk?"

"All right."

"You want to go for a walk?"

"All right. But my clothes are kind of dirty. So am I."

"What's that got to do with anything?"

"I thought you should know."

"Oh. Well . . . thanks. But, come on, Red. Okay?"

"Now?"

"Yes. You feel all right?"

"Feel fine," he said. "I didn't want you to think I was being snobby or standoffish. Just, you know, I slept in these."

They walked out on the path leading through the prickly pear north of the Johnson house. She said it led to a spring. It was a narrow path and they went along it single file, she ahead and upwind of him. The thaw had entered their bones; no longer hunched against that interior cold they rolled along loose-gaited and intensely young. The ground was notably softer underfoot, and the air savored of new grass and heartening sage but was crisp enough still to fire their cheeks. The boy was able to speak quite freely to her back, and he went so far as to tell her in brief the story of his life, that he'd only barely been legitimate, and that he'd been the child of a child, and then his grandfather's captive audience and a dishwasher and then, "I let things get out of hand almost right away, soon as I got promoted. And I kind of liked it when they did, it was sort of exciting, so now there's a guy who wants to come and shoot me." He went on to tell her about a man with a hotel in Riverton and how he meant to go there to work, or at least to stay.

"Leaving?" she said. "Really? When? Why?"

"I don't know. Tonight, maybe. I'm done at the Alhambra."

"You don't have to. We could do something better than the pump house. I'm sure we could fix you up a little better than that. If you don't have work, well, there's just never any shortage of it around here. I'm sure you've seen that by now. Might be kind of boring for a guy like you. But it'd be a place to stay until you're back on your feet."

"Back on my feet," he said. "How did I ever get off em in the first place? I'm a junior in high school and I'm already a failure. That's nice of you, though. To offer."

"I suppose," said Dove Johnson, "that it would be monotonous here for somebody who wasn't used to it."

"I wouldn't think so," he said.

"I like it. I guess that's the main thing. I like it well enough that I'll stick here. So . . . all I'm saying is you wouldn't have to go. If you didn't want to."

"What if I came back?"

"Do I make you nervous, Red?"

"Yes."

"Come back? Now where did you dream that one up? Come back."

"I would," he said.

"Why?"

"I'd like to come back."

"Why?" she said. "I'm tired of not having a boyfriend. Is that being too blunt?"

"You want a boyfriend?"

"Not just anybody. Not the first poor guy who wanders along. Come to think of it, though, I guess you are about the first one to come by. You must think I'm the commonest penny you've ever seen."

"I'd like to come back," he said. "To see you."

"Why? For what?"

"I'd be a lot cleaner," Red Capich said.

— ◦ —

April 1937

The Buick was a great-hearted car. He had remounted the front seat eight inches rearward, and so the cabin fit them well. They'd slept in it when, very briefly by the roadside, they'd slept. Commanding the machine had done much to undo the effects of Savage's brush with humility; he put out on the open road from which he had been absent for so many years, and in celebration he drove them to Alberta. Nearly all this north-ward passage was accomplished over high plain, a long sigh of a land-scape that rolled along under an unavoidable sky. When they stopped for gas they would also relieve themselves and take on light provisions, fill their canteens. Dates, walnuts, candy bars, and alkaline water. Miles spooled up under them; hours passed when nothing quite like a thought entered the old man's head. In Medicine Hat, Radé bought a six-pound round of white cheese. They continued north from there on lesser routes, several hundred aimless miles until it seemed they were sailing a yellow sea, an ocean without ports; antelope littered the prairie. Sav-age turned west, to the mountains, and when he had them in sight he turned south, back toward the States.

They crossed back into Montana and went down to West Glacier, where Savage had the Buick loaded onto a Union Pacific flatcar. A long black Mallet was to drive a colossal plow over Marias Pass, where, they were told, new cornflower snow lay in ten-foot drifts over long runs of the track. Behind the juggernaut were the usual amenities. Upon board-ing the train, Savage and his grandson repaired immediately to the din-ing car. A vain old man in livery showed them to their table and produced a paper rose in a fluted vase. Long, ginger tufts of his hair were combed across a mole-splattered skull and plastered into place. He wore a cummerbund under a linen jacket. "May I have Herrick pour you gen-tlemen a sherry?" He told them he was Palmer House, Palmer House wherever he may roam, and those were his standards of service, and he asked them repeatedly how he might make them happy. Savage ordered veal scallopini and liver and onions and for his grandson two Empire Builder oyster platters and trout almondine. They had the sherry, then another with their bisque. The boy sucked cautiously at spoonfuls of the soup. He tried to appear thoughtful. "Can we cover this?"

"Yes. Just. With champagne, cigars, and a gratuity. I will have the chocolates as well, though they sometimes cause me headache." Chocolate medallions minted with a likeness of England's erstwhile king, they were free, compliments of the Great Northern Way, wrapped in pink foil and set out in bowls at every table.

"Wouldn't it be better to get a sandwich? Have a little gas money when we get off this thing? We're a long way from home, a long way from anything here."

"It is never improvident to eat well. One seizes every opportunity to eat well, Radé."

"Okay. But what next?"

"What would you like to do?"

"I was kind of set on that hotel thing."

"The fellow is dead."

"Can you believe the luck? I thought I'd have room and board— maybe have to sweep the lobby a little. That would have been—"

"Humiliating. You are a young man. A young man. What is that to you?"

"Sort of a problem."

"And where do you think the solution might be found?"

"I don't think there is one."

"The girl."

"I'm no ranch hand, Danny. Not for long I couldn't be."

"What will you be?"

"Broke in about an hour. Then what?"

"Why must you be always plotting, plotting? Something will suggest itself."

"Be one of those guys selling apples."

"How can you be so dismal? Is this something they taught you at the gymnasium? Look. Look where we have come." Outside, densely timbered slopes stepped back and up and back and up to a lacy sky. Cornices of translucent snow flared in great runs over rock escarpment. As they ate they were borne up until they were eye to eye with the source of a hundred small drainages, the headwaters of the Marias, the head-waters of the Flathead.

"Within memory of man, during the late ice age, a sea formed here. Lake Missoula, dammed at its southern end with ice. At intervals of thousands of years the ice would break, and the sea would sweep every-thing before it, running to the Pacific. That must have been sensational."

"How do you know that? Where do you get that kind of thing?"

"One knows the gross geology of one's continent."

"No. Just you, Danny. Most of us don't know that kind of thing. I'm not sure I even want to. When I think of that sea, I think that I'm the guy, probably, who'd have his hut built right in front of it. You ever think it might be possible to know too much?"

"If it is," said Savage, "we are none of us in imminent danger. You had better go and take up with the Johnson girl, Radé. You will need some-one to keep you safe, I think. Go back to high school. Shall we go for-ward? I'd like to see this plow at work."

"Up to the front? Will they let you?"

"Of course," said Savage.

"Isn't it kind of greasy up there?"

"You'll never know unless you come and see it."

"I can pass. We're down to two dollars and nineteen cents. I can't af-ford to get greasy now."

He went through the club car and a passenger car and into the cab of the Mallet where the engineer looked him over significantly but didn't bother to try and make himself heard over the boilers and the engine and the wheels squealing. The train man pointed to the back of the train. Savage stepped out instead and onto the catwalk jerry-rigged along the side of the engine, the articulated boilers. He went forward through steam and smoke, and he could see nothing past the nose of the engine for the snow flying up. The forward driving wheels chuffed hugely beneath him, the track clicked beneath them. Nearer the front, the spray became thicker, whiter, louder, closer. He crawled into the mounting bracing behind the plow and, with the blue and alien mountains all around looking solemnly on, he rode there at its cleaving point, at the heart of a battering roar.